A HANDFUL OF STRAW

Mary Rensten

SCRIPTORA

D1328869

Published in Great Britain 2013 by

SCRIPTORA
25 Summerhill Road
London   N15

in association with The Society of Women Writers &
Journalists

ISBN 978-0-9562494-6-3

Printed and bound by Witley Press Hunstanton PE36 6AD

Remembering Christabel and Sybil

- 'never too late'-

I wish to thank the following people for the help, advice and information they have given me during the writing of this book: Pat Alderman for her editing and encouragement; Val Dunmore, whose knowledge of horses was invaluable, as were the documents found for me at the Royal Veterinary College, Swanley Bar, Herts.; the staff at HALS (Hertfordshire Archives and Local Studies), and at Hertford Museum; Dr. Janet Woodall for checking the historical accuracy of my manuscript; Glyn Hughes at the Met Office, Ken Griffin, Alan Greening, Sarah Adamson; Doreen, Terry and Carey. Also Yvonne Sint for her beautiful cover painting, and Diana Athill, who inspired me to keep on writing.

1

Sir Henry Chauncy read the letter again and smiled to himself. The darkness of the oak-panelled room, the smoking fire that refused to blaze and the damp February day outside were of no account now.

"She's coming!" he called out, and as if in answer to the rise in his spirits the fire sprang to life, throwing a rosy glow over the previously gloomy scene - the heavy oak settle, the worn Turkey carpet and the dusty bookshelves - and highlighting the red brocade of Sir Henry's chair.

"I know," answered an irritated voice from across the room.

"Not in two weeks' time. The day after tomorrow… she'll be here!"

It was a long while since Arthur had heard such enthusiasm in his father's voice. He turned from the mullioned window, from the sight of the sodden parkland and the dripping trees beyond.

"Oh," he said. "Why is that?" Not that he was interested in the visit of Caroline Newell. She was nothing to him, not now, but Sir Henry's obvious joy required some kind of response, and a third person in the house, whoever it was, always eased the stiff relationship between father and son.

Sir Henry chuckled. "She doesn't say it in so many words, but I would hazard a guess that one of her London suitors has discovered where she is staying."

"In Hertford, you mean?"

"No, not Hertford! She left there and went to Bengeo. She's at Lady Poynter's, you know that."

Sir Henry did not like being interrupted, especially by Arthur. It took very little to annoy him where Arthur was concerned.

"As I was saying, Caroline is probably fleeing the attentions of some man. You know how popular she is." The words hung in the air like a question.

"Yes," said Arthur. "I do." He knew what was coming next.

"If you had anything about you, Arthur, you would court her. A beautiful widow, barely thirty, just the right age for you; charming, intelligent, well connected, and with her own money."

"Father, I know all that."

"Well then, here's your chance. Do something about it. Oh, don't look at me like that, as if you were the village idiot!"

"I'm sorry, but…" He was not going to be pushed into any kind of marriage, not yet. In two years' time he would be thirty. Maybe then he would think about it.

"Which I sometimes think you are! You've had a good education, and all you seem to do is mope around the village, ogling - and goodness knows what else - the village girls."

It was true that he had no ambition. He was content with his life, living at Yardley Bury and finding his amusement in nearby Walkern. Was that such a bad thing? He could never hope to emulate his father, a famous historian and a magistrate too, so why bother to try. As for the village girls…

well, they were, to say the least, accommodating, in ways that he was sure Caroline would not be.

She had not always been a sophisticated London lady, the owner of an elegant house in Clerkenwell and an estate just over the border in Essex. Arthur remembered her visiting Yardley Bury with her mother, her younger sister Emilia - Millie, she called herself - and their little cousin Rupert. The four children had played together, the older ones, Caroline and Arthur, forming a pair - a naughty pair, he recalled with a grin - who delighted in tormenting the younger children.

"You find it amusing, do you, that you are idling your life away?" His father's tone was harsh.

Arthur looked across at the old man, formally dressed in black as always, every curl of his black wig in place, his eyes, under their pronounced brows, surveying him sternly.

"I was thinking of…" Arthur hesitated.

Much as his father irritated him, he didn't want to upset him: he might stop his allowance. "I was thinking of Mother, and how much she loved Caroline, and the fun we had here as children." He paused. "I miss her too, you know."

"Of course you do," Sir Henry said gently.

It was six years since his dear Elizabeth had died, at the age of sixty, and he still missed her every day. He ought to move away from Yardley Bury; this old, rambling Tudor house was too big for just him and Arthur. Nothing had been done to it for years and there seemed little point in bothering now. They had few visitors and - the thought brought him up sharply: where was Caroline to sleep? Was there a bedroom in good enough condition for a lady, a room without peeling paintwork or cracked panelling or moth-eaten hangings?

Sir Henry got up from his chair and poked the fire; it had died down again. Flames, springing up briefly once more at the touch of the poker, lit the shabby room. Not that shabbiness here mattered: this was his study, his snug.

"Caroline must have that big room at the front; it's the only one that isn't damp. Speak to Bessie, will you, and get her to organise a thorough cleaning of it. Oh, and get Jacob to see to this fire."

"Is she coming on her own?" Arthur asked, moving to the door.

"No. She will have a maid."

"Oh yes… a lady's maid," Arthur said scornfully. "Well, *she* can go in that little room next to mine."

"No, she can't! There'll be none of your village behaviour in this house!"

Sir Henry looked at Arthur with disdain. How had he ever come to have such a wastrel of a son? There was nothing of the gentleman about him, despite his clear-cut features and tall, athletic figure. If Elizabeth had lived longer things might now be different; he had neither the time nor the inclination to give Arthur the attention he needed. His only hope was that some good, sensible woman would take him on. His thoughts went back to Caroline, and for a few moments he allowed himself to dream: she and Arthur were married and living at Yardley Bury; there were young children riding their ponies in the parkland, boating on the lake, running up and down the wide staircase, sliding down the banisters, sitting with him in the library or the snug, reading, one of them on his lap, the other leaning against his knees.

"It's all arranged." Arthur's voice brought the dream to an abrupt end. "And Jacob will be here in a minute."

"Thank you. That was well done." Perhaps there was hope for Arthur after all. "We shall have to give some thought to meals while Caroline is here; she won't want to eat the plain country food that we have."

"I think she will enjoy eating country food; she always did as a child."

But once again Sir Henry wasn't listening; he was trying to recall the last time he had seen Caroline. It must be all of ten years ago! Yes, it was: the day of her wedding to Robert Newell, in London, a week after the coronation of Queen Anne. April 1702. Dear Caroline. It will be so good to see her again.

"Mary, do get on with the packing."

"I don't know what we should take." Mary, her arms full of garments, looked helplessly at Caroline. "It's the country, mistress. I don't know what they wear there. Not any more," she added, before Caroline could remind her of her childhood on the Amley estate. "Besides, it's not Essex, it's *north Hertfordshire!*"

"Oh, anything will do!" Mary was a lovely girl and she had become a most efficient lady's maid, but there were times when Caroline wished she had a personal servant who was less talkative and more submissive, and even occasionally downright dull. "We're not going to be there long."

"Thank goodness for that."

"All right. That's enough. I am quite aware that you'd rather be here... and so would I... but I must visit Sir Henry."

"In February, mistress?"

"Yes!"

Sir Henry Chauncy was nearly eighty years old and might not have many more years of life; for the sake of her mother Caroline had felt she needed to see him just once more. Two of her mother's elderly friends had died recently, and she regretted not having made the effort to visit them; she had known they hadn't long to live. There was another old Hertfordshire friend she would like to see, Colonel Plumer, not far away at Gilston, but there wouldn't be time on this short visit.

"So just get on with the packing, will you?"

"Yes, mistress, but I still don't know what we should take."

"Oh, just use your common sense - if you have any!" Caroline was losing patience. "We are going to an old house, one that is cold and draughty; they probably still have rushes on the floor!"

"No!"

"Well, maybe not." She couldn't recall the floor coverings from her childhood visits. "But it is way out in the country, miles from anywhere, except for a small village across the fields. We are not going to see anybody of importance; there will be no balls or parties, not even good conversation probably. I shall doubtless have to pay a visit to the local vicar… and that is about all the socializing I am likely to do." She paused. "Now, does that answer your question?"

"Yes, mistress." Mary sighed and turned to the array of clothes on the four-poster bed. Caroline watched her for a moment, then abruptly left the room.

Downstairs her sister-in-law, Lady Lydia Poynter, was enjoying a tisane.

"My dear, come and join me," she called cheerily as Caroline entered the elegant drawing-room.

"Oh yes," sighed Caroline, almost collapsing on to the cushioned walnut settee in front of the fire. "I am in need of some refreshment."

Lydia reached forward from her chair to ring a silver bell on the table by the marble fireplace.

"I'm sorry you have to go," she said, looking intently at Caroline. She had always been fond of her brother Robert's wife, now sadly his widow. In the two and a half years since Robert's death on the battlefield at Malplaquet Lydia and Caroline had become close friends and confidantes. Lydia understood Caroline's feeling of restlessness now she was on her own, her need always to be on the move, constantly seeking some new interest, new people to meet; anything to take her mind off her grief and her anger at the manner of Robert's death, killed by a horse, a horse that had kicked out furiously at the kind, gentle man applying a poultice to the gaping wound in its flank.

"Couldn't you risk just one more day here?" Lydia asked.

"No," said Caroline. "I daren't. With a swift horse he could be here tomorrow! I must leave at first light." She smiled weakly at Lydia. "I'm not a very merry widow, am I?"

"The right man will come along, don't worry." Perhaps this was not the best thing to have said, but Lydia hated to see Caroline so alone. Her normally sparkling blue-green eyes were dull, her cheeks pale despite a carefully applied touch of colour, and her dark wavy hair lacked its usual lustrous sheen.

"I don't know that I want *anyone*. I know what people say: 'You shouldn't be on your own, you need a man to look after you.' But I don't, Lydia. I don't need a man." Vehemently she went on, "Especially not that odious creature who is pursuing me! I thought I had shaken him off by getting away from London for Christmas. Ugh." She shuddered. "The very thought of him, with his smelly wig and his bad breath!"

Sir Gilbey Rowlands had been pursuing Caroline "as though I was a fox at the chase" for the best part of a year, and although she felt she had made it quite clear that she wanted nothing to do with him, he persisted in his attentions. She knew why; it wasn't her he was interested in, although, of course, it would flatter him to be seen with an attractive younger woman - much younger, he was all of fifty - on his arm. No, it was her land he wanted, her country estate at Amley, with Robert's beautiful horses and orchards and magnificent woodlands.

She felt calmer, and at the same time more positive, after a few sips of the tisane that Lydia's maid had placed on a small table beside the settee. She looked across at the older woman sitting in her comfortable wingchair; how content she seemed, how settled in *her* widowhood. But then she had been on her own much longer and now, with this new house, she was happy to stay in one place. Lydia's likeness to Robert was striking: the same soft grey eyes, the same broad forehead, the same fair hair; even the same sunny temperament.

"I shall spend no more than three days at Yardley Bury," she told Lydia, "and then I shall return to you."

"With the greatest of pleasure, you know I love your company. But please don't come," Lydia said firmly, "until I have sent a rider over to Sir Henry's to let you know the coast is clear."

"Oh!" exclaimed Caroline, "how dreadful if I should return to find that detestable man still here!" She stood up and began to pace the floor.

"Still here?" Her sister-in-law's eyes widened in horror. "You don't imagine I would allow him to *stay* here, do you? Heaven forbid! Not even for one night. I loathe the man."

"But you can't send him back to London the same day!" Caroline stopped pacing and stood looking down at Lydia. "I would not wish a journey like that on anyone," she said, "not even Sir Gilbey Rowlands!" and she was off down the room again.

"Do sit down! You are making me feel quite giddy." Obediently Caroline went back to her seat. "That's better." Lydia smiled mischievously. "I shall send him off on a wild goose chase," she said. "It will be such fun!"

"Well yes, it would be. But where?" The thought of Sir Gilbey roaming the Hertfordshire countryside, and possibly, just by chance, turning up at Yardley Bury, was most disturbing.

"Let me think." Lydia raised an admonitory hand to Caroline, got up from her chair and began to pace the room as Caroline had done, but more sedately, her heavy brocade skirt making a gentle swishing sound on the polished boards. Up and down she went, past the sash windows, her hand trailing first on the inlaid tables below them and then over the front of the lacquered bureau at the end of the room, till finally Caroline could remain patient no longer.

"Oh Lydia, don't keep me in suspense!"

"I have it!" Lydia called, clapping her hands in delight. She came swiftly back to the fireside. "I shall send him off to Lady Cowper at Hertingfordbury!"

"Oh no!" The two women looked knowingly at one another. "Oh Lydia!"

"She does so love an audience for her sermons," Lydia said.

"He could be there for weeks! Oh, what a wonderful idea!"

Later, snuggling down into the feather bed in Lydia's best bedroom, hung with silken tapestries, Caroline felt strangely carefree. She was setting off on an adventure, something she loved to do. Yes, it was the wrong time of year and Yardley Bury would probably be dull and dreary... but that was tomorrow. She would not let those tiresome thoughts intrude and prevent her from sleeping. She would put aside reality: she was a lady at the court of Gloriana and she had just been introduced to the famous courtier, Sir Walter Raleigh.

This escape into fantasy had begun in her solitary early childhood - Emilia was five years her junior - and continued throughout her adolescence. She had had no recourse to it during her happy years with Robert, but now, on her own again, she had returned to it as a kind of comfort. It didn't always work. Her storytelling was fine for lulling her to sleep at bedtime, as she was doing now, but not in the small hours of the night, when thoughts Caroline did not *want* to think raced around in her head as her brain flitted from one disturbing subject to another: Robert's death, the future of Amley, the children she had lost, especially Hannah, darling

Hannah, who had lived only two and a half years. She *dreamed* of Hannah, too, and awoke in tears. "It will get better," everyone said, but when? "When the spring comes." "When summer comes." Spring and summer came and Caroline felt no better. Perhaps they meant next spring, next summer… or the one after.

It was winter now, and if you labelled your feelings according to the season, then yes, she *was* at her lowest at this time of year. Perhaps it was the lack of light and sunshine that caused it. Gloomy days encouraged gloomy thoughts and there were days when no diversion could lift her spirits. Not even the festivities of Christmas. In some ways that was the worst time. It was in early December that Hannah had died, and although spending this past Christmas in Hertford with Emilia and her husband Richard and their three children had been a joy, her days there were tinged with sorrow. The sight of young Anne and Charles and Edwin, all lively and healthy, exchanging gifts and playing games, made Caroline long for her own little one to be there, frolicking with her cousins.

She joined in the fun, of course; it was relatively easy to appear cheerful and bright, even sparkling, in company - she had always been something of an actress. It was when she was alone that she felt the hollowness inside, the emptiness of life without Robert and Hannah.

To counteract this empty feeling, she had led a selfish life since Robert died, constantly seeking pleasure as a means of diverting herself from her sorrow.

Now she was about to do something selfless: her visit to Sir Henry she saw as a duty. Perhaps this visit would also be a form of healing for her.

She had felt inwardly at peace in the company of old Doctor Bloxham and his comfortably proportioned wife Sarah, when she had stayed overnight at their home in Cheshunt on her way to Hertford. How Caroline wished she could be like Sarah, content to take every day as it came, trusting in God and asking no more of life than to be the wife of a provincial doctor.

Dear Doctor Bloxham, who had been Robert's mentor. He had insisted that Caroline and Mary took his carriage for the next stage of their journey; he had been quite appalled to learn that they had travelled from Clerkenwell to Cheshunt in a hired vehicle which they had shared with other people. "So dangerous, my dear," he had said, "and, if you don't mind my saying so, not really the thing that a lady in your position should be doing." Perhaps not, but she had felt quite safe, and it *had* been interesting. Of course it had not been comfortable - no one expected travel on winter roads to be *comfortable* - and she had had to hold a scented handkerchief to her nose for most of the journey to counteract the odour arising from the stale straw on the floor.

From Cheshunt Caroline and Mary had travelled to Hoddesdon in the doctor's own comfortable and clean carriage, with the doctor and his wife accompanying them; the kind old man would not hear of them travelling alone. From Hoddesdon to Hertford Caroline had gone on horseback - Richard's young brother had ridden over to meet her - and Mary, with the luggage, had followed in a carter's wagon. They had spent almost the whole of December at Emilia's and all January with Lydia in Bengeo. The inner peace she had felt in the company of the unworldly Bloxhams quickly evaporated in the excitement of

Christmas, followed by all the social gatherings that Lydia laid on for her; a little austerity, such as she expected to find in Sir Henry's home, would be good for her soul.

Tomorrow morning she would ride, with Lady Poynter's groom, John, at her side, to Yardley Bury, and as before, Mary would follow with their boxes, not in a carter's wagon this time but in Lydia's carriage. If she got stuck on one of the muddy tracks that passed for roads in this part of the county, she would just have to make the best of it. She was, after all, a servant. If she didn't always behave like one, well... Caroline knew it was *her* fault, if fault it was, that Mary was so forward.

A year after her marriage to Robert, becoming bored with what seemed to her a life of idleness as the 'lady of the manor', Caroline decided to do something she considered worthwhile: she would teach the children of the estate workers to read. Robert, though in favour of the scheme in principle - unlike other nearby landowners, who did not want their workers to become literate - doubted whether it would succeed. There were five children in Caroline's class to begin with, but gradually the numbers dwindled until there was only one pupil. That pupil was Mary, a slim, fair-haired girl, who, at ten, took to reading like the proverbial duck to water. Caroline, disappointed not to have made any progress with the other four children, was delighted with Mary.

"She is a very bright little girl," she told Robert. "Unusually so, I would say, for a country child. And she's good at sewing; she has the most delicate fingers."

"Yes, well..." Robert hesitated. "The fact is... oh, you may as well know... she's... she is not the cowman's daughter."

"Oh?"

"No. It's a sorry tale, and not one I'm proud to tell you."

Caroline's heart began to beat wildly. "Robert? Oh no, please say you're not."

"Not what?"

She could hardly get the words out. "The... the child's father..."

"Is that what you're thinking?" His eyes widened in disbelief.

She nodded, *her* eyes full of tears.

"Oh, Caroline. Of course not." Although he spoke tenderly she felt he was admonishing her.

"I'm sorry," she said, as he took her in his arms.

"Young Mary is certainly not my child, but I do feel partly responsible for her being in the world."

Eleven years earlier Robert's younger brother Harold, a wild young man, handsome, good with horses, but "without a grain of sense in his head" had brought some of his equally wild friends to Amley for the hunt, and, as Robert delicately put it, "one of them made free with young Susan, who was to marry my cowman, Thomas Butcher, and well... Mary was the result of the..."

"You don't need to go on," Caroline said.

"The cowman stood by the girl and married her." That will make Caroline feel better, thought Robert.

"Good," said Caroline. "And what did you do for her?"
"Me?"

"Yes, it's your estate; the man was your brother's friend."
"That's true, but..."

14

"Don't you think you should have supported her in some way?" She couldn't believe he could have been so uncaring; this was not the Robert she knew.

"We did, at first," he said. "Then Harold died, as you know, in a brawl." He looked at Caroline defiantly. "After that… well, I didn't want to think about the kind of young man he had been - he was a disgrace to the family - and I suppose we just forgot about the child." He paused. "I'm sorry, I know it's not good enough." He smiled and took her hand. "I'm so glad you are doing something for her now."

Caroline took her hand away. "And I intend to do more! Mary is too clever, *and* too sensitive," she added forcefully, "to be left to run wild around your estate and end up in a cowshed! I shall educate her, and when she is old enough she shall become a lady's maid."

Oh, how cross she had been that day. And how contrite Robert had been… and a bit unsure of her, too: he had never seen her so determined. He had yet to learn that Caroline was never so happy as when she had a cause to fight for.

2

"Mistress, you should be up! Mistress, do wake up!"

Mary's insistent pleas broke into Caroline's dream; she had been picking apples at Amley, with Hannah at her side, laughing as leaves came fluttering down from the trees when Robert shook the branches.

"What? What time is it?"

"Eight o'clock, mistress. I have been trying to wake you for hours."

"Don't exaggerate, girl! What time did you say... eight o'clock? We should be on our way by now! Are my clothes ready?"

"Yes, mistress, and your breakfast is ready, too."

"Good. I'll eat first and dress after."

A small table had been drawn up by the fire and on it Mary had placed Caroline's breakfast: a dish of tea, porridge, soft rolls and marmalade and a big slice of chicken pie.

"I haven't time to eat all that!"

"Oh please, mistress. Her Ladyship specially chose the rolls and the marmalade."

"Her Ladyship? In the kitchen?"

"No, mistress. She sent word."

Caroline sighed. She knew Lydia would be disappointed if all the food went back to the kitchen. "All right, I will eat a couple of rolls." Seeing Mary's look, she said, "And some marmalade. You can put the pie in a napkin; I can eat it when I get there if there is nothing else."

"They will feed us, won't they?" Mary, wrapping the pie in a linen napkin, looked up, distress all over her young face. "Should I get some more food from the kitchen?"

Caroline laughed. "Of course we'll be fed!" She sipped at her tea, then seeing Mary's miserable face, "What is the matter now?" she asked.

"I know we will have *some* food, but…"

"But what?" Caroline put down her tea.

"Her Ladyship's housekeeper says… they only have country food up there."

"Nonsense. Sir Henry is a cultivated man; I am sure he keeps an excellent table." Mary looked unconvinced. "He has a house in Hertford, for goodness sake; you've seen it, one of the best houses in the town."

Caroline drained the last of her tea, rose from the table and hurriedly wiped her mouth and hands on a hot cloth Mary was holding out to her. She moved away from the table and began to take off her robe.

Mary surveyed the still full breakfast table. "Could you not eat some porridge, mistress?"

"You are worse than a nursemaid sometimes, Mary! No, I do not want any porridge; there's no cream."

"It's winter, mistress, you don't get cream in…"

"I know! Get another napkin, and put the rest of the rolls in it for the journey. There, will that satisfy you?"

"Yes, mistress." Mary smiled and set about her task.

"Good, because I am not going to risk being trapped by that dreadful Sir Gilbey for the sake of a bit of breakfast. Now, help me dress."

"Yes, mistress." She understood Caroline's impatience. Mary shuddered at the thought of Sir Gilbert Rowlands' pudgy, age-spotted hands on Caroline's creamy skin, and as the maid of Mistress Newell she knew only too well how those fingers felt. What gave these so-called aristocratic men the right to think they could touch and humiliate any servant they came across! Mary had never told her mistress that she had been on the receiving end of Sir Gilbey's 'caresses'. Caroline loathed him enough as it was, without adding to her distaste.

"Come on, Mary, stop dreaming. Bring my clothes! I can't stand here for ever, unclad. Apart from anything else, I am getting cold!"

Caroline, dressed in only her nightgown, had washed her face and brushed her teeth, and she was indeed now shivering despite the steam rising from the perfumed water in the porcelain bowl on the wash-stand.

Mary lifted Caroline's warmed clothes from the rail by the fire and helped her mistress to dress, first in her long-sleeved chemise, then a petticoat.

"Leave it loose," Caroline said.

"But, mistress, it will fall down."

"I said leave it loose! I can't bear tight clothing when I'm riding."

"But you will wear your stays, won't you?" Mary enquired hesitantly, about to slip Caroline's arms through the shoulder straps.

"Yes, but don't do *them* up too tight; and don't take too long about lacing them either. Give me my stockings first."

Mary handed Caroline a pair of long silken hose, knitted so thickly they could almost have been wool. When Caroline had her stockings on, and the garters in place, Mary began lacing the stays.

"I wasn't sure which riding habit to put out," Mary said. "I didn't think you would want your best Bourgogne outfit today, so I…"

"Well of course I wouldn't, you silly girl! I'm going to be riding across fields! I want an ordinary wool skirt and a jacket, and a plain cravat. And a cape, of course. Or better still, a long cloak. I'll have the brown one." Mary turned to the walnut chest of drawers and started to take out the clothes Caroline had asked for.

"But first… I have some *other* robing to do."

Mary paused in her task. "Oh yes, of course."

"Well, look away then."

"Look away?" Mary had been dressing and bathing Caroline for nearly two years; she knew every inch of her shapely body. "Why, mistress?" She looked genuinely puzzled.

Caroline groaned. "We have been over this, Mary." Then, slowly, as if talking to a small child, "If you haven't seen me put them on, you can't swear that I am wearing them, can you? Should anyone ask."

Mary's puzzlement gave way to a grin. "No, I can't," she answered firmly. Then, in her best 'lady's maid' voice, she said, "I am just going to slip out for a moment, mistress…"

"Oh?" said Caroline, playing the game.

"I'm going to look over the banisters and make sure that Lady Lydia is not waiting in the hallway for you."

"Oh, how very thoughtful of you, Mary. Thank you."

19

With her eyes sparkling and her lips trembling on the edge of laughter, Mary curtseyed and left the room, shutting the door behind her.

A few moments later she returned. "All is well, mistress. Is all well with you?"

"All is very well, thank you, Mary. Now, help me finish dressing."

Warm in a woollen skirt, jacket and cloak, Caroline was almost ready for her journey. "All I need now is the hat," she said.

Mary handed her a large, floppy velvet hat with a plume. Caroline put it on.

"There," she said, looking at herself in the mirror. "I shall be warm… and with Lady Poynter's hat, quite disguised too, don't you think?"

How could just a hat disguise anyone? "Oh yes, mistress. If Sir Gilbey gives chase, he will think you are Her Ladyship."

"Cheeky girl! Come, let's not waste any more time. Is the groom ready?"

"Yes, mistress. And the horses."

"Good. I shall just say a quick farewell to Lady Lydia and I shall be on my way. And you know what you are to do?"

"Yes, mistress!" Sometimes, thought Mary, she treats me as if I am an intelligent equal; at other times, as now, it's as if I haven't a brain in my head! "I shall follow in Lady Lydia's coach, and take great care of the luggage." It was almost exactly as they had travelled from Hoddesdon to Hertford, Miss Caroline riding ahead and Mary following with the boxes. Nothing had been lost or damaged; there really was no need for her mistress to fuss.

"Good girl." Caroline swept out of the room, down the wide flight of polished stairs to the ground floor and into the morning-room, where a crackling log fire dispelled the gloom of the winter day outside.

Lydia rose from the chair in front of her writing desk to greet her.

"Goodbye, my dear. I wish you a safe journey." She embraced her sister-in-law, then letting go, she drew back and looked at Caroline. "You certainly won't be cold; you seem to have enough clothes on!"

"Well, yes." Caroline smoothed down her skirt. "I know how bitter the wind can be in these country places." It came out more sharply than she had intended.

"However many petticoats have you got on?" enquired Lydia, surveying Caroline's well-padded figure.

"One," said Caroline curtly.

"One?"

"Oh, possibly two."

"Don't you know?"

"Two, yes." Nothing got past Lydia; she would have to offer some kind of explanation. "Mary was dressing me and I was trying to eat my breakfast at the same time. I really didn't notice."

A slow smile spread over Lydia's face. "You never were a good liar." It was said with affection, but Caroline knew that Lydia could not be fobbed off with less than the truth. For a moment she held her sister-in-law's gaze, then looking down at her skirt, she said, "Oh, very well. If you must know," she paused, "I'm wearing breeches."

"I thought so!" Lydia laughed, but then shook her head. "Oh, Caroline, you really…"

Caroline cut her off. "Don't say I shouldn't! I've got them on now and they are going to stay on!"

This was not how she had expected to part with Lydia; she had a good mind to go now, before any really harsh words were said. The two women had always been frank with one another, but this was not the moment for one of their cut-and-thrust arguments, arguments that nevertheless nearly always ended in laughter rather than tears.

"And you won't make me change my mind," Caroline added firmly.

Equally firmly, Lydia replied, "You're not going to set off from here astride, are you?" She looked and sounded genuinely worried.

"No, of course not. It's only for when we are riding through the fields."

"But why?"

"For speed. It will be so much quicker, Lydia. I don't want to be out in this wintry weather any longer than I have to be, and besides, if Sir Gilbey *did* have a fast horse…"

"Nonsense! You ride side-saddle every bit as fast as you could astride. You know you can."

"All right. Yes, I can." This was all wasting time. Caroline was anxious to get away.

"You won't ride astride through anyone's parkland, will you?"

"Oh Lydia!" How could her sister-in-law show concern for the possible reaction of the local gentry at such a time of crisis for Caroline? "I shall not be going anywhere near the estates of your friends! And any riding on public highways will be done in the most decorous fashion, as befits someone wearing Lady Poynter's hat!" She looked defiantly at Lydia. "Now, are you satisfied?" she added in a gentler tone.

"Yes. All right." Lydia nodded, then shook her head. "You always did like to flout the rules."

"And I shall continue to do so, if I think the rules make no sense!"

"Where did you… where did you get them?"

Caroline had hoped that Lydia wouldn't ask this. "They are an old pair of Robert's," she said, and seeing the sadness in Lydia's eyes, she lightened the moment by adding, "You didn't think I had borrowed them from your groom, did you?"

"Well, I did wonder."

"Oh Lydia! I do *know* how to observe the proprieties."

"You will be careful, won't you?"

"Careful? About what?"

Lydia knew there was no dissuading Caroline once she had set upon a course, but at least she could try. "About riding astride without the proper sort of saddle. If that pommel were to go into your stomach…"

"It won't!" Caroline said. "I've done it before, you know."

"I'm sure you have. Just be very careful, that's all."

"Dear sister, I must go," Caroline said, hugging Lydia warmly.

"Come back as soon as you can," Lydia said, holding on to Caroline, reluctant to let her go.

"I will." Caroline pulled away.

Together they walked to the door. They clung to one another again briefly, then Caroline left the room. Lydia crossed to the table by the fireplace, lifted the little silver bell and rang it, summoning her maid: she felt in urgent need of a soothing tisane.

Caroline, sedately riding side-saddle on a black mare, set off from Lydia's stable yard with Lydia's groom, John, on a grey mare, at her side. Within a few minutes they were clear of Bengeo, and once out of sight of the road, Caroline dexterously swung her right leg across the horse's back and hitched up her skirts.

It would have been more comfortable - and safer too, Lydia was right about the danger - if she had had the proper kind of saddle, or even none at all - but she had chosen to adopt this unladylike style of riding for a reason she had not given Lydia: Sir Gilbey might be nearer than her sister-in-law believed, even now following her - Heaven forbid! - and two riders astride would be seen as gentlemen out riding for pleasure; certainly not as a lady and her groom.

The countryside was bleak and cheerless and the wind, coming from the east, whistled through the leafless trees and hedges. Underfoot it was still muddy from yesterday's heavy rain. Skirting Ware Park on their right they followed the course of the River Beane on their left, taking to the road as they approached the parkland of Woodhall. With Caroline riding side-saddle again, their progress was further slowed by the appalling condition of the track. The winter rains had washed away most of the beaten surface and at times it was hard to be sure that they were actually on the road. Caroline hoped Mary would get through without mishap. A carriage wheel getting stuck in a deep rut, or coming off completely, could hold her up for hours, even till the next day.

Once past Benington Place to their right, Caroline and the groom cut across the fields and Caroline dared to ride astride again. Keeping well clear of the village of Walkern they rode due north to Yardley Bury, approaching the house from the rear and entering the grounds through a gate leading from one of the paddocks. Lydia's groom had not been happy with this, a lady arriving at the back door like a common higgler or stable lad, but he knew, and respected, Caroline's need for secrecy. To have approached Yardley Bury from the front, and been seen riding through the imposing stone gateway and along the drive to the gabled entrance, would have alerted the villagers of nearby Yardley to the presence of a stranger at Sir Henry's house, a rare occurrence, and as such an occasion for gossip in the neighbourhood, which Caroline did not want. Visiting Sir Henry in normal circumstances, as she had planned before she knew that Sir Gilbey was stalking her, she would not have minded, but not as things were today.

She was glad to be in the cobbled stable yard. It was not that she was tired or saddle-sore - she was an accomplished horsewoman - but the rain had returned just as they rode past Walkern, and then, becoming torrential in the past ten minutes, it had all but soaked her through to the skin. Her sodden clothes were spattered with mud and the jaunty plume of Lydia's hat drooped lifelessly, sending a trickle of chilly green dye down the side of her neck and on to the front of her cloak.

It was not how she had wanted to arrive at Sir Henry's door, not even his back door. He would not mind, though, she was sure of that. As for Arthur, he had become such a country bumpkin - so she had heard from Lydia - that he would probably think, if he noticed at all, that a streaked cloak was the height of London fashion.

Thankfully, with John helping her, Caroline dismounted in the shelter of the stable yard's clock tower. The groom, holding the reins of both horses, called loudly for assistance, trying in vain to made his voice heard over the noise of the rain pelting down on the cobbles. There was no one about, just two horses, a chestnut and a grey, arching their heads over their stable doors, eager for attention. They began to whinny, and it was most likely that, rather than John's second "Hulloa, there", that brought two young stable lads scurrying out from another of the stalls, both of them looking as if they had been up to something nefarious. John had once been a stable lad and he knew how dreary the long winter days could be for young boys in a poorly run yard, as this, surprisingly, appeared to be - wet straw lying around, a rotting door with rusty hinges, a stale odour coming from one of the stalls - so he was lenient with the lads, not rebuking them for failing to appear at his first summons.

"You," he said to one of the lads, handing over the reins, "give them a good rub down and a small feed."

"Yes, master." John smiled to himself; so elegant was he in his groom's livery that these yokels thought he was a gentleman. He pointed his riding crop at the other boy.

"And you," he said, "run to the house and tell one of the staff that we are here and that the lady requires an umbrella."

"Yes, sir," the lad said, staring open-mouthed at John's finery.

"Well, don't hang about. Go!" The boy touched his forelock and began to run towards the house. "And make sure Sir Henry knows his guest has arrived," John called after him.

"Yes, master, I will." The boy squared his shoulders and saluted. Amos had only got to feed the horses; he, William, was taking a message direct to Sir Henry.

John turned to Caroline, suddenly aware of how forlorn she looked. "Oh, madam, I hate to leave you in this dreadful place."

Caroline laughed. "It's not dreadful, John. Just old and badly in need of repair."

"I'd pull it down if it were mine," John said.

"Well, it's not, and it's not for you to say," said Caroline, more brusquely than she had intended.

"No, madam. I apologise."

"But I do tend to agree with you," she said, relenting, and before John could make any further comments, she added, "It's the day, of course. Nowhere looks appealing in weather like this." The wind was blowing strongly now, and even under the archway Caroline could feel its impact. "How much longer do I have to stand here? Where is that boy who's supposed to be fetching an umbrella? Do go after him, John."

"Yes, madam." Lady Lydia would not have sent him across the courtyard in this terrible driving rain, so intense now that as fast as it came down it was bouncing back up again from the cobbles.

Before John could do Caroline's bidding the stable lad reappeared, at the now open back door of the house, holding a large black umbrella. He opened it and came running across the yard.

"Here you are, madam," said John, taking the umbrella from the boy.

But Caroline's gaze was fixed on the doorway.

"Arthur," she called, "Is that you?"

"Yes," he answered from the shelter of the house, "It's me."

How doltish he sounded. "Well, don't just stand there! Come and help me."

"Oh. Yes." How was *he* to help? She had an umbrella… and a groom by the look of it.

"Oh, you are a useless creature! Get out of the way. *I'll* go and help her." There was no mistaking Sir Henry's deeper tones, nor his indignation.

"No, Sir Henry, no! Please don't come out in this awful weather. I'll come to you." Picking up her skirts, and with John holding the umbrella over her head, she splashed across the stable yard.

Sir Henry backed away from the doorway, giving her room to enter.

"My dear, dear girl. Oh, it is so lovely to see you," he said, embracing her, not caring one bit that her wet clothing would soak him. "But what an unceremonious way to greet you - at the back door and in all this rain. What must you think of me?"

"Dear Sir Henry," Caroline said, laughing. "I know you're a magistrate, but you are not responsible for the Hertfordshire weather! Nor for my being such an idiot as to ride over here instead of travelling in a closed carriage."

"Come by the fire, and tell me all about it. Arthur, take Caroline's cloak."

"I must take off these boots first," Caroline said, looking with dismay at the mess they had already made in the passageway. Fortunately the stone flags were strewn with rushes. Caroline had made a joke of it to Mary, but here they were; still, it was the back door, and maybe they were just put down in wet weather to stop people slipping on the stone.

"No, no. It doesn't matter. The important thing is to get you dry and warm. Come with me, my dear. Arthur, tell Bessie to bring some hot punch to my study. And see to the groom as well, will you."

John, hovering in the doorway, was unsure how far into the house he was supposed to venture.

"Oh John," said Caroline guiltily, turning round, "make sure you get thoroughly warm before you ride back to Bengeo."

"Don't worry, Caroline. Arthur will look after him. Won't you?"

"Yes, Father, I will." Anything to stop you finding fault with me. Marry Caroline? Never! A stroppy woman if ever there was. Now, what was he to do? Oh yes, see to the groom, and speak to Bessie. "Punch, did you say, Father?"

"Yes, Arthur, punch. And food for Lady Poynter's groom." Sir Henry sighed.

Beckoning to John to follow him, Arthur went in search of Bessie.

"That boy will be the death of me," said Sir Henry, watching him go.

"He's young," said Caroline.

"That's the trouble. He's not, but he still behaves as if he is. My dear girl, what am I thinking of! I'm as senseless as my son. Here's you cold and wet, and we're standing in this chilly passageway." Taking her arm he began to hurry her out of it. "Come, let's get you by the fire." They turned a corner and the passage gave way to a hall with a tiled floor and wood-panelled walls. Though still cold, and smelling of damp, it was at least out of the draught from the back door. Stepping ahead of her, Sir Henry flung open a door to his left and drew Caroline into the warmth of what appeared to be a library.

"Oh!" Caroline exclaimed. All she could see was books, so many books: on shelves, on tables and chairs, and piled high on the floor. She had expected something a little more spacious, a little more elegant perhaps, even in this remote country house. Then, moving round a high-backed oak settle which stood halfway across the room, she saw the fire, the flames from the logs, apple by the smell of them, leaping up into the wide chimney above the stone fireplace, and a comfortable, though shabby chair on either side. "Oh, Sir Henry, how lovely!" and drawing off her gloves she ran and knelt down in the front of the fire and held out her hands to its warmth. "Oh, this is so good." She turned and looked gratefully at her host. "To be warm again!"

Sir Henry stood, looking at her. The dear girl was here, in his home, by his fire, kneeling on the hearthrug, just as she used to do when she was a small child.

"I hope you don't mind my bringing you in here, rather than into one of the other…"

"Oh, Sir Henry, how could I mind?"

"Well, it's so cluttered and…"

"It's warm and it's cosy, and it's… it's the room where we used to play! As children."

"Yes." What memories this room held.

"But... all these books? I don't recall them being here."

"No, they weren't." Would she remember whose room this had been?

Caroline got up from the floor and looked about her, at the faded blue curtains, the old carved chairs, the mantel clock, the piquet table ...

"The piquet table!" She turned round and smiled at Sir Henry. "Of course! Aunt Elizabeth's sitting-room."

"Yes." He smiled back at her. "She did so enjoy a game of piquet."

"Oh, Sir Henry, how wonderful that you have made it your... library?" It was surely a bit disorganised to warrant such a grand name.

"More my... snug, I think."

"Yes, that's exactly it! Your snug. Because it is! A good place in which to read, it would seem," she added mischievously, before sitting down again, this time in one of the two armchairs in front of the fire.

Sir Henry chuckled. How lovely to have someone here who had a bit of spirit, who would joke with him and not be sullen or sarcastically reverential.

"I bring the books *in* here," he said, lowering himself into his red chair, pleased that Caroline had chosen the other one, "but I never seem to take them back to where they belong, in the library at the front of the house."

"I could do that for you," Caroline said.

"I should like that."

"On one condition."

"Oh, and what is that? Not that I don't bring more books in here, surely."

"That you read to me, like you used to."

A small charred twig detached itself from the blazing pile of logs in the fireplace and fell on to the hearth. Caroline leaned forward to pick up the fire tongs, but before she could get to them Sir Henry had risen from his chair and pushed the twig back towards the fire with the side of his boot; he was sprightly for a man of his age.

"It would give me great pleasure," he said. Oh, so much. Books and reading were a major part of his life.

"Dear Sir Henry. It is *so* good to see you again." Caroline stretched out her hand to him.

Bending over her, he took the proffered hand, raised it to his lips and pressed a gentle kiss upon it.

"How very gallant." Arthur, entering the room with a steaming cup of punch on a tray, knew that his voice was sharp. But really… the old man was such a fool. Kissing her hand, indeed; he wouldn't put it past him to start fondling her! Not that she'd let him, he was sure of that. There was little that was soft and womanly about Caroline Newell; well, not to Arthur's eyes, anyway.

"Oh, Arthur," said Caroline, her face glowing from the warmth of the fire, "that looks so good. So warming and welcoming." She rose from her chair and took the punch cup from the tray. "You are a dear," she said impulsively, and, as much to her surprise as his, she pecked him on the cheek. He drew back, his eyes widening in alarm. "I'm not going to eat you!"

Recovering himself quickly, and aware of his father's chuckling, he said, "Of course not. It just took me by surprise, that's all." Whatever should he say now? "It's… it's nice to see you. It's been… um… quite a long time…"

"It has indeed." She took a sip of the punch. "Mmm. This is lovely. Did you prepare it?"

"No." This was so embarrassing. How long must he stand here, close to her, making polite conversation? "Bessie made it."

"Bessie?" She turned to Sir Henry. "Do I know Bessie?"

"No, I don't think so. She was our cook, and when Elizabeth died she… she became my, well… I suppose housekeeper is the right word."

"Yes! I do remember her. Bessie. Of course! A somewhat rounded person, I recall."

Sir Henry laughed. "Yes, that's Bessie. A bit like one of her famous puddings."

"Oh yes, Bessie's puddings! Does she still make that wonderful pudding with pears and honey?" Caroline licked her lips at the thought of it.

"I don't know," Sir Henry said, laughing. "She doesn't cook now, but I believe she does still like to make cakes… and the occasional pudding." Domestic details of this kind were not Sir Henry's province, but if Caroline wanted a particular dish, she should have it. "I shall certainly get her to make the pear and honey one while you are here."

"I should like that very much," said Caroline.

Arthur groaned to himself. How boring this all was.

"Dear Bessie. What a clever idea to make her your housekeeper! She knows the house and the family… and all your needs." Caroline turned her brightest smile on the old man.

"It was *my* idea," Arthur said. He didn't expect his father to remember, but he'd make damn sure he didn't take the credit for it.

"Yours?" Caroline hadn't *intended* to sound doubtful.

"I do have ideas sometimes, you know." Arthur sounded aggrieved.

"Oh Arthur, I didn't mean anything… unkind." Oh dear, was he going to be like this, tetchy and awkward, all the time she was here? She remembered him as a pleasant, though not very bright, boy, by turns shy and then suddenly boisterous, as if he wasn't quite sure what was expected of him as the son of such an eminent man. How he had ever managed at university she couldn't imagine. And here he was, gauche, obviously disgruntled, and seemingly at odds with his father. Oh well, she could put up with it for a few days. She would try to be nice to him. "I meant… you are to be congratulated." She might as well lay it on. "I would never have thought of doing that." Good, he was beginning to relax. "So nice for your father," and she smiled at Sir Henry. At least you two can be civil to one another while I am here. She turned to Arthur. "Come and sit by the fire. Tell me all the news."

"The news?"

"You know, the gossip. The talk! About what goes on in Walkern… and Yardley."

"Well…" began Sir Henry, then stopped.

Arthur shrugged his shoulders. "Nothing really," he said.

"There must be something," persisted Caroline. "There must be some… interesting people. People you know?" she said hopefully. People she might visit, people who might visit her.

"There's the rector," said Arthur.

"The rector?"

"The Rev. Godfrey Gardiner," supplied Sir Henry. "An educated man, though somewhat unsophisticated, as befits a country parson."

"Yes, of course, I shall be pleased to meet him."

No more names were offered, and although comfortable by the fire, Caroline felt she had reached the limit of easy conversation for now, at least with Sir Henry and Arthur together. Separately, she hoped they would have more to say. "I am so lovely and warm, perhaps this would be a good time to see my room," she said. "I can take the warmth with me."

"Your room has a fire, Caroline," said Arthur, with more than a touch of sarcasm.

"Of course; but I don't expect the passageways in between have, do they?"

"No, but you wouldn't expect that. *Would* you?"

Caroline was pleased to find he had some mettle.

"No," she said.

"Oh, do you not have fires in the passageways of your home in Clerkenwell, or in your grand estate at Amley?"

"Arthur, stop this." Sir Henry was not amused by the banter. "You are being offensive to Caroline."

Hardly, she thought, but she knew better than to contradict him, certainly not in front of his son.

"Get Bessie to show Caroline her room."

"Yes, Father. I will do that." The words came out in a sharp staccato. He took the punch cup Caroline held out to him. "Thank you," he said curtly, and made a hasty retreat, shutting the door noisily on his way out.

"At least he shows some spirit, Sir Henry. You can't complain about that."

"Oh, I am not. He hasn't shown that much in ages."

Caroline laughed. "Perhaps I'll be good for him."

"You will. And for me." He sighed and his eyes darkened. "You have no idea how dreary this place has become since…"

Gently Caroline put a hand on his arm. "I know," she said. "Why do you not spend more time at your house in Hertford?"

"I would, but most of my books are here, and I am the local magistrate, as you know, and things come up that I have to deal with."

"What sort of things?" This might be interesting, amusing even.

"Oh, farmers' complaints, disputes about land and tenants, fishing rights, village feuds. All very dull really, but someone has to legislate, and that is my job, I'm afraid."

Not quite what I had in mind, thought Caroline, deciding to ask no further questions. They sat in companionable silence for a few moments, then Caroline stood up. "My room, I think," she said, and as if on cue, there was Bessie at the door.

"Bessie! Oh, it is so good to see you." She held out her hands to the old woman. She was indeed well rounded.

"Miss Caroline." Bessie smiled stiffly and bobbed a curtsey. "I am sorry, I mean Mistress Newell." How formal she was, unlike the Bessie Caroline remembered. "This way, please," she said, holding the door open.

"Thank you." Caroline turned to Sir Henry. "I shall see you at… luncheon, would it be?" Seeing him hesitate she went on hurriedly, "Or whatever meal you have in the middle of the day. I shall just tidy myself up, and then we'll meet again, shall we?"

"We don't usually eat until about four o'clock." He seemed embarrassed to be discussing his domestic arrangements. "If you are hungry Bessie could have something brought to your room."

"No, no. I am not hungry, but I should like a rest."

"Of course. It must have been a tiring journey."

Not tiring so much as uncomfortable, and she did need to remove the breeches.

"Come back in here whenever you are ready," Sir Henry said. "It's the warmest room in the house. Apart from the kitchen."

"Ah, the kitchen! I remember the kitchen." Bessie making puddings and cakes, we children clustered around her, begging to be allowed to lick the spoon, or better still, the bowl with the remains of some delicious uncooked mixture clinging to the sides; hiding from the grown-ups under the big deal table... and Bessie swearing she had not seen us; turning the roasting spit, only one turn each, no more; hot fat might get on to our clothes... and then we'd be in trouble, and so would Bessie.

"I spend very little time in there now. My duties, as housekeeper" - said with studied emphasis, in case Caroline had not been informed - "take me all over the house."

"Oh. Yes. Of course." Yes, you run the house now and I must not get on the wrong side of you. This is not the Bessie I knew. Without Elizabeth, Yardley Bury seemed to have lost its heart; the joy and warmth she remembered was no longer there. Two days here, just possibly three, would be quite enough.

Caroline's bedroom belonged, like the rest of the house, to a bygone age. The old queen, Elizabeth, who had died more than a century ago, would have felt quite at home here: an oak four-poster bed with a silk tester, now sadly in shreds, a cabinet with bulbous columns, an elaborately carved oak chest at the foot of the bed, a most uncomfortable-looking straight-backed wooden chair and, a more recent addition, a walnut table with a mirror on it. Worn rugs, their once bright colours dulled with age, covered the floor, and dusty damask curtains, that might originally have been a bright yellow, hung at the small mullioned windows. The redeeming feature of the room was the fireplace, where logs that smelt of pine were sending joyful, crackling sparks up into the wide chimney. The fire was doing little to take away the chill - it looked as if it had not long since been lit - but the mere sight of it made Caroline feel warm again after the trek from Sir Henry's snug to this room at the front of the house, a room that was seldom used by the feel of it.

Now, at last, she could remove the breeches - how men could wear them all the time she found difficult to understand; all that cloth bunched up between your legs! - but having done so, where was she to secrete them? It would never do for Bessie to find them - she would think Caroline had a man in her room! The oak chest, that would be the place. She lifted the heavy lid and peered inside. She was astonished to find a velvet cloak, richly embroidered with a design of ripe red strawberries, and bees sewn with gold thread. To whom did it belong? It was certainly not Bessie's and she couldn't imagine Aunt Elizabeth wearing it, not out here in the countryside. Perhaps Arthur would know. In the meantime the chest would be a good hiding-place for her own, offending, garment. Carefully she lifted the cloak and placed it on the floor, then laid the breeches in the bottom of the chest; the cloak had been the only thing in there. She was tempted to try it on, but common sense prevailed. Suppose someone - Bessie? - caught her wearing it? She must try to find out, discreetly, whose it was, and why it was there. Carefully she laid the cloak back in the chest - it really was exquisite - and closed the lid.

The room was beginning to feel warmer, and Caroline, who *was* weary after her journey, began to feel drowsy. The bed looked inviting; she pulled back the velvet coverlet and climbed in, drawing the coverlet over her, as much for the sense of being *in* bed as for the warmth it gave her. She sank down into the soft feather mattress. It was good to relax and not have to *make* conversation, which was how it had felt with Sir Henry and Arthur, and with Bessie too. Perhaps she had been wrong to come. It had seemed such a good idea when she had been at Lydia's - spend a few nostalgic days at Yardley Bury, see Sir Henry while she could. She had reckoned without the effect that the absence of Elizabeth would make. Robert had loved Elizabeth too, and he had enjoyed meeting her, both at Emilia's house and the Chauncy home in Hertford. He had not cared for Sir Henry, finding him too rigid in his opinions, unwilling to accept change. Though a man of impeccable probity and great standing in the community, both of which Robert respected, the two men had little in common. Chauncy was a scholar and historian, nearly always looking back to the past; Robert was a man of action, with his focus on the present and the future and all the knowledge that this new eighteenth century was bringing to the fore.

Robert had been far *too* fond of action and innovation, Caroline thought. It was because of Robert's desire - no,

39

Robert's need - always to be at the heart of things that she was now a widow. They had had only seven years together, seven bitter-sweet years, sweet because of the love they had for one another, a love that encompassed not only a deeply fulfilling physical relationship but also intellectual companionship, so rare in a marriage, and laughter and silliness, too. Together they were complete. The bitterness was on account of the children they had lost, two before they were a few months old, and then their darling Hannah. Two years, seven months and four days had been the extent of her life.

They had never really recovered from that tragedy. Caroline could not, would not, talk about it; Robert, on the other hand, went over and over it, first aloud to Caroline, then, as she closed herself in, to himself. He was a doctor, for heaven's sake! If a doctor couldn't save his own child what use was he to anyone? He had been away from home the night Hannah died, attending to a sick child on his estate; that child had lived. For that reason alone Caroline could not speak to Robert: how could she reproach him for saving the life of a child? Wasn't that child's life worth as much as Hannah's? She knew he was suffering too, but she felt unable to reach out to him. Every time she tried, and she did try, she saw in her mind's eye that living child - she didn't even know her name - in her husband's arms, and then, in her own arms, Hannah, dead. Robert felt that he had failed her, and Hannah too. Even more distressing for Caroline was *her* terrible feeling that he *had*.

It was this overriding sense of failure and guilt that had finally caused Robert to forsake his wealthy human patients and concentrate on the welfare of his animals. For some time he had felt a growing impatience with old women grown too fat on an over-rich diet and little exercise and old men with gout from too much drinking. They were not *ill*, he told them, they were self-indulgent and lazy.

"A horse does not pretend to be ill to get my attention!" Not surprisingly, they sought another doctor.

Then came the day, not long after Hannah's death, when he had successfully treated two hunters, both severely injured following a collision in which the riders suffered only minor bruises. "I couldn't save my daughter's life," Robert said to Caroline, "but I can save these beautiful creatures."

And so he had gone to war, but not to fight with Marlborough against the French - he cared nothing for the flamboyant officers in their fancy uniforms, wielding their swords and shouting their huzzahs. It was their horses that concerned Robert. Terrified and wounded, they were often then abandoned: a stricken steed was no use in battle. Some of the officers *did* care for their animals - it would be wrong to think otherwise - and sometimes the man went down with the horse. Some of the mounts were beyond help, and the kindest thing to do was to shoot them, but many of them could be saved, and relieved of their pain too, which was why Robert was there.

Knowing only too well where these thoughts would lead her - to Robert's own death on the battlefield - Caroline determinedly switched her focus to her present situation. If only Mary were here she would be able to change into fresh clothes, something warm… and plain. On the other hand, the yellow silk with the frills would cheer her up. Or there was the blue satin, and with the satin dress she could wear those nice new beaded slippers that Lydia had given her.

Soothed by these comforting trivialities, Caroline drifted off to sleep.

She was awakened by a sharp knock on the bedroom door and a voice calling her name.

"Miss Caroline… are you awake?"

The dream - of beautiful gowns floating around a garden, and young girls shivering in their shifts, trying to catch them - receded, and Caroline awoke to find herself cold and stiff, with the fire burnt down to its embers.

"Mary! Yes, of course I'm awake."

The door opened and Mary, still in her travelling clothes, entered the room.

"Oh, Miss Caroline, you have no idea how relieved I am to be here!"

"Why?" asked Caroline, drawing the coverlet around her shoulders for warmth, "Did you have a bad journey?"

"Bad? It was terrible! The driver got lost."

"No!" Lydia's coachman, surely not? "Put another log on that fire, will you?"

Mary moved to the fireplace, talking as she went. "Oh yes! And I was supposed to be safe with him, wasn't I?" Mary poked the fire and threw a small log on to the embers. A flame sprang up and she added another one.

"Well, you obviously were safe or you wouldn't be here," said her mistress, getting off the bed and drawing near the fire. "You're not hurt, are you?"

"No, mistress."

"Good."

"But I might have…"

"No! I don't want to hear about it now. You can tell me later. What I want now is some fresh, *warm* clothing, so get your cloak off and find someone to bring my boxes upstairs."

Mary looked disappointed; she did so love to tell a tale, and she was quite good at it, Caroline had to admit.

"I promise to hear your story, Mary, but not *now.* You'd do better to go to the kitchen and get yourself a hot drink… and then come and unpack my boxes."

Dressed in clean clothes, the warmest ones that had been packed, and refreshed by a tisane which Mary had persuaded Bessie to allow her to take upstairs, Caroline went in search of company and conversation, although she doubted she would find much of either.

The winter afternoon was drawing in. As she made her way down the wide oak staircase, through the narrow windows above the panelling Caroline could see daylight among the bare, dripping branches of the trees, but inside the house it was almost as dark as night.

"I don't like this house, mistress, it's creepy," said Mary, following closely behind Caroline.

"Nonsense, girl. It's just dark. We could have done with a candle."

"Do you want me to go back and get one?" asked Mary, hoping she would not have to walk along the shadowy passage on her own. It had been bad enough in full daylight, finding her way, first upstairs to Caroline's room, then down a narrow back staircase to the kitchen, and then back up again.

"No, we're nearly at the bottom now. Don't worry, there'll be plenty of light in the main rooms, you'll see."

"I hope so," Mary said gloomily. "It's so damp everywhere, too."

Caroline, just ahead of her at the foot of the stairs, stopped so abruptly that Mary nearly ran into her.

"Mary! Stop this! I know you don't want to be here, but you are, so make the best of it. Tomorrow, when all these rain clouds have cleared, everything will look much brighter." She paused, and mustering a smile, which they both knew was false, she continued, "and we can begin to enjoy ourselves."

3

Daylight brought relief from the rain, and although it was still cold, by nine o'clock the sun was shining brightly out of an almost clear blue sky.

Just the sort of weather for a ride in the country, Caroline said at breakfast, looking pointedly at Arthur. Reluctantly he agreed to accompany her, to Sir Henry's satisfaction: he had parish matters to attend to this morning, but he would look forward to having Caroline's undivided attention later in the day.

Arthur proved to be a competent, if not stylish, horseman, and he knew every inch of the countryside around Yardley Bury. A new barn they passed belonged to Farmer Gilbert, he told her; that five-barred gate was the one that the rector's maidservant, Anne Thorn, had leapt over; that was the Chapman farm where they were trying out something new… a seed drill, Arthur said proudly, anxious to show Caroline that even though Walkern was some thirty miles from London it was not completely behind the times. It had been invented by a man called Tull, he said. How very interesting, Caroline had commented, although, of course, she knew this; they had been using seed drills at Amley for a good seven years.

Encouraged by her apparent enthusiasm, Arthur suggested that they ride north to Cromer, so that she could see the mill there in action. "Not something you can witness in Clerkenwell," he said over his shoulder, as they galloped across a stretch of higher ground from which the water had drained away, leaving it sufficiently dry for both riders and horses to enjoy a brief burst of speed without getting splashed.

The Cromer windmill was indeed impressive, towering over forty feet into the sky and dominating the countryside around. They reined in their horses a little distance from the mill, so that Caroline could watch the shuttered wooden sails going round rhythmically; quickly, too, in the stiff breeze which had now blown up.

Arthur wanted to take Caroline right down to the mill so that he could introduce her to the miller, "a good sort of fellow, quite respectable; reads books, so I'm told".

"Thank you, Arthur, that's a kind thought but I really think we ought to turn back," she said, pointing with her riding crop to a small, dark cloud that had appeared, most obligingly, on the horizon. "I should hate to be soaked again, as I was yesterday." And I do not want everyone in the neighbourhood to hear, thanks to the miller, however nice he might be, that "there is a London lady staying at Yardley Bury, a Mistress Newell, a friend of Sir Henry". It was just the sort of information that the Cliffords, who had a house in a village only a few miles north of Cromer, would pass on to their son, Roger, a young man - around twenty years old, Caroline thought - with extravagant manners and foppish dress, coupled with a strange, to her unpleasant, sense of humour. He had looked so angry, she recalled, so vengeful, when she had failed to be amused by a trick he had played upon one of her friends. Perhaps there was a nice young man underneath all the artifice and seeming malice, but Caroline was not going to be the one to find it. No, best to turn around now; besides, it really did look as if it might rain.

Arthur was obviously disappointed not to be showing off his sophisticated riding companion to one of his friends. Friends? Yes, it was quite possible that he liked to have a drink with the local tradesmen. And why not? Caroline hated the rigid class divisions that English society demanded. Why should a skilled joiner or weaver, or any man who worked with his hands, be considered lowlier than someone who could read Latin and Greek? Caroline's father had brought her up to treat everyone equally, regardless of their station in life. Whatever work they did, he would say, whether it was baking bread, rearing livestock or sweeping chimneys... as long as they did it well and were honest, they deserved respect.

"It isn't going to rain *just* yet," Caroline said. "Show me some more of the countryside on the way back. It is very like Essex here, you know. But more hilly... and therefore more interesting." Arthur gave her a grateful smile. Poor young man, all he needed was a bit of encouragement. And a bit of polish. A few weeks in London would soon put that right. Should she suggest it now? Perhaps not; it would be best to see if they really got on before committing herself to anything. Besides, he might not want to come. London theatres and pleasure gardens might have no appeal for him, and it would be silly taking him to such places if he was not enjoying himself.

"Do you know why it is called Walkern?" Arthur's voice broke into her musing.

"I'm sorry, what did you say?"

"Walkern. It's called Walkern because the Devil told the people to build the church near the river, not where they wanted to build it. He told them to walk on." He paused, waiting to see if Caroline had got the point. "You know, walk on, Walk-ern."

"Yes. Oh yes, I see," said Caroline. She couldn't *really* see the point of the story - there must be more to it than that - but she was pleased that Arthur had volunteered it. "It's a good story."

"It's *true*," Arthur said. Caroline looked at him quizzically. "It is. The Devil can do strange things, you know."

"Yes, of course." Religion, good and evil; was that what interested Arthur? Well, there were plenty of churches in London that he could visit, the new St. Paul's among them. About to ask him what he thought of the work of Sir Christopher Wren, she realised he was out of earshot and ahead of her. Oh dear, had she upset him by her scepticism? She gave her horse a gentle tap with her crop; a quick canter over the tussocky grass brought her to Arthur's side and a warm smile seemed to restore her to his favour.

They crossed the River Beane close to Walkern, where clear water ran over large stones. On a summer day Caroline would have loved to halt and let her horse have a drink, but today she was glad to be up on the other bank.

Suddenly the quiet of the morning was disturbed by the sound of angry voices close by, just beyond the trees that fringed the stream. Caroline reined in her horse. Through the bare branches she saw a handful of people, common villagers by the look of them, all in drab fustian, some of them with sticks in their hands, crowded together outside a thatched cottage. As she watched they began banging their sticks on the heavy wooden door and on the casement window to the side.

"What *is* going on?" asked Caroline, intrigued. Was it a riot, such as she had seen in London? Surely not. "Does someone live there, Arthur? I do hope not."

"Oh, it's just old Jane Wenham's house; they often do that." On his own Arthur would probably have joined them; it was just the sort of excitement he enjoyed. But not now, not with Caroline at his side. Perhaps later, if they were still there. "Come," he said abruptly, turning his horse away from the stream and into the lane by the church. "I'll take you home."

Caroline had no choice but to follow him; she had no wish to become involved in a village fracas - the people had looked really angry. "Why are they banging on the woman's door?" she asked as she caught up with Arthur.

He didn't stop, but rode on, turning off the lane into the field that led up to Yardley Bury.

"Arthur, I asked you a question!" Caroline said crossly. They were side by side now. "Please answer me." Caroline stretched out her hand and grabbed hold of Arthur's reins.

"They're just..." Arthur said, coming to a halt. He wasn't sure that he could give an answer, not one that Caroline would find acceptable. She was certain to laugh if he told her the truth; he had seen her look of amusement when he told her the story about the Devil.

"They're just what? Come on, Arthur, you know why they're there. I can tell by your face."

This was so awkward. He couldn't look at her; he could only look down at his hands on the reins.

"Arthur, look at me!" He lifted his head. "Who is Jane Wenham?"

"She's just an old woman, that's all."

"And is that why those people are banging on her door? Because she's old?"

"Well, no…"

"What, then?" Her horse, sensing her rider's impatience, was pawing the ground fretfully. "I am not moving, and nor are you, until you tell me."

Arthur looked away. When he looked back, Caroline's eyes were still fixed on him.

"She's a witch!" He hadn't wanted to say it. Now would come the mockery.

"Oh Arthur! A witch?" She laughed. "What nonsense!"

He turned on her fiercely. "I know you live in London, but you don't know everything!"

"Well no, I don't." Caroline was taken aback by Arthur's hostility.

"It's time to get back," he said gruffly. "I don't want my father to be worried."

"No, of course not." Such concern for Sir Henry? It seemed quite out of character. It was more likely that he did not want Caroline to go tittle-tattling back to his father. A witch indeed! Sir Henry would not be pleased to hear that his son held such arcane views.

Caroline released Arthur's reins. Without even looking back to see if she was following him, he urged his horse into a gallop. Oh, let him go, thought Caroline. The mood of the day was broken and it was not up to her to mend it.

By the time she rode into the stable yard Arthur was off his horse. He came towards her and took her reins.

"If you dismount I will see to your horse," he said brusquely, guiding her to the mounting block.

"Thank you." She took his outstretched hand and he helped her down. "Arthur," she said, keeping hold of his hand.

"Yes?" What now? More questions, more laughter?

"It was a lovely ride."

"Oh."

"I did enjoy it, you know." She let go of his hand.

"It was a pleasure," Arthur said stiffly, leading her horse away.

That young man is not happy, Caroline thought as she walked across the yard; it would do him good to get away from here.

"Well?" she asked later that day. "What do you think? Will you come to London?"

They were sitting in the snug, warm after food, Caroline on the hearthrug playing with a pile of fir cones and occasionally throwing one into the flames and watching it spit and crackle, Sir Henry in his favourite chair, puffing at his long-stemmed clay pipe, with Arthur opposite him, also smoking. She was pleased that neither of them indulged in the new habit of taking snuff; she found it unpleasant, almost nauseating, to see a man take a pinch of the black or brown powder between his thumb and finger and sniff it up into his nostrils.

Arthur had, up to now, been most companionable, even drawing forth laughter from his father at a story about one of his village friends. For friends they were; he appeared to have no close association with anyone of his own class.

"I don't know," said Arthur, warily, not looking directly at Caroline.

"You could at least say thank you." Sir Henry could not hide his displeasure at Arthur's churlishness.

"Thank you." If only they wouldn't both keep looking at him like that, waiting, wanting him to be pleased.

"You would have a wonderful time, Arthur," Caroline enthused. "There is so much to see and do. I can show you all the sights and introduce you to lots of interesting people. And, do you know, there are over a thousand coffee houses you could visit!" In Heaven's name, why was she saying all this? Couldn't she let well alone? Did she *really* want Arthur to come to London, or was it because she knew instinctively that the more she and Sir Henry pushed it the less likely he was to accept?

"This is very kind of Caroline, you know," Sir Henry said. His pipe had gone out.

"I know that, and I'm grateful." But I'm not going just to please either of you.

"Now is not the right time, though."

"I didn't mean now," said Caroline. "I'm not expecting you to come back with me. This is an idea for the summer, or… or whenever you would like to come."

"Of course you can go now," said Sir Henry, gently tapping his pipe on the hearth. "There's nothing to keep you here; you don't *do* anything here. The best thing *is* for you to return with Caroline. You can escort her to Clerkenwell. That, at least, is something useful you'll be doing!" He reached out for his tobacco jar on the small table beside his chair and began refilling his pipe.

"Ah. Well…" began Caroline, wishing to goodness she hadn't put herself in this awkward situation. "I wasn't planning to go back to Clerkenwell just yet; I need to spend some more time with my sister-in-law."

"He could travel with you from Bengeo." Sir Henry was determined not to lose an opportunity for a closer relationship to develop between his son and Caroline. "You only have to send word and he could ride over and join you."

Caroline was unsure what her next words should be; she was going to displease one of them no matter what she said. The entrance of Bessie saved her having to decide.

"There's a crowd of village people coming across the park, Sir Henry," Bessie said, bursting into the room. She was very agitated. "They don't look happy, neither. They's waving sticks and some of them's got pitchforks!"

Calm, reserved Housekeeper Bessie was gone; a frightened old servant had taken her place.

"Oh no," Sir Henry said, wearily. "I've been dealing with village problems all day. I don't want any more." He put the tobacco jar back in its place, and bending down to the hearth he picked up a pair of wrought-iron ember tongs with which to relight his pipe from the fire.

"What am I to do, sir?" Bessie asked, quite reasonably, Caroline thought.

"Send them away, Bessie." He replaced the tongs and drew on his pipe.

"I would, sir…" Bessie hesitated. "… but I don't think they'll take notice of me."

A loud knock at the front door echoed down the passageway to the snug, together with the sound of angry, raised voices, one of them louder than the other. Caroline and Arthur rose from their places by the fire.

"That sounds like John Chapman." Sir Henry sighed. "Oh dear, I suppose I shall have to see them." He allowed himself one long, satisfying puff of his pipe, then laid it carefully down in a china bowl on the table. He started walking reluctantly towards the door. "Tell them I'm coming, Bessie."

"Yes, Sir Henry," Bessie said, and left the room.

"I'll come with you, Father," said Arthur.

"You stay here," Sir Henry said. "If *you* join in, it will take twice as long."

"I just thought I might be able to help…"

"Help? With a village dispute? All you'll do is make it worse." Then, in a gentler tone, he said, "Stay with Caroline. Please."

Poor Arthur; his father did disparage him so. No wonder he was unsure of himself.

"Do you think these are the same people we saw earlier?" Caroline whispered as Sir Henry was leaving the room.

"What did you say?" Sir Henry paused and turned towards them.

"Arthur and I saw some people… when we were out riding… and I wondered if…?"

"They were banging on Jane Wenham's door," said Arthur.

"Oh, not Jane Wenham again. I heard enough about her this morning."

The voices at the door became more urgent.

"I had better sort it out," Sir Henry said, and left the room.

"Your father said *John* Chapman. Is that the Farmer Chapman you mentioned on our ride?"

"Yes," Arthur said. "He's always having rows with Jane Wenham."

"Why?"

"Usually because she's bewitched one of his animals."

Caroline laughed.

"Don't laugh. He lost cattle worth *two hundred pounds* last year. It's a serious thing for a farmer if there's something wrong with his livestock."

"Well of course it is, but… bewitched?"

"Wait till my father comes back," Arthur said brusquely. "See what he has to say." He walked over to the fire.

"I will," said Caroline. She sat down in Sir Henry's chair.

"You'd better not sit *there.*"

"I'll move… when Sir Henry comes back. He won't mind if I sit here now."

"If it's *you*, I don't suppose he will." He turned his back on her.

There was an awkward silence, with Arthur staring at the fire and Caroline, equally fixedly, looking at the window and the rain now beating on it. After a few moments Caroline got up and moved to the other armchair; there was no sense in annoying Arthur unnecessarily.

"Probably better if I sit here."

"Sorry," said Arthur gruffly, still facing the fire. "It's not easy, you know," he said, swinging round, "… pleasing my father."

"I know." She smiled at him. "It seldom is, with parents. I had arguments with mine. They thought I was too independent for a girl; they were so relieved when I married

Robert." She was tempted to say more, explain to Arthur that half the problem was because he was still living with his father at the age of twenty eight, when he should be running his own home... but that might lead to the question of marriage, a topic she did not wish to discuss.

"Does the farmer really think the old woman is a witch?" she said instead. If she could discover why Arthur still believed in witchcraft - as he seemed to do - she might understand him better.

"Of course he does," Arthur said. "The whole village does."

"Not everyone, surely?" There must be some educated people here who don't.

"You'll not find many who don't, and those few will be afraid to say." Sir Henry spoke from the doorway, then crossed the floor and retrieved his pipe.

Caroline was amazed to hear those words from him.

"But... this is the eighteenth century!" she said.

Sir Henry relit his pipe and sat down. "This is not London, my dear. Old ideas take a long time to die out in a place like this."

"So... they really do believe... that the old woman is a witch?"

Sir Henry nodded. "Oh yes. They do. You'd be surprised how many cases of suspected witchcraft are brought to me."

"What has she been up to this time, Father?"

"She's bewitched one of Farmer Chapman's men."

Caroline looked at Sir Henry in disbelief. The idea of witchcraft still being practised both intrigued and appalled her. It was almost dark now in the far corners of the room away from the light of the fire. Caroline shivered involuntarily; she must return to practicalities.

"A moment ago, Sir Henry, you mentioned cases being brought before you…? Is that as magistrate?" Caroline spoke calmly. She knew she would learn more from Sir Henry if she could resist becoming emotional again.

"Yes."

"Cases of witchcraft?"

"Yes." He sat back in his chair and drew on his pipe. Normally he enjoyed a good discussion, which this promised to be, but the day had worn him out, and he wanted nothing so much as to be left in peace to smoke his pipe and….

"Are you saying that people, women, are still being tried for witchcraft?"

"Oh yes," said Arthur, with enthusiasm. He had left the fire and was standing by the window. "If someone is practising witchcraft they must be punished."

"In what way?"

"Well… hanged, of course."

"No!"

"Francis thinks they should be, doesn't he, Father?"

"Francis? Who is Francis?" asked Caroline, looking first at Arthur, then at Sir Henry.

"My grandson by marriage," said Sir Henry from the depths of his armchair. "The Reverend Francis Bragge. Bragge by name and brag by nature, I'm sorry to say."

"Not a favourite grandson, I take it," Caroline smiled at her host.

"You take it correctly, my dear," Sir Henry said, sleepily. Arthur could tell Caroline all she might want to know about Francis. He put down his pipe and shut his eyes.

"Does he… Francis… know about Jane Wenham?" Caroline enquired, looking across the room to Arthur.

"Oh yes," he said eagerly. "He knows everything about her." He's enjoying this, thought Caroline with dismay. "His father dealt with Dissenters."

"Oh?"

"She's bound to be one. They are."

"Oh." Not totally understanding what Arthur meant, and wanting to get away from the unpleasant-sounding Bragge family, but stay with the subject of witchcraft, Caroline asked, "What exactly is the old woman supposed to have done to Farmer Chapman's man?"

It was no good. The thought of Francis, who was sure to be visiting Yardley Bury any day now - news of a witch at work would soon bring him running - had quite put Sir Henry off his sleep. He might as well answer Caroline's question.

"She put a spell on him, so the farmer says, and he ran across the fields without his shirt on, and then he couldn't work."

Caroline laughed. It all sounded so ridiculous, and yet she could see that Arthur took it seriously, and from Sir Henry's matter-of-fact tone, to a certain extent so did he.

"And that makes her a witch, does it?"

"You shouldn't joke about something like this." Arthur was angry. And possibly a bit frightened? She knew she shouldn't but she couldn't resist taunting him.

"Why, what will you do? Get your witch to put a spell on *me*?"

"Tell her, Father," said Arthur, "tell her not to say things like that." He had gone pale; he *was* frightened.

58

"Reserve your judgment, my dear. 'There are more things in heaven and earth…' "

" '…than are dreamt of in your philosophy.' " Caroline finished the quote for him.

"Yes," Sir Henry said solemnly.

"You're serious, aren't you, both of you? You really believe this woman is a witch."

"As I said, reserve your judgment. Go down to the rectory tomorrow; Arthur can take you. Mr. Gardiner will be questioning Jane Wenham, and the farmer and the farmer's man. Listen to what everyone has to say, and then, when you are better informed, you will be able to make a more *considered* judgment."

Caroline's cheeks flamed red. Although Sir Henry's voice was soft and gentle, she knew she was being reprimanded. No doubt she deserved it, but she was not going to apologise for not accepting his, surprisingly old-fashioned, beliefs. She was, however, a guest in his house and she must be courteous to him.

Smiling at Sir Henry, she said sweetly, "I should like that. It sounds as if it will be most interesting, and I am sure I shall learn a lot." She felt no similar need to be polite to Arthur; she didn't have to look at him to know that he was smirking.

"I know Mistress Gardiner will be pleased to meet you," Sir Henry said.

"Mistress Gardiner?"

"The rector's wife."

"Why should she want to meet me?" Oh no. Not to spread news of me around the county; no, please not. Then, a sudden, alarming yet relieving, thought:

"Please don't tell me she wants to hear about all the new churches in London, the new embroidered altar cloths and painted windows. I have seen so few of them!" She felt quite ashamed that she would be unable to oblige Sir Henry.

He chuckled. "Nothing so uplifting, I'm afraid. It is not the churches she is interested in, our good rector's wife; it is the clothes worn by the congregation. Mistress Gardiner, a somewhat timid lady, as you will find, is a keen follower of fashion, and you, my dear Caroline, will be able to tell her what is being worn in London this season."

"Oh, Sir Henry." Caroline giggled. "How lovely. The secret passion of the rector's wife, and you have discovered it! Well, I shall have to make sure I don't disappoint her... in what I wear tomorrow, I mean. Don't sneer, Arthur," she said, turning to him.

"I wasn't." How could he not sneer at this silly banter?

"Clothes can be important, you know. They say things about people."

"Oh. Do they?" How much longer must he stand here listening to this rubbish when there was a witch to be dealt with!

"Oh yes. The clothes you choose to wear, and the way you wear them, can tell people who are looking at you what sort of person you are *inside.*"

What nonsense she does talk!

"So," Caroline went on, walking slowly across to him and gently removing a tiny piece of straw from the front of his riding coat, "you shall help me to choose what I shall wear tomorrow." Arthur drew back. "Don't worry, I haven't forgotten the reason we are going to be there; at the same time, though, I want to wear something that will be pleasing to Mistress Gardiner."

Arthur looked aghast. He stepped well away from Caroline. "I will escort you there," he said, stiffly, "but I am having nothing to do with your clothes!" and he fled the room, not even stopping to shut the door behind him.

Caroline turned to Sir Henry. "That was naughty of me, I know." She bowed her head in mock humility. Then looking up, her eyes sparkling with fun, she said, "I'm sorry, Sir Henry; I couldn't resist it."

Oh, what a wonderful daughter-in-law she would make, the old man thought.

"Candles," he said, briskly, getting up from his chair. "That's what we need. Light." He went to the open door, and called, loudly. "Jacob! Candles!"

From the distance came Jacob's voice, "Just bringing them, sir."

"Now, my dear," Sir Henry turned to Caroline, "what do you say to a game of piquet?"

"I say yes, Sir Henry. Thank you. I should like that very much."

4

The bedroom was strewn with clothes: on the bed, draped over the chairs, on the oak chest.

"What do you think, Mary? Shall I wear this one?" Caroline asked, looking in the mirror and holding against herself a heavily flounced grey and black taffeta dress. "Or the blue silk, perhaps?"

"That one, mistress," answered Mary, "the one in your hands."

"Not too elaborate?"

"No, Miss Caroline. Mistress Gardiner will like that one."

"Oh," said Caroline, turning from the mirror. "How do you know? Have you met her?"

"Yes, mistress."

"When?"

"When you were out riding." Knowing that was not enough of an explanation for Caroline, she went on, "Bessie took me."

"Bessie?"

"Yes, mistress, she is… quite friendly … with Mistress Gardiner."

"What a peculiar friendship," said Caroline. "Oh well, they seem to *do* odd things here."

She put the grey and black dress down on the bed, and took the blue one from Mary. "What is she like, Mistress Gardiner?"

"It's not for me to say, mistress," Mary replied. "Do you not want this one?" she asked, lifting the taffeta gown from the bed.

"Don't change the subject. What is she like?" She held the blue gown against herself. "Tell me!" She spoke to Mary's reflection in the mirror. "For Sir Henry's sake I have to make the right impression."

"She's just a quiet lady, Miss Caroline, but…"

"But what?" said Caroline, spinning round from the mirror and facing Mary directly.

"She's… she's sort of secretive."

"I'm not surprised. A country rector's wife, who, if Sir Henry is correct, follows the fashions, needs to be secretive."

"Why, mistress?"

"Because, you silly, dim-witted girl, anything out of the ordinary in a place like this is regarded as… well, sinful, probably, 'the work of the Devil'."

"Don't say that mistress, please." Mary sounded suddenly fearful.

"What… Devil?"

"Yes. Don't say it!"

"Why?" Mary had gone quite pale. "Why are you looking so anxious?"

"They… they spoke of the Devil" - Mary whispered the word - "in Mistress Gardiner's kitchen; Bessie and Anne Thorn, she's the rector's servant, and her mother, too."

"Yes. Well?"

"They said… they said the..." Again she whispered the word, "the Devil was everywhere, and most of all, she was in that old woman, Jane Wenham."

"Oh, nonsense!" exploded Caroline, tossing aside the blue dress and snatching up the grey and black one from the bed. "I want no more talk of devils and old women who might be…" She glared at Mary. "Oh, I know what they call her. A witch. Don't tremble like that! It's just a word." She shook the dress at Mary. "I shall wear this one. Very fashionable. A bit courtly, one might say. Just the thing to wear at court, especially if you are a courtesan!" Mary's eyes opened wide. "Don't worry, girl, Mistress Gardiner won't think that… and if she does, well, it will give her a bit of a thrill, won't it!"

"Yes, mistress," answered Mary. She didn't really know *what* to say. Had Miss Caroline taken leave of her senses? It must be this dreadful place. The sooner they were back in Hertford the better.

"You know, Mary," Caroline said, easing herself, with Mary's help, into the chosen dress, and adjusting the neckline so that it showed more of her breasts than was strictly appropriate for the time of day, "What with a witch and a fashion-conscious rector's wife, rural Hertfordshire might turn out to be quite amusing after all."

"Yes, mistress," Mary said. It's all show, she thought. What was that lovely word she had found in a book and Miss Caroline had explained to her? Oh, what was it? … Bravado, that was it. It's all bravado; my lady is as nervous as I am.

Sir Henry and Arthur were waiting for them in the entrance hall.

"You look splendid, my dear," Sir Henry said.

"You should not be wearing *that*." Arthur looked alarmed.

"It's not for your benefit, you know. It's for Mistress Gardiner."

"It's too smart," he said grumpily. "For the rectory."

"I'm glad you acknowledge its smartness, Arthur. Thank you for that. I shan't change it, though."

"Come along," said Sir Henry, who had been watching this interchange between Caroline and Arthur with amusement, "the carriage is ready for you."

"Oh no!" Caroline sounded alarmed. "No, I am not travelling in a carriage, not just to the rectory. I shall walk."

"Walk?" said Arthur scornfully. "Dressed like that?"

"Yes," replied Caroline. "I shall wear a dark cloak; I have no intention of strutting through the countryside like a peacock. Besides, I should be cold in just a dress."

Turning to Sir Henry, she said gently, "Thank you for being so solicitous, but it would be ostentatious to travel to Walkern in your carriage, and as you know, I don't want to excite curiosity in the neighbourhood." She had told Sir Henry, but not Arthur, why she had come to Yardley Bury earlier than planned.

"Huh," said Arthur, nodding at her gown. "What else do you expect in that attire? This is not your Vauxhall Gardens, you know."

Caroline sighed. She didn't like to admit it, but Arthur was right. "Forgive me, Sir Henry. I will go and change," she said quietly. "Then you and I, Arthur, will walk to the rectory together."

"Thank you," Arthur said. Good - he had scored a point there. Thought herself so grand, so far above all of us here.

Just wait. She'd see soon enough that there were more important matters than London fashion and gossip. There were *dangerous* matters afoot here; a loathsome witch was upsetting good hard-working folk. She must be stopped and Arthur would see that she was. And Caroline, soberly dressed please, would see how he wielded his authority in the community. He was, after all, the son of the magistrate.

It was under a mile across the fields to the rectory, and they were there within twenty minutes. They were greeted at the door by Mr. Gardiner, who seemed quite troubled to see a lady arriving with Arthur.

"A friend of my mother," Arthur said tersely, having introduced Caroline to the rector. "She is interested in our local affairs," he added ungraciously.

"Mr. Gardiner," Caroline said, smiling at him and extending her gloved hand. "I do hope you don't consider my presence here an intrusion."

"On the contrary, Mistress Newell, we are honoured to have you with us. My wife will be delighted to meet you. Please do come through to the parlour and I will fetch her," he said, backing away and bowing at the same time.

"No, please, please," Caroline remonstrated. "I am most happy to come into your kitchen. That is where you are meeting, I believe."

The rector halted in his backward progress. He looked appalled. "It would not be fitting for you to be entertained in the kitchen." It was almost as if she had asked to sit in the cowshed.

"Mr. Gardiner," Caroline said meekly, "if I am causing you a problem, I shall not stay. I shall just have a word with

Mistress Gardiner, and then Mr. Chauncy and I will return to Yardley Bury."

"No," said Arthur. "I have to be here."

"You can't let Mistress Newell return to Yardley Bury on her own," Mr. Gardiner said helplessly.

"Mr. Gardiner," said Caroline, delicately placing a hand on his arm, an action which made him feel so uncomfortable that he drew back sharply, leaving Caroline's hand poised in mid-air, "I shall come into your kitchen, with Mr. Chauncy."

"But…" he started. There were no rules in his book to deal with this sort of behaviour.

"Not another word, please. I *love* kitchens. Besides, your wife won't want the villagers and the farm-workers… and the old woman, of course… she won't want them in the parlour, will she?"

"No, she won't, but…"

We can't go on like this, thought Arthur. "Mr. Gardiner," he said, "could we not use your morning room? It is large enough to accommodate us all, and it would be more suitable for Mistress Newell than your kitchen. And probably warmer than your parlour. Am I right?"

"Indeed, Mr. Chauncy, indeed. Thank you." Poor man, he sounded so relieved.

"That is an admirable solution. Mistress Newell," he said, inclining head towards her, "This way, if you please." He stretched out his arm and ushered Caroline down the hallway and into a smallish, low-ceilinged room with oak panelling. A girl in a mob cap and a coarse, woven apron was kneeling in front of the fire.

"That's enough, Anne," said the rector kindly. "It's caught now, it doesn't need any more sticks."

The girl looked from the rector back to the fire. "But I've got more," she said.

"You can use them another time. Now, put them in your apron, take them to the kitchen and put them on the woodpile."

Awkwardly the girl stood up and Caroline saw that one of her legs was twisted. Her face was pale and she seemed to have difficulty focusing her eyes. Poor child, Caroline thought, she must be about the same age as Mary, but how very different. She reached out to the girl, but she shied away from Caroline's gloved hand as if it were some strange creature approaching her, and fled the room at a surprising pace considering her deformity.

"If you will excuse me, Mistress Newell, I will fetch my wife," the rector said.

"That was well done, Arthur," Caroline said, when Mr. Gardiner had left the room, "suggesting we came in here." She removed her gloves and warmed her hands at the fire. "You showed great diplomacy there."

"I'm not the fool you think I am, Caroline," he said, sharply, "as you will see shortly!"

She had touched a raw nerve there. Had she sounded sarcastic, a bit like Sir Henry? She hadn't meant to be.

Before she could say any more - she was certainly not going to apologise - Mr. Gardiner returned, followed by a woman whom Caroline presumed was his wife.

A more meek and mild little person Caroline had rarely seen. If she were to be equated with an animal, Mrs. Gardiner would be a field mouse: she had small, darting, brown eyes, which she lowered the moment Caroline looked at her. She wore a cream lace cap over her greying hair and a brown dress so unadorned that Caroline wondered if it was a finished garment; a closer look revealed a lighter brown lace collar and cuffs. Even so, was this the woman who was fascinated by London fashion?

"May I present my wife to you, Mistress Newell," the rector said, bowing.

"Mistress Gardiner. I am so pleased to meet you." Caroline stepped forward, smiling warmly.

"You are most welcome, Mistress Newell," the rector's wife said hurriedly, as if it was painful to be speaking to her visitor. "Please, do be seated." She waved vaguely at the only upholstered chair in the room.

"Thank you," said Caroline. "It is most kind of you and Mr. Gardiner to allow me to be here. Would you not like this chair, Mistress Gardiner?" Caroline felt she could not sit in comfort while this frail creature stood or perched on one of the wooden chairs or stools ranged around the room.

"Oh. No, thank you," said Mrs. Gardiner, looking to her husband for guidance; she seemed quite perturbed to be addressed in such a solicitous manner by someone she no doubt considered her social superior.

"Come along, Mr. Gardiner, let's get this hearing started," said Arthur.

Caroline shot him a grateful look, which he didn't see, being engaged in drawing - almost pushing, she felt - a motley assortment of villagers into the room.

"Jane Wenham, you sit over there," Arthur said, pointing to a stool on the far side of the room.

Caroline watched, fascinated, as an old, bent, grey-haired woman, dressed completely in dull, faded black except for a piece of frayed sacking over her shoulders, shuffled across the room to the stool which Arthur had indicated. So this was the woman they said was a witch: she didn't look any different from any other old woman you might see in a country lane or in a market place. But what did she, Caroline, know of witchcraft?

"I'll take over now, Mr. Chauncy," the rector was saying, ushering everyone to their places. His former diffidence had gone: he was on firm ground here. "Farmer Chapman, there, please. You, Matthew, next to him." A woman who looked to be in her thirties was pushing her way into the room; there was an older man behind her. "There's no need for you to be here, Susan Aylott. Nor you, Thomas Adams. This is only a hearing, not a trial."

"But, Mr. Gardiner sir," Thomas Adams began. The rector cut him short. "If it comes to a trial, then you'll have your say, but not today." There were murmured protests from the other villagers in the doorway. "Go home, all of you."

Reluctantly Thomas left the room, muttering to himself, "It's not right; I should be here."

"And you, Susan," the rector said politely, holding out his hand to indicate that she should leave.

"I'm staying," the woman said, swaggering across to one of the stools.

She looked Caroline up and down. Caroline returned her stare. She was a good-looking woman, in a common sort of way. The woman's eyes were now on Arthur. "The witch done me harm, too. You know that, don't you?"

"Yes. But this is not about you, Susan," Arthur said calmly. "This is solely to do with Matthew and Farmer Chapman."

"There's things I know that they don't." Her tone was surly.

"Yes, I'm sure there are," said Mr. Gardiner, "but we do not want to hear them today. Come on, off that stool."

The woman shrugged her shoulders and stood up, adjusting her clothing in what seemed to Caroline a provocative manner.

"Good-bye, Mr. Chauncy," she said, smiling, and emphasising his name in a way that suggested she did not usually address him so formally. This was surely not one of the village women that Arthur was said to be chasing. No, it couldn't be; she was far too old, and the smell coming from her was… well, of the farmyard, not exactly unpleasant, but not something you would wish to be close to. To give Arthur his due he did not respond to the woman's smile.

"Oh, all right," she said petulantly. "I'll go now, but I have got things to say, you know… about the witch." There was a movement from the old woman. "Well, you are! And everyone knows it."

"Mistress Aylott, will you please leave," the rector said quietly.

"All right. I said I'm going." She walked, with deliberate slowness, to the door. "Don't think, though, just 'cos you addressing me politely, you'll get rid of me." She turned away from the rector and looked menacingly at Jane Wenham. "I ain't done with you," she said and made to leave the room. Before she could get through the door she was pushed aside by a dark-skinned, fair-haired girl in a torn silk dress. Rushing into the room, she made straight for Caroline. Close behind her came a young man, also with a dark complexion.

71

"Pretty, pretty," the girl said, touching the skirt of Caroline's gown.

"Polly!" the young man shouted angrily, grabbing hold of the girl by her arm, pulling her away. In a gentler voice he said, "You're not supposed to be in here! I'm sorry, Mr. Gardiner, sir." He turned to Caroline. "Sorry, madam. Very sorry."

"It's all right, Jem," said the rector calmly. "Take her away."

"Pretty, pretty," the girl went on saying.

"Thank you, sir," said the young man. "Sorry, ladies. Sir." He nodded, first to Caroline and Mrs. Gardiner, then to Arthur, and with his arm round the girl he left the room, closing the door quietly behind him.

"Who was that?" Caroline mouthed to Arthur.

"I'll tell you later," he mouthed back.

Caroline was intrigued: a good-looking, polite, *very* well-spoken boy, and a girl - his sister by the look of her features, although her hair was fair whereas his was raven-black - in a *satin* dress, albeit it an old, shabby one. Were they gypsies, perhaps? The honey-brown skin colouring was right, and the dark eyes... Or someone's bastards, maybe? That dress had once been very beautiful; it was a lady's dress, too.

There was no more time for idle thoughts. The hearing was about to begin.

"Now then, Mistress Wenham," the rector said, turning to the old woman, "what's all this about?"

"It's him, Mr. Gardiner, sir." The old woman pointed a thin, dirt-encrusted finger at the farmer. "'E says I've bewitched 'im; Matthew there," she said, directing her accusing finger at the young farm worker.

John Chapman, a heavily built man in his mid-forties, looked angrily at Jane Wenham.

"I only said it because it's true!"

"Let Mistress Wenham speak," said Mr. Gardiner, raising his hand, the open palm towards the farmer, halting him. "You'll have your say in a minute." He turned to the woman. "Well, go on. What is it you're supposed to have done to Matthew?"

"I'll tell you what she done," John Chapman interposed, getting up from his seat and advancing on the old woman. "She given him a cold, she did. Made him so 'e can't work!"

"Sit down!" shouted the rector.

Grumbling to himself and twisting his cap fretfully in his hands, the farmer subsided on to his chair.

"I did no such thing." It was Jane Wenham's turn to rise from her seat. " 'E got a cold 'cos he been running 'bout with no clothes on." She looked around the room, her dark eyes flashing. Focusing them on Caroline she said, "If you was to run 'bout in winter with no clothes on, you'd get a cold!"

"I certainly would," said Caroline. So would anyone, she was about to say, but Mr. Gardiner was already rebuking the old woman.

"Jane Wenham, I will not have you being impertinent to my guest." It was not easy to conduct a serious questioning with this fancily dressed lady from London sitting in the room, and it didn't help that his wife couldn't take her eyes off Caroline's gown. "Go on," he said to Jane Wenham. "What else?"

"That's it. There ain't no more."

"There is. There's a lot more!" The farmer was up on his feet again. "Ain't there, Matthew?"

"That's right," nodded Matthew.

"There's bound to be more. Come on, let's hear it," said Arthur, standing beside Caroline's chair, with an arm across its back. Almost as if he thinks he is having his portrait painted, Caroline thought, turning round to him. She couldn't believe how aggressive he looked; and sounded, too. At the same time, he seemed excited. Caroline found it disturbing.

"Thank you, Mr. Chauncy," Mr. Gardiner said, determined to maintain his authority and conduct this hearing as calmly as possible, which would not be easy, knowing how Arthur Chauncy loved to stir things up and how belligerent the old woman could be if she was opposed.

"Now, Matthew. You've told us Mistress Wenham made you take off your clothes... so you got a cold... and you couldn't work." The rector spoke slowly and deliberately. "Is there anything else?"

"She asked me for some straw."

"Yes?"

"I didn't give it her. So she helped herself."

"What was so terrible about that?" Caroline couldn't help interrupting.

"Ah well, you see, Mistress Newell," John Chapman said, pleased to have a chance to speak again, "you wouldn't know this, ma'am, not being from round here, but she'd be wanting the straw to sell it. To the straw plaiters."

Caroline nodded. She'd heard about Hertfordshire straw plaiting.

"And it weren't the first time she'd done this. New Year's Day she begged him for straw." He turned to his farm worker. "Didn't she, Matthew?"

"That's right; she did. I didn't give her none then and I wouldn't give her none now!"

"I don't want you to go over things you've told me before, Matthew. Let us concentrate on what has just happened." The rector paused. So far, so good. Just a few more questions, and then, if Mistress Newell did not interfere again, he would bring this hearing to an end. "Is there anything *new* you need to tell us?"

"I came over all funny."

"Funny?"

"Queer-like. She mumbled at me, see, and I had to go to Munders Hill."

"Munders Hill?" interjected Arthur. "That's over three miles from here."

"I know, sir." Matthew turned gratefully to Arthur. Mr. Chauncy wouldn't hurry him along like the rector was doing. Mr. Chauncy would want to hear everything; he knew about witches, Mr. Chauncy did. "I had to go, though, she made me. I ran all the way there and I got wet crossing the river and when I got to Munders Hill I asked for some straw."

"But you had straw," said Caroline. "Why did you…?"

"Mistress Newell, if you would please…"

"I'm sorry, Mr. Gardiner. I do apologise." How much longer was this ridiculous interrogation going on? Caroline was beginning to wish she had not come. It didn't help to have the rector's wife staring at her continually. What was the woman doing? Trying to memorise every detail of Caroline's dress, so that she could tell her dress-maker - if she had one - and get an exact copy made? No, that was unfair, and unkind. She smiled across at Mrs. Gardiner, and was pleased to receive a warm, though hesitant, smile back. Perhaps Mrs. Gardiner was as tired of these proceedings as she was. If only they could both escape to the parlour, or the kitchen even, and talk about fashion!

"Did you get some straw, Matthew... at Munders Hill?"

"No, Mr. Gardiner, sir. They wouldn't give me none. It was her done it. Just 'cos I wouldn't give *her* no straw, she put a spell on me."

"It's all lies, Mr. Gardiner. I never put no spell on him." The woman began to mumble. "I never did... don't put no spell... no spell."

"Mistress Wenham!" The rector was losing patience. "Let Matthew tell his story please."

"That's all it is, story. It ain't no truth."

"All right, all right. Just let him tell us." This was getting nowhere. "So what did you do then?"

"I took some," Matthew said, "from a pile of dung," as if that was the only possible answer.

"Ugh!" Caroline exclaimed.

"It wasn't his fault," said Arthur quietly.

"They have strange powers, ma'am," the rector said. "Witches." He whispered the word as if almost afraid to utter it. "Go on," he said wearily, to Matthew.

"Well, like I said, I took the straw... then I took off my coat and my shirt and my breeches." He looked at Caroline. "Begging your pardon, ma'am... I put them round the straw, wrapped them like... and I came home."

"If that isn't witchcraft, I'd like to know what is," said the farmer, looking defiantly, first at Caroline and then at the rector.

"It is a very odd thing," replied Mr. Gardiner, slowly and carefully, as if he was weighing each word as he said it. "I do agree with you there, Farmer Chapman, but whether or not it is witchcraft, I am not sure… and I don't really see how you can blame Mistress Wenham for what befell Matthew."

"Not blame her! Who else is there to blame?" the farmer asked angrily. Hadn't the rector been listening? "The woman is a witch, you know she is!"

"I do *not* know that she is, that is the whole point," replied Mr. Gardiner.

The farmer had more to say. "You remember that sheep, the one that stood on its head… You do, don't you, Mr. Chauncy?… That was her."

To Caroline's dismay Arthur was nodding and murmuring affirmation of John Chapman's words.

"And Susan Aylott's baby," the farmer went on. "*That* was her. It died 'cos of her."

"And Mary Ireland's baby," chipped in Matthew. He looked menacingly at Jane Wenham. "You touched it… and it died."

"She talks to the Devil, she do," said the farmer, now well into his stride, "and that is a wicked and sinful thing to do. You told us that, Mr. Gardiner, sir."

"Well yes, it is. Very wicked, but…"

"Definitely a sign of witchcraft," said Arthur, crossing the room to stand by the rector. "Don't you agree, Mr. Gardiner?"

"It *can* be, but there really is no proof that Mistress Wenham has been…"

Matthew and John Chapman started to protest and Mrs. Gardiner, whose face, up to now, aside from the smile she had given Caroline, had been expressionless, began to look anxious; her husband might bandy words but if it came to fisticuffs he would have a problem.

"I *saw* her!" Matthew was shouting. "She had on that cloak! I saw her, I tell you!"

Mrs. Gardiner's face went quite pale.

"He *saw* her," said Arthur. "You can't argue with that, Rector."

"That is enough!" Mr. Gardiner raised his voice sonorously. It silenced them all, even Arthur. The rector turned to his wife. "Are you all right, my dear?" he asked. "If you would rather leave…"

"No, no. Thank you. I am well."

"Are you sure you wouldn't rather go…?" asked Caroline, getting up from her chair.

"No. Thank you, Mistress Newell. I will stay. My husband needs me at his side." Despite your moment of faintness, you are a determined woman, Caroline thought, sitting down again.

The rector cleared his throat, put his hands together, as if about to pray. "It is my opinion," he said solemnly, "that Mistress Wenham cannot be held responsible for your behaviour, Matthew… and therefore I ask you, Farmer Chapman, to give her a shilling for all the trouble you have caused her."

They all began to speak at once, as the rector had known they would.

"A shilling!" Jane Wenham said, and the farmer echoed her. "A shilling?"

Arthur made a sort of noise in his throat - he looked disappointed - and Mrs. Gardiner murmured something nobody heard and fanned herself. The rector, having made his pronouncement, looked quite pleased with himself.

"Yes, a shilling," he said.

"What about me?" queried John Chapman. "What about all *my* trouble? My man not working, and me losing cattle! Two hundred pounds worth of stock I lost! And you want me to give *her* money?"

"A shilling," the old woman said, going up to the farmer and all but spitting the words in his face. "You come to my house, you bang on my door, you ruin my name…"

"You don't get no shilling from me!" The farmer sneered at her and made for the door.

"You'll not get away with this!" Jane Wenham screeched after him.

"Oh, Mr. Gardiner," said his wife, trembling all over, "you should have offered her more."

"No, no." Mr. Gardiner shook his head.

"More?" said Matthew. "Farmer won't pay *one* shilling, never mind more. If it was me, I wouldn't pay her one penny!"

Mrs. Gardiner appealed to Arthur. "We should be giving her more. She'll turn on us, Mr. Chauncy, I know she will."

"You're right, Mistress Gardiner. This is a bad day, a very bad day. I fear we shall all suffer for what Mr. Gardiner has done."

Caroline looked at him in disbelief; she would deal with *him* later.

"Mistress Gardiner, it has been a delight to meet you. I bid you farewell," and she smiled and nodded, in as pleasant a manner as she felt she could muster. "Mr. Gardiner, thank you for allowing me to be present this morning. I commend your decision."

"Thank you, Mistress Newell. I do hope it was the right one." He took her outstretched hand, and inclined his head in a small bow. Caroline smiled at him warmly, then turning to Arthur, her smile gone, she said icily, "Take me back to Yardley Bury."

"Oh, Mistress Newell, will you not take a dish of tea with us?" Mrs. Gardiner asked. Her visitor was leaving and she did so want to ask about the elegant dress she was wearing. "I was hoping to ask you about…"

"Not today, thank you, Mistress Gardiner." Caroline knew she was being rude, but she had had more than enough of the rectory and the Gardiners for now. "I will perhaps come another day, if I may. Or, better still, I will send my maid, Mary; I think you have met her. She knows more about the London fashions than I do."

Mrs. Gardiner stood open-mouthed as Caroline swept out.

"That was unpardonably rude, Caroline," Arthur said, following her out. "She might appear to be a silly woman to you, but she did not deserve that."

"No, she didn't." Caroline stopped abruptly on her way to the front door. She turned and nearly collided with Mrs. Gardiner as she emerged from the morning room. "Mistress Gardiner," said Caroline, in the humblest of voices, "Do you think we could take that dish of tea together tomorrow? What time of day would suit you best?"

"Oh, Mistress Newell." This was almost as upsetting as Caroline's rudeness.

"Oh. Yes. I should like that. Oh. Any time. Whatever is convenient for you. I really don't…"

There was only one way to bring this dithering to an end. "Shall we say eleven o'clock?"

"Oh. Yes. Yes. That would be… yes, that will be very nice. Thank you," and she curtsied.

"Oh please, Mistress Gardiner, don't." It was so embarrassing. Caroline took the woman's hands in hers. "It has been a very trying day, I think."

"Yes. It has."

"Till tomorrow then." Caroline released Mrs. Gardiner's hands, and made her exit as speedily as she could.

"There," she said to Arthur, when they were outside the door, "was that better?"

"Much better," Arthur said, offering his arm to her. He was pleased; all he had to do was be firm and she would be as submissive as the village girls. He smiled at her.

"I am not looking forward to coming back," she said, as they began to make their way across the fields, "but for the sake of your father I do not wish to fall out with the rector or his wife… or anyone in this village."

Arthur's smile faded. His father, not him; he should have known.

Caroline did not make her promised second visit to the rectory. Mr. Gardiner had sent word that, unfortunately, his wife had one of her megrims, a complaint from which she suffered from time to time. She hoped Mistress Newell would pardon her.

Caroline was relieved, but at the same time slightly annoyed. Now, dressed to please Mrs. Gardiner, she had nothing to do. Arthur was nowhere to be seen and Sir Henry was busy in the library. Had he been in the snug she knew he would have been happy to talk, but his presence in the library indicated work of some kind, and she did not wish to interrupt. She could go for a walk, she supposed, but on her own that would be dull. The snug was empty and there was a good fire. She would sit in there; she could read and write letters, to Lydia and to Emilia.

Comfortable and settled, her morning passed quickly. Jacob brought her hot chocolate and some small cakes that Bessie had just baked.

"Mmm. Almond." Caroline said, biting into one of the little cakes.

"One of your favourites, I am told."

"Yes they are. Please thank Bessie for me."

"I will, madam. Is there anything else I can get for you?"

"No thank you, Jacob. I am quite content."

And she was; it was not such a dull morning after all. It might have interesting, though, to see Mrs. Gardiner again, if only to find out why, if she was so interested in fashion, she had made no attempt to wear anything remotely up-to-date yesterday. But then, of course, she had not been expecting to meet Caroline. Poor woman, she must have been mortified to be found in her dull morning gown. I must make an effort to see her again before I leave, Caroline thought.

Had she gone to the rectory Caroline might have witnessed the unedifying sight of the Gardiners' sixteen-year-old maid, Anne Thorn, dressed only in an underskirt and a chemise, screaming uncontrollably and, between her screams, accusing Jane Wenham of bewitching her when she'd been to fetch some peas from a neighbour.

This much Caroline learned from Mary, when she came bursting into the snug later in the morning. Why Mary had been at the rectory that morning was not explained. Caroline would get to the bottom of that later, but for now she must let Mary tell her story - a ridiculous story, Caroline thought - about bundles of sticks and crooked pins, and twigs being burnt to make the so-called witch appear... which she did. A crowd of villagers had thronged the rectory kitchen while all this was going on. Mary knew all their names: there was Thomas Adams, whose sister grew the peas, Susan Aylott, who loathed Jane Wenham for some perceived mischief in the past - Caroline nodded, she knew *those* names - and Elizabeth Field, a more sensible, older woman who said very little. There was also a young man called Jem, who worked for Farmer Chapman, looking after his horses. Jem, that dark-haired boy, with a strange sister. Interesting, thought Caroline, but said nothing. Mary had more to tell. There had been talk of the witch wanting Anne Thorn's blood, and a black cat, which Anne had seen, a cat that was the witch's familiar.

"Familiar?" asked Caroline. She knew the word, but not in connection with a witch, or a cat. "What is that?"

"I don't know, mistress," said Mary, "but it's what Mr. Chauncy said."

"Mr. Chauncy? Arthur?"

"Yes, mistress."

"What was he doing there?" As if she needed to ask.

"I don't know, mistress. I expect he had gone there with Mr. Bragge."

"You mean the Reverend Bragge?"

"Yes, mistress, he was asking most of the questions. It was him what said the old woman really is a witch."

Caroline decided to let Mary's lapse of good grammar pass; she wanted to hear the rest of the story.

"And you saw all this?"

"Yes, mistress." Oh dear, was she in trouble? Should she not have said anything? It had all been very strange: that girl Anne who was said to leap over gates even though she'd had a broken leg… and then her saying the old woman had been coming after her when she wasn't anywhere near. Mr. Chauncy said it was all because she was bewitched. It was frightening as well… all those village people shouting and pointing at the old woman. And that parson, that Mr. Bragge - he could make anyone feel afraid. He knew just the words to use to make you feel sinful, and he looked at you as if he could *see* the sin inside you. Oh yes, he had noticed Mary; he had run his eyes up and down her silk dress several times. She had had hostile looks from the villagers too, all except the young farm lad, Jem. He had smiled at her. She hadn't smiled back, although she would have liked to; he was very good to look at, in a country sort of way, of course.

"What were *you* doing at the rectory?"

"I was taking some ribbon to Mistress Gardiner."

"Not *my* ribbon, I hope!" Though why not? A bit of ribbon would brighten up Mrs. Gardiner's drab gown. Not that Caroline would have taken it there herself - that would have been most patronising. On the other hand, if a lady's maid gave her ribbon, that would be acceptable.

"Yes, mistress. I'm sorry."

"No, don't be. It was a kind thought, Mary. And I can well spare a piece of ribbon." She smiled at her maid. "I told you something interesting would happen, didn't I? And it has: a witch-hunt and a …"

"Please don't mock, mistress, not about the witch. Or the Devil. Mr. Bragge says we must not let him win… and that we are all to pray for Anne's soul."

"Yes, do that," said Caroline, "but I don't want you going to the rectory again."

5

When Caroline walked into the dining hall later that day she was surprised to see three men rising from their seats at one end of the long oak table: Sir Henry, Arthur and a short, stocky young man she had not seen before.

"My dear, come in." Sir Henry greeted her affably. "I was not sure that you would be joining us today."

"Oh, I am sorry. Am I late?" Caroline asked. "I slipped up to my room to put on something warmer. Compared with your snug this room is cold, Sir Henry."

The tall, narrow windows of the dining hall faced east. Even on a day which began with sunshine, all natural warmth had gone from the room by noon, and what light there was was swallowed up by the almost black oak-panelled walls. The only relief from this darkness was the cream plaster of the ceiling, too high up to be of any practical use in bringing brightness to the room.

"It is indeed," Sir Henry said, "and you ladies never seem to wear as much as we men do."

A cough from the table alerted him to his duty.

"Allow me to introduce my grandson," Sir Henry began, turning to the young man standing beside Arthur. "Caroline, my dear, this is…"

"Madam." Before Sir Henry could finish his introduction, his grandson had interrupted. "The Reverend Francis Bragge at your service," he said, stretching out his arms behind him in an extravagant gesture and at the same time bowing low, the luxuriant curls of his full-bottomed wig swinging forward as he bent his head. Without doubt this was a man who took snuff; she could just see the flamboyant way he would do it.

"Francis," Sir Henry said, sharply, "kindly me allow me to finish what I am saying!"

"Sir Henry, I do beg your pardon." Another bow, another swing of the curls, a hand placed delicately on his very fine lace cravat. "The charm of your visitor... Mistress Newell, I believe," he said, with an inclination of his head towards Caroline, "quite made me forget my manners. Madam, my apologies." Again the curls swung forward as the young man bowed. "Do, pray, continue, Sir Henry," he said unctuously.

"Mr. Bragge." Caroline returned his elaborate salutation with the merest nod of her head. If the man chose to behave as if he were an actor in one of Mr. Congreve's comedies, that was his concern. Caroline saw no need to respond in a similar fashion. It was a relief to turn away from him and smile at Jacob, as he placed a chair at the table for her.

"Thank you, Jacob," she said. She was pleased to see several dishes - meats and fish, pies and puddings - laid out on the table; she was feeling hungry and the food both looked and smelled appetising.

She sat down and the three men resumed their seats, the Reverend Bragge with an exaggerated flip of his fashionable, pleated coat tails.

Sir Henry said, "As you will have gathered, my dear, my grandson is proud of his newly acquired title. He is a curate in Bedfordshire, in the town of Biggleswade."

"How very nice for you," said Caroline, having no idea, and caring less, whether or not a curacy in Biggleswade was a worthy post for Francis Bragge.

She was seated opposite Arthur and Francis and in the space between them she could look out through the long windows at the park. Even on a wet February day it was a pleasanter sight than the faces of the two men in the foreground of her view.

"Will you take soup, my dear?" Sir Henry asked.

"Thank you. I will."

"Jacob. Soup for Mistress Newell."

"Yes, Sir Henry." Jacob ladled mutton broth from a large tureen and placed a bowl of it in front of Caroline. She lifted her heavy silver spoon and dipped it into the steaming soup. It was good. She put the spoon down and reached forward for a piece of bread on a platter in the centre of the table. Before she could pick it up Francis had stood up, lifted the platter and put it down again, quite unnecessarily, nearer to her.

"Allow *me*, Mistress Newell," he said.

"Thank you."

Sir Henry seemed disinclined to talk, as did Arthur, who had not said a word since she came into the room. Was he in awe of his… what was he, Francis, to Arthur? A cousin? No, a sort of step-nephew, from Sir Henry's second marriage. Caroline concentrated on the food in front of her; she had no wish to begin a conversation, particularly not with Mr. Bragge.

At last, when the silence was becoming oppressive and Caroline felt she must break it, Francis spoke.

"I believe you live in London, Mistress Newell." He made it sound a most undesirable place. "Are you enjoying your visit to the country?"

"I am indeed," Caroline said. "As to London… it is a magnificent city in which to live."

"Oh?" He sounded both bored and disbelieving. Well, she would see to that.

"Oh yes. Just think what there is to do and see. The wonderful theatre with so many amusing plays and…"

"I have no time for the theatre."

"Oh, that is sad… that your work does not allow you time for pleasure."

"I do not mean time in that sense, Mistress Newell." Was this woman a fool, or was she just being provocative?

"In what sense do you mean it then, Mr. Bragge?"

"Francis means that he has no *use* for the theatre," Sir Henry said. "He disapproves of it."

"Oh," said Caroline. She had finished her soup and was helping herself to a slice of cold ham pie. "Perhaps architecture is more to your liking." She smiled across at Arthur - she had had a similar conversation with him - but there was no response. "The glorious new churches designed by Sir Christopher Wren, for instance. And Mr. Hawksmoor."

"They *would* be worth seeing, I am sure."

"You have not seen them?" Caroline opened her eyes wide in mock amazement. "A clergyman such as yourself! Oh, Mr. Bragge, you should. They are so beautiful, so spacious, so uplifting."

He was becoming irritated, Caroline was pleased to see.

"I have far too much to do, Mistress Newell, to go gallivanting to London to look at new churches, however *uplifting* they may be."

"Your parish work, I presume," Caroline said agreeably, smiling at him fleetingly before returning to her food. "This is a delicious pie, Sir Henry. Is it one of Bessie's?"

"No!" said Francis, cutting across Caroline's remark to his grandfather. "I have more important matters to attend to than my parish."

"Oh? What could be more important than the care of souls in… Biggleswade, is it?"

"It is not just the souls of Biggleswade I care for, Mistress Newell!" No, she was not a fool; well, neither was he, and he would take no more of her provocation. "I care for the soul of anyone, anywhere, who is tempted by the Devil… and by sin!"

"I see," said Caroline, recoiling from the intense, fiery look the curate gave her; this man was not to be trifled with.

"Francis is here to seek out the sin in Walkern," said Arthur calmly, as if it was quite a normal topic of conversation for a mealtime. "He is here to help us with the witch."

"Arthur," said his father sternly, "you must *not* use that word if you are referring to Mistress Wenham. Nothing has been proved." He turned to Caroline. "No, it is not one of Bessie's."

"Oh. Well, you have a very good cook, then. I shall have some more, if I may," and she helped herself to a second slice. Goodness, she was eating a lot; it must be this fresh country air.

"If I may speak, Sir Henry?" said Francis, loudly. He was very angry.

"About what? The pie?"

"No!" He banged his fist down hard on the table. "Of course not the pie! I wish to speak about the sins being committed here, in Walkern."

"Francis, this is the dinner table, not the pulpit," said Sir Henry, wearily.

"I beg your pardon, sir." Though seated, he somehow managed to bow to his grandfather, "Your guest seems ignorant of the matters afoot here, and I wish... nay, I feel it is my duty... to inform her." And before Sir Henry could even draw breath, he went on, "Contrary to what you say, and it gives me no pleasure to contradict you, Grandfather, on the evidence I have seen this morning, I feel we can say with a considerable degree of certainty that the woman Jane Wenham *is* a witch, and a dangerous witch at that." He leant across the table, picked up a chunk of bread and bit into it viciously.

Caroline waited until he had finished chewing, and then said, "And what evidence is that, Mr. Bragge?"

"I doubt if you would understand, Mistress Newell," he said condescendingly. "This is a spiritual matter."

"Are you suggesting I have no sense of spirituality, Mr. Bragge?"

Sir Henry might not wish to have a serious debate at his dinner table, but he could not let Francis's imputation pass.

"I should hope not," he said. He was not going to have the young coxcomb being rude to Caroline, even though she was being most unladylike, taking over the conversation and taunting him. "Come along, Francis, do Caroline the courtesy of giving her a proper answer."

Francis, controlling his contempt for Caroline and his annoyance with Sir Henry for putting him in his place like this, took his time in answering, elaborately chewing every morsel of food in his mouth before he spoke.

"The evidence is manifold, Mistress Newell." He paused for effect.

"We don't want a sermon, Francis. Just tell us, in plain language, why you say that Jane Wenham is a witch. That is all Caroline wants to know. Isn't it?" asked Sir Henry, smiling at her.

You are enjoying this, despite your apparent irritation, she thought, as their eyes met. She smiled back.

"Of course," she said, looking across the table at Francis. "I know nothing of these matters, and you obviously do, so tell me, please."

"I questioned the woman," Francis said, as if speaking to a child, "and with the answers she gave me, added to the information I had been given by the rector's young servant and the villagers who were present, there was no other conclusion to be drawn." And as far as Francis was concerned, that was that. "Are the pears from your orchard, Sir Henry?" If you want to talk about pies, well, I can ask about pears.

"Yes," said Sir Henry sharply.

"Information," said Caroline. "You mean by that, I suppose, the talk of crooked pins and twigs in an apron and… What else was there? Oh yes, something about the twigs being burnt to make the witch… to use *your* word… to make her appear. Was this your *information*?"

"It was."

"Mr. Bragge," said Caroline slowly, leaning across the table and looking at Francis intently, "are you telling me that you believe these phenomena to be significant and valid?"

"Indeed I do. Do you doubt my word?"

"Oh no. Not your word."

"Well then, you have your answer."

Caroline sat back in her chair. She looked across at Arthur; he seemed excited, his eyes shining; did he think Francis had thwarted her? She turned her attention to Sir Henry, who was staring down at his plate as if he hoped to find an answer in the remains of the food he had pushed to one side.

"Sir Henry, what is your opinion of this?"

"I reserve judgment, my dear. As I said to you before, there are strange things going on in the village, but I do not know why they are happening."

"They are happening, Sir Henry," Francis shouted angrily, again pounding his fist on the table, this time so ferociously that the silverware clattered and a glass fell over, "because there is a witch abroad!"

For a moment no one spoke. Arthur picked up the glass that had fallen and set it upright. Francis and Sir Henry sat, tense, not looking at one another. The old man was no longer amused.

"I think… Francis," said Caroline gently, "that your grandfather would like this discussion ended."

"Thank you," said Sir Henry wearily. "I shall go to my room."

He stood up, a little unsteadily. Caroline began to rise from her chair, to go his aid.

"Allow me," said Francis, leaping up and springing to Sir Henry's side before Caroline could get there.

"I am not an invalid." Sir Henry shook off his grandson's arm and began walking towards the door. "I will see you all later in the day," he said.

"We shall look forward to that," said Caroline.

Sir Henry didn't turn, just waved one hand over his shoulder in acknowledgment of her words, and was gone.

Arthur by now had got to his feet too, and the three of them stood, seemingly unsure what to say or do next. The meal was not really over, but no one wished to resume any kind of conversation.

"I trust you are satisfied, Mistress Newell." Francis spoke angrily. "We were having a pleasant, quiet meal together, until you chose to spoil it with your rancorous questioning."

"Rancorous, is that what it was? Well, you shall have no more of it, I promise you, Mr. Bragge. Arthur," she turned to him, "I cannot stay at Yardley Bury. This is no place for me. I don't know which century you and Mr. Bragge belong to, but I am now firmly in the eighteenth century, the age of Sir Isaac Newton and Robert Boyle: I am sure you have heard of them. Witches and crooked pins play no part in *my* life! Excuse me, gentlemen," she said, and gathering up her skirts to speed her progress, she swept out of the room.

"Mary!" she called. "Mary!" Her voice echoed down the hallway. "Where are you? I need you! We are leaving!"

Sir Henry's carriage was waiting in the drive, with Jacob standing by. In the entrance hall Caroline, dressed in her travelling clothes, was pacing up and down impatiently.

It was the morning after the 'rancorous' meal, an occasion which had left Sir Henry exhausted, Francis self-satisfied, Arthur confused, and Caroline so furious she had been hell-bent on departing from Yardley Bury there and then, despite there being no more than an hour of daylight left.

Unable to find Mary, she had gone in search of Sir Henry, to say good-bye and apologise to him for leaving so peremptorily. She had found him in the snug, stretched out in his red brocade chair, his eyes closed.

"Please, Caroline, don't do this," he had said. "If you *are* determined to leave, at least stay until tomorrow morning, I beg of you. I shall not be able to sleep, thinking of you out there in the dark."

"Oh, Sir Henry," Caroline had said, laughing, "I shall not be riding."

"Oh? How do you intend, then, to get to Bengeo?"

"Ah. Well…" She had hesitated; she knew she was being presumptuous. "I was hoping I might have the use of your carriage."

"With pleasure." What else was he to say? With the mood she was in, if he refused her his carriage, she would simply get on a horse and *ride* away from Yardley Bury.

"Thank you." She was still set on leaving as soon as Mary could be found to pack her boxes. "I shall be quite safe, Sir Henry," she had said. "There are lanterns on the carriage."

It was Sir Henry's turn to laugh. "A fine lot of use they will be if you are waylaid by a highwayman!"

Though not afraid for herself, Caroline did not want to upset Sir Henry any more than he already was.

"Very well. I will go in the morning."

"Thank you, my dear." He had shut his eyes and leaned back in his chair. Caroline had taken it as a signal for her to leave him to rest.

"I think I shall keep to my room for the rest of the day," she said.

His eyes still shut, Sir Henry had replied, sleepily, "Yes. That would be wise."

Caroline had kept her word; she had eaten in her room and not come downstairs again until this morning. She had said goodbye to Sir Henry, but she had not seen Francis or Arthur since she'd swept out of the dining hall the day before. Good manners told her she should seek them out and, if not make her peace with them, as least bid them farewell. Her feelings of outrage, though somewhat muted now, coupled with a sense of having perhaps made an exhibition of herself, made her unwilling to go in search of them. If they came to the door to see her off, she would, of course, be polite. She hoped it would not happen - better to slip away quietly. It was bad enough to know that Sir Henry was hovering somewhere nearby, probably in his library just off the entrance hall; she hoped she could be resolute and not give in to any last-minute pleading for her to stay.

"Oh, where is that girl?" she said out loud. She was anxious to be away. Jacob, still waiting by the carriage, was moving from foot to foot to keep warm: there had been a frost overnight. "She was here five minutes ago."

"I think she is in the kitchen with Bessie." Caroline swung round. Sir Henry was standing in the doorway of the library. "She and Bessie seem to have become friends," he said.

"Yes, I'd noticed," Caroline said. Not only was she an impolite house guest, she was also a cruel mistress, separating her maid from her new-found companion. Poor Sir Henry, he looked so hurt. For two pins, she'd… No, she wouldn't. She would not stay in a house where she could not speak her mind. "Oh, come on, girl!" What was she doing with Bessie? Bidding her a long, tearful farewell? For someone who had made such a fuss about coming to the country for a few days she had adjusted to its life remarkably quickly. It couldn't all be due to Bessie. It had something to do with the rectory. There must be some reason why her maid wanted to trip down there at every opportunity… and it wasn't, Caroline felt, just because Mary wanted to help Mrs. Gardiner to make her dresses more fashionable. "Oh, there you are!"

Mary, breathless, holding her cloak round her shoulders with her hands, came running down the long passageway from the back of the house.

"Where have you been?" Caroline asked angrily.

"I'm sorry, mistress," Mary said, struggling to get her breath back and fasten the clasp of her cloak at the same time. "I had an errand to run."

"An errand? For whom? Stop fiddling with your cloak and look at me."

Mary looked up; her eyes were filled with tears. "For Mistress Gardiner," she began. "I was just taking her some…"

"Enough! I don't want to hear any more. Get into the carriage. And stop looking so miserable! You should be pleased: we're going back to Hertford."

"Yes, mistress."

Caroline turned away, only to see another sad face. Sir Henry was still standing by the library door; it was warmer there. Caroline, wrapped in her travelling cloak and fuelled by her impatience to get away from Yardley Bury, was impervious to the cold air coming in through the open front door. Sir Henry had another reason for staying where he was. He was unaccustomed to a scene of this nature - a visitor departing, upset and in a rush, after only three days - and he was unsure how to act. If Elizabeth were here, *she* would not be letting Caroline leave. It was such an unhappy situation; there must be something he could do to remedy it.

"My dear," he said, stepping away from the shelter of the doorway, "I do wish you would reconsider..." He felt suddenly dizzy, and reached out a hand to support himself on the long case clock that stood by the library door. Fortunately Caroline hadn't seemed to notice; she answered as if she thought he had come to the end of his speech.

"I'm sorry. I can't."

Sir Henry's dizzy spell, brought on by the contrast in temperature between his over-heated library and the cold front hall, soon passed, and he said, as much to himself as to Caroline, "That grandson of mine has a lot to answer for."

Thankfully she appeared not to have heard. She and Francis Bragge were poles apart and Sir Henry knew that there was nothing he could say that would bring them together. He could though... perhaps... persuade Caroline to stay a bit longer at Yardley Bury. The house was big; she and Francis had no need to meet. Mary had gone out to the carriage - he could see her through the open door - and was arranging warm rugs on the seat for herself and her mistress. Sir Henry had time for one more plea; he would try another tack.

"Is it Arthur, my dear… as well as Francis… who has upset you?"

This time she had to answer. She walked over to him, took both his hands in hers. "It's not Arthur, it's not Francis; it's me. I feel so… so out of place here." She had said all this before - was there any point in repeating it? "Do you not see, Sir Henry, how ludicrous all this talk of witchcraft is? Arthur is an educated man, so is your grandson. They are not country yokels; they should not be part of this. And Jane Wenham, as far as I can see, is nothing more than a very sad, old woman, so poor she has to resort to stealing. If you were that poor, might you not steal too? I know I would."

For a moment the old man said nothing. A lot of what she said was true.

"You will come back, won't you, when this trouble has died down?" He was trying not to beg.

"I will," Caroline said brightly. She was feeling guilty about leaving him. "Of course I will."

"That's my girl." He squeezed her hands tightly, then let them go. "Now, where is Arthur?" he said. "He should be here to bid you farewell."

"No, please…" She did *not* want to see Arthur. Too late. There was a sound of heavy footsteps in the passage from the back of the house and Francis, with Arthur following close behind him, both of them in cloaks and riding boots, came striding into the front hall. The faces of the young men were flushed and angry.

"Mistress Newell!" Taken by surprise at the sight of her, Francis stood rooted to the spot, then, recovering himself quickly, executed an elaborate bow.

"Caroline," said Arthur, and smiled weakly at her.

"Ah, good," said Sir Henry. "I'm glad you are both here. Caroline is about to leave us, as you can see… and I wish you to bid her farewell." And you will speak in as calm and polite a manner as possible, his tone of voice and stern look informed them.

"Yes, Father." Arthur extended his hand to Caroline. "I am sorry you have decided to go. I should like to have shown you more of the countryside."

She took his hand. "I should have liked that too."

"Is there no chance that you might …?"

"For goodness' sake, Arthur, let her go! You have more pressing things to do than show Mistress Newell around." Francis turned abruptly away. Arthur might be prepared to talk pleasantries with the woman, but he had no time to waste on them: there was a village in imminent peril and it seemed that he was the only person who appreciated how grave the situation was! "Sir Henry, I must speak with you. There are matters pertaining to the witch that require your immediate attention."

"That was most discourteous of you, Francis. Will you please say goodbye to Mistress Newell as a gentleman should."

"Mistress Newell. I do beg your pardon." His face was stony, his eyes dead, his bow no more than a nod; she was not worth his attention.

Caroline inclined her head towards him. She was so angry she could not trust herself to speak. Quickly she turned away from him.

"Now, my dear," said Sir Henry, "allow me to escort you to the carriage." He gave a little bow, and crooked his elbow for her to take his arm, in such a gallant fashion that it was, to

Caroline, if not to Francis, an obvious mimicking of his grandson. She took his arm and they moved towards the door; it was only a matter of a few steps and she would be out of the house and into the carriage.

And away from Yardley Bury.

A sound from Francis, a mixture of impatience and disdain, brought her round sharply. She disengaged herself from Sir Henry's arm.

"Mr. Bragge."

He turned towards her. "Mistress Newell." The disdain she had heard from him was now to be seen in his face.

"I do not take kindly to being dismissed in such a fashion," Caroline said.

"Oh, and what fashion is that?" countered Francis.

They are like two fighting cocks, Arthur thought excitedly.

"You know very well. You have been peremptory and rude."

"I do beg your pardon, madam." He saw the look of admonition on Sir Henry's face; it wouldn't do to upset him. "It was not intentional, I assure you. I would not dream of being rude to Sir Henry's guest…"

Caroline was ahead of him: "… whatever she might think."

For a fleeting moment Francis was taken off guard. Before he could speak again, Caroline weighed in. "My opinions, Mr. Bragge, are every bit as valid as yours, even on the subject of supposed witchcraft, with which you appear to be obsessed."

"On that, Mistress Newell, I would beg to differ." A smirk spread across the curate's face. "I am a man of the cloth, an ordained clergyman of the established church; you, madam, are merely a woman, a fashionable, educated one, I grant you, but a woman nevertheless, who can have *no understanding whatsoever* of what is going on in Walkern at the moment... *The terror! The fear! The sin!...*" With every horror named his voice rose. "*The worship of the Devil!!*" His arms were flailing, his eyes were aflame.

"Francis! Stop!" Sir Henry took hold of his grandson's waving arms. "You are not in the pulpit now, and heaven help your congregation if that is how you behave when you are!" He let go of his grandson's arm. He was shaking with fury. "Now... say goodbye to Mistress Newell in a civilised manner. Then, when you have done so, we will discuss your concerns in an equally civilised manner."

Poor Sir Henry, all this was taking it out of him, thought Caroline.

"I beg your pardon, Sir Henry." Francis looked for a moment as if he was surprised to find himself in the entrance hall of Yardley Bury.

"Mistress Newell." His flamboyant bow was interrupted by his grandfather.

"Oh spare us that, Francis, please. Just say goodbye. That's all we need."

Francis chose to ignore the rebuke; he completed his bow to Caroline. She could feel Sir Henry's anger... and Arthur's disbelief. It was one thing to be rude to Caroline - that was understandable - but not to his father, not when he was a guest in his home.

"I do beg your pardon, dear Mistress Newell. I tend to forget myself when I become caught up in some worthy cause, such as I am here, in this frightened, most needy company of souls." His smile sought her understanding, which he was certain she would give. She was, after all, a well-bred lady, despite her faults; she would know how to respond to his courtly gesture and his apology, spoken with such depth of feeling.

"If only it were, Mr. Bragge."

"I beg your pardon?"

"Condemning an old woman to death for stealing a few turnips or a handful of straw. You call *that* a worthy cause?"

Sir Henry groaned; he wished Caroline had not said that. She had no way of knowing, of course, that for Francis it was not just a matter of an old woman and a bit of straw. He had been waging war against witches and Dissenters - he coupled them under the same heading - ever since he was a boy in the vicarage in Hitchin. To disparage his campaign in Walkern was to disparage the man himself: witch-hunting had become his *raison d'être*.

"This is nothing more than a joke to you, a mere diversion in your social round!" He stepped menacingly towards her. "Well, let me tell you, Mistress Newell…"

"Francis! Desist, please!" His grandson might attack Caroline with words, but a raised fist could not be allowed.

"No, Francis!" Arthur, much as he supported Francis's views, was horrified to see him approach Caroline in such a belligerent fashion.

Francis lowered his fists. For a moment no one spoke, no one moved; it was as if they were puppets with no will of their own.

"Are you coming, mistress?" Mary's small, sad voice, calling from the open carriage, broke the tension.

Caroline relaxed her shoulders, and walked to the door. "No, Mary, I am not."

"But, mistress, it's getting cold. Can I shut the door?"

"No. Leave it open. Climb down and help Jacob to get the boxes back to our rooms. We are staying."

"Staying? Oh, mistress..." Mary was out of the carriage in a flash, her face alight with joy. "Oh, Miss Caroline. Thank you."

"I am not doing this for you!" All that radiance just because the girl was staying at Yardley Bury? Caroline would get to the bottom of that later, but now...

The three men were standing, just as they had been when Caroline went to the door. "Now, Mr. Bragge, this cause of yours, to get rid of the old woman you deem to be a witch. Am I right?"

"Well, yes." What is she playing at?

"The woman whom *everyone else* in the neighbourhood believes is a witch?"

"They do." How dare she interrogate him like this!

"Nevertheless, in England we also believe in the rule of law. Do we not?" Reluctantly, Francis nodded. "We no longer consider it right," Caroline continued, "for people to be persecuted for their opinions and their beliefs, as happened in the past."

"There are times, though..." Francis began.

"Allow me to finish, please, Mr. Bragge." She gave him the briefest of smiles.

"Thank you." To her surprise she found herself trembling. She took a deep breath, glanced at Sir Henry, trying to interpret the look on his face: was he cross with her, was he in agreement? Had she gone too far? Well, she couldn't stop now, even though she seemed to have lost the thread of what she wanted to say, and the impetus too. "It is because so many of you..." she hesitated, "... because you are all against her, that poor old woman... and because I do not believe the things you say about her..." The nerves had calmed now and she was getting back into her stride. "This theory that you have, that she is a..."

"It is not a theory, madam! It is a fact!"

"Fact or theory... Jane Wenham needs someone on her side... and that someone is going to be me!" She began to tremble afresh. She had never intended this to happen: she had foolishly set herself up as the old woman's champion. What could she, Caroline, do against the power of the church... for that's what it was, in the person of the Rev. Francis Bragge... and if the case came to court, no doubt the jurors, whoever they were, would be as superstitious and prejudiced as the people of Walkern. As for Sir Henry, what must he think of her? First she's leaving, then she's not... Would he forgive her for making such a spectacle of herself in his house? Would he want her to stay now? She hadn't asked him; she had just assumed she could. When would she learn to think before she spoke? So many times had Robert taken her to task for doing exactly what she had done today. "Just because you think your cause is right, it doesn't mean you are the right person to fight for it," he had said. She wanted to run away and hide.

"Well said, Caroline." Sir Henry clapped his hands together and nodded his head in approval. "You should have been christened Portia."

She couldn't judge his mood - was he mocking? That would be unlike Sir Henry, but who knew... this whole situation was so uncharted, so bizarre. "If you gentlemen will excuse me, I shall go and remove my outer garments; it has become somewhat overheated in here, don't you think?" How stupid and trivial that sounded! She must take herself away from them quickly; from Arthur and Francis and above all, Sir Henry. She needed to think.

She inclined her head towards the men - neither Arthur nor Francis had said a word since her pronouncement, and not one of them had stirred, not even Sir Henry, as if waiting for her next move - then, with her head held high, she walked swiftly across the tiled floor to the wide staircase, put one hand on the banister and began climbing the stairs. She would not look behind her; she did not want to see the expressions on their faces.

Arthur looked puzzled, as if he couldn't quite comprehend what was going on. Francis's face was flushed and angry, his breath coming fast and his chest heaving. Sir Henry, with a smile spreading slowly from ear to ear, to the point where he was almost grinning, was nodding his head. He waited until Caroline was out of earshot, then, composing his face with difficulty - this was, after all, no laughing matter - he said to Francis, "I think, my boy, you are going to have quite a fight on your hands."

6

In the middle of the afternoon it began to snow, not heavily, but enough to make Caroline decide against taking a walk. She couldn't, though, stay in her room all afternoon. Aside from the fact that she was beginning to feel cold - the fire needed making up - it would be discourteous to Sir Henry if she isolated herself any longer. She had done her thinking, and if Sir Henry would allow her to stay she would do what she could to prevent Francis from persecuting the old woman. How she would do this she didn't yet know, but she *would* find a way, even if meant contacting some enlightened people in the neighbourhood - there must be *some* - and risk Sir Gilbey discovering her whereabouts. Compared with what was going on in Walkern, being hounded by an aged suitor was of no importance. Besides, he had probably lost interest by now, or had found another, younger quarry.

Caroline set off in search of Sir Henry. There was no one about - she hoped she wouldn't suddenly be confronted by Arthur or Francis, or worse still, both of them - and her footsteps sounded loud to her ears as she walked across the tiled floor towards the back of the house. The most likely place to find Sir Henry was in his snug. She opened the door quietly. Yes, he was there, fast asleep in his red armchair. She crept in, ready to settle herself in the other chair by the fire. First she must get something to read; if she just sat, she too might fall asleep. Which book should she choose, from among so many? Something that could be reached easily and lifted from a shelf or table without making a noise. There was a slim volume on the little table beside her chair, *The Topography of Hertfordshire.* That would do. Perhaps it had even been placed there specially for her: Sir Henry was keen to impart knowledge about his county. She sat down and carefully lifted the book. She had barely started reading - she wasn't sure it was a good choice: it seemed, from the first few pages, to be the kind of book that would send her to sleep! - when a small log fell from the fire on to the hearth and broke into pieces. Caroline put her book aside, knelt down on the hearthrug and began to sweep up the fragments of charred wood into a small metal scoop that lay on the hearth.

"You shouldn't be doing that, Caroline."

"Oh, Sir Henry! I'm sorry if I disturbed you." She sat back on her heels and smiled at the old man. He looks tired, she thought; he shouldn't be having all this worry at his time of life.

"You didn't. I sleep lightly and I heard the log fall."

"All cleared up now," Caroline said, getting to her feet and shaking out the skirt of her dark green velvet dress.

"That's a very becoming gown," he said.

"Thank you. I usually wear brighter colours than this, but…" No, she wouldn't tell him she was wearing it because it was the warmest one she had brought with her. Even so, she had needed a woollen shawl around her shoulders for the cold passageways between her room and the snug.

"My father liked bright colours," Sir Henry said, not appearing to notice that Caroline had not finished her sentence. "He was quite a peacock; he liked bright hangings in the house too."

"Did Aunt Elizabeth like colourful clothes? I can't quite remember... though I do seem to recall a gown with butterflies and flowers embroidered on the skirt." Was this a good moment to mention the cloak in the chest upstairs?

"Oh yes. She loved embroidery. She was very skilful at it herself."

"Now *that* I don't remember. Did she have other embroidered clothes? As well as that skirt, I mean."

Sir Henry chuckled. "So you've seen it; I thought you might have done."

"I wasn't prying," Caroline said hastily. "I was looking for somewhere to put some of my own clothes and... and I saw it."

"Do you like it?"

"Oh yes, it's beautiful. Was it... was it Aunt Elizabeth's?"

"It was intended for her... but she never wore it."

"Oh? Why ever not?" She was doing it again, being impatient, pushing, prodding, when she should just wait; if he wanted to tell her, he would.

"It came too late." A look of great sadness came over his face. "By the time it arrived she was too ill to wear it."

"Oh, my dear." Caroline slipped off her chair, and knelt down by Sir Henry. She took the old man's worn and knotted hands into her own soft ones and lifted them to her face. "I am so sorry. I have brought back unhappy memories for you."

"Not at all. You have brought back a very *happy* memory."

"Oh?"

"She saw the cloak, and loved it. She stretched out her hand from the bed… and smiled. She hadn't done that for some days."

"Oh, Sir Henry."

"So, you see, it's a happy memory."

"Thank you for telling me that." She wanted to know more but was not sure that she should ask. "Why… why do you keep it there, in that chest?"

Sir Henry pulled a wry face and looked away.

"I'm sorry, it's none of my business. Please let's talk of something else."

How tactless she had been!

"My dear girl, there is nothing to be sorry for." He patted her hand reassuringly. "I only paused because… I thought… if I told you why it is there, you would think me a foolish old man."

Caroline waited; let him take his time.

"When I am feeling sad, when I'm missing her… I miss her always, but there are days when…"

"Yes," Caroline said. "I know." There were days when the thought that Robert had gone from her life forever were more than she could bear. She would go then to visit Hannah's grave, as if a second heart-wrenching pain could somehow make the first one more bearable. "I do, I really do."

Holding the cloak that he had bought for Elizabeth, seeing again her smile as she touched it, the ache for her would tip over into tears, and in the tears he found some release from his pain. And so, of course, the cloak had to be kept hidden away, in a room where no one in the house would look for him.

For some moments they sat there, hands joined, not speaking, their thoughts in sympathy.

"Now isn't that a cosy scene."

Arthur's harsh, sarcastic tone shattered the peace of the fire-lit room. It was the second time he had interrupted a tender moment between his father and Caroline. They let go of each other's hands and Caroline began to get to her feet, then changing her mind, she sank back on to the hearthrug by Sir Henry's chair.

"Yes, isn't it," she said. It was only Arthur, what did it matter what he thought of her? But it wasn't Caroline he was looking at, it was his father, with whom he had probably never shared such intimacy. Poor Arthur, no wonder he sought out the village girls; he enjoyed no love at home.

"Come and join us," she said, patting the floor beside her. "It's so warm just here, and you look as if you could do with warming up."

Arthur did indeed look chilled; his nose had gone an unattractive shade of blue and there were drops of sleety rain on his hair.

"No thank you," he said sharply. "I have no time to sit." He turned on his heel and left the room, banging the door shut behind him.

"Arthur!" called his father, struggling to his feet. "I won't have this rudeness!"

"Shall I go after him?" Caroline asked.

"No, my dear." Sir Henry subsided into his chair. "Let him be. I shall speak to him later." He sighed heavily. "I sometimes think I should have been stricter with him when he was a boy; he might have turned out better… but, there you are… I didn't, and now I have to live with it."

"It's not too late for him to change." Caroline hated to see the old man so downcast about his son, on top of everything else.

"I don't think he will," Sir Henry said slowly, "until he finds a really good woman, someone who is prepared to take him in hand; a strong woman, but one who will also love him."

"Goodness," Caroline said, jumping up from the floor, "it's getting very dark in here. Shall I ring for Jacob and have candles brought in?"

"Thank you, my dear, that is very kind." He wished he hadn't said that about Arthur; he hoped he'd not annoyed her.

Having rung for Jacob, Caroline went over to the window. The feeling of closeness she and Sir Henry had shared was now gone, and it was difficult to know what they should talk about. She was about to make a trite remark about the weather - the sleet was driving against the window now - when Jacob entered, with an already lit candelabra; he would have known the reason for a summons at this time on a winter day.

"Are there chamber-sticks in the hall?" Caroline asked, as he closed the curtains.

"Yes, madam. I have put out several; they are on the table."

"Then I shall take one and go up to my room. Sir Henry, if you don't mind, I will…" She smiled to herself - he had already picked up a book, and appeared to be engrossed in it. Caroline took it as a polite signal that he wished to be left alone for a while.

112

She would stay in her room for the rest of the day; she did not wish to have another meal in the company of Francis, they would only come to blows, again... and that would upset Sir Henry.

7

Caroline, having breakfast in her room, became aware of the distant sound of angry voices, coupled with a loud banging, as if someone was trying to break down a door.

"What now?" She went to the window overlooking the long front drive.

Mary, repairing a mysteriously torn frill on one of Caroline's petticoats, looked up from her sewing, but said nothing; she didn't want her mistress finding her any more jobs to do, just to stop her going down to the rectory.

"Goodness," said Caroline, "there's a crowd of them out there, and there are more coming! The Reverend Francis Bragge has a lot to answer for, stirring everybody up like this."

Mary joined her mistress at the window. "It's not Mr. Bragge, mistress, it's the old woman."

"Oh Mary… you don't believe all that nonsense, do you?" It was said with tenderness, as if Caroline was addressing a small, beloved child.

"Well, no. Not really." Mary was trying hard to make her answer sound true. "No."

"But…?"

She had never been able to lie successfully to Caroline. "It was Jem, mistress, he said…"

"Jem. Ah. The young man who helps one of the farmers."

"Yes, mistress." Mary turned her head away; she did not want the rising colour in her cheeks to be seen.

"And what has *Jem* been saying?"

"He just said... "

"Yes?"

"He said there *are* funny things going on, things you can't explain. So... so maybe the old woman is to blame."

"Do *you* think she is?"

Mary was silent for a few moments. Caroline waited, looking steadfastly at the girl; her high colour was now subsiding.

"No, mistress," Mary said at last.

"Good girl, that's what I hoped you'd say." She turned back to the window. "There's Mr. Gardiner! Oh, this must be serious."

Renewed knocking and shouting had at last brought someone to the front door. A great blast of sound came surging up the stairwell and through the open bedroom door.

"Shall I shut the door, mistress?"

"No! I want to know what's going on." Caroline strode to the door and on to the landing from where she could look down into the front hall. She could see Sir Henry, and behind him, Francis.

"More trouble with the witch, no doubt," she heard Francis say.

"*You'd* like that, wouldn't you?" Caroline said softly.

"Mr. Gardiner, do come in," Sir Henry said.

The rector stepped into the hall, but the villagers hung back. Their fear and anger had made them bold enough to come to the front door, but not one of them would cross the threshold without a direct invitation from Sir Henry… and he was not about to issue one.

"And the rest of you… go home."

There was grumbling, but no movement, from the villagers.

Mr. Gardiner turned to them. "Do as Sir Henry says, all of you."

Still they didn't move. Then a man at the back of the group spoke out.

"We're not going… till we know that you're going to *do something*… 'bout the witch." There were murmurs of agreement from the crowd.

"Quite right," said Francis. "They need to know."

"Leave this to me, Francis," Sir Henry said, firmly. "Mr. Gardiner, would you be willing for them to wait at the rectory?"

"Yes, Sir Henry, of course."

The rector gave his instructions to the villagers and reluctantly they departed. Sir Henry led the rector, followed by Francis, into his library.

"Oh, now what?" said Caroline, from her vantage point on the landing. "I must find out."

In the library Sir Henry was seated behind his desk, with Mr. Gardiner in front of him. Francis stood, gazing through the window. The villagers, looking back every now and then towards the house, were walking slowly along the drive.

"Caroline, my dear." Sir Henry rose from his chair as she entered the room. Mr. Gardiner began struggling to his feet and Francis spun round from the window. That dratted woman again!

"Why are you here?" he asked, approaching her angrily.

"Francis!" Sir Henry exclaimed.

Caroline stood her ground: the man was vile, but he did not intimidate her.

Ignoring Francis, she spoke to Sir Henry. "I do beg your pardon. I will leave immediately. I didn't realise this was a private meeting."

To Francis's annoyance, Sir Henry said, "Come and sit down, my dear." He gestured to a chair by the fireside. "Of course this is not a private meeting." His words were for Caroline, but he was looking at his grandson. "We shall be glad of your opinion." His tone of voice changed: he issued an order. "Francis, apologise to Mistress Newell." This was the second, if not the third, time he had had to ask Francis to do this.

Good manners, or possibly respect for his grandfather's standing in the county - it would not be politic to go against him, certainly not just now - briefly overcame Francis's dislike of Caroline. "I apologise," he said. He waited for her to sit down, then flicking up his coat tails, seated himself on an upright chair near the window.

"Now, Mr. Gardiner," Sir Henry said. "You say Anne Thorn has tried to drown herself."

"Oh, poor girl." Caroline lifted her hand to her mouth. "How dreadful."

"Did you see this happening?"

"No, Sir Henry, but my wife did, and Susan Aylott, and some of the other women."

"Mm…" Sir Henry was looking dubious; the testimony of a few excitable women would not justify the arrest of Jane Wenham, if that was what they were after.

"And Farmer Chapman's men, too," the rector said, interpreting the magistrate's hesitation correctly. "It was one of them that rescued Anne." He turned to Francis.

"She had a crooked pin with her again."

"Ah," said Francis, standing up. "Now…"

"Oh no, not more of those." Caroline knew she should not speak, but she had seen the look on Francis's face at the mention of a crooked pin. How could she be expected to sit quietly and listen to this superstitious rubbish?

"Don't mock, Mistress Newell." Francis didn't even give Caroline the courtesy of looking at her; his eyes were fixed on Mr. Gardiner. If there was a crooked pin, there could be something else; a cat perhaps or an incantation of some kind.

"No, please ma'am, don't." The rector was trembling.

"You really are frightened, aren't you?" Caroline said.

"Yes. Everyone is afraid."

"Mistress Newell, as I have pointed out before" - how tedious this woman's behaviour was becoming - "does not appreciate the seriousness of this situation."

"The whole village is in an uproar," Mr. Gardiner said. "If you don't arrest Jane Wenham soon, Sir Henry, I don't know what they'll do. They could kill her! It wouldn't surprise me if they weren't at her house now."

"They were told to go to the rectory."

"They are in an angry mood, Sir Henry. I don't think they will wait peacefully at the rectory; I'm not sure they will even have gone there. They could easily have cut across the field to her cottage."

"Very well. I will make out a warrant for her arrest," Sir Henry said. He didn't *want* to do this, but he felt he had no option; he was the magistrate and, with the constable's help, it was up to him to keep the peace in the neighbourhood. "Send the constable to me, Mr. Gardiner."

"I'll take the warrant to the constable for you, Sir Henry," said Francis.

"Thank you, Francis, but it would be more appropriate if the constable were to come here."

"That will take far too much time. Anything could happen while we are waiting for him to come here and then for the warrant be taken back to Walkern."

"If it would make the old woman's life less at risk..." Caroline was addressing Sir Henry. "Mr. Gardiner said the village people might kill her..."

Sir Henry nodded.

At the risk of annoying him, Caroline went on, "Perhaps Mr. Bragge *should* take the warrant."

"How very sensible of you, Mistress Newell, supporting my suggestion." Francis rose from his chair and bowed to her.

"If you like, Sir Henry," Caroline continued, as if Francis had not spoken, "I could accompany him." And keep an eye on him for you, her look said.

Sir Henry, interpreting it correctly, said, "Yes, I think that would be most satisfactory. In fact, if you take charge of the warrant, you can give it to Arthur, he'll be there."

"Why Arthur?" began Francis. What standing did Arthur have to warrant such trust?

Sir Henry stopped him with a raised hand. "... and that will leave you, Francis, free to assist Mr. Gardiner... in leading any prayers that might be necessary. The people will need spiritual guidance, will they not, Rector?"

Mr. Gardiner nodded. "They will," he said.

Sir Henry turned to his grandson. "You could perhaps pray with the villagers who may have gathered at Mistress Wenham's cottage, Francis, while Mr. Gardiner succours those who have gone to the rectory."

"Yes, but…" Francis tried again.

"… and Arthur, meanwhile, can take the warrant to the constable."

A very neat arrangement, thought Caroline. She would love to have smiled at Sir Henry and given him a thumbs-up sign; instead she just nodded her head gently.

"Oh, very well," said Francis. He couldn't resist adding, "But I do think Mistress Newell's presence will be unnecessary… and inappropriate."

"Nevertheless, she is going. Caroline, my dear, while *you* are preparing yourself for the walk, *I* shall prepare the warrant. Mr. Gardiner, I shall be glad of your assistance."

He took a sheet of paper from a drawer in his desk, and began to write.

Francis and Caroline, avoiding contact with one another, left the room.

Conversation with Francis on the way to Walkern being non-existent, Caroline used the time to study the man as he strode, fractionally ahead of her, with short, quick steps, suited to his short legs and stocky build. Head up, arms pumping up and down - she could see his closed, angry fists each time his arms moved away from his body - he walked in an absolutely straight line; heaven help any person or object that got in his way! If Caroline were to fall in one of the many rabbit holes that dotted the meadow they were crossing, she doubted whether the curate would stop to assist her.

"Mr. Bragge," she said at last, when she could stand the silence no longer.

"Mistress Newell." He half-turned towards her but kept on walking. "Are you having trouble keeping up with me?"

"Not at all. I enjoy walking. I wanted to ask you, before we reach Mistress Wenham's cottage…"

"Yes?" He stopped sharply and swung round to face her.

"Why do you find it necessary to be so cruel?" She had not intended to put the question so bluntly, but his look of loathing - of her or the old woman, or both of them perhaps - had forced those words out of her.

"I have been put on this earth to do God's will, and if that requires me to be, as you put it, cruel… to a sinner, to a person possessed of the Devil, then that is what I shall be." Nothing, Caroline felt, could touch the man; there was no appealing to his better nature, if he had one. She would have to find another way to rescue that poor creature from his grasp; he was like a poisonous spider that had caught a fly in its web.

No more was said. They came out on to the lane and turned right by Walkern Church, with Francis still ahead. It was slightly less cold down here and the wind had dropped. The lane, though, was muddy after the rain of the previous day, and Caroline had to be careful where she trod. If only she had put on her riding boots; her shoes, which were perfectly adequate in London, were of no use here. The long grass of the fields had already soaked them and her stockings, too. The discomfort and annoyance she felt was quickly put aside, as she spied, on the other side of the lane, the crowd of villagers gathered outside Jane Wenham's cottage, just as they had been when she took her ride with

Arthur. This time, though, there were more of them, and the mood was different. Then they had merely been taunting the old woman; now their voices were threatening, and the people sounded afraid, as well they might be if they thought they really were at the mercy of an evil creature. Caroline herself felt no fear of the old woman but she could understand the villagers' anxieties. If *she* lived in a remote place, far from the civilising influence of a city like London, she might well feel the same.

As she and Francis neared the house - Francis now dashing ahead, splashing through the stream that crossed the road - Caroline could make out the words, emphasised by blows on the door, being directed at the old woman.

"Come out, you witch!" A woman's voice.

"Bitch!" A man now, with a heavy piece of wood, banging at a window.

"You won't get away this time, Jane Wenham!" Another woman.

Then another voice, "Out of the way, I say." It was Arthur, right in the middle of the mob.

"Arthur!" called Caroline, but she was too far away for him to hear her.

Rather than wade through the water, she crossed the stream by a rickety bridge with a rough handrail on one side.

Francis by now had reached the cottage and was pushing his way through the crowd to the door, against which two of the men were thrusting their shoulders in an attempt to break it down.

"Stop! Stop!" yelled Francis. "This is not the way to do it!" Those on the fringes of the crowd - there must have been about thirty people there - turned towards him, and sensing his authority, even if some of them didn't know who he was, drew back. Among them was a tall, dark-haired young man, whom Caroline thought looked familiar, but couldn't quite place. Beside him stood a slim woman in a rough cloak with a hood pulled down over her face. Something about her also seemed familiar to Caroline; perhaps it was the girl she had seen at the rectory, Mr. Gardiner's servant, Anne... It couldn't be her - a flounced hem was peeping out from under her cloak. A village girl in an apricot silk gown? Oh no! She recognised the dress: it was one of hers, one she had given to Mary. Surely not... not after all that Caroline had said to her... and the young man was Jem, the mention of whose name had caused Mary to blush.

"Mary?"

There was no need to shout. By now Caroline was standing almost next to her, and the crowd, in response to Francis's intervention, had gone quiet. Mary, turning quickly at the sound of her name, looked directly into her mistress's eyes.

"Miss Caroline!" Her mistress was the last person she expected to see here.

To be caught disobeying her was bad enough, but to be caught wearing a peasant's cloak that she had borrowed from one of the maids at Yardley Bury *and* to be found in the company of Jem Dakers, "Oh, mistress..."

"Yes, you may well look mortified." Caroline surveyed the young man. "And who is this?"

"This is Jem, mistress." Who else would it be?

"Jem. Yes, of course. You were at the rectory, weren't you... with your sister, I believe it was."

"Yes, madam. I was." His gaze, though direct, was respectful.

"I hope you are looking after Mary."

"Yes, madam."

"Good. What I'd like you to do now, Jem, is take my maid back to Yardley Bury."

"Yes, madam."

"But, mistress…"

"No, Mary." Caroline shook her head. "You will do as I say."

On the other side of Jem was one of the village girls. She looked to be about Mary's age; she had dark eyes and sallow skin. While Mary was being reprimanded she had looked pleased, but when Caroline asked Jem to accompany her maid to Yardley Bury the girl's expression became sullen, and at the same time anxious.

"And what is your name?" Caroline asked gently.

The girl said nothing, just stared at Caroline. Was this lady of quality speaking to her?

"Come along, tell me your name."

"Please, ma'am, it's Margaret." It was little more than a whisper.

"Margaret."

"Yes, ma'am."

"Well, Margaret, I should like *you* to do something for me, too." There was no response.

"Go on, Margaret, speak to the lady," Jem said, pushing the girl forward. The hood of her homespun cloak fell back, revealing lank, brown hair.

"Yes, ma'am," the girl said, her voice still only a whisper.

"That's better," said Caroline. She sensed how anxious Mary was becoming.

Was Miss Caroline going to abandon her and make this half-witted country girl her lady's maid? Surely not, not just for one misdemeanour.

"Now, Margaret… I want you to walk with Jem… and see that Mary gets back safely to Sir Henry's house. Can you do that?"

"Oh yes, ma'am." Margaret's eyes lit up. And by the way she was looking at Jem, it was plain to see how she felt about him.

Mary flashed her mistress an angry look: how could Miss Caroline humiliate her like this… in front of all these people. Those in the crowd nearest to Mary, diverted from their attack upon the witch, were enjoying the spectacle of the fancily attired lady's maid who had turned Jem Dakers' head receiving a dressing-down from her mistress.

"Good girl. When you get there, Mary will take you and Jem into the kitchen, and Sir Henry's housekeeper, Mistress Sawyer, will give you some… What would you like? Some freshly baked bread perhaps, or some fruit, or a cake. Anyway, you choose what you would like… and you, too, Jem… and then you can bring *Margaret* back to…"

"I don't need anything, thank you," Jem interrupted, his voice just on the edge of being rude. "I have work. I work for Margaret's father, Farmer Gilbert."

"Oh." Jem's proud words and demeanour suggested that he aspired to being far more than just a farmer's lad: well, if he had his sights set on her Mary, he would have to be.

Caroline smiled at him. "That's good," she said. "Now, go along, the three of you." Her smile had gone. "Mary... I will see you later."

"Yes, mistress." Indignation, anxiety, shame and embarrassment: they were all there in Mary's answer.

Caroline watched them leave, Margaret triumphant, Mary downcast, and Jem, who now seemed amused by the situation, in the middle, carefully not walking close to either of the girls.

Renewed banging on the cottage door and windows brought Caroline up sharply. Heavens! She had almost forgotten the reason she was here!

"Mr. Chauncy," she called loudly, "I need to speak to you!"

Arthur turned from the cottage doorway. He had seen Caroline arriving with Francis - how could he not have done, a well-dressed lady amongst all the villagers - but he had chosen not to acknowledge her presence. It would be too embarrassing... *and* he would have had to assume some responsibility for her .

What was Francis thinking of, bringing her here! Now she was waving some sort of paper at him... and he couldn't ignore her.

"Yes, what is it?" he barked.

"I have a letter for you... from Sir Henry."

"Oh?" A reprimand, no doubt, for following the mob to the cottage; nothing got past his father. "I'll come for it," he said, and pushing aside those villagers who were in his way, he strode across to Caroline and held out his hand.

"It is for the constable," Caroline's voice was little more than a whisper. "It is a summons for the old woman's arrest."

"Oh!" Arthur could not quite believe it. A summons… brought to him, by Caroline?

"Take it," she said, thrusting it into his hand.

"Yes. Of course." He looked down at the paper... then up at Caroline. He smiled. "Thank you." His father had sent the summons to him! He squared his shoulders. "Thank you," he said again. "I shall take it to the constable directly."

As if at a signal, all the shouting and banging had stopped and Caroline and Arthur's words fell into the space created by the silence; the eyes of all the villagers were upon them… and those of Francis Bragge, too.

"Now that you have delivered your message, Mistress Newell," the curate said, "you may leave us."

"I will," Caroline said crossly. She had no wish to stay; she could feel the villagers' hostility towards her. How she was to return to Yardley Bury was another matter: could she - should she? - set off and walk there on her own?

As if he read her mind - an appalling thought! - Francis said, "It was short-sighted of you to send your maid away. You need her now. Don't you?"

Arthur could hear the sarcasm in his voice. He is annoyed that my father had the summons delivered to *me*, he thought, and not to him.

"Mistress Newell has my protection," he said gallantly. "I will see that she comes to no harm." He took her arm. "Come with me, Caroline. We shall go together to fetch the constable."

"You've no need for that, Mr. Chauncy."

Arthur turned round sharply, to see Susan Aylott standing so close that she must have heard every word he and Caroline had spoken. The foul smell that Caroline had been aware of at the rectory, coming from the woman's body, was still there, but less so in the open, chilly, air. Even so, Caroline instinctively drew back from her, then guiltily forced a smile to her closed lips.

"The constable's here," Susan said, nodding her head and pointing down the road. As one the crowd turned, their relief palpable. All would now be well; the constable would execute the warrant in Mr. Chauncy's hand, and the witch would be taken to gaol… or, at least, to the Cage.

Where she will be safe from the mob, thought Caroline. "I had better go back to Yardley Bury now," she whispered to Arthur.

"You can't," he said, whispering back hoarsely. "Not on your own. Wait, this won't take long, and I'll come with you."

If only she hadn't sent Mary away. What did it matter if Mary was with Jem?

She hadn't been taunting Mistress Wenham, only looking on, like a bystander at a fire. For all Caroline knew, Mary had gone there to aid the old woman; she was well aware of her mistress's views on the subject of 'the witch'. Caroline shook her head ruefully. Yet again she had acted on impulse… and where had it got her? Stuck in a muddy lane with a fanatical parson, an angry crowd, very cold feet… and no immediate means of escape. Arthur was right: she could not set off across the fields on her own.

The constable, a tall, broad-shouldered, stern-faced, bearded man in his forties, opened the warrant and read it.

"Yes," he said. "Let us do it." He refolded the warrant and placed it in a pocket of his coat, then walked purposefully across to Jane Wenham's door, and knocked upon it with his oak staff.

"Jane Wenham, I have a warrant for your arrest." He spoke the words slowly, weightily - there was no mistaking their importance. "Open the door and come out."

There was no need for him to say who he was; they had crossed swords many times in the past few years, and the old woman knew the constable's voice well.

Not a sound came from the house, nor from the crowd in the lane. The constable spoke again.

"Jane Wenham, you are required to come out of there." There was authority in his voice, but no emotion.

"Go away. I am not coming out." The old woman sounded weary, as if all the fight had gone from her.

"Yes you are!" Susan Aylott picked up a small stone from the ground and threw it at one of the windows.

"That's right, you tell 'er." Thomas Adams, beside her, found another stone to follow Susan's on to the window-pane.

"Stop that!" the constable said. He turned back to the cottage. "I have a warrant for your arrest, Jane Wenham." He spoke very deliberately.

"I don't care if you have ten warrants, I am not leaving my home!"

"If you don't open that door… and very quickly… I shall break it down."

The words were greeted with a great cheer from the crowd, and the constable continued, "I've plenty of strong men here to help me."

"Oh no." Caroline tugged at Arthur's sleeve. "What is the point of getting a warrant if he's going to use violence?"

"Thomas, Matthew, James… are you ready?"

"Go away, the lot of you!" The old woman's voice was stronger now.

"If they couldn't break down the down the door before, why should they be able to do it now?" Caroline asked.

"They weren't trying before," said Arthur. "Not really. They were too afraid of what the witch might do to them, but now…"

"Now they feel the law is on their side," said Caroline.

"Yes. And it is." Arthur let go of Caroline's arm. "I shall go and help them," he said forcefully, and he joined the men at the door.

With the arrival of the constable and his demand for strong men to assist him, the women in the crowd had drawn aside, and now formed a group of their own, with only Susan Aylott standing aloof, not allying herself with either the men or the women. Her eyes had followed Arthur, and she made a move to join him.

"Get back, Susan." The constable had seen her. His glance took in Caroline, also standing alone. "Look after the lady," he said.

"I'm all right," Caroline said quickly.

Susan Aylott gave her a sneering shrug. Here was a woman, thought Caroline, who was no respecter of person or class. The latter aspect appealed, in theory, to her egalitarian leanings, but she wished the woman would not be quite so brazen about it. I should like to teach her some manners and have her put in a good hot bath. Caroline smiled to herself at the thought.

"What you grinning at? It's not funny, you know, having a witch living down your road. It's not a show, put on for the likes of you."

"Of course not, Mistress Aylott. I know that. But unlike you, I do not believe that Mistress Wenham *is* a witch." There, she had said it - in public, in front of a crowd of angry villagers who believed fervently that witchcraft was being practised in their midst - and she had said it so loudly that Arthur, on the point of adding the weight of his shoulder to the others about to be thrust at the cottage door, turned round to her.

Before he could say anything, however, Mr. Bragge, who had been surprisingly silent up to now, stepped forward.

"Mistress Newell, this is no concern of yours. Please do not offer your opinions here!"

"I have *made* it my concern, Mr. Bragge, as you well know… and I shall offer my opinion whenever I think fit!"

There was no time for Francis, or Arthur should he have wanted to, to respond to Caroline's broadside. At that moment the constable, with his three stout villagers and Arthur, broke down the door of Jane Wenham's cottage, to the delight of the women and the rest of the men, who cheered and clapped, and then hissed, as the constable, with Thomas on his other side, brought the old woman, struggling and spitting, out of her house.

"Take your hands off me!" she screamed. Though her arms were held, her feet were free; she kicked out with them in all directions, her fear and anger giving her the strength and agility of a much younger woman.

"You'll be sorry for this, you will, all of you," she said, and her narrowed, hate-filled eyes raked the mob from one side to the other, as if she were aiming arrows of venom at those who tormented her.

Caroline, who had been included in the woman's scan, shivered involuntarily.

There was something here that was very unsettling, but whether or not it was malevolent, she couldn't say. If you believed the woman was a witch, and you had been provoking her, then yes, her look *was* malevolent, and frightening, too, and the sooner someone who eyed you like that was locked up the better.

Despite the efforts of five sturdy men to keep her under control, the old woman was still struggling.

"I should tie her up if I were you, Constable," said Arthur.

"I got some rope," Thomas said. He let go of Jane Wenham long enough to pull out a length of thick cord from a bag slung across his shoulder. She immediately began to flail him with her free hand, at the same time lashing out at him with her tongue.

Caroline blushed at the epithets that came from Jane Wenham's throat, farming and animal allusions, most of them.

"While you're about it, get something you can use as a gag!" cackled Susan Aylott. "We can't have... a lady..." - she made the word sound distasteful - "... hearing things like that, can we, Mr. Chauncy?"

Arthur had his own concern: what should they do with the witch now that they had hold of her? Where was she to go? To the Cage here in Walkern, or the gaol in Hertford... or up to Yardley Bury? His father's warrant had given no specific instructions.

"Where are you taking her, Constable?" he asked.

"To my house, sir, to the Cage."

"No! No!" The mob did not want that.

"We should take her to the rectory," Thomas Adams shouted, once again firmly grasping the old woman. "Let her see what she done to poor Anne Thorn."

"Anne nearly drowned 'cos of you!" a woman called out.

"Yes, take her there!" A man's voice, echoed by murmurs of agreement from the crowd.

"I'm not going!" yelled the old woman, and turning her head she spat full in Thomas' face.

"You'll go where the constable tells you, witch!" said Thomas, wiping the spittle from his face with his hand, then plastering it over Jane Wenham's sleeve. He would like to have spread it on her face but he was afraid she might bite him... and goodness knows what terrible harm that might do him.

A woman in the crowd shouted, "Witch! Witch! Put her away, the bitch!" and, as more villagers joined in, it became a chant, "Bitch! Bitch! Put away the witch!", drowning the prayers that Francis, standing in their midst, with his eyes closed and his hands raised aloft, was offering up to the Almighty.

Arthur looked across at Caroline. He could see that she was trembling. It didn't take long, Arthur thought, for her civilised veneer to wear off. Faced with the raw emotions released in the struggle between good and evil, which were totally outside her own experience, she was frightened. It made him feel superior, but at the same time protective; she was, after all, his father's guest and her mother had been a dear friend of his mother. However much he might enjoy watching her layers of sophistication peeling away, he could not let her stand there and suffer.

"Take her first to the rectory, Constable, and then to the Cage." Arthur's voice was authoritative and strong. "Mistress Newell, you will come with me to the rectory..." Sensing Caroline's anxiety, he softened his tone. "You will be safe there... and once I have made sure the witch is secured in the Cage I shall take you back to Yardley Bury."

"Thank you," said Caroline. She nodded approval at Arthur; he had taken command of a difficult situation and made a bold, forceful decision.

He had, however, reckoned without the tenacity of the old woman: she kicked, she spat, she struggled free of the rope that bound her, and once free she scratched with her long jagged fingernails at Matthew's face, all the time shouting and screaming in a mad frenzy. If ever the crowd needed proof that the woman possessed unnatural powers this was it; she was not behaving, in their eyes, like a normal person.

Caroline watched in horror, but also with understanding; she had witnessed the same behaviour once at Amley, when a beautiful bay mare, trapped between the shafts of an overturned cart, had not only managed to break free, but had snapped one of the shafts, and still attached, had dragged it with her out of the ditch and into a copse. Whatever had been flowing through the creature's body and producing her panic had also given the terrified animal the strength to break free of its bond. Caroline had been dumbfounded, but Robert had taken it calmly.

It is what animals do under great stress, he had told her. He didn't know why, but he suspected that they produced some substance in their bodies... in their blood or their bones, he wasn't sure which… that gave them, briefly, extraordinary and unaccountable energy. And now Caroline was seeing the same phenomenon in a woman of more than seventy years of age.

Jane Wenham's bid for freedom did not last long. Her abnormal burst of energy had exhausted her. She collapsed, weeping, on to the ground in front of her cottage, and now, without any resistance, she was tied up with Thomas' rope and led away by the constable.

Caroline found herself shaking afresh. All around her were shocked, frightened faces, mirroring, she was sure, her own expression. Even Francis, arrogant, sarcastic Francis, was trembling; never in his life had he seen such a powerful demonstration of demonic power. His body and his soul thrilled to the excitement and passion of the incident he had just witnessed.

"Arthur," Caroline called softly. His eyes had been on the old woman; he, too, was amazed. He started now, as if waking from a dream, and turned to Caroline.

"Come," he said, reaching out his hand to her. "Come to the rectory and get warm. It's all over now."

All over? Francis looked at Arthur with disbelief and disgust. Is that what he thought? Take the woman into custody… and that's that? Oh no. Far from being over, it was just beginning. *This* was a witch-hunt like no other!

8

Caroline sat huddled up close to the bedroom fire with a woollen shawl wrapped tightly around her shoulders. Even so, she could not stop trembling. The things she had seen and heard at the rectory were troubling her greatly, frightening her... and the very fact of finding herself frightened by them was in itself disturbing. If only she could bring common sense to bear upon the situation, think about it rationally, as the rational, common sense sort of person she knew she was... but she could not.

Her brain was a jumble of images:

Jane Wenham struggling and cursing.

Francis, raising his voice in prayer.

That horrible woman Susan Aylott, leering at Arthur.

Mrs. Gardiner, shrieking and almost fainting.

Anne Thorn, screaming, leaping at Jane Wenham, scratching her forehead, tearing at the skin as if to pull it away from the bone; the cries of pain from the old woman; the horror and disbelief of everyone there, Caroline included, as they had stared at Jane Wenham's forehead - despite the ferocity of her attack Anne had drawn no blood!

Above it all, like an evil chorus, the yowling of cats.

Then, suddenly, silence... everyone tense, taut.

No one moving, no one *daring* to move... nor speak.

It was as if, for whatever length of time the silence lasted, they were under a spell.

Into the silence had come the calm, official voice of the constable: "You know what this means, Mr. Chauncy, sir?"

The spell was broken; they could all breathe again.

"Yes," Arthur had replied. "It means she *is* a witch. You had best take her to the Cage."

There, it had been said: the woman *was* a witch.

Such mundane words…

But now, at last, something would be done; she would be imprisoned and punished and they, the villagers, would be free of her.

Caroline, too, had given a great sigh of relief. In strange and difficult circumstances she felt she had acquitted herself well. She recalled Arthur's words of warning on the brief walk from the cottage to the rectory; once they got there on no account was she to utter a word to anyone. Already chilled by both the weather and the sense of being caught up in something she did not understand, something completely outside her own experience, she was only too ready to comply with Arthur's wishes: the sooner she was back at Yardley Bury the better, and if keeping quiet would speed her arrival there, she would be happy, for once in her life, not to offer an opinion or interfere in any way. And in the rectory kitchen - all niceties befitting a lady were today set aside - even if she had wanted to speak, she would have been hard put to make herself heard above the din. At least it had been warm in there, but soon, with the press of people, it had become *too* warm. As they shouted and shook their fists and prayed aloud, and as their clothes and their bodies thawed out, the stench had become intolerable. Caroline had been on the point of getting up, and regardless of safety, pushing herself through the throng; she felt she would do anything, scream if necessary, just to draw in a breath of fresh, untainted air. But then... Arthur pronounced Jane Wenham a witch. For now, the inquisition was over and Caroline didn't have to stay in that foetid atmosphere any longer. Selfishly it was all she could think of at that moment. She began to gather her skirts together, ready to depart - she would push through the crowd whether they liked it or not - when the old woman, breaking free of the constable's hold - he had had her arm in a grip throughout the questioning - all but threw herself at Arthur. "I am not a witch!" she screeched.

Her eyes flashed angrily; her face, even in the heat of the kitchen, turned deathly pale. "I am not going to any Cage," she hissed, desperation in her voice. "You say I'm a witch... Prove it. Put me to the test! Go on! Now! Look for the Devil's mark! Why don't you?" She turned to the women. "Go on, Susan, you look... and you, Elizabeth Field. Pull my clothes off! It's what you want to do, isn't it?"

"No, no!" Mr. Gardiner intervened hastily, but Jane Wenham ignored him.

"You want to see if I got three nipples? Eh, Thomas? Go on. Look!"

Tied at the wrists she managed to jerk the slack of the rope sufficiently to allow her to get the fingers of one hand to the lacing of her tattered dress - no one had thought to give the poor soul a coat for the trek to the rectory - and pull it fractionally undone. "I could have a spider's mark... or a toad's foot! Look under my arms, Matthew Gilston... see if the Devil's drunk my blood! See if I got teats there... It's what witches have, ain't it?" and Matthew, who had ventured too near, got a faceful of Jane Wenham's rank spittle.

With Susan and Thomas and others clamouring at the tops of their voices for these tests to be done, it had been hard for Mr. Gardiner to bring order to the proceedings. Eventually, with the help of Arthur, he quietened them down. "Let us not have any more of that," he said. When he was certain they were all listening he went on, "Now, does anyone have a *sensible* suggestion?"

For a moment no one spoke, then, hesitantly, Elizabeth Field volunteered, "We could swim her."

"Oh, that's right." Jane Wenham cackled - her voice had made Caroline shudder: there was something so... she baulked at the word, even saying it to herself now in the safety of her room... something so witchlike about the sound. "You do that, see if I swim!"

"Course you will," Susan had spat out the words. "You're a witch!"

And if she *drowned* that proved she *was* a witch. Caroline knew of this ancient punishment, but had never seen it executed. "You cannot do that." The constable's voice was firm. "Ordeal by water is not allowed, not any more." He paused briefly. There will be no argument, his look said. "So you'd best let me take her to the Cage."

Caroline recalled how relieved she had felt at that moment. Now it *was* all over: the old woman would be taken to the local lock-up, and there she would be safe.

The feeling of relief hadn't lasted long. "Must be something we can do." The frustration in Susan Aylott's voice was matched by the looks of disappointment on the faces of the other villagers... and on Arthur's face, too,

Caroline was horrified to see. For them it was not good enough simply to put her in the Cage; *she* might be all right there, but what about them? Were they just to go home without the satisfaction of putting the witch through a proper test?

Much to Caroline's surprise, and discomfort, it was Mrs. Gardiner who had spoken next... in a small voice, which, nevertheless, everyone in the room heard.

"We could get her to recite the Lord's Prayer," she said. Her husband had taken her hand and looked at her with so much gratitude and tenderness, it had made Caroline's heart swell. "Yes," he said, "*that* is a right and proper thing to do."

"Indeed it is." Francis stepped forward eagerly. "Allow me, Mr. Gardiner, Mistress Gardiner," he said unctuously, somehow managing, to Caroline's amusement - it was good to have a brief moment of light relief in the midst of all this anguish - to execute one of his extravagant bows, despite the crush of people around him.

And so Jane Wenham had begun to recite the prayer, with everyone in the room following minutely what she said, all of them ready to pounce on her the moment she made a mistake, however slight. At first everything went well - from Jane's point of view, not her persecutors; they were disappointed. She knew the words - she wasn't supposed to, she was a witch, and probably a Dissenter, too - but then, when she came to the passage about temptation and evil, a most important passage... she got it wrong, spectacularly wrong. To the satisfaction of her inquisitors, she asked God to lead her into temptation, not once but twice. She pleaded tiredness, but the crowd just scoffed; she couldn't say the Lord's Prayer correctly because the Devil wouldn't let her...

and that *proved* she was a witch! Francis nodded smugly and the rector and his wife put their hands together and lifted their eyes to heaven in a joint gesture of thankfulness to the Almighty.

The villagers, though, wanted more. Yes, of course Jane Wenham was a witch! *They* had known that all along, and now *she* had proved it… and therefore, there *must* be witch marks on her body… and it wouldn't hurt, would it, just to have a look. A couple of the women began to pull at her clothes. "Enough!" Mr. Gardiner shouted. "I will have no more of this. Mistress Wenham is tired," and when the women started to grumble and eye the rector boldly and aggressively, in a manner they would never have presumed to do in normal circumstances, he reprimanded them even more firmly. "This is not the way to treat any person, whatever you may think of them. I will not have any more questioning… or searching for marks. Susan Aylott, take your hands off Mistress Wenham. Do not look at me like that! Constable, take Mistress Wenham to the Cage… and if you women don't behave some of you will find yourselves there, too!"

Although he had no legal authority to punish the villagers, the rector's words sobered the women, and as the constable, accompanied by the two clergymen, led Jane Wenham away, they hung back, for the moment subdued. The last place they wanted to be was in the Cage with the witch! The men, though, were not so easily put off; they would follow her to the Cage, they said… "There is no law can stop us!"… and there they would stay, all night, taking turns to make sure she did not escape.

Gradually the rectory kitchen had emptied. The women, keeping well out of the rector's way, followed the men down the lane to the constable's house and its Cage, and fresh, cold air, coming in through the open front door, replaced the stench left by unwashed, sweating bodies. Only Mrs. Gardiner, Arthur and Caroline remained behind; even Anne Thorn had disappeared in the throng. Pleading the onset of a megrim, Mrs. Gardiner made a hasty retreat to another part of the house and Arthur escorted Caroline to Yardley Bury, walking her there at great speed. So urgent was his desire to get back to the village... "to ensure that the witch has been locked up securely, according to my father's orders"... that he made no attempt to see her into the house despite her obvious fatigue, casually depositing her at the back door, like a parcel, before sprinting back across the fields to Walkern.

Caroline had made her way quickly to her room: she wanted to see no one. Now, though, her initial fear calmed, she craved company and sustenance. She dragged herself to the landing and called over the banisters for Mary to bring her a tisane. Whether or not Mary had heard her she did not know; she staggered back to the fireside, and lowered herself carefully into her chair - she was feeling faint now, as well as shaky - trying to breathe as deeply as she could. Her mother had always told her to do that if ever she was afraid or too excited, even too hot or too cold - it was her mother's cure for almost everything. She needed, at this moment, not to feel afraid, here in this old, dark house, with no one of her own to turn to. Oh, how she needed Robert! He would have put the whole matter into perspective for her. She could almost hear him: "An old woman making a nuisance of herself and a lot of ignorant peasants spreading ridiculous stories and proclaiming her a witch? Pull yourself together, Caroline. There is nothing here that can harm *you.*" Of course not. And yet, as the early darkness of the winter afternoon began to fill the wainscotted room, Caroline shuddered again; there was something in this place, this village, that was... *evil.* It was not an easy word for her to say... or even think; it sounded so primitive, so... so sinister, as if just by saying it, by admitting its possibility, she was evoking danger. She drew closer to the dwindling fire.

Miraculously, Mary, on her way through the entrance hall to the library - Sir Henry had said she could borrow a book whenever she pleased - *had* heard her mistress calling, and appeared within minutes with a ginger tisane, Caroline's favourite, and just the thing, Bessie had said, to warm her up on a cold day.

Mary had been aware of Caroline's unceremonious return to the house - she had been in the kitchen - but hadn't dared to step out into the passageway to greet her after her humiliating dressing-down in front of Jem.

That had been so awful, tramping back to the house, with Jem saying nothing ... not a word, all the way!... and Margaret sniggering and grinning on the other side of Jem. And when they got to the house he wouldn't come in; he just took hold of Margaret's arm and dragged her back across the stable yard. Jem would not forsake her, though, would he? Surely not... not after the looks he had given her when they stood in the crowd outside the old woman's house. He had even touched her hand - and he hadn't taken his fingers off hers straight away, as he should have done. But then Miss Caroline had appeared. Mary didn't think she had seen their hands touching; she hoped not. Things were bad enough without *that*. Bringing a warm drink to Miss Caroline's room with such alacrity could be just the way to get back into her mistress's favour: how lucky to have been where she was at the very moment Miss Caroline had called for her.

The sight of her lady, shivering, hunched over the fire, shocked Mary.

"Miss Caroline, you have a fever!" she said. What else could it be?

"Oh, Mary." There were tears in Caroline's eyes. She held out a trembling hand to her maid. "Dear Mary."

"Mistress! You are ill!" She had to be; Miss Caroline did not behave like this.

Unsure of what was required of her, Mary reached out her fingers and tentatively stroked the back of Caroline's hand.

"What are you doing?"

"Nothing, mistress… I thought, if you have a fever…?"

"I do not have a fever! How dare you! Go away and leave me alone!"

Mary scuttled to the door. This was no time for argument, and she would certainly not risk offering more comfort. She fled the room, closing the door quickly behind her.

Caroline, left alone, felt ashamed of herself. Yes, she had had a disturbing experience… but it was over now. There was no need to have shouted at Mary like that. She had treated her as if she were some ignorant scullery maid! She would have to call her back. It would not be easy; Mary was most probably by now in the kitchen, sobbing into Bessie's apron. Caroline would have to shout very loudly to made herself heard. She stepped out on to the fast-darkening landing; there was not a gleam of candlelight anywhere.

"Mary!" she called, and then again… "Mary!" Where *was* everybody? Sir Henry, Arthur… even the appearance of Francis at this moment would be welcome. The passages leading from the landing to other parts of the house stretched away in silent gloom. Caroline's heart began to race wildly and she started to tremble afresh. Trying hard to breathe deeply she scurried back into her room and shut the door. The fire was of little comfort now. It had died down to a few embers… and it was almost too dark to see if there were logs, or better still twigs - they would catch quickly and give her some light - piled by the hearth. She began to cry, and unable to stop, she hugged herself and gave way to her misery, hot tears raining down her cheeks.

A sharp rap at the door both startled her and jolted her out of her abject state. Hastily wiping away her tears she called out, in what she hoped was a strong, normal voice, "Come in."

The door opened and warm candlelight flooded the room. Behind the light came Jacob, bearing a tall, branched candlestick.

"Oh, Jacob." Relief flooded through her. "Thank you."

"I thought you might need some light, madam. It has got dark very early today."

"Yes, indeed it has." How joyous to have such a mundane conversation with the old servant. "Would you do something about this fire for me, Jacob, while you are here?"

"Of course, madam." He set the candlestick, with its sweet-smelling beeswax candles, down on a small table and moved to the fireplace. "Ah, you seem to be out of logs. I will fetch some."

"Thank you, Jacob. Oh, and could you ask Mary to come up, please?"

"Certainly, madam." He bowed and was gone.

Caroline wiped away the rest of her tears, blew her nose loudly - who cared if it was unladylike - smoothed down her tousled hair and sat erect in her chair.

"Come in, Mary," she said in answer to the timid-sounding knock on her door a few minutes later. Mary entered slowly, and stood just inside the doorway, as if ready for flight. "Come here," Caroline said, her voice as soothing as she could make it. She reached out a hand to Mary. "Come and sit on this stool," and with her other hand she patted the small embroidered footstool by her chair.

"Yes... mistress." Mary's voice was low and uncertain. Miss Caroline's words *sounded* pleasant enough... but 'sit on the footstool'?... it was such an odd thing to be asked to do.

"Mary, Mary dear," Caroline began, once her maid was seated. "I... I am so sorry, I really am..." .She leant over and took Mary's hand in her own.

"Why, mistress, what for?" Miss Caroline really *was* ill. It must be this place, this village; it made people peculiar.

"For the way I spoke to you." Caroline patted Mary's hand, drew her own hand back and sat up straight. "Now," she said, in a firm voice, "We have both been foolish... but we've now got to pull ourselves together and be sensible."

"Yes, mistress," Mary said. Be sensible? What about? Jem probably.

"The reason I changed my mind about leaving here the other day was because I felt someone should help that old woman they are calling a witch. Everyone seems to be against her and she really ought to have someone to speak up for her... and I said that I would... not in so many words, but, well, I made it quite clear to Franc... Mr. Bragge... that he wasn't going to have it all his own way in this affair. But, as you know, instead of speaking up for Mistress Wenham today, I allowed myself to be frightened by a lot of silly nonsense at the rectory... Oh yes, I was frightened, just as much as those village women..."

"Oh, mistress..."

"Surprised, are you? Not as surprised as I was, to find myself sitting here shaking and quaking. Anyway, that's over."

"Yes, mistress." So... could she go now, back to the kitchen? Bessie was waiting for her... and Jem might come back later when things had calmed down.

"So what we are going to do now..." Caroline was interrupted by a knock at the door. "Ah, that must be Jacob with the logs. Come in," she called, loudly. Jacob entered with a basket of logs and kindling and bent down by the hearth. Mary and Caroline, neither of them saying a word, watched as Jacob expertly brought the fire back to life.

"Thank you, Jacob," Caroline said, as the old man straightened up. "That is much better."

"We can't have you getting cold, Mistress Newell. Sir Henry wouldn't like it."

Caroline smiled at the old man. "No, he wouldn't."

As soon as Jacob had shut the door behind him, Caroline turned to Mary.

"Now Mary, before we get interrupted again... I want *you* to be my eyes and ears... in the village... and especially... at the rectory. Find something you can do for Mistress

Gardiner… it doesn't matter what it is, a bit of sewing… or you could read with her… just so long as you keep up with what is going on."

"I thought you didn't want to me to go to the rectory?"

"I do, now. But don't tell anybody… and I do mean *any*body… why you are really there."

"No, mistress."

"Mistress Wenham shouldn't have to go through any more of that dreadful testing, and if I can stop it, I will. If you don't want to come back alone… Jem, if he's there, may walk with you."

"Oh yes, mistress!"

"Walk, that's all. Straight here… and then, if I want you to, you go straight back again. Now… help me to get dressed. It's high time I joined Sir Henry in the snug… or wherever he is."

"Jacob said he's asleep, mistress."

"Oh. Well, in that case, I shall stay up here for a bit longer. In fact, I don't think I will go down at all. It's warm in here now. Mary, bring me some food; some hot soup and soft rolls would be nice, and a little fruit… and a portion of one of Bessie's puddings, too. And bring something for yourself. And while we are eating, we can think how best to help the old woman."

"Yes, mistress."

"Oh, and on the way, have a look in the snug, and if Sir Henry is awake, apologise for me, will you. Say I've a headache or something. He'll understand, after what's happened today."

"Oh mistress, I can't do that!"

"Why not? Oh, all right, I'll write him a note. If he's still asleep you can just leave it on his table."

"I'm not going in there, mistress! I'll give the note to Jacob."

"You've been in there before."

"Not when Sir Henry was asleep. He might not be wearing his wig!"

"Ah. Yes." Caroline smiled. It would be embarrassing for both of them if Mary were to see the old man's shaven head, an intimate sight which only Jacob and Arthur would be allowed to behold.

"You go and get the food then, and I'll write to Sir Henry." Caroline suddenly felt deflated and weary. "Goodness, Mary, how dull I have become… that a quiet supper and an early night sound enticing."

"You are just tired, Miss Caroline. Tomorrow you will be…"

"On the war-path again?"

"Yes, mistress, you will."

"Oh, I will! I won't let *anyone* stop me from doing what I know is right! *You* know that, don't you, Mary?"

"Oh yes, mistress. I do."

9

It was the perfect morning for a ride in the countryside - a duck-egg blue sky with little tufts of cloud and just the hint of a breeze - and Caroline had taken full advantage of it, riding fast and fearlessly almost as far as Cromer. Now, with her spirit and her body refreshed, she was returning to Yardley Bury. She trotted into the stable yard, dismounted almost before her horse had come to a halt, and tossed her reins to a grinning William. The stable lad had been party to her sudden desire to gallop off on her own - "Not a word to anyone!" she had said to him. Removing her hat and shaking free her hair, she strode to the back door. *Now* she was ready for breakfast! If she had stopped to eat earlier she would have lost her momentum, and somebody, Sir Henry or Arthur, would no doubt have tried to prevent her from starting out on her solo ride. The ride had done more than invigorate her, it had given her time to think over the plans she had laid with Mary the evening before; together they hoped to bring a little enlightenment to this dark corner of Hertfordshire.

Caroline pushed open the back door and stepped into the flagged passage. As her eyes accustomed themselves to the gloom of the grey stone walls after the sunshine outside, so too did her ears adjust from the gentle sounds of the stable yard - the neighing of horses and the clucking of hens - to the hubbub of angry voices coming from the front entrance hall.

She was about to seek refuge in the kitchen - she did not want to come face-to-face with a crowd of villagers - when, abruptly, the clamour ceased, as the heavy front door shut with a thud.

For a moment all was still. Caroline held her breath. The villagers might have gone, but there must be someone - whoever had shut the door so forcefully - still in the hall.

"Will there be anything else, Sir Henry?"

"That's all for now, thank you, Jacob. No, wait a minute, there is something. See if you can find out if Mistress Newell has come downstairs yet."

"No need, Sir Henry!" Caroline called out before Jacob could answer. "I'm here!" and running lightly on her toes, like a young girl, she skipped into the hall and made a deep curtsey in front of Sir Henry.

"Goodness! You're very lively this morning." The old man smiled broadly. "Do I take it that you are fully recovered from yesterday's ordeal?"

"Yes indeed, Sir Henry." She took his arm. "Not an ordeal, more… an interesting experience, shall we say." The last thing Caroline wanted was Sir Henry, with well-intentioned concern for her security, preventing her from further involvement with Jane Wenham. "Do you think I might have breakfast in your snug?" She looked enquiringly at Jacob. "It's not too late, I hope?"

"Not at all, madam. I will fetch it for you."

Caroline, sitting on one side of the fireplace in the snug, smiled at Sir Henry seated opposite her in his red chair.

"That was delicious… and so welcome," she said. With a linen napkin she wiped from her cheek the very last crumbs of the warm scone. She had already circled her lips with her tongue, determined not to waste even the tiniest smear of plum jam.

"Now," she said, folding her napkin neatly and placing it on top of the empty plates on the tray. She had eaten everything that Jacob had brought: coddled eggs with cinnamon, cheese, fruit... and all the scones. "Tell me... The village people at the door. Was that about Mistress Wenham again?"

Sir Henry surveyed her for a moment before answering. Their topics of conversation throughout Caroline's breakfast - the cold weather, storing fruit, feeding animals in the winter - were bound to give way to what she *really* wanted to talk about.

"You should let it go, my dear," he said. "There is no need for you to concern yourself about *her*." He knew, the instant he spoke the word, that he had said the wrong thing.

"Oh, but there is! I stayed on purpose to champion her! I want to know what I can do." Better to ask than tell him that she and Mary had ideas of their own.

Sir Henry took so long to answer that Caroline began to wonder if he had either not heard her or had no intention of acknowledging what she had said. Well, *that* would not do!

"There must be something..."

Sir Henry raised his hand to stop her. "Let me tell you what happened this morning... and then perhaps you will be able to understand that there really is nothing you can do for her."

"But..."

"No, Caroline. Allow me to speak, please."

"Of course." Caroline sat back in her chair, her hands folded modestly together in her lap.

"Those people were here this morning at my request. Mistress Wenham and Mr. Gardiner, Farmer Chapman and Matthew, and some of the village women."

"Was the girl here, too?"

"The girl?"

"Anne, the rector's maid."

"No, no." He paused. "It will be much easier, my dear, if you let me finish. *Then* you may ask your questions."

Caroline nodded her head meekly. It was Sir Henry Chauncy the magistrate speaking; she must give him the respect he was due.

"What we had here this morning, in the library, was a judicial examination of the facts of the case."

Caroline sat, quiet.

"The facts being," Sir Henry went on, "that John Chapman and Matthew Gilston had accused Mistress Jane Wenham of witchcraft, and having tested her in various ways, as you know, they had come to the conclusion that she *is* a witch. However, the method of testing her and the way it was carried out did not satisfy *me...* " Caroline nodded in agreement. "... and I felt that the woman should be tested again on the Lord's Prayer, but this time without an audience, just Mr. Gardiner, and Mr. Strutt – he's the Vicar of Yardley – and possibly Francis. Of course, as you might expect..." Sir Henry dropped his official tone, smiling ruefully at Caroline, "... the villagers didn't want that; they wanted to be there. They'd been watching her all night, you know, most of them, including Arthur." Sir Henry's mouth turned down in disgust. "They could have let the poor woman sleep!" He reached for his pipe.

Judging that his speech was over, Caroline cleared her throat.

"May I ask a question?"

"Not yet." His tone was brusque. He held the pipe, unlit, in his hand and tamped down the tobacco with his thumb. Then, in a gentler voice, he said, "Be patient, Caroline. I know it's not in your nature, but remain quiet for a few more minutes, please..." He got up from the chair and took the ember tongs from the hearth. "... and I think you'll find that your questions will be answered." With the tongs he plucked a small glowing coal from the fire and lifted it to his pipe. When the pipe was alight he sucked deeply upon it, placed the tongs back in the hearth, and sat down. He smiled at Caroline through a haze of comforting tobacco smoke. "So, tomorrow morning, at ten o'clock, at the constable's house, Mistress Wenham will be examined on the Lord's Prayer. I can't be there, I have to be in Hitchin for a hearing." He sat back in his chair and looked steadfastly at Caroline. "Would *you* like to attend? Just as an observer. *Not* to speak."

"Oh yes, Sir Henry, I would. Very much."

"I thought you might."

A look of understanding passed between them: he had had this in mind all the time.

"It is only right that there should be another woman present."

"Yes." There was no need to say more. Caroline understood the implication, although she doubted whether Francis or the rector - or the unknown Rev. Strutt - would stoop to doing anything unseemly to reach the verdict they desired.

"Just remember, though, you are not there to speak up for Mistress Wenham, much as you may want to. There will be somebody doing that…"

"Oh."

"… a cousin, William Archer."

"I didn't know she had any family."

"Oh, she has family; they just don't have much to do with her. She has a daughter, somewhere. She's put two husbands away, you know… in strange circumstances. She's not a pleasant woman, Caroline."

"Perhaps she hasn't been given a chance to be."

"That may be so, but it is not of significance at this moment. It is purely a case of possible witchcraft that we are considering, nothing else."

"Yes, Sir Henry."

"I must emphasise, Caroline, that you are not to interfere in any way with the procedure, but… if you do feel that Francis - if he *is* taking part, and I don't doubt that he will - is becoming too enthusiastic in his examination of Mistress Wenham, as well he might…" He was not finding this easy to say: the boy was, after all, his grandson. "… I shan't be too cross, if you do speak. You're a sensible woman… and a sensitive one, so… use your discretion, my dear, and your common sense."

"I will, I promise you." Caroline was touched that Sir Henry found such qualities in her. "I won't let you down."

"Good girl."

Caroline waited; she felt sure Sir Henry had more to say.

"I don't want this thing to come to a trial. There has most certainly been a breach of the peace…" He drew deeply on his pipe, released the satisfying smoke, then slowly placed the pipe on the table at his side. With his elbows now resting on the arms of his chair, he laced his fingers together and put his hands against his mouth, as if to prevent any unconsidered words from creeping out. He lifted his head but kept his hands together. "As for witchcraft… well… I really do not know, Caroline. I wish I did."

10

There was a good chance, at this time in the morning - it was now half-past ten - that Jem would be at the rectory: the rector's horse was always needing attention, and the rector's wife would have a warm drink for him after his labours. This much Mary had gathered from Jem as they'd stood together outside Jane Wenham's cottage. You could have knocked her down with a feather when Miss Caroline suggested last night that they include Jem in their plans to help the old woman!

If he wasn't there she would glean what information she could from Mrs. Gardiner, or Anne... though *that* was likely to be very biased... and then, if there was nothing forthcoming from them - she was under strict instructions *not* to speak to Mr. Gardiner - she could, legitimately, go in search of Jem elsewhere. She hoped she wouldn't have to go to the Gilbert farm. Farmyards were dirty, smelly places at the best of times and in the middle of a wet winter, as this was, they were thick with mud as well.

Not wanting to call attention to herself either on her walk across the fields or on arrival at the rectory door, Mary had borrowed a plain grey worsted skirt from Sir Henry's kitchen maid, Dora. How foolish she had been to wear her apricot silk, one of Miss Caroline's recent cast-offs, to the village! If she had dressed in something less noticeable, her mistress would probably not have spotted her that day. Now, wearing the same maid's cloak with the hood up and a wicker basket over her arm, Mary could pass for any country girl out on an errand.

It was quite fun, this dressing up, pretending to be someone else - no wonder Lady Poynter's friends were always having fancy dress balls! How strange it was, Mary pondered as she made her way to the rectory, that she, a servant, had nothing in her clothes chest that was considered by the villagers as suitable for a maid to wear. But she was a *lady's* maid and as such she could be at home in fine company as easily as among her own class, which, of course, these country people were not. *They* were peasants; most of them could not read. Could Jem read? She didn't know. They knew nothing of music or going to the play... and as for washing themselves! And when the Queen's soap tax was brought in they would have even more reason not to wash! Jem, she had been pleased to discover, was very particular about keeping himself clean, as much from necessity as choice she imagined. If he wanted to be let into the rector's kitchen for that warm drink or a slice of pie he *had* to make himself clean. Mrs. Gardiner was a most finicky lady, and if he had entered her kitchen smelling of the stable or the pigsty, she would have banished him immediately.

Mary, now in the rectory grounds, and on her way to the back door, glanced in at the kitchen window. She could not believe her eyes: Jem was standing in front of the hearth singing his heart out... and Mrs. Gardiner, sitting by the fire, her normally sallow cheeks rosy-pink, was looking up at him entranced, clapping her hands and tapping her feet to the haunting, foreign-sounding melody. Mary, eyes and mouth wide open in amazement, stood rooted to the spot. Jem, still singing, took Mrs. Gardiner by the hands, pulled her up from her chair and twirled her round until her skirts flew above her ankles.

Mary blinked: was she dreaming? As Jem twirled Mrs. Gardiner yet again, he saw Mary through the kitchen window. He stopped dancing so suddenly that Mrs. Gardiner was almost thrown off-balance. Her eyes, following Jem's, went immediately to the window. She froze, but quickly recovered herself - it was only a servant girl - and assuming a more suitable expression for a rector's wife, shooed a laughing Jem from the room and returned to her chair as if nothing, absolutely nothing, untoward had passed between her and Mr. Gardiner's farrier. Calmly she smoothed down her black bombazine dress, patted her hair back into place and took up her darning from the workbox at her side.

Mary needed to make a quick decision. Should she turn round and go straight back to Yardley Bury… or continue on her way to the back door of the rectory? Hesitating outside the kitchen window and trying hard not to look in, her course of action was decided for her when Jem appeared, pulling on his coat and laughing, at the back door. He called to her to come in.

"Should I?" she asked.

"Of course," Jem replied. "I was just on my way out."

"Hm. It didn't look like that to me."

"Well, I was." Mary's expression of disbelief called for an explanation, not that he needed to explain; she might be a *lady's* maid, but she was *only* a servant. Whereas *he*, although his work might be lowly, was definitely *not*. Looking at the girl now, standing there with what could only be described as a haughty expression on her dainty face, he fancied he could see something of the lady in her. He knew a lot about breeding, breeding horses that was, but with people too, there was a lot in the breeding... and this young filly with the bright blue eyes and the springy golden hair peeping out from under her hood was *not* just a peasant girl brought up by city folk. He felt certain of it. There was something about her cheek-bones, something structural, the race-horse, rather than the carthorse. "Sure, a few twirls won't do the old lady any harm... and that's *all* she was getting!" Jem's eyes twinkled and Mary felt herself blushing. "You've no need to be jealous."

"Jem Dakers, how dare you say such a thing!" Excited as she was by Jem's words, the sooner she got herself inside, with Jem firmly outside, the better. "I have business with Mistress Gardiner," she said primly, "and it does not concern you... so please get out of my way and allow me to go in."

"Oh, now, listen to it, Miss Hoity-toity! So that's what a lady's maid is... a maid who think she's a lady!"

"It's no such thing..." Mary began, crossly - the cheek of him, a farm lad speaking to *her* like that! - but she couldn't go on. Jem was grinning broadly; she couldn't be angry. She *wasn't* angry, she was enjoying herself. Jem was flirting with her... and it was very nice. Dangerous, yes - not at all what Miss Caroline would want, or permit - but very nice.

Boldly, Mary said, "I need to speak to Mistress Gardiner, but I should like to talk to you later, Jem." She knew her colour had risen dramatically, but she hoped Jem would put this down to the cold wind which was rattling the bare branches of the trees in the rectory garden and piercing Mary's thin cloak.

"Would you now? Well, that might be arranged." Enough amusement; a serious look was called for now. "And what would you like to talk to me about, the state of farming in the county, the best horse for a lady to ride… or the prospects for a young farrier, perhaps?" No, he shouldn't have said *that;* goodness knows how she would interpret it.

"None of those," said Mary calmly. She would not rise to any bait he offered. She was pleased to see a faint blush on his cheeks: he knew he had spoken out of turn there.

"Oh," said Jem, to her surprise stepping closer. "Was it something more…?"

He's going to say 'personal' or 'intimate' thought Mary, alarmed, yet thrilled. I can't let him, not yet!

"I need your help," Mary plunged in, "for my mistress."

"Oh?"

"She wants to help the old woman… the witch." She felt breathless, and a shiver went through her. Just saying that word… although it might, of course, be the cold wind. She was getting so chilled standing outside it was becoming hard to tell what was real and what was not. She had never been able to stand very cold air… and if she didn't get inside soon, into the warmth of the kitchen, she would get a chill, a real chill, with a fever… and then she would be no use to Miss Caroline… and Jem wouldn't want to look at her, with red eyes and a runny nose.

"Does she now?" Jem was saying. "Oh."

"… And she wants you to keep your eyes and ears open and see that she comes to no harm, and if you hear of anyone who plans to hurt her in any way, you are to report to her, through me." Oh, Miss Caroline, it's all I could think of - I do want to see him again, and I am getting cold, truly I am - and in a way it's true, because it's what you told me to do, keep my ears and eyes open, *and* you said Jem could help me. And it won't matter, will it, if in the end, we get the result we want?

"Sure I'll help you, Mary." She did like the way he said her name. It didn't sound a plain, ordinary name when Jem said it. "And if I take it right, you wouldn't want anything I could discover told to you in front of anyone else, now would you?"

"No." Oh, what had she said...

"So, if I had something to tell you, for you to pass on to Mistress Newell, it would be best if we were to meet somewhere, say... between Walkern and Sir Henry's house?"

"Yes, I suppose so." Mary's heart was beating fast, and she no longer felt cold; she felt too hot - could she have caught a fever so quickly?

"That little spinney perhaps, just at the edge of Sir Henry's parkland. D'you know the one?" Mary nodded. "There's a couple of tall holly bushes there, too, so you'd not be seen from the house."

His eyes were fixed on hers; in imagination she was already there... in the spinney... with him. A strange feeling overcame her, as if she were being flushed right through with something warm and tingly; it was disturbing, but at the same time... Oh, it was so lovely.

"Yes, that would do," Mary said, as sharply as she could. "Now, if you will let me pass, I shall go into the house." She really wanted to go straight back to Yardley Bury, to the comfort of Bessie's arms, to the familiarity of Miss Caroline's demands, but if she did that he might follow her and… She put her head down and charged forward. Like a bull at a gate, as Miss Caroline would say. She didn't care; she just had to get away from Jem.

"Not so fast." Jem laid a hand on her arm, and that deliciously troubling feeling ran through her again. She daren't look up. "How do we arrange these meetings?" *These* meetings… not just one! "Do we have a signal of some kind?"

"I don't know." Mary's voice was hoarse. "I'll have to think about it. Let me into the house, please."

"The door is open." He took his hand from her arm. "All you have to do is walk in."

Mary looked up. So it was. She was swiftly through the entrance and Jem shut the door behind her. She could hear him, first laughing, then whistling, on the other side of the door. She could still feel the imprint of his fingers on her arm. She stood in the flag-stoned passageway and took a deep breath. Always breathe deeply, Miss Caroline had told her, if you think you are about to cry or scream or say something you shouldn't. She should have taken the deep breath earlier, before she had said some of those silly, compromising things to Jem. If Miss Caroline were to find out that she had arranged to meet him… in a spinney where she was hidden from view! Miss Caroline must *not* know, but if she *did*… well, Mary was only doing what her mistress had asked of her, helping her to give support to the old woman. Why else would she be meeting Jem? He was nothing to her; she was a lady's maid, he was only a farm lad. She sighed. A farm lad had no right to be so well-spoken, so good-looking.

Mary pushed back the hood of her cloak, took another deep breath, and walked into the rectory kitchen.

"Mistress Gardiner," she said, gently, from the doorway. "May I come in? My mistress has sent me with something to show you, something she thinks you will like."

"Oh." It would be best, Mrs. Gardiner decided, to act as if nothing had happened; there had been no singing, certainly no dancing. Who would believe the girl anyway, if she did say anything? As for Jem... he wouldn't speak of it to the rector; he wanted to keep his job. Looking after horses here and there brought in the extra money he needed for looking after Polly. Poor child, without Jem she would probably have starved to death by now. "Well, bring it here."

The rector's wife sat upright in her chair, and held out her hand for Mary's basket.

Mary advanced into the room, until she was standing directly in front of Mrs. Gardiner. Out of the corner of her eye she caught sight of a cat curled up on the hearthrug and another one on the padded chair next to it. Thank goodness neither of the cats was black! She didn't want the witch-woman's familiar listening to her conversation with Mrs. Gardiner. She didn't really believe that a black cat could be a witch in disguise... but in a place like this it was best to be careful.

She put her hand into the basket and drew out a small package. She placed the basket on a nearby stool and began to open the package, carefully turning back the four corners of a silk cloth to reveal a tiny doll nestling in the centre.

"A doll! What would I want with a doll? Take it away!" Mrs. Gardiner sat back in her chair, drawing herself as far away as she could from the object that Mary was holding. "I don't want a doll! I'm not a child!" There was scorn in her voice; there was also fear.

Mary lifted the doll from its wrappings and held it out to Mrs. Gardiner. She placed the silk cloth back in the basket.

"Take it away, I said. Don't you think I have enough to put up with at the moment without you bringing me a doll?"

Mary was perplexed. Mrs. Gardiner *was* a strange lady, she already knew that but… afraid of a doll? If she took it back, not only would Miss Caroline be cross with her, but she would no longer have access to the rectory; after today Mrs. Gardiner would probably never let her into the rectory again. She would have one more try.

"It's a fashion doll, Mistress Gardiner. From Paris." She touched the doll's blue velvet dress. "See, she is dressed in the latest Paris fashion… and her hair is done in the new style."

"Oh… A fashion doll, you say."

"Yes. Some of the London ladies have them… to see what is being worn in France…" Mrs. Gardiner was listening and nodding her head. "… so that they can have their dresses made in the same style… and…" If what she had been told about Mrs. Gardiner was true this should do it. "… and keep up with the fashion."

It wasn't the exact truth. The doll that Mrs. Gardiner was handling, almost reverently Mary thought, was not a real French fashion doll, *poupées* they were called, and some of them were life-sized. This was a tiny replica that Miss Caroline's dressmaker had clothed for her, as she often did, so that her mistress could see for herself before she ordered a gown how it would look when it was finished. They were beautifully dressed these dolls… miniatures, Miss Caroline called them… and she now had a collection of them. "It's

165

nice to remember exactly how my gowns looked long after I have discarded them," she had said.

"A Paris gown, you say?" Mrs. Gardiner looked up at Mary, her watery grey eyes almost bright.

"Yes, a copy of one."

"It's very beautiful." Mrs. Gardiner stroked the skirt of the doll's gown.

"Would you like me to dress one for you?" Mary asked.

"For me?"

"Yes. If you have an old doll... I could make a dress for it... a dress that is in fashion now... and then, if you wanted, you would be able to copy it... or have it copied... to make a dress for you." Mary waited, tense. Would Mrs. Gardiner respond as she hoped? How could she fail to want something so appealing... and to her, so exotic... as a Paris-designed gown of her own?

"Why yes, if you would." She handed the doll back to Mary. "Oh..." and she clapped her mottled hands together, as she had done when Jem was singing to her; then, remembering that Mary had seen her through the kitchen window doing just that, behaving in what might be thought an unseemly manner for a rector's wife, Mrs. Gardiner quickly put her hands in her lap. "A Paris gown... in Walkern. Fancy that," she said, as sedately as she could. She was finding it hard to contain her excitement.

Mary put the doll back into her basket and leant forward. Gently she touched Mrs. Gardiner's folded hands. "Not just any Paris gown, Mistress Gardiner... *Your* Paris gown."

"My...?" Mrs. Gardiner drew back. "Yes, well, we'll see." It was Mistress Newell with whom she should be talking about the fashions, but oh dear, it was so much easier to talk to Mary. "That is very kind of your mistress… and you, too, Mary. Thank you," she said, withdrawing her folded hands from under Mary's and patting the girl's hand with her own.

"I'm glad you are pleased," said Mary, withdrawing her hand quickly; if this went on they'd soon be playing pat-a-cake. She stood up and carefully re-wrapped the doll in its silk cloth. "It's time I went," she said, "unless… " She hesitated purposely. "… unless you have some other sewing you would like me to do?"

"Oh. Yes. I do. But…" It was Mrs. Gardiner's turn to hesitate. "Well… not just at the moment."

"If I came back tomorrow would you have some?" Mary enquired quickly. She needed a practical reason for returning to the rectory; she had a feeling that the dressing of a fashion doll would be kept secret from Mr. Gardiner.

"Tomorrow? Yes, I would." She lifted one hand to the shoulder of her drab brown dress. "This does not fit well," she said. "Would you be able to alter it for me?"

"Oh, easily," said Mary, determined not to lose the opportunity to return to the rectory. "I shall see you tomorrow, Mistress Gardiner."

"Oh. Yes. And the… um…" She nodded towards the basket.

"The doll?"

"Yes." Mrs. Gardiner's hands crept up to her mouth. Was she not going to get her Paris gown? Had this been some trick? There were so many strange things happening at the moment, it was hard to know what was true and what was… witchcraft.

167

Mary was thinking fast. "When I come to alter your gown, I shall... I shall bring some fabrics with me... and you can choose which one you would like to have *your* doll dressed in." Please God, Miss Caroline would let her bring more than one piece of spare cloth to show Mrs. Gardiner.

"I see," said Mrs. Gardiner, much relieved. "That's how it is done, is it?"

"Yes," Mary replied, "That is how it is done. Good-bye, Mistress Gardiner. I must go."

Waving her hand in a cheery manner at the smiling rector's wife, she took herself out of the kitchen, into the passageway and out of the back door as fast as she could. She pulled up the hood of her cloak - a few flakes of snow were starting to fall and the sky had that leaden look that suggested that more was on the way - and headed for Yardley Bury.

She was so intent on getting back to what felt like normality, away from this pretending business... cloak-and-dagger, Miss Caroline called it... that she failed to notice a grinning Jem watching her from the shelter of one of the stables.

The snow was coming down quite heavily now; big flakes tossed by the easterly wind swirled around her. This country snow wasn't like the snow you got in London; that didn't lie around for long and it soon turned to a brown sludge as the cart wheels went back and forth over it. This stuff was white and glittery and it hurt Mary's eyes to look at it. And it was settling on the ground, making it hard to see whether she was stepping on a clump of grass or about to fall down into a rabbit hole. Should she turn back, or go on? She paused for a moment and looked up; she must have been walking more quickly than she would have thought possible, for there, ahead of her - the snow was easing now; it had almost stopped - she could see the spinney where she would be meeting Jem one day soon: bare-branched trees, and holly bushes half-coated in snow. She was, thank goodness, not far from Yardley Bury. She pressed on, using the spinney as a signpost. Keeping her head down, out of the wind, but glancing up every now and again to make sure she was going in the right direction, Mary made straight for the clump of trees. She would stop there, for just a moment, taking shelter behind the holly bushes. There was a stone, or something like it, in her left shoe; it would be a relief to get it out. Balancing on her right foot she lifted up her left one and, with an effort, pulled off her shoe. Yes, it was a tiny, sharp stone. She shook it out and was putting her shoe back on, hopping on her right foot to stop herself from falling over, when she was startled by a voice, an unmistakable, low male voice, close to her ear. Jem! She looked up sharply, and if Jem hadn't been there to grab her arm, and help her to keep her balance, she would certainly have landed on the snow-covered earth.

"Can I be of some assistance to you, madam?" Jem asked, his black eyes twinkling at her.

"Jem! What are you doing here?" He still held her arm. There it was again, that same feeling that made her feel so strange and excited. They had some funny diseases out in the country, with all the animals about; she hoped she wasn't going down with one of them.

"I'm preventing you from falling on the snow."

"I wasn't *going* to fall on the snow," Mary said, shaking off his hand, "not till you came along and gave me a fright. See you don't do that again."

"No, ma'am, I won't." He bent closer to her. "I won't need to, because next time we meet here you'll know I'm coming... won't you?"

"I don't know what you mean," said Mary, as haughtily as she could.

"Yes, you do. *This* is the spinney, or did you not realise that, city girl?"

"I am *not* a city girl!" Mary turned on him fiercely, "I was born and brought up in the country, same as you!" His eyes were so dazzling and mischievous it was all she could do to turn away from him... but she knew she must. If Miss Caroline were to be looking out of one of the Yardley Bury windows, with all this snow on the ground two darkly-clad figures, so close together, would stand out a mile. She stepped away from him, taking care not to overbalance again. "Now, if you will excuse me, I must be on my way," she said in her most ladylike voice.

"I do beg your pardon, madam," Jem said, giving her the most elaborate of bows, his hands waving in the air like the sails of a windmill.

"Oh, stop bending over like that," Mary said, laughing - how could she not? "You look like that dreadful Mr. Bragge." She clasped both hands over her mouth. "Oh, I shouldn't have said that."

Jem's face was instantly solemn. "No, you shouldn't, young lady." He wagged his finger at her. "That is no way to speak of the Lord's anointed."

"Jem Dakers! The sooner I get away from you the better!" Mary giggled; she could have stayed there all day, talking like this. "I'm going," she said, "before you say anything else that a lady... a lady's maid should not hear."

"Away with you then, Mary Butcher. I'll be seeing you very soon."

Was he going to reach out his hand to her again? No. Just as well… it would only start up that funny feeling. She moved away from him and began to walk down the incline towards the house.

"Good-bye," she called over her shoulder, as casually as she could.

It was only when she was entering the back door a few minutes later that she thought… How did he know my surname? Has somebody been talking about me? It was not a feeling that Mary liked, not in a village where there was an old witch-woman. Mary shivered; she brushed the snow off her cloak and made her way into the warm kitchen.

11

It was far too cold, Bessie decreed the next morning, for Caroline to walk to the constable's house as she had planned. Although the snow had almost gone, leaving only thin strips along the sheltered edges of the grass verges of the lanes, the wind was still blowing hard from the east.

Sir Henry had a small cart for local journeys and it was in this that Caroline rode to Walkern, with young William holding the reins. She was perfectly capable of driving herself, but Bessie insisted she take the boy.

"It is more fitting, Mistress Newell, for you to be accompanied," she said.

"By a stable lad?"

"Well, no, madam… but Jacob has gone with the master… and there is no one else. I have told William that he has to take it very slow and watch out for any patches of ice."

William obeyed Bessie's instructions to the letter, and Caroline missed the start of the proceedings.

When she entered the small room where Jane Wenham's examination was taking place, Mr. Gardiner and Francis were standing over the old woman, one on either side, as she sat at the far end of a table on which there was a large book and several papers.

Caroline looked around her. There was almost no warmth coming from the small grate, and weak sunlight, slanting through windows high up in one wall, was the room's only illumination. There was not even a rag rug on the stone floor. It was as inhospitable as a room could be.

To one side, in the shadows, sat a thin, upright, grey-haired man. Presumably this was Mr. Archer, the woman's cousin. The man began to rise from his seat and Caroline quickly waved him down with her hand. He subsided on to the bench, and Caroline slipped unobtrusively on to a stool close to the door.

"Come along," Francis was saying irritably. "I'm not going to wait all day for you. Say the prayer!"

"It's no good, sir. I can't say it." Jane Wenham sounded both weary and resigned.

"You slept last night, didn't you?" Francis asked.

"Yes sir, but…"

"Well then." He banged his fist down on the table. "Say the prayer!"

"I can't, sir! My brain's that muddled, what with the questions and… Mr. Gardiner, sir…" She looked pleadingly at the rector.

"Try just once more," said Mr. Gardiner, in a kindly voice.

"I know it, sir," said Jane Wenham, "but… but I can't *say* it." Trembling and on the verge of tears she turned to Francis. "Oh please, sir, don't make me do it again."

Francis sighed deeply. He took his hands off the table and stood fully upright, rotating his shoulders to ease the tension built up from leaning over. "All right. No more testing. For the moment, anyway."

"Oh, thank you, sir." The old woman gave him a weak smile.

"There's nothing to smile about, Mistress Wenham." Francis leant over her again. "We have to arrive at the truth, *today*, and if you refuse to be tested on the prayer, then you must confess. For the good of your soul!"

"Much you care about my soul!"

Francis sighed. "If you are *not* a witch, Mistress Wenham…" his voice was soothing, treacly, "then why…" he banged his fist on the table - he's fond of doing that, thought Caroline - and his voice was now loud and rasping, "why can you not say the Lord's Prayer? Um? Tell me that?"

"I don't know, sir." It was little more than a mumble.

"Don't know? Of course you know." Francis loomed over her menacingly. "You are held in the power of the Devil… and he won't let you say it. That's what is happening here."

"No, sir…"

"Tell him, Jane. Tell him you speak to the Devil." William Archer's voice was calm, placatory.

"I don't speak to him!" Jane was on her feet now, waving her arms and glaring at her cousin. "He speaks to me!" She sat down heavily.

"Ah. Now we are getting somewhere." Francis was jubilant. "And what does the Devil say to you… umm… Mistress Wenham?"

"I don't know."

"Oh come, Mistress Wenham." Francis was enjoying himself, as Sir Henry was afraid he would. Why did Mr. Gardiner not speak up? And where was Mr. Strutt? If this went on, Caroline would have the greatest difficulty in keeping quiet.

"If the Devil speaks to you, you must know what he says."

"I don't, sir. He just seems to take me over... I have a temper, sir..."

"Oh yes, we know that!" There was vicious scorn in Francis's words. He'd had enough of being in this dreary room with this silly old woman. "You get angry when the Devil is in you... and you bewitch those about you..."

"No, sir..."

"... as you bewitched Anne Thorn."

"She made me angry."

"So you called on the Devil... to help you?"

"No, sir. I didn't."

"I think you did, Mistress Wenham... and with his help you bewitched Anne Thorn, just as you have bewitched others in the past. I understand from Mr. Gardiner..." and he nodded, almost humbly, to the rector, "that for twenty years you have troubled the people of this village. If I may trouble *you*, Mr. Gardiner... that paper in front of you... if you please."

Mr. Gardiner, his hand shaking, held out the paper to Francis.

Francis took the paper and began to read from it. "Richard Harvey's wife twelve years ago. Thomas Ireland's child before that..."

"Elizabeth Field had charge of that child. Why don't you question her?"

Francis laid the paper down on the table. "And there are many more," he said.

The old woman said nothing, just sat, looking down at her hands.

"I said," Francis shouted at her, "there are more names."

"I heard."

"Then why don't you confess?"

"You should, Jane." Her cousin spoke as quietly as before. "Your husband would be alive if you hadn't bewitched him."

"Ah. So you agree with us, Mr. Archer?" Francis gave the man his warmest smile.

"I do, sir."

"You're s'posed to be here to help me… not go against me," Jane pleaded.

"I'm not against you, Jane, but I must tell the truth."

"Quite right, Mr. Archer," Francis said. "Now, if you would be so kind… tell us about Mistress Wenham's husband… or should that be *husbands*. I believe she has had more than one."

William Archer looked uncomfortable. Nothing had been proved concerning the deaths of Jane's two husbands, Edward Wenham and, before him, Philip Cooke. There had been rumours, but no charge had been brought against Jane on either occasion.

"I don't know a lot about that, sir, her husbands, but I do know she has been a witch for a long time," he said.

"How long?" Francis smiled. This could be useful.

"A good ten years, sir, I should think. Perhaps more."

"More? Oh. Thank you, Mr. Archer." Francis turned to Jane. "Fifteen years? Twenty ? Is that how long you have been a witch?"

"I don't know," replied Jane hesitantly, startled by the sudden sharp tone of his voice.

"Come now, Mistress Wenham. Let us not prevaricate."

Francis, assuming an air of boredom, looked up at the rafters.

"What?"

It was not a word that Jane had ever heard, as Francis well knew.

Slowly Mr. Bragge brought his gaze down from the rafters and fixed his eyes, piercingly, on Jane. "How many years have you been a witch?" he boomed.

"Ten," Jane said breathily.

"It's longer than that, Mistress Wenham."

"Thank you, Mr. Gardiner. Mistress Wenham… more than ten?"

"All right. Twelve… sixteen."

"Sixteen?" Francis turned to the rector. "Would that be about right?"

It was Mr. Gardiner's turn to look uncomfortable. "Er… it will do."

"Thank you, Mr. Gardiner." Francis turned back to Jane. "Sixteen years… since you became a witch?" he hissed.

"Yes. Sixteen!" she hissed back. "There, is that what you want?"

"Write it down, Mr. Gardiner." Francis's voice was smug. "We'll get her to sign it in a minute. Now…" He turned back to Jane. "Tell me about your familiar." He perched nonchalantly on the edge of the table and folded his arms. "Your cat, Mistress Wenham." His voice was soothing, gentle and friendly. "Is it black?"

"You got a very short memory, Mr. Bragge. I told you that three days ago, at the rectory."

"Don't be impertinent, woman!" What was the point in being nice to someone like this? He got off the table. "This is a formal examination," he barked, "and I want proper answers from you!" He leaned over her. "Now... is - your - cat - black?"

"Yes!"

"Good. So you have a cat, a familiar."

"It catches mice. You could say it's familiar with them." She glanced across at her cousin, to see if her levity found favour with him. At the same moment she saw Caroline. The sun, moving round the room, had caught her in a shaft of light.

The old woman's gaze alerted the clergymen; they turned round and stared at Caroline. Mr. Gardiner rose hurriedly to his feet, and Francis executed a sweeping bow.

"Mistress Newell, what brings you here?"

His sarcastic tone encouraged Caroline to reply in a similar vein.

"Are you referring to my mode of transport, Mr. Bragge... or are you enquiring as to my reason for being here?"

"Your reason for being here, obviously. I care not how you travel!"

It was very tempting to go on parleying with him - it was so easy to tease him and get him riled: the man had no sense of humour - but a serious examination was in progress here, and she must not reduce it to a charade, whatever she felt about him personally.

"I am here at the invitation of your grandfather... as an observer, nothing more. I shall make no comment on the proceedings, so please, do carry on with what you are doing." Leaning forward, she said, "I'm sorry if I startled you, Mistress Wenham."

Jane Wenham smiled weakly at Caroline. Was this London lady friend or foe? She had no way of knowing, but at least with a friend of Sir Henry present she might not be treated too roughly.

Francis was boiling inside; Sir Henry had sent this detestable woman to spy on him! What did he think Francis was going to do? Murder the witch? Outwardly calm, but still seething with anger, Francis turned to Jane Wenham and resumed his questioning.

"As I was saying… your cat, your *black* cat, is your familiar."

"If you say so."

"No, Mistress Wenham, not if *I* say so. If *you* say so. Do - you - have - a - familiar!"

"Yes." The clergyman obviously wanted more from her. "Yes! Yes! Please can we stop?"

But Francis was not ready to stop; he was almost there. "What is it you have? Say it!" His face was very close to hers, blocking Caroline's view of the old woman. "Come on, *say it* !"

"I HAVE A FAMILIAR!" Jane screeched. "I have a familiar, I have a familiar, I have a familiar! Is that enough? I can say it more if you want!"

"No, thank you, Mistress Wenham, that is enough. Mr. Gardiner, have you got that down?"

"Yes, Mr. Bragge."

"Good. Now… what about confederates?" Francis asked beguilingly.

"Con-fed…?"

"Helpers, assistants. Other witches who work with you."

Mr. Gardiner looked up from his writing; he appeared to be distinctly troubled.

"Er… Mr. Bragge… Do we need to know this?"

"Of course we do! The more information we have the sooner we can stamp out this pernicious witchcraft which is blighting your village. Now come along, Mistress Wenham, give me some names."

"I never knew their names," Jane mumbled.

"Ah. So you did have helpers!" Francis looked triumphantly at the rector.

"You must have known their names, Jane," ventured her cousin.

The woman looked angrily at him. Helping her, was he? He was no help.

"Well, I don't know them now!"

"Stop playing games with us," said Francis. He sounded bored. "We must have those names."

"If I might…" began Mr. Gardiner, lifting his hand as if he were a small boy in front of a stern schoolmaster.

"By all means. If you can get some sense from her… please go ahead." He turned away from the table, looked around the room, letting his gaze fall briefly and mockingly on Caroline. "Well, come along, Mr. Gardiner, ask your question. We don't want to be here all day. Constable, do you think we could have a little more wood on this fire. It is very cold in here. I am sure the lady is finding it so," he said, inclining his head towards Caroline.

"Thank you, Mr. Bragge. I am quite warm… but I am concerned for Mistress Wenham. You seem to have taken away her cloak. Perhaps you could return it to her… at least until the fire is made up."

"Get your cloak," Francis said sharply.

Jane stood up and retrieved her cloak from a peg near the door.

"Now, Mr. Gardiner…" Francis said when Jane was back on her stool.

The rector turned to Jane, and in the kindliest of voices, as if asking a dear child how many sweet buns she had just eaten, he said, "How many were there?"

"Two, I think. Could be three."

"And who were they? Can you tell us their names?"

"Well… there was Margery Gill. I think she used to do it." This gentle approach was working. "Only not all the time. Not in the summer."

"I see," said Mr. Gardiner, patiently, writing it down. "Margery Gill. Winter only."

Francis began to pace the room.

"And the others?" the rector asked, his pen poised to write down the names as Jane gave them to him.

"There was… Mary Allen… and Agnes Hyde."

Mr. Gardiner put down his pen; he shook his head. "No. No, Mistress Wenham, Mary Allen is not a witch; she has never been a witch. Nor Agnes Hyde." He looked across at Francis, who had paused in his pacing to warm his hands at the meagre fire. "I regret to say, Mr. Bragge, that this is pure invention; these women are not witches."

"Ha!" snorted the curate, walking smartly to the table. "Trying to put the blame on others, are you?" He stood over Jane, looked at her fiercely for a few moments, then receiving no response, turned abruptly to the rector. "On the other hand, Mr. Gardiner, she has named them… and therefore we must examine them. I will get them called here immediately."

He turned to the constable and began to issue his order for the arrest of the women, but his words were drowned by two overlapping voices, the firm one of Mr. Gardiner, who was rising hastily from his chair - "No, Mr. Bragge, that is neither practical nor possible," - and the croaky tones of a man standing in the doorway: "No, you can *not* do that."

"I beg your pardon!" Francis wheeled round angrily. "Who are you to tell me what I may or may not do?"

The newcomer, not deigning to answer Francis, began to unwind a long muffler wrapped around his throat and face.

Mr. Gardiner, coming forward quickly to help the gentleman, said sharply to Francis, "This is Mr. Strutt. The vicar of Yardley."

"Of course," said Francis, suavely. "Mr. Strutt, I do apologise. I didn't recognise you under all that... er... facial wrapping." It would not do to be impolite to his grandfather's vicar. "We did not expect to see you. I understand that you have not been well."

"I am still not well, Mr. Bragge," the vicar said. "If you could place a stool for me by the fire that would be a great help."

"Most certainly." With a flourish Francis lifted a stool that was by the table and placed it close to the fire, dusting it off with his sleeve before offering it, with both hands open and extended in front of him, to Mr. Strutt.

"Thank you. But before I sit down, will you please introduce me to this lady," the vicar said, bowing, not effusively as Francis did, but politely, to Caroline.

Having been introduced to Caroline with the ceremony that Francis thought fit, Mr. Strutt took his seat and proceeded, very calmly, to take over Francis's self-chosen role as the chief interrogator, ascertaining the names of all Jane Wenham's assistants and exactly where they lived.

"If it is deemed necessary for them to be examined, and in Walkern, we will first need the authority of the magistrate, and this, of course, will take several days," the vicar said when he had listed the names of all the women.

"I don't care how long it takes, Mr. Strutt, as long as we get at the truth."

"Quite so, Mr. Bragge, quite so."

Dismissing Francis, who was, Caroline felt, about to make a speech, the vicar smiled at the rector, and said, most cordially, "Now, Mr. Gardiner, who shall we ask to see first?"

While Mr. Gardiner was hesitating - he was pleased to have Mr. Strutt there, but at the same time he was not the Walkern parson - William Archer spoke.

"If you don't need me no more, I'd like to be going. It's quite a step from Sandon." He picked up his hat and stood up.

"You walked?"

"Yes, sir. I walk everywhere."

"Just one thing before you go," said Mr. Strutt, from his seat by the fire. "Are you satisfied with your cousin's confession?"

"Yes, sir." William Archer looked puzzled.

"You agree that it was freely given?"

Before the man had a chance to answer, Francis interposed. "Mr. Strutt! I find that offensive. What are you suggesting?"

Taking his time, Mr. Strutt turned himself around on his stool until he was facing Francis. "I am not suggesting anything, Mr. Bragge. Unfortunately I was not present during the actual testing of Mistress Wenham's ability to say the Lord's Prayer… and therefore I am enquiring as to whether, in Mr. Archer's opinion, it was conducted fairly. He is, after all, here to support his cousin, not to support *us*."

In Mr. Strutt Francis had met his match for pomposity, but that, Caroline felt, was all it was, pomposity. She could detect no malice or menace in his words.

"That don't help me none," Jane said. "Support? Huh, what support's 'e given me? Can't you say nothing that'll help me, William?" she begged.

"I'm not telling lies for you, Jane. These gen'lemen know you're a witch, you told them so."

"Well said, Mr. Archer." Francis smiled at him.

"It shames me to have a cousin like you, Jane."

"Well, you shame me, William Archer… so we're equal!" Jane said, and she spat at him. "Waste of time, you comin' here."

"I think we can let Mr. Archer go." The vicar had no wish to get into a family row. "Thank you for coming."

With Mr. Archer now out of the room, Jane calmed down, though she was right, thought Caroline: the man had been of no use to her.

Now what was going on? Francis was waving a paper at her, Mr. Gardiner was holding out a pen, and Mr. Strutt, who had got up from his stool, was saying, "All you have to do is sign it, Mistress Wenham."

"You said, sir… but what is it?"

"A paper," said Francis sharply, "that says you agree with our findings."

Jane looked up at Mr. Gardiner, then at Francis, then across to Mr. Strutt. She knew that saying was one thing, writing was quite another. When you wrote something down on paper it was there for always, and even if you said you didn't mean to sign your name it was there, on the paper... and that made it... they called it something, these man who knew these things... they said it was ... binding. That was it; it tied you up.

Mr. Gardiner said kindly, "We just want you to sign, to say that Mr. Bragge and I..." Mr. Strutt cleared his throat noisily. "... and Mr. Strutt... have examined you."

"Is that all?" asked Jane. It didn't seem much to ask: they *had* examined her.

"That is all," said Francis quickly, placing the paper in front of her and snatching the pen from Mr. Gardiner.

"Mr. Bragge!" the vicar of Yardley remonstrated. "There is surely no need for this rush."

"We have spent far too long on this one woman, Mr. Strutt. We have other witches to see! Come along, Mistress Wenham. Write your name there, if you can. If not, just put your mark."

Jane took the pen from Francis, and looked at it.

Can she write her name? Caroline was thinking... or is it that she can't read and has no way of knowing what the paper says?

"Just here, Mistress Wenham, if you please," said Francis, pointing to the place where Jane should sign.

"Might I have a look?" interrupted Caroline, standing up and walking forward to the table. All eyes were immediately upon her, Francis's frankly hostile, those of the vicar and the rector questioning, Jane Wenham's uncertain. Was this lady someone who could force her to sign, some important person from London who could tell vicars and rectors what to do? It didn't matter that she was a woman, Queen Anne was a woman, and she could tell folks what to do, even people like Mr. Bragge. Quickly she made her mark.

"Yes, ma'am, if you want to," she said, putting the pen down and holding out the document to Caroline.

"I protest." Francis was most displeased at this turn of events.

"Why, Mr. Bragge?" asked Caroline, sounding as naïve as she dared. "Thank you, Mistress Wenham." She smiled and took the paper from the old woman.

"Because, Mistress Newell, you are not officially part of this examination."

"I see. But I am here with Sir Henry's knowledge... and when I report back to him..."

"When you do what?" Francis exploded.

"I'm sorry, I put that badly. When I tell him what I have done today... he will enjoy hearing about it... I wish to give him an accurate account. Of course, I do realise that if I had been present at the beginning of these proceedings, I should have known what was on the paper, as, no doubt, you would have explained it to Mistress Wenham before you commenced your examination."

Francis had no riposte for her - how could he? - and in the ensuing moments of silence Caroline read the document that Mistress Wenham had signed. Oh dear, oh dear, Caroline thought, the woman has confessed to being a witch... and there is nothing I can do about that. I can protest I suppose, and say that three clergymen have taken advantage of a simple-minded old woman. But is she? Perhaps she is a witch... and they are right. Who am I to pit myself against three highly educated clergymen? Caroline felt out of her depth, her strongly held convictions about witchcraft suddenly in disarray. She wished she had left well alone and had not asked to see the paper. She had promised Sir Henry she would not interfere. Well, she hadn't. The deed had been done... and she had had no part in it. And that gave her no satisfaction, either. She handed the paper to Mr. Gardiner. "Thank you," she said, and picked up her reticule from the floor by her stool. She must now leave, with dignity.

The clergymen watched her depart and then resumed their seats.

"You may go, Mistress Wenham," said Mr. Gardiner.

"Go?" said Jane. "Go where?"

"To your home," bellowed Francis, collecting up his papers, keen to get away.

"Don't I have to go to no court then?"

"Of course you have to go to court, but not today."

Caroline, in the small entrance hall of the house, had overheard this conversation. She waited, certain there was more to come.

"Next month, would you say, Mr. Gardiner?" Francis asked.

"Probably. Yes."

"Next month, Mistress Wenham. March," and he said the word very clearly.

"I know what next month is, and the one after."

"And in the meantime, go home... and see to it that there is no further trouble."

"Take Mistress Wenham back to her cottage, Constable," Mr. Gardiner said gently.

Caroline looked out into the street; there was no sign of young William or the cart. She was loathe to ask Francis to escort her back to Yardley Bury, but there seemed no alternative. She was about to re-enter the examination room when the constable appeared in the doorway, holding Jane Wenham firmly by the arm. She was looking down at the floor and mumbling to herself.

"I shouldn't 'a done that. I shouldn't 'a said I was a witch, I shouldn't."

"Come on now, Jane, let's get you home."

"Oh, Mistress Wenham..." Caroline began, in a low, uncertain voice, extending a hand, equally uncertainly, to the old woman. "I am so..."

"Excuse me, madam," the constable said, inclining his head towards Caroline as he escorted Jane past her. "I have my duty to perform."

"Yes, of course," said Caroline, drawing back.

She watched them leave. There was still no sign of William. She moved to the doorway of the room.

"A good day's work, Mr. Gardiner," Francis was saying.

"Yes. Indeed. Thank you, Mr. Bragge. And you too, Mr. Strutt."

The vicar simply nodded and began to wrap his long muffler around his throat and face. There was no longer any sunlight coming into the room and sleety rain was starting to coat the window panes.

Francis turned to Mr. Strutt. "I am most obliged to you, sir, for turning out on such a cold day in your present perilous state of health." He offered one of his best bows to the vicar.

"It was my duty, Mr. Bragge. I am, after all, the vicar of Yardley, Mr. Gardiner's adjoining parish... whereas you, I believe, are a curate in Biggleswade. Is that right?" He managed to make the name of the town sound so ridiculous that no serious-minded man would wish to live there. Mr. Gardiner allowed himself a wry smile and Caroline caught a twinkle in Mr. Strutt's eye before it was all but hidden by the woollen muffler.

To have to travel back to Sir Henry's with Francis would be unbearable, Caroline thought, making her way uncertainly out of the front door; it would be preferable to walk alone, even in this horrid weather. Oh, thank goodness... there, clip-clopping along the village street, was William and the little cart; he could not have timed it better.

"Well done, William. Now, take me back to Yardley Bury as fast as you can. I am cold and I am hungry... as I expect you are."

"No, ma'am, I've been at my mother's."

"Ah. Lucky you."

"Should we not wait for Mr. Bragge, ma'am? He's just coming out."

"Certainly not. Mr. Bragge will walk."

12

Being bounced along in Sir Henry's cart, Caroline wished she were on her way to Lydia's bright, comfortable modern home in Bengeo instead of returning to Tudor Yardley Bury. Her heart sank at the thought of spending yet another night and day there. Snowdrops and primroses by the roadside, and a few impatient leaf buds on old apple trees leaning over garden walls, tantalised her with a faint promise of spring, when in reality it was still winter; damp, depressing, cold winter.

She must stop this and think positively! Jane Wenham had been allowed to return to her home on the understanding that she behave herself. If she did obey and there were no more witchy - was there such a word? - activities in Walkern did that mean that the villagers would let bygones be bygones and live in harmony with her? Caroline doubted that a reprimand from the three clergymen, and a confession from Mistress Wenham that she *was* a witch, would be enough to satisfy the likes of Susan Aylott and Matthew Gilston. They wanted revenge for perceived harm either in the present or in the distant past. No, thought Caroline, as they approached Yardley Bury, it was very unlikely that they would leave the old woman in peace, however well she behaved.

Entering the long drive of the house Caroline suddenly leaned forward and tapped William on the shoulder.

"Stop here, will you. I want to walk." She climbed down from the cart and William set off at a swift pace for the stable yard.

Left on her own, Caroline walked slowly; there must be something she could do to help Jane Wenham. But what? If only she could talk to Lydia or one of her London friends. There must be someone she knew in the neighbourhood, someone who would give her impartial advice. There were the Cliffords, but that might mean exposing herself to the attentions of foppish young Roger. Who else was there who lived not too far away, whom she could visit, and return to Yardley Bury within a day? She was already more than halfway up the drive when it came to her:

"That's it!" she said out loud and for a moment she stood still. "Colonel Plumer at Gilston Park, he's the man to help me!" and then, hot on the heels of her first good thought, came another one: until her trial next month Jane Wenham could stay on Colonel Plumer's estate! Removed from Walkern entirely, the old woman would be safe and the villagers would be free of their witch: it was the perfect solution.

By the time Caroline reached the front door she was aglow, from both the exercise and the inner satisfaction that, at last, she had found something she could do to help Mistress Wenham. She couldn't wait to tell Sir Henry; he would be delighted.

Sir Henry, of course, was not at home; he would be in Hitchin all day. She whiled away the hours writing letters... to Emilia, to Lydia, to friends in London.

In the late afternoon she spoke to Sir Henry, in his snug. Briefly she told him what had taken place at the constable's house, then, brimming over with enthusiasm, she revealed her plan.

"I don't know if that would work," Sir Henry said slowly, when she had finished speaking.

"But why not?" He was not showing the enthusiasm she had anticipated.

"Well, to begin with..." He drew on his pipe. "... we can't be sure that Colonel Plumer will be willing to have the woman there. If word got out that he was harbouring a witch on his estate the situation could become very difficult for him."

"Then we must make sure that word does not get out!" Oh, why did men always have to make a simple thing so complicated?

"My dear Caroline... you are jumping too far ahead. First we must seek Colonel Plumer's agreement... and if he gives it..."

"He will, he will! I know he will!"

"You know nothing of the sort. Now... stop being so... so impatient." He had wanted to say 'childish'. He had had a hard day in court - a difficult case, with half the witnesses not turning up - and the last thing he wanted was an argument about the old witch-woman. It had been as much to humour her as anything else that he had suggested Caroline attend today's examination and report back to him. It was good to know that Francis had behaved himself, more or less, but that was all he had wanted of her. He did not want her involving someone like Colonel Plumer in her Good Samaritan schemes.

"I know you mean well, my dear." He sighed, and gave her a weak smile. "But there really is nothing you can..."

"Yes there is!"

She was interrupting him again. He would have no peace until she had had her say.

"Go on, then," he said wearily.

"I can go over there," Caroline said. "To Gilston… and talk to Colonel Plumer. I do know him, Sir Henry."

"Very well, if that is what you want to do. Don't commit him to anything, though."

"I won't, I promise you." Caroline got up from her chair, leant over Sir Henry and kissed him on his forehead. "I'm going to leave you now," she said. "Have a good rest. You must be tired after your day in Hitchin."

And tired of your badgering. "I will," he said, patting her hand. He shut his eyes.

Caroline slipped out of the room, closing the door softly behind her.

The only person Caroline felt she could take with her to Gilston was Mary, with young William driving the cart. She would have preferred to ride - a good gallop across the fields would have helped to blow away the cobwebs of Walkern that seemed to have gathered themselves around her - but it was not practicable. She could not go alone and she was certainly not asking Arthur, or Francis - heaven forbid! - to accompany her.

Having made her arrangements with Mary and William as soon as she had left the snug, Caroline was ready for an early start the next morning. After a quick breakfast she came downstairs fully dressed for her expedition. She had not expected to see Sir Henry in the entrance hall as she turned the corner of the staircase.

"Sir Henry, you are up early."

"And so are you, my dear. Where are you going, so elegantly attired?"

Had the occasion been different Caroline would have enjoyed responding to the flattery - she knew her dark blue brocaded cloak and gown were to be admired - but today she had more serious concerns.

"To Colonel Plumer's, of course." She paused two steps from the bottom of the stairs. Sir Henry was looking both surprised and dubious. Had he forgotten their conversation of the previous evening?

"Not without prior warning."

"What do you mean… warning?"

"Does Colonel Plumer know you are paying him a visit today?"

"No. Why should he?"

"My dear girl, you can't… Oh, do come down, Caroline, it's hurting my neck having to look up at you."

Caroline descended the remaining stairs.

"That's better. You weren't thinking of driving over to Gilston on the off-chance that Colonel Plumer would receive you, were you?"

"Well… yes. Why not?" If only she had got up an hour earlier!

"Why not? I cannot believe you can be so ill-mannered. Nor capable of such impropriety."

"Impropriety?" What was he talking about? She was simply calling on an old friend; what was wrong with that?

"Come into the library, Caroline." It was an order. Sir Henry strode across the hall. Meekly Caroline followed him.

"A lady," he said, turning to face her, "does not visit a gentleman on his estate without first sending to enquire whether or not he will receive her. Even if she does know him!"

"Would you not ride over to…?"

"We are not talking about me, we are talking about you! *A lady does not visit a gentleman's estate uninvited!*"

"Are you forbidding me to go?" Now *she* was angry.

"Yes, I am!"

"But…"

"Please don't tell me I can't. I know you are thirty years old and mistress of your households, but here, at Yardley Bury, you are both my guest and my responsibility. I will not have you disporting yourself in such an inappropriate manner." His anger was making his language as flowery as that of his grandson.

"Put simply, Caroline, I require you to behave… as a lady should."

"I will do as you wish."

She had no choice but to agree. It was galling, and if anyone else had attempted to curtail her activities in this way he would have received short shrift from her, but she could not be rude to Sir Henry. She needed to phrase her next words carefully.

"May I then send William, or Amos if you prefer, with a note to Colonel Plumer asking if I may visit?"

"No, you may not!"

"How else then am I to make contact with him? Should I send a carrier pigeon, perhaps?" She would not be thwarted in her plan just because of some silly bit of country etiquette. Seething, she walked over to the window. It was a beautiful morning; if only she had got up hours ago she could have ridden over to Gilston and Sir Henry would be none the wiser. "I won't give up, you know," she said, swinging round to face the old man.

A smile began to spread across his face.

"It is not funny, Sir Henry. I am trying to do something useful, something worthwhile, and you are putting obstacles in my way! Why? I thought justice mattered to you."

"Come and sit down."

"No, I won't. I'm sorry, Sir Henry, but…"

"Well, even if you will not… I will."

He walked across to a chair by the fire. Caroline stood, looking at him. They seemed to have reached an impasse. Caroline took a deep breath.

"Tell me, please, why I may not send William or Amos with a note?" She spoke as calmly as she could.

"Because, my dear, it would not be appropriate."

"Appropriate be hanged! Is that all you care for, that what is done is appropriate? It's appropriate, is it, to call an old country woman a witch, but *not* appropriate to send a stable lad riding over the fields with a note?" Her heart was beating fast and her cheeks were burning.

"Calm down. Please." Sir Henry waited until he judged she was less agitated. "Caroline… listen to me." Still she would not look directly at him. "I will write to Colonel Plumer, explaining that you are here, staying with me, and that you wish to visit him, at his earliest convenience."

"And then?" She wanted action, not just words.

"And then I will instruct Samuel to ride over to Gilston…"

"Samuel?"

"My coachman."

"Yes, I know, but…"

"I know he is old, but he is a very good horseman… and he is the right person to do this." He sighed. "I do wish you'd trust me."

"I'm sorry."

"Samuel will deliver my letter directly to Colonel Plumer … and then wait for his reply. Now, does that satisfy you?"

"Yes. Thank you." Why couldn't he have said that in the first place! He was right, though, on two counts. He, Sir Henry, should be the one to write the note, and a stable lad was perhaps not the - yes, she had to use the word - appropriate person to deliver it.

"I am sorry to have given you so much anguish," she said, looking him full in the face at last.

"Not anguish, my dear, just annoyance. Unnecessary annoyance!"

"Yes. I'm sorry." Caroline hung her head and clasped her hands together. She both looked and sounded penitent. Sir Henry observed her for a moment. It would take more than a few cross words from him to kill her spirit. Thank goodness.

"Right," he said loudly. Caroline's head jerked up, and their eyes met. Any animosity there was before had gone. "Leave me to write to the colonel, and *you* … go and undo any arrangements you have made with William. I love to have you here, Caroline… " There was a twinkle in his eye. "… but you really must not take over my household!"

"No, Sir Henry." She smiled at him. "You *will* send the note today?"

"Yes. I will send it today, and I will ask Colonel Plumer if you may visit him tomorrow."

"Thank you." She felt suddenly embarrassed. She *had* behaved badly and Sir Henry had taken it well. "I hope to see you at dinner," she said. She gave him a quick curtsey - she had never done *that* before, why was she doing it now? - and before he could question her about it, or laugh at her - he had raised his eyebrows as she bobbed in front of him - she fled into the hall, leaving the library door open.

Slowly Sir Henry got up from his chair, walked across to the door and looked out into the hall. Caroline was nowhere in sight, but he could hear her footsteps racing along the landing and then a distant door banging shut. He stood for a moment: would she come charging down again with another question for him? No, all was quiet above. He smiled to himself and walked back into the library, closing the door gently behind him. He sat down at his desk; there was a pile of writing paper in front of him. He lifted a quill pen from the rack, checked to make sure it was sharp, dipped it into the silver inkwell... and began to write.

Caroline lay down on her bed and stared up at the canopy. She was angry with herself - she should not have spoken as she had to Sir Henry; she was a guest in his house, he was a magistrate, a man of stature and he was fond of her. But at the same time she needed to have *her* say; she would not keep quiet just because she was a woman, because she was young and he was old. If she felt strongly about something, as she did about the treatment of Mistress Wenham, she had to speak out... and if somebody thought she was wrong to do so... *and* to take action... well, that was unfortunate, but it would not stop her. She would apologise to Sir Henry, but she would still go ahead with her plans. She might have to modify them, but she would *not* give them up. As for the apology, she couldn't face Sir Henry again today - she doubted if *he* would want to see *her;* she would write him a note. She sat up and looked about her for pen and paper.

There was none that she could see; it was a poorly appointed room. She would need to call Mary to fetch them. Oh no! Mary would be waiting, with William and the cart! Could she creep downstairs and hope that Sir Henry would not come out of the library at the wrong moment? Gingerly she opened the door. She stepped out on to the landing and was about to descend the staircase when Mary emerged from the passageway leading to the kitchen. Looking up she saw her mistress.

"Miss Caroline! I was just coming up to you. The cart is ready. Shall I get William to bring it round to the front door?"

"No. We are not going."

"Not going? But... why?"

"It is not your place to ask questions, Mary," was the sharp answer. "Just tell William that he will not be wanted today. Now," she said, softening her tone slightly, "bring me a tisane, feverfew I think, I have a headache. And bring me pen and paper, too."

Having written to Colonel Plumer, Caroline stretched her back, flexed her fingers... and yawned. There was nothing more she could now do to expedite her plan - Mary had taken the letter down to Sir Henry, for him to despatch - until she received the colonel's reply. Such unnecessary formality! She yawned again and lay down on her bed. If she wasn't going anywhere she might as well have a sleep...

An excited Mary awoke her in the late afternoon; it was five o'clock and just beginning to get dark. The village people had been to the house - "Did you not hear them, mistress?"- begging Sir Henry to do something about the witch woman. She had not stayed quietly in her cottage; she was rampaging around the village causing more trouble to Anne Thorn, and Mr. Chauncy had killed a cat at the rectory, and Anne's urine had been boiled over the fire in a stone bottle with a cork in the top, and the old woman had been in pain but when the cork burst out of the bottle, with a noise like a pistol going off, she stopped hurting and...

"Stop!" pleaded Caroline, putting her hands over her ears. "I don't want to hear any more!" She took her hands from her ears and reached for her tisane on the bedside table. It had gone cold; she must have taken just a few sips and gone straight to sleep. She remembered writing the note to Sir Henry and handing to it Mary... and then nothing until now.

"I have more to tell you, mistress."

"I don't want more! Didn't you hear me? Just fetch me a fresh tisane. Ginger, with honey. Well, go on, don't just stand there!"

"I have a message for you, mistress, from Sir Henry."

"Why didn't you say that in the first place... instead of all that horrible stuff about cats... and bottles of urine. Ugh!" Caroline shuddered. "Well, what *is* the message?"

"Sir Henry says will you please come down to the snug; he has a letter for you."

Caroline's letter was from Colonel Plumer. She was invited to take luncheon with him at Gilston Park the following day, and furthermore, if Sir Henry could spare her, to extend her visit into the following week.

"Oh, thank you so much, Sir Henry, for writing to him," Caroline said, looking up from her letter. She was standing on the hearthrug and Sir Henry, with his pipe in his mouth, was in his beloved red chair. "You are so good to me and I don't deserve it." She dropped him a brief curtsey.

"Come, come, let's not have any of this false modesty, Caroline. It does not become you. And do stop curtseying!"

"Do you prefer it when I am aggressive and troublesome?" she asked mischievously.

"Yes, I think I do. But not all the time; it's tiring." He beckoned her towards him.

"Come and sit down. Not on the rug, on the chair."

Obediently Caroline seated herself on the armchair on the other side of the fireplace.

"Tell me," said Sir Henry, when she was settled, "Do you have anything definite in mind for Mistress Wenham? It would be as well to marshal your thoughts on this before you speak to Colonel Plumer."

"I will. I will think it through, I promise. I am just so pleased that we can do something for her."

"Caroline, you are jumping ahead again. Don't do it! You don't know that Colonel Plumer will agree to *anything* that you suggest. He may not be prepared to have such a troublesome creature on his land, and whatever happens, no one in Walkern... and I include my son in this... no one must know of your plans. This is between us, and no one else."

He reached out for his tobacco jar.

"Not Francis?"

Sir Henry paused in his movement towards the jar. "Definitely *not* Francis."

He smiled at Caroline and began to refill his pipe. When the task was done to his satisfaction - Caroline knew better than to interrupt this important routine - and the pipe was drawing well, with a small cloud of aromatic smoke curling upwards from the bowl, Sir Henry continued, "You do know that the witch has been taken into custody again?"

"No, I did not. But that's good. Is that because of all that nonsense Mary was talking about, Arthur killing a cat and… other unpleasant things. Mistress Wenham will be safe in the Cage."

"She's… er… she's not in the Cage."

"But you said…?"

"She is at the rectory at the moment."

"You said she was in custody."

"She is. The constable is with her."

"I don't understand."

"They are doing some more tests. Some different ones."

Sir Henry looked away. He was obviously uncomfortable with the situation.

"Who are?" She knew the answer.

Sir Henry sighed. "Arthur and… and my grandson."

"Oh no! Oh, Sir Henry, how could you let them?"

He was finding it difficult to give an answer. Finally he said, "I had very little choice, my dear. It's better, if they do want to test her, that they do it with the constable present. He's a reasonable man, a man of probity, aware of his duty, and he will make sure that Mistress Wenham is treated properly."

"And so will I!" Caroline jumped up from her chair.

Sir Henry took his pipe from his mouth. "I don't see that you can do anything," he said.

"Oh, I can. I am going there, to the rectory, right now!"

Sir Henry sat straight up in his chair and put his pipe on the table beside him.

"My dear girl, you cannot *do* that. Aside from anything else, it will be dark within an hour."

"All the more reason to go straight away. I'm sorry, Sir Henry, but I must do this. Please don't try to stop me."

She dashed from the room, calling out as she went, "Mary, come here quickly!"

Sensing from the moment she had spoken of the letter awaiting her mistress in the snug that something... exciting, important, she wasn't sure which... was about to happen, Mary had been hovering in the entrance hall. She was shivering with cold and wishing she were in the warm kitchen, but unwilling to leave her listening post in case she missed anything.

"I'm here, mistress."

"Good girl. Tell William to saddle a horse for me. And one for him. Then fetch my dark brown cloak... and my boots. And hurry!"

Sir Henry, coming out of the snug, had heard most of Caroline's speech.

"No, Caroline, no! If you must go, take the carriage."

"No, Sir Henry, there isn't time. I don't want to disobey you... but I have to do this. Heaven knows what dreadful tests that poor woman will be suffering at the hands of Francis and Arthur!" She took his hands in hers. "Oh, my dear, dear friend... I am so sorry to do this to you."

Mary, returned from giving Caroline's instructions to William, was flying up the stairs.

"Will you not reconsider?" Sir Henry clasped her hands tightly.

"No. I can't, Sir Henry, I can't." Caroline pulled her hands free. "I will see you when I return," she said, and walked quickly away from him. Before she was even out of the entrance hall Mary was there with Caroline's cloak over her arm and her riding boots in her hand. She scurried after her mistress, down the passageway and past the kitchen.

"You're not going alone, are you, mistress?" Mary asked anxiously, draping the cloak around Caroline's shoulders and helping her into the boots.

"No, William's coming with me. I hope you told him to saddle a horse for himself. I told you to."

"Yes, mistress, I did," Mary said, forlornly. She didn't want Miss Caroline to see the disappointment in her eyes.

"If you want to follow me on foot... that's up to you."

Mary looked up eagerly. "Yes, mistress, I'll do that."

"He might not be there, you know."

"Who, mistress?"

"The Lord Mayor of London. Who d'you think?"

Mary blushed and looked away.

"I'll see you at the rectory."

"Yes, Miss Caroline." Mary hesitated. "It's just that I don't like to think of you going down there on your own."

"Of course you don't. Go on, go and get your cloak!"

"The horses are ready, ma'am," William called from the back door.

"Good. I'm coming."

Caroline mounted swiftly. With William following her she rode out of the stable yard, into the parkland and then galloped across the fields to the rectory. William, on a slower animal, had difficulty keeping up with her.

"Did you bring a lantern?" Caroline called over her shoulder.

"Yes, ma'am, I did," William answered proudly. He didn't, though, tell the lady that it was Amos who said he should take the lantern. Next time there was an adventure like this he would let Amos come with him... if the lady didn't mind.

It took little more than five minutes to reach the rectory. Almost before her horse had come to a stop Caroline was out of the saddle. "Look after my horse, William," she said, flinging the reins towards him and running across the wide, curved drive to the front door. She might be making an unorthodox appearance, but it wouldn't do for her to add to it by turning up at the back of the house.

Caroline pushed open the front door; there was no time to wait for a servant or the rector himself to usher her in. She strode down the hallway towards the sound of raised voices flowing out of the kitchen door. Briefly she paused on the threshold. The room was lit only by the shrinking daylight and the firelight, and but for the colours of the villagers' clothes, drab though they were, Caroline felt she could be looking at an illustration from a book of medieval history she remembered from her father's library. It was a scene both fascinating and repellent.

The central figure was Anne Thorn, seated by the fire. Her face was drained of colour, her mouth slack and dribbling; she was trembling, in an odd, jerky way.

Mr. Gardiner stood over her, his hands steepled in prayer, while Mrs. Gardiner wiped the girl's face with a cloth. Another woman, with her back to Caroline, knelt in front of Anne. Framing this tableau on one side was the constable, holding firmly on to Jane Wenham, and on the other side was Francis, eyes closed, head back, arms raised, also praying, fervently and loudly. Clustered around these central figures were Susan Aylott and Elizabeth Field, Thomas Adams and Matthew Gilston, together with other people from the village that Caroline did not recognise. Amongst them was Arthur, tense and impatient, bobbing from one foot to the other, like a caged animal ready to spring.

"Thy will be done, on earth as it is in heaven," intoned Francis. "Give us this day our daily bread, and forgive us our trespasses." The rector spoke *his* words in an undertone - he was talking just to his God, his wife and the stricken girl; Francis was addressing a full congregation - and like a chorus, the villagers echoed the words.

Anne suddenly opened her eyes, and seeing Jane Wenham, she began to scream. Francis broke off from his prayer; the holy man was gone, the witch-hunter was back.

"Stop that!" he shouted. There was no mercy for a sick child in his voice, just anger.

Mr. Gardiner, as if in a trance, continued to pray, with a dwindling chorus of villagers accompanying him. For some of them, to keep on praying in such frightening circumstances was the safest thing to do; others were not going to miss the excitement of the moment, however dangerous it was, by keeping their eyes closed.

"Mistress Thorn, stop your daughter from making that noise. We can't help her if she is screaming."

The woman kneeling in front of Anne turned round to Francis.

"I'll try, Mr. Bragge, sir, but it's having the witch here what's done it."

"Yes. I know. Of course it's the witch. But we still can't have her screaming like that."

Caroline, watching unobserved from the doorway, could keep quiet no longer.

"The girl is terrified, Mr. Bragge. She's also had a fit; can't you see that?"

She stepped into the room and made her way to the hearth. Regardless of the gasps and stares that greeted her, she knelt down beside Anne and put her hands on either side of the girl's head, gently turning her face towards her own.

"Anne, listen to me. Nobody is going to hurt you. You have had a fit, that is all, and you have come out of it. And now… you must rest." She turned to the rector's wife. "Mistress Gardiner, could you get Anne a nice warm, sweet drink, please. Milk with some honey in it would be good."

Mrs. Gardiner, totally at a loss, began to stammer. "Bu… but…"

Keeping one hand on Anne, Caroline held out the other one in supplication to Mrs. Gardiner. "Please. It would be so helpful."

Slowly Mrs. Gardiner got up. She looked uncertainly about her, as if waking from a dream.

"A warm drink, yes…" and she began to move away from the hearth.

Francis quickly moved into the space left empty by Mrs. Gardiner.

"How dare you come here, interfering!" He stood over Caroline, one arm raised.

She looked up at him. "Don't you raise your hand to me, Mr. Bragge."

The curate had the grace to lower his arm, but he remained standing over her, his eyes blazing with fury.

"This is no concern of yours! Mr. Chauncy, will you please take Mistress Newell back to your father's house at once."

"Well…" began Arthur, from the back of the room.

"I am not going back, Arthur," Caroline said, "not until I have seen that this poor child is all right."

"This poor child, as you call her, is bewitched, Mistress Newell, not ill. It is because the witch is *here* that she is now recovering."

"Anne's not ill," one of the women said, "'cept for her knee, what comes out sometimes; then the bone-setter has to put it back."

"Mistress Wenham has taken the spell off now," Arthur said. "That's why Anne is better."

"And is that why she screamed? Because she is better?" Caroline felt bewildered. Was she missing something here? Was there something the two clergymen and the villagers knew that she did not? She could see from their eyes that everyone in the room believed what Arthur had said.

"I don't understand," she began hesitantly. There was no point in being aggressive with these people, and she was not going to change their minds with modern science or a basic knowledge of medicine, or even common sense.

Better to listen to what they had to say. Suppressing her dislike of him, Caroline looked appealingly at Francis.

"Of course you don't," he said condescendingly. "I will explain."

"Thank you, Mr. Bragge," Caroline said humbly, "But would you first allow Mistress Gardiner to give Anne her warm drink. That, I am sure you will agree, will do no harm?"

Francis nodded his acquiescence, and for a few moments the attention was on Mrs. Gardiner as she administered the milk and honey, a spoonful at a time, to Anne. Caroline got up from the floor, dusted off her skirts and sat down on a stool hastily vacated by one of the village women. She was relieved to see an out-of-breath Mary appearing in the doorway. She acknowledged her arrival with a quick nod and a fleeting smile, then turned her attention to the curate.

"Now, Mr. Bragge," she said, "I am ready for your explanation."

"Madam." Francis gave her a curt bow. Damn the woman! She seemed able to turn everything to her own advantage. Putting him on the spot, was she? Well, he'd see about that! "The explanation is simple: the girl is in the witch's power, and therefore, she will do whatever the witch asks her to do."

"I do wish you would stop calling her that!" Caroline hadn't meant to interrupt, but, really, she could not let that pass. "Mistress Wenham is innocent until she is proved guilty, in a court of law."

"We all *know* she is a witch, don't we?" Susan Aylott's scathing words were greeted by a chorus of approval.

"Not now, Mistress Aylott, if you please," said Francis. "Mistress Newell, not having your faith, nor your understanding of the situation, does not believe that we have in our midst a witch, a woman capable of all manner of depraved and sinful behaviour, and being a lady acquainted, no doubt, with modern science... which I understand does not take things on trust or face value, but requires proof... Mistress Newell will not be satisfied until it is proved to her that this woman is a witch. And therefore... I shall give her proof." He paused. Yes, he had her full attention; he would so enjoy the next few minutes. "Mistress Thorn, be so good as to give me that pin in your daughter's hand."

Elizabeth Thorn uncurled Anne's fingers and carefully extracted a small, black, twisted pin that lay in the palm. She handed it to Francis.

"Thank you, Mistress Thorn." He started to make a bow, then checking himself - this was only a country woman - he turned abruptly to Jane Wenham. "Have you been tested with pins?"

"No, sir."

"Then it's time you were. Mr. Chauncy..." He smiled at Arthur. "I think you should do this." If there should be any blood, Francis did not want it on his fingers. He held out the twisted pin to Arthur, who took it eagerly.

"What are you going to do with it?" Caroline asked anxiously.

"You'll see," said Arthur. "Mistress Wenham, hold out your arm."

Obediently Jane lifted her scrawny right arm. Arthur pushed her sleeve up to the elbow, then held the pin poised over the mottled, papery skin.

Caroline leapt up from her stool. "Arthur, you can't do this!" She looked to the constable for help. He made a hesitant move forward.

"I'm not sure you should do this, Mr. Chauncy. Sir Henry didn't say anything about pins..."

"It's all right, constable. I take full responsibility for this." Francis spoke in assured tones.

"*I* will take the responsibility, not you," said Arthur. He would not let Francis humiliate him! "Now, Mistress Wenham…"

"No!" yelled Caroline, reaching out to grab the pin.

"Let him do it, ma'am." Jane Wenham sounded weary and resigned. "I've made my confession, and whatever happens they'll send me to court."

Caroline looked at the roomful of expectant faces, all eager to witness, and gain satisfaction from, this promised moment of barbarity. Only Mrs. Gardiner's head was bowed. Surely *she* must have some feeling for the old woman.

"Mistress Gardiner, you can't let this happen."

Mrs. Gardiner looked up, her face full of pain. "The woman is a witch, Mistress Newell. The pin won't hurt her." Mrs. Gardiner brushed her hand across her forehead.

"Of course it will hurt her! Mistress Gardiner, I appeal to you!"

"If you had heard those cats…" The rector's wife was almost in tears. "Oh, I must lie down." She pushed herself through the knot of people around Jane Wenham and made her way to the door.

"My wife is not well, Mistress Newell. Please excuse her."

"Of course, Mr. Gardiner."

It was no wonder she was not well, with all that was going on in her kitchen.

The villagers watched her go. Francis cleared his throat, drawing their attention back to the testing of the old woman.

"It wouldn't surprise me if Mistress Gardiner weren't bewitched," said a man at the back of the room. "They's no respecter of persons, witches."

"That may well be so, Mr. Ireland," said Francis, "but at the moment we must concentrate on the needs of young Anne. Now, Mr. Chauncy, if you would please continue."

Standing directly in front of her, with his left hand firmly grasping Jane's arm, Arthur drove the pin deep into her flesh. The old woman remained perfectly still and looked straight into Arthur's face.

"Oh, how could you!" Caroline flinched and turned her head away. When she looked back Arthur was withdrawing the pin from Jane's arm.

"Now, let us see if there is any blood." Francis took hold of Jane's wrist and lifted it, waving her arm about as if it was an inanimate object, not a part of a human being. "There. Nothing. Not a drop. Just a bit of watery fluid. I knew there'd be no *blood*." He let the arm drop. Slowly the old woman's sleeve slid down.

"Did it not hurt you?" Caroline asked. Her first concern was Jane Wenham's suffering. She would come to the test itself in a minute; there was so much she did not understand.

Jane shook her head; she did not look up.

How could this be? She had seen Arthur driving that pin deep into the woman's flesh, not just running it under the skin, as you might do to remove a splinter of wood, but straight in, for at least an inch. It was not possible that the woman would not bleed, and yet *there had been no blood.* Not a single drop. And this, said Arthur and Francis, and the Rev. Gardiner, was proof that Mistress Wenham was a witch. Did witches not have blood, did they never bleed? If they did not bleed, they were not human; even animals bled. So what were witches?

This is so wrong! There must be some logical explanation for the lack of blood in the woman's arm. Robert would have known the answer. If only she knew more about medicine; if only she had listened more carefully when Robert had explained how blood was circulated around the human body. But what if there was no *logical* explanation?

"There you are, Mistress Newell," Francis was saying. "What more proof do you need?"

"Is this… proof?" She felt the eyes of the villagers upon her. Somewhere a cat yowled.

"I saw a cat," said Anne Thorn in a sing-song voice, and she began to scream.

A shiver ran through Caroline. Oh, it would be so easy if she could agree with these people, accept their findings and leave Mistress Wenham to their mercy.

What was it to her if the woman went to prison? Caroline suddenly felt defeated; she had had enough of Walkern with its superstition and its problems. It was time to return to civilisation. But she couldn't, not just yet. Sir Henry, at her insistence, had arranged for her to visit Colonel Plumer at Gilston, yet another remote place.

Well, she would go, it would be discourteous to Sir Henry if she didn't, but she would make it a purely social call.

"Yes, Mistress Newell. It is." Francis waited. Surely now this woman would retreat, and if she didn't, he was ready for her; he made the list in his mind: all the other tests they had done, the statements of the villagers, the catalogues of ills going back twenty years, the suffering of poor Anne Thorn. What more could she want?

"Then I apologise for thrusting myself in here among you," Caroline said. She made a move towards the door, then stopped. She could not leave without speaking to Jane. Whether she was a witch or not, she was still a very unhappy old woman.

"Mistress Wenham." The woman lifted her head and looked at Caroline. "I wish you well."

"Thank you… ma'am. You… are… very kind." The words were dragged out slowly as if it was a great effort for Jane to speak at all.

Impulsively Caroline took the old woman's hands in hers. "I'm so sorry I have not been able to help you."

Feeling herself on the verge of tears she let go of Jane's hands, turned on her heel and left the kitchen, calling to Mary to follow her. She fled down the passageway and out of the front door. William was there with the horses. She took the reins of her mount from him.

"Mary, get up behind William."

"But, mistress…"

"Do as I say! I need to get away from here, and I want you with me."

Without waiting to see if Mary had obeyed her, Caroline mounted her horse, gave a sharp tug on the reins, and was off, round to the back of the rectory and across the fields at a gallop.

Jem, arriving at the rectory in time to see Caroline riding off, and Mary, flushed pink with embarrassment, clambering up with difficulty behind Sir Henry's stable boy, cursed himself for being on foot. If he had had a horse under him he could have whisked Mary away from William's clumsy hands and set her up in front of him on *his* mount. As it was, it was better to keep out of sight until they had gone.

He could, of course, take the rector's horse and go after them, but judging by the look on Mistress Newell's face, his intervention would not be welcome. Besides, he had other, more pressing things to do: Polly had gone missing, again. Usually she turned up within a very short time, often with her skirts wet; she loved water and could never resist a stream or even a puddle, and there were always plenty of those about. She had never strayed beyond the confines of the farm until today. He worried that one day she would wander further afield… and drown.

The Beane just here was shallow, but just a little way downstream it became too deep for wading… and Polly could not swim.

He had been looking after her on his own for six years now, since he was twelve and she was seven. Old enough to be employed, Jem had worked his way down from Norfolk to Hertfordshire, picking up a few days' work here and there in villages such as Barley and Sandon, and ending up in Walkern. No farmer had wanted a lad with gypsy looks on their land for long, and Jem was constantly moving on, until a winter day five years ago when, shivering with cold, he and Polly knocked on the back door of Joseph Gilbert's farmhouse.

It was the farmer's wife, Alice, who had taken them in and fed them, and persuaded her husband to let them sleep in one of their barns, at least for a night or two, until the really bad weather, with snow and strong winds, had ceased. It could all be gone by next week, she had said to her husband; and them with it, he had muttered. But the weather didn't change; huge drifts of snow piled up against the hedges and the outbuildings and all the tracks and paths became impassable: Jem and Polly had no choice but to stay where they were. Each day Jem made his way across from the barn to the farmhouse where Mrs. Gilbert had warm food waiting for them. Joe Gilbert insisted they took it back to the barn; he wasn't having gypsy children in *his* kitchen. But they could move into the stable, if they liked; they would be warmer there, with the horses. This weather was as trying for them as it was for humans. Without any exercise they became restive, stamping about in their stalls and tossing their heads, at times quite violently.

Mrs. Gilbert hoped the children would be safe there. They were only *gypsy* children, and not her responsibility, but she wouldn't want anything bad to happen to them, especially that little girl, Polly; she was such a frail, pale child, not really like a gypsy child at all. The boy was, of course, you could see that: black hair, dark eyes, swarthy skin. At a guess only one of the parents had been a gypsy, probably the mother, who'd been seduced by a farm worker somewhere and then banished by her own people; the girl would have committed two sins in one, coupling out of wedlock and with a non-gypsy.

Joe Gilbert noticed how quiet the horses had become once the children were settled into the stable. Quiet and calm; it was uncanny. At first he thought it was just because they had company. But it couldn't be that: the stable lad saw to them twice a day, and *he* hadn't been able to dispel the animals' distress at being trapped in their stalls. And then he saw Jem, talking to them, soothing them, and the little girl, without any fear, stroking and patting them. Well, never mind the girl, but that boy, twelve years old… Joe Gilbert could do with him on the farm. He needed someone who could look after the horses; they were sensitive beasts, they deserved better care than they got from his stable lad. And so, once the intense weather eased and the snow could be swept from the paths, the farmer installed Jem and Polly in an old run-down cottage on his land, and set Jem to work as his second stable boy. It wasn't long before Jem was in charge. He understood horses, and under his tuition, the other boy learned to understand them; they became a team. Farmer Gilbert trusted Jem - he'd never thought he would trust a gypsy lad, but this boy was different. There was something special about him, and the way he looked after that poor little sister of his impressed the farmer. Soon Jem was in demand at other farms in the neighbourhood: he could always be relied upon to cure a sick horse or turn a bad-tempered one into a creature a child wouldn't be afraid to ride. Joseph Gilbert was pleased to loan him out. His skills brought the farmer an extra source of income, which he had the sense to share with Jem.

Within minutes of Caroline's departure, people had begun to stream out of the rectory. Maybe someone here knew where Polly was; she might have seen people she knew walking down the lane and followed them, Matthew perhaps, or Thomas Ireland. No, they had not seen her. And if they had, they were too taken up with the witch to give any thought to Polly. Elizabeth Field *had* seen her, she thought, earlier, not on the walk here, nor in the rectory, but somewhere nearby.

Outside the washhouse, perhaps? Of course. The obvious place. Jem found her bending over Mrs. Gardiner's washtub, filling and emptying jugs and pails of water; her clothes were soaking wet and she was shivering… but happy, humming to herself contentedly.

Jem took her into the rectory kitchen, now almost deserted, and Elizabeth Thorn helped him to wrap Polly in a blanket. They sat her down by the fireside and Elizabeth rubbed warmth back into the girl's frozen fingers. Mrs. Gardiner, coming into the kitchen, her megrim now eased, was startled to see Jem there with young Polly. It seemed as if you got rid of one problem - she was relieved that the witch and the constable and everyone else had left her house - only to be faced with another one. Remembering the good effect of the milk and honey drink she had given young Anne, she set about preparing a similar concoction for Polly.

Poor child, her lips were blue with cold and she was shaking all over - please don't say the witch had got at her, too. She wouldn't be surprised if Jane Wenham wasn't responsible for all the megrims she was having, one nearly every day. The sooner that woman was out of Walkern the better.

When Polly had recovered sufficiently to go home, Jem lifted her, still wrapped in the blanket and with a thick shawl around her shoulders, on to the rector's horse. He was about to set off, cradling Polly in front of him, when Mrs. Gardiner rushed out of the back door. Would Jem go to Yardley Bury, with a message for Mary: she needed help with some sewing. Yes, he would ride there tomorrow morning, early. And maybe bring Mary back? Jem kept that thought to himself.

Tonight, though, he must concentrate on his sister. He gave a flick to the reins and rode off.

13

Caroline's drive to Gilston in Sir Henry's carriage was uneventful. Mary, reluctant and almost sullen when they set out, suddenly brightened up as they neared their destination; she seemed to be bubbling over with some inner excitement. Caroline was accustomed to Mary's volatile temperament, but this was extreme. No doubt she would be given an explanation in due course: Mary rarely kept her thoughts to herself for long. Meanwhile she had plenty of her own to occupy her.

In the rectory kitchen she had been caught up in the atmosphere of hatred and fear, and the absolute belief of everyone present that Jane Wenham was, and always had been, a witch. Away from the hysteria Caroline was able to think clearly again. Why did all these obnoxious tests - being pricked with a pin to see if she bled, reciting the Lord's Prayer over and over, being checked to see if she had extra teats - why did they prove a woman was a witch? Might she not have some strange, unnamed, even unknown, sickness, or, in the case of the Lord's Prayer, have been too tired to say the words in the correct order?

Enough of this! There was nothing she could do by worrying - 'Worry worries worry' her mother used to say - she must just hope that Colonel Plumer could be of practical assistance to her. She didn't know him well, but he had thought highly of Robert and approved of his concern for animals. It was through Robert that Caroline had met him and they had taken to one another immediately; the last time she had seen him was at Robert's funeral at Amley, nearly two and a half years ago. She had not had much conversation with the colonel that day but she remembered him putting an arm around her shoulders and saying, as people do on these occasions, that if he could ever be of service to her, she must not hesitate to call upon him. Well, here she was, doing precisely that, though giving shelter to a self-confessed witch was probably not what the colonel had had in mind.

Caroline allowed herself a small smile, and turning to Mary found her grinning from ear to ear, her eyes wide open and sparkling.

"Whatever is the matter with you, girl? Anyone would think you were off to the fair with your sweetheart from the look on your face! What is going on?"

"Nothing, mistress." Mary tried, without much success, to bring a more sober expression to her features.

"Go on. What is it? Tell me."

"It's Jem, mistress."

"Jem?"

"He followed us. He's here." She pointed out of the window, and sure enough, there he was, astride the rector's horse, with a grin on his face as wide as Mary's had been a few moments earlier.

"Mistress Newell." Jem doffed his cap. "Good morning."

Caroline looked at the young man. He was very good-looking; no wonder Mary's head had been turned by him. "Good morning to you," she said, unsure what tone to adopt; the lad was a farm boy, nothing more, and yet… he *was* very personable.

"This is some plot of yours, isn't it? The pair of you." Caroline looked sternly at Mary.

"No, mistress, truly. I didn't know he was coming. Honest."

The carriage turned into the drive of New Place, Jem keeping pace with it.

"Hmm. Do you really expect me to believe that?" She turned to the window and put her head out. "Samuel, stop the carriage please." The horses began to slow. "Young man, come here." The carriage came to a halt and Jem drew up beside the open window.

"Yes, madam."

"You can, I presume, explain your presence here?"

"Yes, madam, I can. I was at the rectory yesterday…"

"I didn't see you there."

"No, madam, I arrived just as you, and Mary and William, were leaving."

Oh no, Mary thought. Oh, I hope he didn't see me clambering up behind William.

"I see. Go on."

"Mistress Gardiner asked me to give a message to Mary… to do with some needlework, but I couldn't deliver it till this morning: my sister was … she was not well… and I had to look after her. And when I rode to Yardley Bury this morning Mistress Sawyer said you had gone to Gilston, and so… I was riding Cherry, the rector's horse, and 'cos she needed a good run, she hadn't had one for some days… I thought I would ride over… and… and give the message to Mary. And provide an escort for you, madam."

"Hmm. A likely story! Well, now that you *are* here, you may keep Mary company while I take luncheon… and then, if you wish to be of service to *me*, you may accompany us back to Yardley Bury later in the day."

"Thank you, madam."

"Oh, thank you, mistress."

"Mmm. I still think it's a bit odd. However… Samuel, drive on."

Colonel Plumer's residence, although of almost the same date as Yardley Bury - it had a bust of the late Queen Elizabeth over the front porch - had an elegant interior, recently refurbished by the look of it, with light wood panelling replacing the dark oak that made Sir Henry's house so gloomy.

The colonel, a tall, spare man with bright blue eyes and bushy white eyebrows that contrasted strangely with his flowing brown wig, greeted Caroline in the tiled entrance hall.

"This is a most delightful surprise," he said, his whole face lit up with a beaming smile. He gave Caroline the briefest of bows and immediately took her arm. "Come, my dear, let us go and eat."

How charming, how informal he was, and so apparently light-hearted. This is going to be a refreshing change from the tense atmosphere of Walkern and Yardley Bury, thought Caroline. It was a pity she had come here to talk about Jane Wenham rather than to chat about trivialities.

On the point of ushering her into the dining hall, a large, airy room with long windows looking out over the rolling parkland, Colonel Plumer suddenly turned to Caroline with a look of distress on his face.

"My dear lady," he said, "whatever am I thinking of! Rushing you into luncheon after such an arduous journey." He halted any protest from Caroline with a raised hand. "I know all is well, but no travel is pleasant and easy at this time of year. You must be in need of rest."

"My dear Colonel, I assure you I am not. A little tidying of my hair, perhaps..." the only way she could think of saying that she would be glad to make use of a commode, or whatever facility of that kind was available to her.

"Of course, of course!" He lifted a heavy silver bell from a table by the doorway and rang it loudly. "I have a room set aside for you, my dear. It is a room designed and appointed by my wife for the sole use of lady visitors such as yourself. How thoughtless of me not to have had you escorted there immediately you arrived. I do beg your pardon. Ah, Prudence..." A stout, rosy-faced woman came waddling across the tiled hall. "Take Mistress Newell to her room, will you."

"Yes, master," the woman said, and dropped a curtsey to Caroline.

"And then, my dear," the colonel said to his guest, "when you are refreshed Prudence will bring you to the dining hall. I do so regret that my wife is not here; there would have been no lapse of etiquette from her, I assure you. Sadly, she is away from home at the moment, visiting friends in Lincolnshire." Seeing Caroline's raised eyebrows - Lincolnshire was a considerable distance away - he went on, "She is a very strong-minded lady, my wife, and nothing I could say would persuade her not to undertake such a journey. I rather fancy you are of the same mould, my dear."

Caroline smiled at her host. "I probably am," she said. How the colonel did run on, but it was all very pleasant; she was already enjoying his company.

"Now, you go with Prudence." He beamed at the old servant. "She has been with me a long time, and as you will deduce from her name she comes from a Puritan family... and is none the worse for that. So, yes, go with Prudence, and I shall see you shortly. Oh, and I have someone here whom I know you will like. He is a friend of my... No, I will say no more, I can see that I have exhausted you."

"Not at all, Colonel."

"No, Caroline, no! I can't have you addressing me as *Colonel* all the time! We shall have to do something about that. But not now. No, we shall resolve that over luncheon. For now, I must let you go."

Caroline, who was beginning to feel in desperate need of relieving herself, was at last released. The room set aside for her was as charming and airy as the rest of the house. Even the rugs on the polished boards were light in colour. If there had been more time she would have liked to rest on the comfortable-looking bed with its gleaming woodwork, richly embroidered quilt and soft silk hangings.

Twenty minutes later, feeling refreshed - she had been delighted to find lavender water and scented creams laid out for her - Caroline, led by Prudence, walked into the dining hall. The colonel was seated at the far end of a long table covered in a snowy white fringed cloth, upon which there were equally snowy napkins, gleaming silverware and sparkling crystal glasses. Immediately on his left was a young man of pale complexion and wavy, sandy hair.

On Caroline's entrance both men sprang to their feet, the young man executing a somewhat awkward bow at the same time.

"My dear Caroline," the colonel enthused. "Do come and join us. How lovely you look. I trust you have forgiven my earlier lack of consideration."

"Oh, Colonel, there was nothing to forgive."

"Well, that's as maybe, but now… Now, let me introduce you," the colonel said. "This young man…" He took hold of his arm. "… is a good friend of my son, Will. Have you met Will? I can't remember."

"I don't think I have."

"No matter. Now, Caroline, may I introduce to you Mr. Simon Warrender. As well as being a dear friend of my son, Simon is also my godson."

"Oh."

"Now… Simon's family come from Yorkshire… and they have estates in the West Indies, in Jamaica. Is that not so, Simon?"

"Yes."

"How interesting." Oh, do get on with the introduction, please… so we can all sit down and eat!

"Simon, my boy." He extended his left hand towards the young man and his right hand towards Caroline. "Miss Caroline Newell, a dear friend of Sir Henry Chauncy. She has come all the way from Yardley Bury to visit us. Oh, but you know that, of course you do." He turned to Caroline. "I've told him all about you, my dear. Haven't I, Simon?"

"Yes… you have." Poor young man, thought Caroline; he's blushing to the roots of his hair. It *is* hair, it's not a wig. How unusual; how… how very nice.

"Mistress Newell," said Simon, bowing, again awkwardly, as if it was something he had only recently learned to do and hadn't quite mastered the art.

"Mr. Warrender," said Caroline, inclining her head slightly. She looked up and smiled at him. He gave her a fleeting, embarrassed smile in return. Oh dear, it was going to be hard enough, in the course of one afternoon, to get on to the topic she needed to discuss with the colonel, without trying to make a shy young man feel at ease, which she knew she could easily do by getting him to talk about himself. She had yet to meet the man, young or old, shy or confident, who didn't like to talk about himself, and the colonel's mention of Yorkshire and Jamaica had given her two good openings for conversation. Fortunately she needed neither.

"Good," said their host. "Now… let us all sit down and eat. We are having a light meal which, according to my wife, is the most suitable for ladies in the middle of the day. For myself, I prefer something more hearty, so I trust you will forgive me if I partake of roast meats rather than pies and sallats."

"Of course." There had been no mention of what young Simon was to eat: a mixture of the two, perhaps.

"Daniel, see to Mistress Newell's chair."

An elderly manservant drew back the chair to the right of the colonel's. Caroline sat down and her chair was pushed in.

"Thank you, Daniel," said the colonel.

With the gentlemen seated, they set to and ate. Colonel Plumer, scorning a taste of something delicate to begin the meal, attacked first some shoulder of mutton and then roast pork as if he hadn't eaten for days, seeming to relish even the greasy sauces, that but for a quick dab with his napkin, would have run down his chin. He put as much energy and enthusiasm into eating as he did into talking, and for a while no one spoke, other than to murmur words of acceptance or refusal to Daniel, who served them so discreetly he might almost not have been in the room.

Cautiously Caroline lifted the crust of the slice of pie Daniel had put on her plate; you never knew exactly what a pie crust might be covering.

"It is one of the mistress's favourites," he whispered; there was no refusing it.

It looked like a small bird, a lark most probably. Happy to eat chicken and turkey, partridge and pheasant, Caroline preferred a songbird to be warbling in a tree, not sitting dead on her plate. There is not much I can do for this one now, she thought, and lifted a forkful of the pie to her mouth; cooked with herbs and mustard it was very good. She followed this with a sallat of almonds, currants, sage, lemon, orange and pickled cucumbers. Simon, she noticed, ate little: a small slice of mutton, some peas, a little sallat, a sliver of the lark pie.

When the colonel had eaten his fill and wiped his mouth vigorously on his napkin, he sat back in his chair, smiled at Caroline and Simon, and said, "Now... we have satisfied our craving for food - Daniel, you may clear - so let us now talk."

Caroline looked up, somewhat startled, with her knife and fork poised in mid-air. Simon, accustomed to the colonel's eccentricities, was calmly placing his cutlery to one side of his unfinished plate of food.

"Eating and talking do not go well together, but one follows the other most pleasantly, I find." The colonel beamed at his guests. "So?" he enquired. "Has either of you a topic you wish to discuss?"

"No," Simon answered promptly.

"Well, no… not really." Caroline, unused to being invited to put forward a subject for conversation - how refreshing that was! - felt it might not be polite to plunge in straight away with something as serious as the trouble at Walkern. At a loss, however, to think of anything else to discuss, she began, hesitantly, "I… I should like to talk to you about a problem at…"

"Problems, no. No, no. Not good for you, whatever they are, so soon after eating."

"No, I suppose not."

"No matter, my dear, no matter. I shall use this time, while we gently partake of a little fruit… Thank you, Daniel." A large bowl of stewed pears was placed on the table. "… to acquaint you two young people with one another a bit more. Now, Caroline, let me tell you something more about Simon."

"Wouldn't it be…" She searched for the most polite word. "… easier if Mr. Warrender told me, told us, himself?"

"Ha! Ha! Well, yes, it might…" Caroline didn't think she had said something funny, "… but it would either take a very long time, and you would learn nothing of importance, *or* he would simply tell us nothing at all! Wouldn't you, my boy?"

Simon smiled shyly. "You are right, sir, that is how it would be." He turned apologetically to Caroline. "Conversation is not my forte, Mistress Newell, as the colonel well knows."

"Nor mine," Caroline said, attempting to sound truthful, "so shall we let the colonel proceed?"

"You couldn't stop him if you tried." Simon gave the colonel a broad, beaming smile, which lit up his whole face, a delicate face, liberally freckled, with sand-coloured eyebrows over light blue eyes; it was not a face that would easily withstand the cold winds of north Yorkshire or the glaring sun of the tropics.

"Tush, tush!" laughed the colonel. "He can be a cheeky young fellow at times but I am very fond of him. He is my godson, after all. Oh, I told you that, didn't I?" He leant over and patted her left hand affectionately. She could do no more than nod, her right hand being fully occupied in lifting a spoonful of sugary pears to her mouth.

"Now, Caroline, Simon loves horses."

"Oh," said Caroline, swallowing her pears quickly. The colonel was not eating; it was easy for him to talk. She couldn't do both; she put down her spoon.

"To the point of obsession, I would say." He turned to Simon. "Am I right?"

"Yes, sir. More or less."

"No less about it. Well now, Caroline's... I beg your pardon, Mistress Newell's... late husband was not only a very fine horseman, he was also a doctor to the animals, to the horses. So, you see, you two have a bond there."

What *was* Colonel Plumer doing? Trying to marry them off? Not another old man match-making! Simon was a sweet young man - how old was he? Twenty-one, possibly twenty-two. People with his colouring always looked so young, almost unformed, it was hard to tell. She did feel drawn to him, but only as she would be to a young brother.

Poor boy, he seemed a bit of a lost soul. It was time to steer the conversation on to Jane Wenham - if only she could think of some way of connecting her to horses, or Yorkshire. There was nothing for it but to get straight to the point; if she didn't the afternoon would have gone before she'd had a chance to raise the subject.

"I wondered, Colonel Plumer, if I could…"

"Oh no. No! Forgive me for interrupting, my dear, but we must do something about this *Colonel* business. There is surely something else you can call me." With no response from Caroline, he went on, "What about Uncle Plumer? Um? It's Simon's name for me."

"Yes, if you like."

"Good. That's settled. Now, to get back to Simon."

She would just have to be patient. There were still several hours of daylight left, and if she did have to travel partway back to Yardley Bury in the dark, she at least had the comfort of knowing that young Jem would be riding alongside the carriage.

"Well now, as you can see, he is not a sturdy boy. He finds Yorkshire too cold and the West Indies too hot."

Caroline looked across the table at Simon. He was making patterns with a fork on the white tablecloth; he did not look up. He has heard all this before and learned to accept it, Caroline thought.

"So…" said the colonel, rubbing his hands together, "he has to find somewhere neither too hot nor too cold."

Simon stopped his pattern-making and lifted his head. His eyes met Caroline's. What now? both pairs of eyes seemed to say, before they dropped, hurriedly.

"… and that somewhere is here, in the south of England!" the colonel concluded.

"Yes. Very suitable," Caroline murmured. Simon said nothing.

"So, my dear Caroline, I have suggested he looks for an estate either in Hertfordshire or Bedfordshire, or possibly in Essex, a place where he can breed horses… and I think *you* are just the person to advise him!"

"Me?"

"Yes. Without doubt. You have been sent to us today, I do believe, for that express purpose."

"No no, Colonel, I have not! I have come today because… Well, I wished to visit you, naturally, being in your neighbourhood; it would have been discourteous not to, but… I am also here because…" This was not going well. It was her turn to reach out her hand. "… because, Uncle Plumer…" She patted his hand. "… I have an urgent request, a favour, to ask of you."

The colonel took Caroline's hand in his. "My dear girl, ask away. But whatever it is, it surely won't prevent you from offering some helpful advice to young Simon. You know about horses and you know the countryside."

"Well, only around Amley."

"Exactly! Couldn't be better. There must be quite a number of suitable properties in that area. Near Sawbridgeworth perhaps, or Bishops Stortford, or just over the border, near Billericay, say."

"I'm sure there are." However was she going to get back to *her* problem? A horse-breeding estate could wait, Mistress Wenham could not.

"Good! Very good! I knew you'd be able to help."

Daniel placed a plate of small cakes on the table. "Ah, cakes!" He let go of Caroline's hand. "Good!" He rubbed his hands together. "Oh yes. These are very good; they have almonds in them, and cinnamon, too. You must have one, Caroline." He passed her the plate.

"Thank you," Caroline said, taking one of the small oval pastries.

"Simon, help yourself."

"Not for me, thank you, sir."

"Oh no, of course, you… er… don't care for sweet things, do you?"

"Not a lot."

"And now you, Caroline…" Can we please get away from cakes, and back to… "You have something to ask of me. What is it?"

Now that her moment had come Caroline felt ridiculously tongue-tied, especially with her mouth filled with a sticky sweetmeat.

"Is it something you don't wish to ask in front of Simon? Because if it is, he can…"

"No, not at all, it's…" She swallowed the last of the cake and wiped her mouth on her napkin. She took a deep breath and launched into the speech she had prepared the evening before. "You would do me an inestimable favour, Colonel, sorry, *Uncle* Plumer… if you were able to provide on your estate some temporary accommodation for an old woman who is…" How pompous she must be sounding. She let out the rest of her breath and took another one. Away went the well-rehearsed words. "The thing is, there's an old woman in Walkern, her name is Jane Wenham, and the people there say she's a witch, and they're taunting her, and quite frankly,

Uncle Plumer, I fear for her life." She reached for his hand again. "Can you... will you, help? It's just until she goes for trial in about a month's time. It's just so she can get some rest and not be hounded all the time. They're all doing it, the villagers and a young curate who's there, and Sir Henry's son..."

"Stop, stop! Yes, of course I will."

"Oh, thank you, thank you!" Caroline felt near to tears. She grabbed the colonel's hand and held it tight. "Oh, you are so kind."

"Dear me, you have got yourself in a state about her. Now..." Caroline smiled; it seemed to be his favourite word, and she had noticed that something positive always followed it. "You just let me know when you want her to come, and we'll make all the necessary arrangements here. Won't we, Simon?"

"Yes, of course, sir." He looked across at Caroline and gave her a shy smile.

"Thank you," she said.

"I get the feeling that, in your view, this woman is not a witch?" the colonel asked.

"No, I don't think she is, but... Well, I'm not sure that I know exactly what a witch is. If there are such people, that is."

"Um. I wouldn't want to make a pronouncement on that. There are some very strange people in this world, you know; whether some or them are witches or not, I don't know." He pondered the question for a moment. "Simon, what do you think?"

The young man looked embarrassed at being included in the discussion. "Well... I don't know quite what to say," he began. Not wanting to offend Caroline, or more particularly the colonel, in any way, but sensing that they were both waiting for an honest answer, he said, directing his words mainly at Caroline, "I have seen some strange rituals among the Negro slaves in Jamaica, some of them based on superstition and old beliefs brought over from Africa, things like Obi, which is also known as Obeah... I don't know if you have heard of it?" Caroline shook her head. "And in Haiti, which is a large island nearby, I believe they have a religion which they call Voodoo... but I cannot believe that in modern England something as... as primitive as witchcraft... is still being practised." He paused and looked down. *This* might offend the colonel, but he had to say it. "Nor that any sensible person could believe in it."

"Well said, my boy! Don't you think so, Caroline?"

Simon looked up, relief flooding his face.

"Yes, indeed." She smiled at Simon; there was more to this young man than she had given him credit for. Not hold a conversation? Far from it: he was very fluent.

"He doesn't deny the possibility of witchcraft, but thinks it unlikely that we shall find it here, in Hertfordshire." He turned to Simon. "Very well said and very diplomatic: you please us both. Now... Caroline, when shall we expect this protégé of yours?"

"Oh!" She had never thought it would be this easy. "Well... as soon as possible, I think." Now it had actually come to the moment, Caroline realised she had no definite plan. "In the next few days? If you could send word to me that you are ready for her?"

"Oh, I'm ready now. Goodness me, there are plenty of places, old cottages and barns and sheds, where she will be safe. You just send her over here, or bring her yourself if you want; not on your own, obviously, and we'll make sure your old woman... *what* is her name?"

"Jane Wenham. Mistress Wenham."

"Mistress Jane Wenham. Yes, well... we will look after her for you, won't we, Simon?"

"Oh. Yes, sir, we..."

"In fact..." began the colonel, excitedly, "here's an idea for you! Now, Simon... why don't you ride over to Walkern - tomorrow, perhaps? - and then you can help Caroline to bring the woman back here! Now... isn't that a good idea!"

"Ye-es." Simon and Caroline answered hesitatingly, in unison.

"Good! That's settled." The colonel rubbed his hands together, which Caroline now recognised as his way of showing satisfaction. "Now... why don't you two young people take a walk around the park... it looks quite pleasant out there, not too cold, not a lot of wind either... while I have a little nap. Sorry, my dear, but when you get to my age you find you can't get through the day without one. And when I've had my nap, we'll..."

"Oh, but... That's a very nice thought, Uncle Plumer, but I really should be getting back to Sir Henry's. I should like to be there before dark."

"Of course you would. How thoughtless of me. And foolish of you, my dear, if you don't mind my saying, to come all this way for so short a visit. When you come back, with your old woman, you must stay for several days. It will give you a chance to get her settled, and Simon will entertain you: you can go out riding together, talk about horses... and

235

you can advise him. Now... that *is* a splendid idea." Once again the colonel's hands were rubbed together.

What a lovely man, thought Caroline. He does so enjoy making other people happy. "That would be... very nice. Thank you. I should like that."

It would be good to get Jane Wenham properly settled, but as for spending more time with Simon... she was not sure. He seemed a nice enough young man, and his thoughts on witchcraft did concur with hers, and they did both care about horses... and he had travelled abroad... so it might be quite enjoyable, and interesting, too, to be in his company for, well, say a couple of days. It would certainly be more pleasant than the company of Arthur or Francis! The thought of them brought her down to earth. *She* would not be escorting Mistress Wenham to Gilston; that was the job of the constable. There was no reason for her to come back; the colonel would see the old woman was cared for, he had said so.

"Could you send for my maid, please, Uncle Plumer?"

While Caroline was taking luncheon in the dining hall at New Place Jem chatted to the lads in the stable yard and Mary sat in the kitchen, feeling out-of-place and embarrassed. As in Walkern, no one knew quite how to treat her: she was not a lady, but neither was she an ordinary maid. Surely the colonel's wife had a personal maid? Yes, she had, but she was away, visiting with her mistress - they made it sound so grand - and anyway, she was the cook's niece, so she was one of them. They fed her well enough, but there was only so much bread and cheese, with turnip soup and pease pudding, she could eat at one time. Mary wished Jem was with her, but he was not allowed into the kitchen. The cook could not abide the smell of horses; it made her feel quite ill, and when she travelled anywhere she had to cover every bit of her nose and throat "to keep out the infection, 'cos that's what it is for me. So if he's your young man, I'm sorry, but I can't 'ave 'im in here."

Mary blushed and denied any connection with Jem, then felt guilty for doing so, and reinstated him by saying that he was clever with horses and that her lady thought very highly of him. The maids grinned and the cook cackled, "You can't fool an old bird like me, girl, I can see you're sweet on him. Ain't you a bit too dainty for him, though?" and there was more laughter at Mary's expense. After a while, though, they left her alone, and she sat in a corner and read her book; that in itself was odd behaviour. Then Prudence, who seemed different from the others, took Mary into her room, where she sat reading while Prudence sewed, holding the material close to her eyes. After a while Mary put down her book.

"Would you like me to do that for you?" she asked, and with a deep sigh of gratitude, Prudence handed the sewing to Mary. They sat by the gently crackling fire - Mary stitching and Prudence sleeping - until a sharp rap on the door had them both sitting bolt upright. It was time for Mistress Newell's maid to attend her mistress. Mary gave the sewing back to Prudence, and on an impulse, kissed the old servant's cheek, and left the cosy room. Now she could see Jem again!

A little watery sunshine extended the afternoon light as Caroline and Mary, with Jem riding alongside the carriage, made their way back to Yardley Bury. With luck they would be home before dark. Then, just as they were approaching the great parkland surrounding the estate of Standon Lordship, some four miles from New Place, two young men on horseback, whooping and laughing, urging their mounts forward as if in a race, came charging out of the thicket on the right-hand side of the road and galloped straight across the path of Sir Henry's carriage. The startled carriage horses, neighing frantically, reared up, and shying away from the horsemen jerked the carriage so severely that it began to roll into the ditch at the side of the road. The horsemen, still laughing and yelling, seemingly oblivious of the harm they had done, had already disappeared into the woods beyond.

The two passengers, coming out of a much-needed doze after the strains and stresses of the day, cried out in alarm, Mary more intensely than her mistress, who recovered almost immediately.

"Oh, stop that squealing, Mary; we're still alive." She put her head out of the tilting window. "Heavens! How did we get *here*?"

Jem, bringing his horse to a halt the moment he had seen the horsemen, let out an oath he hoped Mistress Newell had not heard.

"I'll go after them," he said.

"No, no," said Caroline. "Don't do that. You won't catch them, and anyway, we'll need you to get that wheel out of the ditch." She climbed down from the carriage and surveyed the damage. "Samuel can't do that on his own."

Samuel, making soothing noises to his trembling horses, was slowly edging his way down from the steeply sloping box.

"No, Samuel," Caroline called up to him. "Don't try to come down. Jem will see to the wheel, and when I say, you must urge the horses forward."

"Yes, madam." Thankfully the old man clambered back on to his seat. It wouldn't do to show Mistress Newell how much he was trembling.

"Now, come on, Jem," Caroline said, "Get your shoulder behind the carriage and push. And if need be, Mary and I will help you."

"Begging your pardon, madam, but wouldn't it be better if I was to go to the house for help?"

"What house?" There was no habitation that Caroline could see.

"The big house in the park here. There must be a gate somewhere and if not I can jump over the wall."

"And get yourself shot for trespassing? Oh no! Besides Mary and I do *not* want to be left here with a broken-down carriage. We certainly would be a target for highway robbers then!"

"Oh, Miss Caroline, don't say that!"

"No, Jem, you get down in the ditch and put your strength behind that wheel."

"Yes, if that's what you want."

Caroline didn't care for Jem's tone, but she was in no position to take him to task for sounding sulky; he was not her servant and she needed his cooperation. If he were just to ride off and...

"First though, I got to put a strong piece of timber under it."

"Oh?"

"So it don't keep sliding back in the mud! It's muddy in the ditch." He still sounded aggrieved.

"Oh yes, of course." She had misjudged him; this was not going to be an easy job for one man on his own. "All right,

Jem, I'll leave it to you." She smiled at him. "I suppose we're lucky it's not a very deep ditch."

"Yes. We are," Jem said. The awkward moment was over. Caroline moved away.

"I'll help you find the wood," Mary said eagerly, hitching up her skirt and preparing to follow Jem into the thicket.

"You will not!" said Jem. "You will stay here and look after your mistress."

"Oh! Oh, all right then," said Mary, surprised… and a little bit hurt.

Caroline, who by now was at the front of the carriage stroking the horses, smiled to herself; this young man could be good for Mary.

Within minutes Jem was back with a birch log, sturdy but not too thick, to wedge under the wheel.

"All right, Samuel," he called when the log was in place. "Get them moving."

Jem heaved on the wheel while Mary pushed, rather ineffectively, on the back of the carriage and Samuel flicked the reins. Nothing moved, not an inch.

"It's no good," said Jem. "We need more strength."

"I'll push," Caroline said, coming round to the back of the carriage. "Move over, Mary."

"Mistress, you mustn't!"

"Why not?"

"Well… you'll get your dress dirty and…" She was perfectly capable of helping Jem on her own. It was the first time they had been together all day and she wasn't having her mistress there, getting in the way.

"Oh, nonsense. This is an emergency; what does a dress matter? Come on, girl, push. Jem, do you think if all three of us were to push on the back of the carriage we might do it?"

"It's worth a try," said Jem, stepping out of the ditch.

It was no good; the carriage would not budge.

"Oh dear, I am no use pushing," Caroline said, pulling herself upright and stretching her back.

"Miss Caroline, look at your shoes!"

"Oh, never mind my shoes! Samuel!" she shouted.

"Yes, madam?" came the driver's voice from atop the box.

"Get down here and help us to push."

"But... the horses? What shall I...?"

"Leave the horses. I'll see to them. You come and push."

"But..."

"Did you hear me? *Come and push!*"

"Yes, madam."

Reluctantly Samuel climbed down from the box. Although he was in his late sixties, he still had plenty of strength in his shoulders, which Caroline did not. She would be more use sitting on the box and encouraging the horses, who were by now merely fractious, where before they had been frightened.

With Samuel adding his strength at the back, Jem in the ditch levering up the wheel and Caroline encouraging the horses, the carriage began to move, but not enough to drag the wheel out of the mud.

"Mary," said Jem, wedging the log firmly under the wheel, "if you was to come down here and just hold on to the log... you don't have to push it... I think we could get her moving."

"Yes," Mary said, eagerly, scrambling into the ditch.

"Good girl," said Jem. "Here…" He took hold of both her hands and placed them on the log. "You keep them on there."

"Oh yes, I will," said Mary. She felt that same, thrilling feeling washing through her that she'd felt when they were in the spinney together. Jem's hands were pressing on hers. Oh, it was wonderful. Just the two of them, out of sight of Miss Caroline. She turned her head and looked up at him, her eyes shining.

"All right?" he asked.

Mary nodded. Oh, his eyes were so dark, so…

"Yes, that's it," he said, letting go of her hands, and almost in the same instant, climbing out of the ditch.

"But…?"

"It doesn't need two of us to hold a log," he grinned. "I'm going to push, with Samuel."

"Oh." She couldn't keep the disappointment from her voice.

"I'll hold your hands later," he whispered. "They're bound to need some warming up after all this." He turned away from her. "Come on, Samuel, let's get this old chariot moving. It's about time Sir Henry bought something more modern. It must be at least twenty years old."

"There's nothing wrong with Sir Henry's carriage," Samuel said, protectively. "Anyway, old things are best. You young people… Come on, get pushing."

"Yes, *sir*."

Even with the two men pushing and Mary's hands firmly on the log, the wheel remained stuck in the mud.

"I'll have to go down and push on the wheel," said Jem. "Samuel, you keep pushing on the back."

"I have to have a stretch first," said Samuel. "And a 'please' wouldn't hurt! I'm not being ordered around by you, gypsy boy!"

"Sorry," said Jem. This was no time to get into an argument, much as he would relish it. "Yes, we need a few minutes' rest."

"I don't need a rest, I just need a stretch!" The old man was not going to be pacified that easily.

"I do," said Jem. "I don't have your stamina, Samuel."

"No, that you don't. Hm. You don't know what hard work is, you young lads."

"Should I keep on holding the log?" Mary's voice came up to them from the ditch.

"No, you can take a rest for a couple of minutes," Jem called.

"Oh. Good. It was beginning to hurt."

"Hurt…" muttered Samuel. "Huh."

"Have you stopped pushing?" Caroline called from the box.

"Yes, mistress," Mary said, stepping out of the ditch. She walked round to the front of the carriage. "We're having a little rest. Is that all right? It's ever such hard work."

"Oh, I know," said Caroline. "But we must keep trying. We don't want to be here when it gets dark, do we?"

"No, mistress. There could be highwaymen, robbers and…"

"Nonsense, there's no highwaymen here. Give me your hand." Caroline took Mary's outstretched hand and clambered down from the box. "That's better," she said. "A little walk about for just a couple of minutes and then…" She left the sentence unfinished. "What's that noise?" Above the gentle rustle of dry leaves in the thicket and the caw of a crow sitting on a branch watching them, they heard a faint rumbling in the distance. "Horses, I think," Caroline said, after listening for a moment. "If it's those two young rapscallions coming back…" She reached for the whip in its holder by the driver's seat.

"It could be robbers, mistress!"

Caroline ignored her. "Jem! Come here."

"Madam?" Jem got up from the bank where, much to Samuel's disgust, he had been lying, stretched out, arms behind his head.

"It's those crazy horsemen coming back. Here, you take the whip and…"

"It's not them, madam," said Jem. "It's that young gentleman… well, I think it is… that gentleman at the colonel's." And as the horsemen drew nearer, "Yes, it *is* him… and one of the stable boys."

"Oh, thank goodness," Caroline said, restoring the whip to its holder. She stepped out into the middle of the road and began to wave her arms above her head. One of the horsemen, holding his whip high in the air, waved back, then, as he drew nearer, she cried out with relief, "Oh, it is! It's Simon… Mr. Warrender."

"Oh, mistress. Are you really sure it's him?" Mary had been having visions of being captured by highwaymen, and brave Jem coming to the rescue.

"Of course I am. I recognise his…" There was no need to tell her maid that Simon's pale complexion and sandy locks were unmistakable. "… his face, now that he is nearer."

Within seconds Simon had drawn his horse up by her side. "Mistress Newell!" He jumped off his mount, and took Caroline's hand in his. "Are you all right?"

"Yes, of course I am!" I am not a weakling, just because I'm a woman, you know. "… but thank you for asking." She could feel herself relaxing, letting go, knowing there was someone else here, someone who could give orders. She had never been one to sit back and let a man take charge, but now, much to her own surprise, it was exactly what she wanted. "It is so good to have you here, Simon… Mr. Warrender." She clasped her other hand over his and heaved a great sigh of relief. She found herself wanting to hug him. "I don't understand why you are here," she said, instead.

"Ah, well… Tom here…" He nodded at the stable lad, a sturdy, square-built boy with a cheeky grin and hair almost the same colour as Simon's. "… thought one of your wheels looked a bit… well, not quite as it ought to be. He spoke to your driver, and he said there was nothing wrong…"

"And no more there ain't!" Samuel spoke angrily. "I told the boy! I been driving for Sir Henry for thirty years and we never had no trouble, not in all them years. And there ain't nothing wrong now." He looked disparagingly at Tom, who, with his back turned to Simon, stuck out his tongue at Samuel, which luckily for Tom the driver did not see.

"Then why are you in the ditch?" asked Simon, equally angry.

"It weren't me, and it weren't the carriage, it were them…" He spat out the word. "… *gentlemen*, though *I* wouldn't call them that!"

"All right, Samuel, I will explain to Mr. Warrender, but not now. I think we should…" She looked to Simon to take over.

"Yes, indeed. Now…" Caroline smiled to herself at his emphatic use of the colonel's word. "With two more pairs of hands we should soon get her on the road again." He took off his cloak and hung it over the open carriage door.

With Simon in charge and everyone spurred on by his presence, the carriage wheel was soon out of the ditch.

"Time to move on," he said, retrieving his cloak.

"Dear Mr. Warrender, I can't thank you enough." Caroline leant down from the box to put her arms around his shoulders as he struggled into his cloak. There was an awkward moment as Caroline's hands became entangled with Simon's cloak. They drew apart, looked at one another, and laughed.

"I do apologise," Caroline said. She couldn't believe how embarrassed she felt.

"Not at all," said Simon. "Now… we had better get going."

"Yes, of course. The colonel will be getting worried. Please give him my best regards and thank him for sending you to… well, what turned out to be… our rescue. We must be on our way, too."

The pale sunshine had gone and the light was fading. It would be fully dark by the time they got home.

"No, no. You mistake my meaning. I am coming with you."

"Oh!"

"I could not let you travel on your own, after the experience you have had. Your maid, and the young man,

Jem... they have told me all about it. If I ever get hold of those two young rascals... well, I don't use a whip on a horse, unless it's the *only* way to make him move... but those two... It would give me great pleasure, and believe me, Mistress Newell, I am not a violent man."

"Oh, Simon. Thank you."

"Yes. Well." Her use of his first name again, or possibly the vehemence of his outburst, had embarrassed him. He turned away and called to Tom, who was happily chatting to Mary and Jem. Samuel, still chagrined, was feeding the horses with short tufts of grass he had managed to pull from the bank at the side of the road.

"Yes, sir?" said Tom, hurriedly handing his pipe to Jem. "Coming, sir." He wafted away the wreath of smoke that hung around his head. "He don't like smoking," he said to Jem.

"He's right," said Jem.

"I *know*. I'm trying not to, 'cos... well, I want to be... I'd like to be... his man, his servant."

"Tom! Where are you?"

"Here, sir," said Tom, appearing round the far side of the carriage.

"Right. Now... You ride back to Gilston, tell Colonel Plumer what has happened here, get Prudence to sort out some clean linen for me... Are you taking all this in?"

"Yes, sir."

"And then, tomorrow morning, I want you to ride over to Yardley Bury. Do you know where that is?"

"Yes, sir."

"Because..." Simon turned to Caroline. "If you will permit it, Mistress Newell, I will ask Sir Henry to find me a bed for the night. I do apologise," his face coloured, "I should have asked this first. I am so sorry." Simon hung his head; his confidence and masterfulness seemed to have deserted him.

"Of course he will." Caroline bent her head so she could look up into his eyes. "Oh, Simon, he will be so grateful to you for seeing me safely home... How could you think otherwise?"

"Thank you." He lifted his head. It was as if for the past few seconds he and Caroline had been in a small bubble of their own, unaware of anything outside it.

"Right then, Tom. You be on your way. And I will see you tomorrow morning."

"Yes, sir." Tom saluted, then gave a short bow to Caroline.

"Go on," laughed Simon. "Don't start giving yourself airs." He knew, from Prudence, what Tom had in mind, but even with his pleasant manner and ready smile the lad had a long way to go before he could become the personal servant of a gentleman.

"No, sir." Tom mounted his horse and rode away, whistling.

Jem threw the pipe into the ditch. "Come on, Mary, let's get moving." Together they walked to the front of the carriage. "Mr. Warrender, sir, what would you like us to do?"

Oh, thought Caroline irritably, the calm of her moments with Simon gone; just because there's a gentleman here everyone assumes *he* will give the orders.

Well, let him. After all, where would I be without him now? With the carriage still stuck in the ditch, that's where.

Samuel lit the carriage lantern to save stopping again and having to fumble around with the tinder box in dwindling light, then, still grumpy, he mounted his box. Caroline and Mary got back into the carriage, and with Simon and Jem riding alongside, they went on their way.

When at last they turned into Yardley Bury's long drive it was very dark, with dense cloud obscuring any light they might have had from the moon. All the more need to see the welcoming lights at the front of the house…

"That's very odd," said Caroline. "There's not a single light showing." Anxiety began to knot her stomach. She called out of the window. "Samuel, take us round to the back. Quickly, please."

14

"Bessie! Bessie!" Caroline held the trembling old servant firmly by the shoulders. "Quieten yourself down. Take a deep breath. That's it."

"I am sorry, Miss Caroline, but… It has been so horrible… and with Sir Henry… "

"Sh… sh… Not another word, until you're sitting down." Gently she steered Bessie to a chair in Sir Henry's snug.

The distraught housekeeper, alerted by the sound of horses' hooves on the cobbles of the stable yard, had met them at the back door. At the sight of Caroline Bessie had clung to her, sobbing wildly.

Jacob, who had followed Bessie out of the house, had taken her by the arm and pulled her away from Caroline. "Come now, Bessie," he said, "that's enough. Mistress Newell don't want to stand out here getting cold. I'll take Bessie to the kitchen, madam, and you and the…" He peered at Simon in what light there was from the carriage lanterns. "… the gentleman… might like to go into Sir Henry's study. I have kept a good fire in there for when… if… he returns, later tonight." At the worried query in her eyes, he added. "He is at the rectory, madam."

"Oh," said Caroline. *Nothing* here was making sense. However, first things first: she must get warm, offer some hospitality to Simon, and find some way to calm Bessie down. "Jacob, bring us some hot punch, please, to the snug. Mr. Warrender and I will take Bessie with us." Bessie was still sobbing uncontrollably. "Do you know why she is so upset?"

"Yes, madam, I do," Jacob said, "but it would better if she was to tell you."

"All right, Bessie, that's enough crying," Caroline said, once they were in the warmth of the snug. She hoped she sounded firm but not uncaring; she felt far from calm inside. "Take your time; tell us what's been going on while I've been away." She sat down beside Bessie and took the old woman's hands into hers. Then, looking up at Simon, who was standing with his back to the fire, she said, "I'm sorry about this. It's a poor introduction to Yardley Bury, coming in through the back door and having to deal with..."

Simon raised a hand in protest. "Don't give it another thought," he said. "You are here now, and so am I, and between us I am sure we can solve this problem, whatever it is."

How reassuring he sounded, and how naïve. "Thank you." She turned to Bessie. "Well, Bessie, what's this all about? Why were you in such a state just now?"

"Oh, Miss Caroline," she wailed.

"No, Bessie! Don't start again. Just tell me what's happened, *calmly* please."

Bessie sniffed. "Sorry, Miss Caroline, I don't have a handkerchief with me."

"Oh, never mind a handkerchief, just get on with it!"

"Here." Simon held out a folded linen square. "Take this."

"Oh no, sir, I couldn't. Thank you, sir, but..."

"Take it, Bessie! Thank you, Simon."

Jacob crept silently into the room and put a tray with two glasses of steaming punch on the table beside Sir Henry's chair.

"Thank you, Jacob," said Caroline.

"Mistress Newell." Jacob inclined his head to her and then to Simon. "Sir." Simon nodded his thanks and Jacob left the room.

"Now, Bessie," Caroline said, "talk to us. It *is* something you can talk about, isn't it?" A cold shiver went through Caroline. "Is it Sir Henry, Bessie? Has he been hurt?" She daren't let her mind go to any darker place. "Is that why he's not at home?"

Bessie shook her head. "No, Miss Caroline, the master's not hurt. He didn't feel well earlier, but he's all right now, Jacob says. It was what happened that upset him and…"

"For heaven's sake Bessie, *what ?"* She gripped Bessie by the shoulders. "Will you please tell me what has been going on!"

"It was the witch."

"Oh no. No." She sighed. "Go on."

"She's been at Anne again. She made her go in the river… and Anne nearly drowned… and…" Bessie began to wail. "Ohh… Oh, Miss Caroline…"

"Yes… And then what?"

"There was pins… all round poor Anne, and the witch's pincushion, that'd been full at night… it was empty in the morning. And there was the cats… scratching and yowling and making that growling noise… and their crying… it was like young children crying… and one of them… Oh, Miss Caroline… it had the face of a dead child."

"Oh, Bessie."

"And there was scratchings… under the windows and the doors and… "

"How do you know all this? Were you there?"

"No!" She paused. "Susan told me."

"Susan. D'you mean Susan *Aylott*?"

"Yes, Miss Caroline."

"Oh Bessie, you know what a trouble-maker *she* is!"

"It weren't just her saw it, there was Matthew and Thomas and Elizabeth Field… and Mr. Chauncy. He was there."

I'm sure he was, Caroline said to herself. "And Mr. Bragge, was he there, too?"

"Yes… and Mr. Strutt. They was all there, praying, and Mr. Gardiner, too."

"Who are they, these… gentlemen?" asked Simon.

"Clergymen, all of them. Mr. Gardiner is the rector of Walkern, Mr. Strutt is the vicar of Yardley, and Mr. Bragge… is the curate at Biggleswade." She made no effort to disguise her distaste for the man. "He is also Sir Henry's grandson and he is very keen on hunting down witches. He is twenty-two."

"Thank you. Just in case I should meet them."

"You'll certainly meet Mr. Bragge; he is staying here." Oh, it would be such a delight to tell Simon what she really felt about the Reverend Francis Bragge.

Caroline took a deep breath and turned back to Bessie, who was still snuffling into the handkerchief Simon had given her.

"Bessie," she said gently, "This has all happened before; why are you so upset this time?"

"Because… She was bound over again, wasn't she, the witch, and she didn't obey and Sir Henry had to go down… and that's what's made him not well. She wouldn't listen to him, she was screaming and swearing and saying she'd put spells on all of them and…"

"Where was the constable while all this was going on?"

"He *was* there, but he couldn't do nothing."

Caroline nodded. "Once a mob gets it into their heads to riot it takes more than a constable to stop them."

"They wasn't rioting, Miss Caroline." Bessie was now calm and coherent. "They was afraid, all of them. They wanted the witch out of the village; that's why Sir Henry went down. They come up here, begging him to send her to gaol… and he wrote the paper… and then he went down to the rectory and… he sort of fainted, they said… he'd eaten nothing all day… and I wanted to go down there but Jacob said I should stay here till you came back, and we was worried for you, too; it was so late and you hadn't come back and… Oh, Miss Caroline…"

"Don't start crying again, Bessie, please. The important thing is that Sir Henry is all right."

"Yes, Jacob says he is. He's staying there for the night… at the rectory. I hope he'll sleep; he does so like his own bed. Oh, Miss Caroline, he shouldn't be having all these worries at his time of life."

"I agree, Bessie; he shouldn't. And what about the… Mistress Wenham, where is she?"

"Oh, she's gone to the gaol."

"D'you mean the Cage?"

"No, Miss Caroline. The prison. In Hertford."

"Goodness! Who took her, the constable?"

"No, it was Uriah, and Thomas, Thomas Harvey; they took her in the wagon. And they had the paper. Jacob told me this, so you can know it is true… the paper Sir Henry wrote."

"To say she should go to the gaol?"

"Yes."

Caroline looked up at Simon.

"It's over now," he said quietly. "Do you think Bessie could find us some food? It is some time since we ate luncheon, and I am sure you must be…"

"Of course!" She sprang up from her seat beside Bessie. "Oh, Simon. Oh, I am so sorry." She went over to him and put her hand on his arm. "Oh, you poor boy, you must be starving! You ate practically nothing at luncheon." She turned to Bessie. "Could you get us some food?"

"Yes, Miss Caroline. What would you like?"

"Anything, Bessie. Something warming."

"Cook has some broth, I know that. I'll ask her to put something together for you and the gentleman."

Now that her histrionics were over and she had unburdened herself to Caroline, Bessie was no longer just a frightened old woman; she was once again Sir Henry's capable housekeeper.

"This is Mr. Warrender, Bessie." A little more was needed to explain the presence of this stranger in Sir Henry's snug. "He is a godson of Colonel Plumer of Gilston."

Bessie curtseyed. "Sir." Then, straightening up, she said, in her best housekeeper's voice, "If you and Mistress Newell will care to sit by the fire I will get Jacob to bring in a small table and you can have your meal in comfort."

"Thank you, Bessie. That would be very nice. "

"Yes, thank you, Bessie," echoed Caroline. "There's no need for another table, we can use this one."

"That is Sir Henry's smoking table, madam!"

"Oh. Yes, of course."

When Bessie had gone, they sat down, Simon in Sir Henry's red chair.

Caroline smiled across at him from the other side of the fireplace: Sir Henry would not be needing his red chair this evening.

"Oh," said Caroline, stretching out her feet to the fire, "it is so good to be warm and safe again, and now that I know Sir Henry is well... in his absence I hope I can be a good hostess."

"My dear Mistress Newell... there is no need to entertain me. I am just so pleased that I was able to be of service to you."

"So am I, Mr. Warrender."

Silence fell between them. Caroline drew back her legs and sat upright.

Oh, why are we being so stiff and formal, she thought. If only we could restore the closeness we had earlier, when Simon had come to my rescue. Well, we cannot return to *that*; the thought of it was... embarrassing, to say the least. But we can't sit like this until Jacob brings our food; not speaking, not looking at one another. Simon, leaning forward tensely, appeared to find his clasped hands of more interest than anything else in the room. Caroline took a deep breath.

"What became of Simon and Caroline?" she asked.

Simon's head shot up; his face was flushed.

"I am not sure that it is appropriate now." His words came out awkwardly.

"Oh, fiddlesticks to appropriate! I do so loathe that word! If it was *appropriate* when the carriage wheel was stuck in the ditch, I consider it just as appropriate now… unless it is the fact that there is no one here to chaperone us that troubles you?"

"No…" Simon began, "but…"

"You've no need to be worried, I'm years older than you, you know." Oh dear, the more I say the worse it gets, Caroline thought. Oh Jacob, please bring that food!

"I don't think you are." Simon was grinning at her.

"Of course I am. You can't be more than… twenty, at the most."

Simon laughed. "This happens all the time," he said. "It's my fair colouring, and having to keep out of the sun I haven't yet got any lines on my face."

"Are you suggesting I have?"

"No, of course not." He studied her face for a moment."You haven't."

"Well, thank you. If I did have… any lines, that is… I would cover them with a lotion… and then you certainly wouldn't be able to see them!" This was becoming a very silly conversation: only a direct question could stop it.

"So, tell me then, young Simon… how old are you? Twenty-one?" In that case, not a boy but an adult.

"Does it matter… how old I am?"

"No. No, it doesn't. I do apologise, I shouldn't have asked you, it was most…"

"Inappropriate?"

"Stop it!" She turned away from Simon's grinning face. "Oh, where is our food?"

"I am twenty-seven, Caroline."

She looked at him, amazed. He wasn't grinning any more.

"Oh, Simon, I… I…" The snug door swung open, as Jacob, followed by Dora carrying a small gate-leg table, backed into the room, with a china tureen and bowls and bread on a silver tray. "Ah," said Caroline, jumping up. "Lovely hot broth; how good it smells. Thank you, Jacob. Oh, and lovely rolls, too. Did Bessie make these, or Cook?"

"Umm… Cook, I think… madam."

"Yes, of course, I was forgetting; Bessie doesn't make the bread any more."

She dared to look at Simon. "She does make puddings, though. If you have a favourite pudding perhaps she will make it for you, or you could have one of her special ones; honey and pear, that's the one I like." She knew she was gabbling.

"Yes, that sounds… nice."

"Oh, it is. Delicious." Oh stop this, Caroline! "Let us eat," she said, in more measured tones. "Thank you, Jacob, you can leave us now. No, wait a minute."

The old servant turned back from the door. "Where is my maid?"

"She is in Bessie's room, madam."

"Oh, good. And the young lad, Jem?"

"He's gone, madam. He had to take Mr. Gardiner's horse back to the rectory."

"Yes, of course. Poor Cherry, she must be quite tired."

"He will return in the morning, madam, to give us news of Sir Henry."

"Oh, that's good."

"Is there anything else I can do for you, madam?"

"No, I don't think so. Thank you, Jacob."

Jacob turned to Simon. "Your room is ready for you, sir. If you ring for me when you wish to go up, I will show you the way."

"Thank you," said Simon.

Jacob bowed and left the room.

To begin with Caroline and Simon ate in silence; they realised, the moment they tasted Cook's mutton broth, that they were both very hungry. Their first pangs satisfied, the silence, to Caroline, began to hang heavy. He's not going to initiate a conversation, it's going to be up to me, she said to herself. What shall we talk about? What will be a safe topic? She didn't *want* a safe topic, she loved a bit of controversy, but after the faux pas she had made about Simon's age, it would be better if she chose something bland, something... Horses! That was the answer.

Safe, but interesting to both of them, and tomorrow if Simon wanted to, maybe Arthur would ride with him to Cromer, show him a bit of the local countryside, as he had shown her earlier. Arthur... Now there was a thought! And Francis, too.

Little as she wanted to see or talk to either of them, she did hope that one of them would return to the house before she retired to bed. For herself, she didn't care tuppence, but Sir Henry, a stickler for propriety - that dreadful word again! - might not be pleased to learn, as he was sure to do, that, apart from the servants, Caroline and a young man he did not know had slept alone in the house.

Perhaps, tonight, Mary should sleep on the little truckle bed that had been placed for her use in Caroline's room. She didn't like having Mary with her at night; she tended to sleep on her back, and then she snored. Tonight, though, she would have to put up with it... for Sir Henry's sake.

And so they talked about horses: horses in the New World, horses in the army - Caroline told Simon about Robert's untimely death - racing horses and Queen Anne's innovation, a major horse-racing event at a place called Ascot; rearing horses, riding horses, shoeing horses, even the different types of saddle... By the time they had more or less exhausted the topic, without touching on the subject of Simon's proposed purchase of an estate on which to breed horses - that might involve her in a way she wasn't prepared to consider just at the moment - Jacob had cleared their supper dishes and the evening had long since turned to night. She heard the long-case clock in the entrance hall chime nine, and felt that she could, without being inhospitable, beg to be excused and retire to her room. There was still no sign of Arthur or Francis.

Simon, left on his own, looked at the array of pipes on the mantelpiece and wished that he smoked: he didn't know why, but he felt disturbed. He had never met, in England at any rate, a woman quite like Caroline Newell, an attractive but forceful woman who obviously regarded him as a mere boy. And how old was *she*? It was difficult to know; it always was with women. He felt a bit in awe of her, and though they had spoken widely on the subject of horses - he had found her account of Robert Newell's experiences on the battlefield with the Duke of Marlborough both fascinating and harrowing; such cruelty to such noble animals - he hadn't felt able to bring up the question of finding an estate for himself. From Caroline's silence on this, Simon deduced that she had no wish to help him. Well, he would let it be. Perhaps, tomorrow, if Arthur Chauncy was able to go riding with him, he could bring the question up with him. *That* would be quite proper.

Simon smiled to himself: he knew exactly how Caroline… Mistress Newell… felt about the restrictions of propriety. She would like it in the New World, he felt sure; people there, freed from the conventions of the old world, spoke and acted more openly.

Mary was glad to be sleeping on the truckle bed in Miss Caroline's room; it had been a strange, at times frightening, day and she would not have wanted to be on her own tonight. There had, though, been some good bits: Jem holding her hands on the birch log, and later when they got back to Yardley Bury, wrapping his arms around her. He had pulled her into the shadow of the stable archway, and was about to kiss her - she could tell that he *was* - when young Amos appeared, and stood there, giggling at them. If he should tell William, and William told her mistress - he was quite capable of it - she would be in trouble. It had been lovely, though, the feel of those strong arms, that strong body pressing against her. Oh, she could feel it now. And there was that other feeling too, like waves washing through her. It made her want to… No she must not do *that;* Miss Caroline was only a few feet away: she must go to sleep. Tomorrow she would go to the rectory, and then… if Jem was not there, she would go to his cottage! It was only right for her to enquire after his sister; no one could object to her befriending poor Polly.

15

Despite the tumultuous day she had had Caroline slept well, and when she awoke it was past nine o'clock.. There was no sign of Mary - the truckle bed had been folded up and put away - and there was a cold ginger tisane on her bedside table. Caroline reached for her fur-lined silk wrap, which was laid across the foot of her bed, and went out on to the landing, hoping that Mary was within earshot. She called out loudly and was startled to be answered by Sir Henry's sonorous voice.

"Good morning, Caroline."

"Sir Henry!" She drew back, embarrassed to be seen by him in her wrap.

"I am glad that you slept so well," Sir Henry chuckled.

Caroline, not finding the circumstances at all amusing, called back stiffly, "Thank you. I did." Oh, what did it matter if he saw her like this; her body was far more covered than it would be in an evening gown! She leant over the landing railing. "Dear Sir Henry! How *are* you? We have all been so worried about you. Are you recovered? Did you sleep well at the rectory?"

"One question at a time, please!"

"I'm sorry, but… I want to know how you are."

"I am quite well, thank you, but no, I did not sleep well; the bed was hard and lumpy. I'll get your maid, and when you're ready come down to the snug."

"Sir Henry," Caroline called, as he was about to move away. "We have… you have a visitor…"

"Mr. Warrender, yes. I've met him," Sir Henry said. His voice was non-committal. "He is out riding, with Arthur." He turned on his heel and disappeared from her sight under the overhanging landing. I hope I have not upset him, Caroline thought, letting Simon spend the night here.

"Of course, I don't mind that he stayed the night! My dear girl. After what he did for you?" Sir Henry reached across from his red chair and patted Caroline's knee.

"Besides, he's a friend of young Will Plumer. I've known the Plumers for years. A nice lad, Simon, I thought."

"Yes, he is." Caroline was not going to be drawn.

"It'll do Arthur good to have a change of company. Take his mind off the goings-on in Walkern." He sighed. "Oh that boy, when will he grow up? Young Simon's got ten times more sense than he has. And as for my grandson… he spent the whole night in Walkern, apparently, going from house to house, praying with everyone."

"Isn't that good? The villagers must have been quite distressed."

"It's good that they have someone to lead their prayers as well as the rector, but it's the way he does it, so aggressively; I can't see how he can be giving comfort to anyone." He began to fill his pipe with tobacco from the jar on his table.

"You don't… like him very much, do you, Sir Henry?"

"No, I don't! I wish I did; he *is* my grandson, my daughter's child, I ought to like him." He tamped down the tobacco savagely. "It's his father, of course; he's to blame. He was fanatical about Dissenters; he humiliated and punished them in the most degrading fashion... I'm not going into details, they're... they're very unpleasant, and to my mind, very unchristian. And I fear Francis is trying to emulate his father, or at least show him that he can be as ruthless with witches as my son-in-law has been with Dissenters. If I had known what sort of man *he* was I would have done everything in my power to stop that marriage!" He sighed and gave a final tamp-down to his tobacco. "Well, it's too late now."

Caroline sat in silence while Sir Henry went through the ritual of lighting the pipe. She waited until he was sitting back in his chair, puffing contentedly, before she spoke.

"Would you... ?" She was unsure how to say what was in her mind.

"Go on, I'm listening," Sir Henry said, without taking the pipe from his mouth.

"I'd like... I should like to visit Mistress Wenham in Hertford Gaol. I feel I owe it to her, to make sure she is comfortable there and has all she needs. I don't expect you to approve, but..."

"My dear girl..." Sir Henry sat up and took the pipe from his mouth. "Why do you think I will disapprove?"

And if he did, she would still do what she had set her mind to, so why waste his breath - he felt so tired - raising objections.

"I don't know. I... I feel I have already caused you so much trouble, I don't want to add to it. I *would* like to see her,

I feel I *should*, but I won't go unless you… give me your permission." She bent her head; she felt nervous of his answer.

"Caroline. Look at me."

She raised her eyes.

"This is not like you. Asking permission?" Goodness, she was blushing. He would have *no* trouble, he felt, in persuading her to abandon this silly plan. Go to the gaol, indeed! What was the point?

"I have not been the easiest of guests, I know, and I am sorry, and I think it is now time for me to leave."

"Leave? You mean, go to Hertford, and not return here?"

"Yes," Caroline said, in a small voice.

"No no. I will not allow *that*! Go to Hertford, visit the old woman, if you must, and then come back here. I am not parting with you yet! You've only been here a little over a week! Once the village calms down and I have got rid of Francis, I propose to take you out, visiting. I believe you know the Cliffords; they're quite near, and they have a most unusual house. Then there's Sir Philip Boteler at Woodhall… and we can call on Colonel Plumer." He paused. "I've been looking forward to that, Caroline. Don't deny me that pleasure."

Caroline's heart sank, but she managed to muster a smile. "It all sounds delightful." What else could she say? But the Cliffords? Oh no. No! That dreadful boy, Roger, might be there, although he did spend much of his time in London, at the theatre and in the gaming rooms. And she didn't care for any member of the Boteler family she had met. It would be good, though, to see the colonel again. She would have to think up excuses not to visit the other families. "In that case, I will stay for a few days with my sister, Emilia. I expect you remember her."

"Of course I do. Lovely child."

"And then, I'll return." She tried to sound cheerful. "And we can enjoy ourselves. I should certainly like another visit to Gilston." She hoped he would take the hint that the other visits were *not* pleasing to her.

"Splendid. I shall write to my neighbours and arrange to visit them."

"Ah… Shouldn't you wait, Sir Henry, until I do return? To see what the weather is like? It is, after all, still winter… and we might yet have snow."

"You're being very cautious. That, too, is not like you."

"I'm thinking of you, Sir Henry. I know that if you have made an arrangement to visit someone, such as Colonel Plumer, for instance, you will be loathe to let him down by not turning up, whatever the weather and however tired you might be feeling that day." She was making it up, desperately, as she went along, but it began to sound so plausible that by the time she got to the end of her speech she almost believed it herself.

"Oh, very well then. I will wait till you return. But don't make it too long. I shall miss you, you know. I'm very fond of you, Caroline, very fond." He stretched out a hand to her.

"And I of you." Caroline reached out with her hand until it met the old man's. "I must go and look for my maid, so she can begin packing." She got up from her chair and moved quickly to the door.

"Packing? But you're coming back, you promised."

Caroline, her hand on the door handle, turned round. "I shall need to take a few things with me, and so will Mary."

"Yes, of course. Of course." He drew on his pipe.

Caroline turned back to the door.

"Just a minute," Sir Henry said. Caroline paused, her hand about to reach for the handle again. "How are you proposing to *get* to Hertford?"

"Oh… I thought, perhaps I could have the use of your carriage again?"

"For several days? What if I am called on to go somewhere urgently? Why do you not ride, it's how you came here." His voice was sharp.

The old man was upset, annoyed. Did he think she would *not* return to Yardley Bury, despite what she had said? A shrewd man, accustomed to hearing untruths in court, he had seen through her dissembling. She would not hurt him for the world, but neither would she agree to anything that was unacceptable to *her*; she would not have Roger Clifford, or anyone else she didn't wish to see, knowing her whereabouts. A man in a position of authority, Sir Henry was unaccustomed to having his wishes thwarted by a woman. His dear Elizabeth had loved him deeply, but she had never challenged his word. It wasn't that Sir Henry was hard-hearted or cruel: a woman with a mind of her own was new to him and he was finding it hard to know how to respond. He would certainly not give in to her. She would have to find a way round their difficulty, without offending him or going against her own wishes. As Lydia was fond of saying, "Subtlety is what we women use, to get our own way: men do not understand subtlety."

Well wrapped up against the cold, and with her hands encased in a warm fur muff, Caroline took herself and her problem for a tramp across the fields. By the time she had walked to Walkern Church and back again she had solved it.

16

The sun was shining and the air was still when Caroline and Simon set out to ride to Hertford the next morning.

It was Simon's expressed desire to visit the county town and to see Sir Henry's splendid residence, Lombard House, that had decided the issue. Caroline would stay with her sister, and Simon, if he so wished, could make use of Lombard House - there was always somebody there, caring for it, when Sir Henry was away. As for trusting Caroline to Simon… he had already proved himself in Sir Henry's eyes by bringing her safely back to Yardley Bury after that *terrible* experience on the road. Caroline did not disillusion him. If he wanted to think she had been in mortal danger, as a mere woman could be in such circumstances, well, she would let him; it served her purpose now, and Simon, she noticed with amusement, made no attempt to underplay his part in the 'drama'. They would be away for only a day or so, and Emilia's maid could attend to Caroline.

Mary, meanwhile, was to be entrusted to the care of Bessie, even to the point of sleeping in the housekeeper's bedchamber, an arrangement that pleased Mary greatly; unbeknown to Caroline, she had already spent several nights with her.

Mary did not like sleeping alone in that big, old house with its creaky floorboards and rattling windows, nor, however, did she enjoy sleeping on that lumpy truckle bed in her mistress's room. She was to be allowed to go to the rectory each day to help Mrs. Gardiner with her sewing, but she was under strict instructions to return to Yardley Bury before nightfall. If she was not back in Bessie's care by sunset, Jacob was to fetch her in Sir Henry's cart, and she would not be allowed to visit the rectory the next day! Although Caroline trusted Mary, she had seen the glint in her eye at the thought of spending a whole day, even two perhaps, at the rectory: the chances that Jem would be there, on at least one day, were high. Mary had been made to promise that she would behave herself at all times as the personal maid of a lady *should* behave… "and you know what I mean," Caroline had said to her, just as she and Simon were about to leave. Mary had nodded and curtseyed.

"Yes, Miss Caroline, I do."

"I don't wish to intrude, but may I ask what that was about?" said Simon, when they were out of earshot.

Caroline laughed. "She has found herself a sweetheart in the village."

"Oh!"

"A nice young man, very good with horses, I'm told. You've met him. Jem."

"Ah yes, Jem. The gypsy lad."

"Yes. Not that I mind about that, but…"

"You don't want your maid to get too fond of him?"

"No, I don't. Jem's a good lad, but… she's still very young. Besides, I don't want to lose her."

Chatting amiably, they rode at a leisurely pace until they were well clear of Yardley Bury. With the bowl of blue sky above and just a light breeze it felt almost spring-like, but it wasn't long before Caroline became aware of very dark clouds assembling to the northeast; they could soon be engulfed in heavy rain.

"Time for a change of pace!" she said. Simon nodded. With the gentlest tap of their crops they urged their horses into a gallop. Riding hard, and due south, they managed to stay ahead of the rain. On the outskirts of Hertford they slowed their horses to a walking pace.

"We managed that well."

They were the first words Simon had spoken since they began to ride at speed.

Caroline had been relieved that he hadn't wanted to talk. It had given her time to sort out her thoughts, mainly about Mary: was she right to leave her in Bessie's care? As far as Caroline could recall the girl had never been away from her since the day she had become her personal maid. It would probably do her good; it would certainly be a test of her character. Simon's commenting on Jem being a gypsy brought home to Caroline the need, before too long, to tell Mary about her true parentage. Robert, possibly because he was ashamed of his brother's friend, had been against any disclosure, but Mary had been a child then: she was now a young adult, and it was right that she should know who she was, especially if she wanted to marry. Not just yet, though. Heaven forbid! She felt sure Jem was an honourable young man - something told her he was - but she knew how easily passion and need could overtake conscience… and common sense.

Oh, why had she been so set on seeing Jane Wenham? What good could she do her, now? She had come back from that walk with a clear plan in her head, and nothing, and no one, was going to stop her from carrying it out. She hadn't asked Sir Henry, she had told him! So much for subtlety! *And* she had told Simon! How 'improper' was that! Well, there was no point in going over it now; here they were, on the road.

She looked across at her companion, at his calm face, his relaxed yet upright body, his oneness with his mount - he was a very good rider - and smiled. Sensing her eyes on him, Simon turned his head and smiled back. Neither of them felt the need for words; it was… it was soothing, thought Caroline. With all the turmoil that had been going on in the past week and a half, it was good to be with someone who made her feel calm.

It was midday when they rode into Bull Plain, Caroline leading the way. The front doors of the houses on either side opened directly on to the street. They dismounted outside Emilia's house, and Simon held the reins of both horses, while Caroline, straightening her skirt, plucking off her hat and brushing back stray strands of hair from her face, went to the door. She lifted the heavy brass knocker and banged it down hard three times.

"All right! I'm coming. There's no need to make such a noise!" The voice was male, deep and strong. The green painted door was opened by a tall, sharp-featured man, dressed sombrely in black.

Richard Oliver stared with amazement, which soon turned to delight.

"Caroline! What…? This is…"

"It's not like you, Richard, to be lost for words."

"It is not every day you find your sister-in-law standing on your doorstep, and most certainly not when you thought her to be some good ten miles away in the north of the county."

"That's more like it!" If Richard could use ten words where one sufficed, he would. "Well, are you going to invite us in?" She laughed. "Or are we to stand in the street all day?"

"Oh, I do beg your pardon, Caroline. At the unexpected sight of you my wits seem to have left me, and…"

"Yes! Well, get them back quickly, please!" She turned round to Simon, who was standing quietly, seemingly unruffled by the conversation at the Olivers' door. "Richard, may I introduce you to Simon Warrender. He has kindly ridden with me from Yardley Bury, and he will be staying at Lombard House." She indicated with her right hand, to Simon rather than Richard, the large, elegant residence facing on to the far end of the street. "Simon, this is my brother-in-law, Richard Oliver."

"Mr. Oliver." Simon stepped forward, gave the briefest of bows, and took Richard's outstretched hand.

"Welcome," Richard said, placing his other hand over Simon's in such a way that any attempt to withdraw it might appear rude.

"Thank you, sir." Simon bowed again, uncertainly, his slim fingers still held fast in Richard's huge hand. He felt in awe of this tall, imposing man with the booming voice. Caroline had in no way prepared him for such an encounter - all he knew of Mr. Oliver was that he was a scrivener - and he had no idea what to say or do next. He need not have worried: Richard spoke again, immediately.

"No bows and no 'sirs' in this house, young man!" He gave Simon's hand a final pat, then released it completely. "Come in! Come in!"

"But... the horses?" Simon ventured.

"Oh... Just tie them up there." Richard pointed to a post near the door. "I will send my groom to attend to them. He will give them a good rub down... I see they have some mud on their hocks... and some food and water." He took a step towards Simon's horse. "That is a very good animal you have there. It would appear to be from Arabian stock, unless I am much mistaken. The horses we are currently breeding from Arabian stock are proving to be..."

"Richard, we are getting cold! You and Simon can talk about breeds of horses later. Right now I wish to see my sister, and if you are not going to take me to her, I'll go myself!" and she stepped into the house.

"Caroline, wait!" Richard grabbed hold of her arm.

"What is it?" Caroline asked anxiously.

"Let me prepare her."

"Prepare her! To see *me*?"

"Yes, she is... she has not been well."

"Since when? She was perfectly all right at Christmas. Richard, what it is?"

"She is... she is with child again."

"Oh, Richard, how... wonderful!"

"Yes, it is." He sounded uncertain.

"Why did she not send word to me? She must have known when I was at Bengeo."

"She... she did not want to... to tempt fate by telling anyone too soon. I have known for only a few days. She is very fearful, Caroline."

"Yes, she would be." Emilia had lost two babies since the birth of Edwin three years ago.

"I do not wish her to be startled in any way, and the sudden, unexpected sight of you, though of course entirely delightful…"

"… might, you fear, bring on another miscarriage." Over the years Caroline had become accustomed to finishing Richard's sentences, just to get to the point of what he was saying.

Richard nodded. "Yes, so I think that if I were to…"

"Go and tell her, and we will wait here."

"I shall not be a moment. I shall just make sure that…"

"Go!"

Richard remained where he was. "I appreciate that it may seem ridiculous to you, her own sister, that I should feel it necessary to…"

"Oh, Richard! For pity's sake, go!" She took hold of his arm and pushed him forward, towards the staircase.

"… take such precautions, but I would not do it unless I felt…" His voice trailed off as he disappeared around a bend in the stairs.

Caroline let out a deep breath. She turned to Simon, still outside with the horses.

"Oh dear, he does talk, my brother-in-law, but don't let it put you off. He is a kind and generous man, a good husband and a good father."

Simon smiled. "Yes, I'm sure he is." He tied both horses' reins to the wooden post.

"Do you have any family? I mean, sisters or brothers?" Caroline asked, from the doorway.

"No, none," he said, following Caroline into the hallway of the Olivers' house.

"Then this will be quite an experience for you! You had better brace yourself."

As if to underline Caroline's words, there came a burst of squealing and shouting from the floor above and three young children, two boys and a girl, hurtled down the stairs, one of the boys by way of the banister rail, from which he jumped deftly into the arms of Caroline, standing laughing at the foot of the stairs.

"Charlie!" she exclaimed. "You little monkey!"

"Aunty Cara! Aunty Cara!" the boy yelled, hugging her tightly, his legs around her waist. Oh, it was so lovely to have a child in her arms again. Turning her head she grinned at Simon. He smiled back, looking, he hoped, more confident than he felt.

Seconds later there were two more excited children tugging at Caroline's skirts.

"Me! Me! Lift me up!" It was the little girl.

"Anne, you are too old to be lifted up."

"I'm not, I'm not! I am not eight yet. When you are eight you are too old to be lifted up, but not when you are seven and three quarters. I have another three months to go before I am too old to be lifted up!"

Goodness, had this child inherited her father's verbosity? It was to be hoped not.

"All right. Stop! You shall all have a lift up in time. Yes, you too, Edwin." She rumpled the curls of the little boy gazing up at her with big round eyes, eyes so like Hannah's it made her heart miss a beat. "But right now," she said firmly, disentangling herself from Charlie's grasp, "I want to see your mother."

Emilia Oliver, five years younger than her sister, stood at the top of the staircase; her face, though radiant, was tear-stained. She was no longer the fresh-faced girl Lady Lydia had introduced to the newly appointed Hertford scrivener, young Mr. Oliver, then only twenty-four. That had been nine years ago, and now Emilia was a careworn mother.

"Millie, what is it?" Caroline asked, putting the children from her and running up the stairs. She took Emilia's outstretched hands in hers, then let them go to clasp her sister in her arms.

"Oh, Cara, it is just so lovely to see you." Emilia sobbed on to Caroline's shoulder.

"But… I've only been gone from you a week!"

"No, you were at Lydia's for a month." It was said with some pique.

"Yes, but I came to visit you during that month."

"Once." Emilia hadn't wanted to part with Caroline after Christmas, especially not for her to be visiting Lydia, in her lovely modern house, which Emilia so envied.

"Well, I'm here now." She kissed Emila's cheek. "And… I hear you have good news," she said cheerily. She was not about to echo Richard's fears.

"Is it… good news?"

"Another baby! Of course it's good news."

"If I can keep it."

The radiance gone, Caroline could see how grey and drawn her sister's face was.

"Oh, my dearest, you mustn't think like that. This time you will; I'm sure of it." Caroline hugged her close. "Come," she said, taking her hand, "I want you to meet someone." Carefully, walking backwards in front of her, Caroline helped Emilia down the stairs, step by step.

"That is not the most sensible way to walk down the stairs, Caroline. You are setting the children a bad example."

In the presence of a stranger Richard was trying to keep his tone light, but Caroline knew he was displeased.

"A few tumbles won't hurt them," Caroline said, without looking round, "but it might hurt your wife." Still keeping hold of her sister, she turned: they were almost at the bottom of the stairs. "Simon," she said, reaching out her other hand to him, "This is my dear sister, Emilia."

"Madam," said Simon, bowing. Mr. Oliver might disapprove of his action, but Simon would rather the lady of the house thought him courteous than rude. He obviously pleased her: a smile spread across her face.

"Emilia dear, this is my friend Simon… Mr. Warrender, who has so kindly ridden with me from Yardley Bury."

"Mr. Warrender, welcome to our home." Emilia, now safely down the stairs, extended her hand to Simon.

"Mrs. Oliver," he said, and bowed again.

"No bowing, please! We do not encourage it in this house." One bow Richard could ignore, but not a second one.

"I apologise, sir," said Simon, very nearly bowing again, but managing to stop himself just in time.

"You have nothing to apologise for," Caroline said. "Insisting on someone *not* bowing is as bad as insisting that they do!"

"No, Caroline, that is not the case. The act, or action, of bowing by one person to another indicates that the person performing the action is considering himself to be inferior, and I feel sure that Mr. Warrender is not, in any way, an inferior person. There is, in my view - stop tugging at my sleeve, Edwin, I am speaking! - only one person in this realm to whom…"

"Oh Richard, please! Spare us one of your lectures. Come to me, Edwin." She scooped up the little boy into her arms.

"I was about to say that the Queen…"

"My dear brother-in-law. I admire your egalitarian views, as you know, but at this moment Simon and I are in need of food and a fireplace. When we are fed and warm you may talk to us on any subject you choose… and we promise to listen. Don't we, Simon?"

"Er… yes." He had never in all his travels come across a woman like Caroline; lively and intelligent, she spoke her mind without fear and appeared to have little time for the respect due to the head of the household, as he had been brought up to have. And the man's wife… she just smiled, seemingly enjoying everything, not at all troubled by the way her sister spoke to her husband. If this was the way English society was going, he would have to adapt to it. Somehow, he didn't think it was: there was an air of the Dissenter about Richard. Perhaps they would speak about it later. No, not they… He, Mr. Oliver, would speak. Simon would not proffer any views. He felt he must be careful about what he said: Colonel Plumer, though quite happy to employ a Puritan servant woman - dissenting was, in his view, acceptable for the lower orders - believed strongly that the ruling classes must attend and support the Church of England, and nothing else. As for Roman Catholics, the very words terrified the colonel.

Caroline turned to the two older children, who had been standing quietly, listening to the grown-ups. Did Father not like this new man? Should they speak to him or not?

"Anne, Charlie, come here to me," she said, squatting down so that she was on their level, and putting her free arm protectively around them. "This nice man…" She had seen the puzzlement and doubt on their faces. "… who has been very kind to your Aunty Cara, is called Mr. Warrender. Can you say that?"

"Mis-ter Warren-der," they chanted in unison, with Edwin, snuggling into her neck, getting no further than "Mis-ter, mis-ter".

"Good! Well now, Mr. Warrender is Aunty Cara's friend, and we are nice to friends, aren't we?" The children nodded. "So you must be nice to Mr. Warrender." The children looked solemnly from their aunt to her new friend. Under the scrutiny of their three pairs of eyes, to say nothing of the eyes of their parents, Simon managed to produce a nervous smile: he hoped it was the right response.

"I will, Aunty Cara," said Anne, reassured by Simon's smile, "and I will see to it that my brothers are."

"Good girl," said Caroline. "Run along and play now, or…" She looked to Richard for guidance. "… whatever you should be doing at this time of day."

"You may play," Richard said benignly, "but there must be no noise."

"Thank you, Father," said Anne.

"What are *you* going to do, Aunty Cara?" asked Charlie.

"That, Charles, is not your concern," his father said.

Far less biddable than his sister, Charlie wanted an answer from Caroline, and he wasn't going to leave until he had one.

"I am going to talk to your mother and your father, and to Mr. Warrender, and if you are very good I will talk to you, and Anne, later. Come on Edwin, time to get down. Anne, take his hand." Obediently Edwin climbed down from his cosy perch on Caroline's shoulder, which his dribbling had made decidedly wet.

"Oh, Edwin, look what you've done!" Emilia crossed the floor and began to wipe the dampness from her sister's cloak.

"It's nothing," said Caroline, easing herself up from her squatting position. "Go on, children, off you go."

The children dutifully trotted off to another part of the house.

"Oh, Cara, you are so good with them," Emilia said. "It is such a pity…" She stopped herself. "Oh my dear, I am so sorry. What a thoughtless thing to say!"

Simon, still standing awkwardly at the foot of the stairs, looked embarrassed and perplexed. Caroline put a hand on his arm.

"I had a little girl. She died," she said, simply.

"Oh. I'm sorry." Before Simon could say any more Caroline had turned away and was addressing Richard in a jaunty tone. "Dear brother, may we now avail ourselves of a modicum of your hospitality and prevail upon you to provide us with some sustenance in the form of a small but nourishing meal? Preferably by a warm fireside, if that can be arranged without too much inconvenience."

"With pleasure, dear sister," replied Richard, totally unaware that he was being teased.

"Oh Cara, you are so naughty!" Emilia laughed and took her sister's arm. "Richard, take Caroline and Mr. Warrender into the parlour. There's a good fire in there. I will go and see the cook about some food."

Mary was not going to waste one minute of her freedom: no frills to gopher, no stockings to mend, no collars to wash, for three days! It was a strange feeling, though, knowing that her mistress was not here, that, within reason, and so long as she abided by the conditions laid down by Miss Caroline, she was free to go wherever she pleased... and see whoever she wanted to see!

She ran upstairs to Caroline's room, lifted the sewing box from the chest of drawers, wrapped the fashion doll in a length of silk, put the bundle into a brown sacking bag, grabbed her cloak from its hook in her own small room, and within five minutes of her mistress' departure she was on her way to the rectory, slipping quietly out of the back door before Bessie could give her yet another lecture on the need to obey Caroline's rules.

"You put one foot wrong, my girl, and you'll be sorry!" Mary's silk dresses and fancy speech cut no ice with Bessie: Mary was a child in her eyes, and she would treat her as such. "D'you hear me?"

"Yes, Bessie," Mary had replied meekly.

"Mistress Sawyer, if you please!" If this pert little lady's maid failed to behave herself while her mistress was away it was not going to be because of any lack of diligence on Bessie's part! What was Miss Caroline thinking of, going off on horseback, without her personal maid, *and* with a gentleman she barely knew! She had certainly gone down in

Bessie's estimation, and why Sir Henry had allowed her to go, she couldn't for the life of her understand; the old man was not well and Miss Caroline had taken advantage of him. It was most unfair. Going to Hertford just so she could see the witch? Just because she hadn't been in Walkern to hold the old woman's hand when she got taken off to gaol! Her brain must be addled! She'd always had some odd ideas, had Miss Caroline. She remembered a book with a picture of a sad child in it; young Miss Caroline, not more than six years old, had insisted that the book was left open, not closed and shut away on a shelf, so that the child in the picture could see. By the next day, she had forgotten about the picture and was on to something else, thank goodness, or who knows where this might have led: books left open all over the house probably.

Oh well, she would be back the day after tomorrow, and meanwhile... Meanwhile, Bessie thought, she would have a word with the cook about preparing some really nice food for Sir Henry: he could do with feeding up. In fact she might take over the cooking for a couple of days, make some of the master's favourite dishes, spoil him a bit. Poor man, it can't have been easy for him this past week, what with the witch causing trouble, and Miss Caroline here, and that hoity-toity grandson, too. There would be no special dishes for *him*!

Mary slowed her steps as she approached the rectory: she mustn't appear too eager, and she must *not* enquire about Jem. That was going to be so hard; she must just hope he was there.

In the rectory kitchen Mrs. Gardiner, in a sombre grey dress and shawl, was laying out on the big deal table the sewing she wanted Mary to do: two sheets to be patched, a frayed lace collar, a torn skirt, several pairs of hose in need of darning.

"Oh," Mary said, disappointed. "I thought we…" She hesitated to tell Mrs. Gardiner what her expectations had been; perhaps this dull, plain sewing had been Miss Caroline's idea.

"You thought you'd just sit about like a lady, did you, doing nothing?" Mrs. Gardiner's aggrieved tone surprised Mary: they both knew she was there to sew.

"No, but… I thought we were going to do some interesting sewing… perhaps making you a gown. I've brought the fashion doll." She reached into her bag and brought out the silk-wrapped mannequin.

"Oh!" Mrs. Gardiner's tone brightened instantly. "Yes. Oh yes, please." Her beaming face clouded over. "If you are sure Mistress Newell would not mind? She had intended you to…"

"I am sure she would not mind," Mary said. If she did it was too bad; she wasn't here, and Mary was, and she was not going to spend her time mending sheets! A lady's maid did not mend household linen. "Do you have the fabric for making a dress?" she asked.

"I do," said Mrs. Gardiner. "I have some… blue taffeta." Her eyes shone at the thought of wearing a gown of blue taffeta cut and stitched in the latest style.

"Blue taffeta?"

"Oh, is that not suitable?" Anxiety clouded Mrs. Gardiner's face. She had had the fabric for over a year; it had been an, uncharacteristically, impulsive purchase the last time she had visited Hertford, but once back in Walkern she had never dared have it made into a gown. She had shown the material to no one, with the exception of Susan Aylott, in a rash moment, on the summer day she had returned home with it. She had not shown the fabric to Mr. Gardiner.

"It is very suitable," Mary said. "If you give me a small piece of the fabric, I will make a tiny gown, in the style you choose, for the doll, and then later we can sew the full-sized dress." There was no reason for Mrs. Gardiner to know that the designs Mary had sketched were taken directly from her mistress's gowns: it was most unlikely that the two ladies would appear together wearing them. In fact, she doubted whether the rector's wife would ever have an occasion to don the frilly concoction that Mary was sure she would choose from the designs she now laid out on the table.

"Oh, they are lovely." She looked up at Mary. "You *are* a clever girl!"

"Thank you, madam." She gave Mrs. Gardiner a polite smile. This was not the moment to tell the lady that she could also sing and, after a fashion, play the spinet: they might end up drinking tea together! The sooner they started the sewing the sooner she might be able to see Jem.

By the end of the afternoon, Mary had completed the miniature taffeta gown for the fashion doll; she had also cut out and begun to put together the skirt of Mrs. Gardiner's new dress. She had not seen Jem. Nor had she seen Margaret Gilbert, watching her through the kitchen window.

17

At the mention of Sir Henry Chauncy's name Caroline and Simon were admitted into the courtyard of Hertford Gaol.

"We have come to see Mistress Wenham of Walkern," Caroline said, as the wrought iron gates clanged shut behind her.

"The witch?" The gaoler, a stocky man with heavy shoulders and the ears and nose of a prize-fighter, was scornful. "Yes, she's here. A lot of fuss she's been making too, shouting and swearing."

"Oh dear. Nevertheless, I should be grateful if you would show me to her cell... or wherever she is being kept." She smiled at the gaoler.

"You want to see her?"

"Yes! I've just said that! Well... *may* I see her?" The man was no doubt only doing his duty, but Caroline was finding it hard to remain pleasant.

"Yes, if you want. It's just... well, ladies, likes of you, don't normally come to see prisoners, not likes of her anyway."

"I know that," Caroline said patiently, "but I do wish to see her."

"All right, madam... if you say. It's this way."

The gaoler led Caroline, with Simon following, across a courtyard and down a flight of shallow stone steps.

The crisp, wintry air outside had been invigorating and Caroline and Simon had enjoyed the short walk from Bull Plain, but here, inside the building - so different from the entrance with its ornate gates and pillars topped with statues - the air was damp and chilling and the only light came from tiny windows high up in the bleak stone walls. Caroline shivered and pulled her flowing brown cloak tightly around her body.

The gaoler, none too pleased to have his daily routine interrupted, halted outside one of the oak doors that lined the passage.

"She's in here," he said peremptorily. Taking a key from a bunch at his waist, he unlocked the heavy door and pushed it inwards. In the dim light coming through a small barred window, Caroline saw three women, two of them sitting, one lying down, on thin pallets ranged round the sides of the cell, the floor of which was covered with none too clean straw. How ironic, thought Caroline: all this straw, here for the taking... and Mistress Wenham can make no use of it.

Absorbed in their own thoughts or simply in despair at their plight, the women did not look up when the gaoler entered.

"Jane Wenham," the gaoler shouted, and from a pallet at the far end of the room, a head was raised.

"What you want?"

"You got a visitor."

"Who? The Queen?" she cackled. With the light behind Caroline, the woman was unable to distinguish her features. "Not one of them parsons? I'm not saying that prayer no more, not for no one!"

"It's not them, Mistress Wenham." Caroline, loathe to enter the vile-smelling room, yet feeling she should, stood in the doorway.

"Who are *you*?"

"It's a lady, come from Sir Henry Chauncy, so mind your manners, woman," the gaoler said.

"You found something else I done wrong, 'ave you?"

"No, Mistress Wenham, I have come to see if there is anything you want or anything I can do for you, and to tell you…" No, this was not the place to reveal her chief reason for being here.

"There's nothing *you* can do for me; I don't want you. Go away." The woman spat on the floor and turned her back.

Caroline's heart sank: had she made a big mistake coming to the gaol, coming to Hertford at all? No, whatever happened *here*, it was good that she had arrived just when Emilia needed her.

"Just watch your tongue, speaking to a lady like that!" The gaoler might not want Caroline here, but he felt sure this conversation would get back to Sir Henry, and he did not intend to come out of it in a bad light. This wasn't a difficult or dangerous job, not like in the London prison he'd once worked in, where his skill as a pugilist had come in handy, and here he had decent accommodation provided across the street from the gaol.

"Well, you've seen her now, madam," the gaoler said firmly, beginning to pull the door shut, "and there's nothing you can do for her." So you may as well leave, his tone implied.

"I wonder…" asked Caroline, politely - there was no point in antagonising the man - "… do you have a private

288

room where I could speak to Mistress Wenham on her own?" Her voice was warm, but commanding.

This was too much for the gaoler. "You're not from the court! You can't talk to my prisoners on their own!" He was shouting, angry.

"Please don't speak to Mistress Newell like that." It was the first time Simon had spoken since they had entered the gaol.

The gaoler looked at him sourly.

"I am sure Sir Henry Chauncy would wish you to grant the lady's request."

Caroline, although always ready to fight her own battles, was grateful to Simon for his intervention - yet again, she thought.

The implication of what might happen if the gaoler remained uncooperative worked like magic.

"Yes, well... if Sir Henry thinks it's all right... to talk to the woman... then I s'pose you better do it." The man shrugged his shoulders. "You can go in my room, but you're not to be long." He was still in charge here, and any visitors, however genteel they were, should know it. He locked the door of the cell. "Follow me," he said gruffly, moving away.

"But...?" Caroline began, gesturing towards the door.

"My turnkey will fetch her."

He led Caroline and Simon up the stairs, across the open courtyard and into a small room to the right of the main entrance.

"Wait here," he said, adding "please" as a surly afterthought.

"What a rude fellow." Simon coloured with anger. "I've a good mind to..."

"What, give him a thrashing?" She raised her eyebrows at him.

"No, of course not, but…"

"He is in charge here, Simon, and he feels we are undermining his authority, which, when you think about it, we are. Coming here, without any formal request, not even a note from Sir Henry, asking to see a prisoner! In his circumstances I think *I* would have refused. Be nice to him when he comes back."

She reached out and touched his sleeve.

"I'll try," he said.

Caroline withdrew her hand.

The room was considerably brighter than the cell downstairs. A pegged rug covered part of the stone floor and logs crackled cheerily in a small brick fireplace. There were two upright chairs on either side of a deal table; Simon pulled one out and Caroline sat down.

"He looks after himself well enough." Simon nodded towards the high-backed wooden armchair by the fire: a big, grey and white striped cat was curled up, fast asleep, on a knitted cushion.

"For the rats, probably," Caroline said. "They get them in places like this, don't they? So I've been told."

"Yes."

"As for the room… I expect he needs a bit of comfort. It must be a terrible life, spending your days in a place like this."

"According to your brother-in-law, it's a lot better than the old gaol. This one's only been up ten years, he says."

"Sh. She's here," whispered Caroline.

Jane Wenham, her hands tied behind her back, was pushed into the room by a spotty-faced young lad in worn breeches and a grubby coat. The prisoner was dressed, as far as Caroline could make out, in the same dull black clothes she had been wearing at the rectory before her arrest. After the foul odour of the cell, to Caroline's relief, the smell emanating from the old woman was, surprisingly, not unpleasant; there was a scent about her of dried grass and wild herbs.

"Mistress Wenham, it's good to see you," Caroline said, and without thinking she held out her hand to the old woman.

"Is it? You want to have a gawp at me, do you, all on your own?"

"No, Mistress Wenham I have not come to… gawp… at you. Please sit down. Simon?"

Interpreting her look, Simon drew out the other chair. The woman hesitated, but the turnkey nodded at her and she sat down awkwardly, unable to straighten her skirt or her cloak because of her bound hands.

Caroline smiled at the boy. "Thank you," she said. Nodding at Jane Wenham she asked, "Could you… untie her hands? It would be easier for her to sit."

"No," the boy said. The idea seemed to alarm him, as if just being in the same room with the witch wasn't scary enough. With her hands free who knew what she might be able to do.

"It wouldn't be allowed, Caroline," Simon whispered.

"Oh. No. Well, never mind." She turned to the boy. "You may leave us now," she said.

"C-can't do that," the boy stuttered. "I g-got to stay with 'er. M-master said."

Caroline looked up at Simon; she looked set to argue.

"Better than nothing," he said. Instinctively he felt that compromise was not a word Caroline liked; he hoped that on this occasion she would see that it was the best course to take.

For what seemed to Simon a long moment, she was silent.

"Yes," she said at last. She turned to the boy. "All right, you can stay. Now, Mistress Wenham…"

"I don't want *him* here." She nodded at Simon. "'Nother parson, is he? "

"No, he is not a clergyman. He is a friend of mine, and I wish him to stay."

The woman was not appeased; she glared at Caroline. Caroline smiled back at her.

"We have some good news for you, Mistress Wenham," she said.

"Good news! What good news could *you* bring *me*?" She sounded both sarcastic and resigned.

Caroline's shoulders drooped; this was not the reaction she had expected.

"Do you want me to…?" Simon queried.

Caroline nodded. Somehow she had got on the wrong side of the old woman and she felt strangely inadequate. If the news came from Simon, whom Jane Wenham had never met before, she might receive it better.

Simon gave a quick glance at the boy; he seemed not to be listening, lolling against the wall and picking his nose vigorously. It was doubtful, anyway, if he would understand fully what Simon was about to say.

"Mistress Wenham." He leant over her chair, resting one hand on the back rail. "My uncle…" He looked at Caroline for approval of his use of the term; she nodded. "My uncle, who lives at…" The turnkey might have more about him than Simon gave him credit for. "… has an estate on which there is a cottage where you can live in safety… and we will take you there."

The old woman turned her head and looked at Simon, and in her rheumy old eyes Simon could see how pitiful and naïve his short speech had been. The woman could go nowhere until after her trial, and then the only likely place would be the scaffold.

"You will not hang, Mistress Wenham." Caroline leant forward in her chair.

The woman laughed. "What, you the judge now, are you?"

"No, of course not, but…"

"I signed a paper, din't I? You was there! I told them. Said I was a witch."

The turnkey stopped picking at his nose, and trembling, drew himself as far away from the woman as he could. To hear the word from her own mouth!

"What you think they goin' do? " In a mock genteel voice, "Oh, sorry, Mistress Wenham, we made a mistake, you can go now. You can go and live in that nice safe cottage." Then in her normal voice, choked with painful emotion, she said, "You think I'm a fool, what don't know nothing!"

"No, no." Caroline reached her hand across the table. "No, Mistress Wenham, we don't." She looked to Simon for help.

"Mistress Wenham," he said calmly, "Mistress Newell and I do not believe that you are a witch."

The woman shook her head: hadn't the gentleman heard what she said?

"We know you signed a paper, but we both feel that you were forced to do that. And that was not right."

"No, it weren't." She sighed painfully. "But it's done now."

"Yes, but it's not the end, Mistress Wenham." Caroline had found her voice again. "Mr. Warrender and I will do everything in our power to see that you do not... to see that you get to that cottage where you can be safe."

The old woman stared at Caroline with a look of pity and disbelief. She shook her head from side to side and began to laugh. The laugh grew to a loud cackle and, as the tears streamed down her face, the cackle became a wail.

"Sh-sh-she b-best g-go b-back." The frightened turnkey tightened his hold on the rope that attached him to the woman; he began to drag her off the chair.

"Careful there!" Simon remonstrated. "You'll hurt her."

Hurried footsteps echoed across the courtyard and an angry voice called out, "What's going on? What's all that noise about?"

The gaoler burst into the room, his night stick raised, ready for trouble.

"It's all right," said Simon calmly. "Mistress Wenham just got a little bit upset."

"Bit?! They could hear her across the street! Come on witch, back to your cell."

He grabbed hold of Jane by her arm. "Told you it would do no good," he said, turning to Caroline. "You see them out," he said to the turnkey, "and I'll see to her." He looked grimly at his visitors. "And it'd be best you didn't come here no more. Leastways not without you bring a proper letter from Sir Henry," he felt it in his own interest to add.

With the sound of the gate clanging loudly in her ears Caroline walked swiftly away from the gaol, the hem of her cloak trailing in the dirty gravel of the High Street. Not caring a jot for the spectacle she was making of herself, she walked several paces ahead of Simon: she couldn't bear him to see the tears in her eyes.

What a fool she had been! An utter, utter fool! How patronising and ridiculous she must have appeared to the old woman! *She* knew what was going to happen to her: she would be tried, found guilty and condemned to death. Of course she would! What kind of fool's paradise was Caroline living in to think otherwise? A safe cottage on a country estate! No wonder the woman had laughed till she cried! She hadn't meant to say anything about the cottage, not today; she had just gone to the gaol for a little chat, to see how Jane Wenham was, exchange a few pleasantries, enquire about her daughter, ask if she had grandchildren; maybe ask the gaoler if she and Mistress Wenham might have a dish of tea together by the fire. Tea? By the fire? Ha! Where had she thought she was: in a manor house? All she had succeeded in doing was upsetting the woman and angering the gaoler to such an extent by her presence that he would no doubt take his extreme displeasure out on his prisoner. Better not to have gone there at all. But then, nearing Richard Oliver's house, she thought of her sister. There was nothing she could do for Jane Wenham, but she could be of use to Emilia.

Surreptitiously, she wiped the tears from her eyes and half-turned to Simon.

"Well, that was a waste of time, wasn't it?" she said breezily, laughing, as if what had taken place in the gaoler's room was of no consequence.

"I wouldn't say that," Simon began. "The woman will realise, when she calms down, that we have given her something to live for."

"Huh! What use is that, when judge and jury are going to take her life away? I've acted in a thoughtless way, Simon, and it's best forgotten. Now, I don't know what you want to do, but I shall go into the house and attend to my sister." She lifted the latch of the door and walked in, without giving one backward glance to Simon. She knew she was being abominably rude, but she could feel the tears welling up in her eyes again, and she could not bear him to see what a weak, senseless woman she was. Later she would apologise, but now….

"Emilia, where are you?" she called loudly, stepping into the hallway, leaving Simon, bewildered, on the doorstep.

In their highly charged emotional state - Simon was every bit as upset as Caroline but he was better at hiding his feelings - neither of them had noticed that the wind, blowing from the east, was bringing with it tiny flakes of snow, now beginning to settle on Bull Plain.

"It's nothing," said Caroline later, looking out of the window. "See, it's stopped snowing already; this bit on the ground will soon clear away. And even if it's still there, it's not going to stop me taking you to meet my sister-in-law this afternoon."

She beamed at Simon, her earlier distress set aside for the sake of Emilia, and for Simon. It was unfair to inflict her unhappy state of mind on them. It was possible that Sir Henry would be able to do something for Jane Wenham. She would speak to him immediately she returned to Yardley Bury the following morning. But for now, she must put on her cheerful face. "I know you will like Lydia, Simon," she said. "And she has a most charming, modern house, too."

"Hm."

Caroline was unaware that Emilia had entered the room.

"Oh, dearest girl." Caroline put her arms tenderly around Emilia's shoulders. "You mustn't be jealous of Lydia! You have no reason to be. She is a lonely woman, no longer young, with no children of her own; you have Richard and Charlie and Anne and…"

"I know! But we have no money… and it is hard to bring up three - four! - children, and maybe even more, who knows!… on Richard's earnings as a *scrivener*." Emilia still hadn't got over her disappointment that Richard's career had not advanced as she had expected. By now, in his thirties, he should have been an attorney, earning considerable fees and owning a large house.

Though extremely good at rhetoric, he had found it hard to get down to the study required to gain the qualifications he needed.

"Shush, dear. We don't need to talk of this now. Come and lie down." Seeing Simon's embarrassment, Caroline drew her sister out of the room. "I will help you, you know I will," Simon heard her say as the sisters left the room How confusing and complicated family life seemed to be. Would he ever want to embark upon it? It would have to be with the right woman… and he hadn't yet found her. He needed, he felt, someone with the sparkle and intelligence of Caroline, but with the softness of her sister. As for real love… that hadn't happened yet, not in England, anyway. There had been a girl in Jamaica, a beautiful girl, but… no, he could not have brought her home to be his wife.

Smiling, his mind dwelt on her for a moment, her dark eyes, her soft, brown, glowing skin, the curve and swell of her...

"Simon, are you ready?" Caroline's voice broke into his thoughts.

"Yes," he said, hoping his face had not betrayed him.

He needn't have worried: Caroline had felt unable to look at him directly ever since they had come out of the gaol. At luncheon they had been on the same side of the table with young Charlie between them, and riding side by side to Lydia's it would still be unnecessary for their eyes to meet.

"Good," Caroline said. "Then let us go."

Simon did like Lydia, and she was entranced by him. She liked his good manners, his quiet charm, his ability to hold a conversation without dominating it, as so many men did. His appearance pleased her, too: not good-looking in a conventional sense, with those pale eyebrows, and that pale skin, so admired on a woman but not on a man, but his tall, muscular, well-built frame more than compensated for them. They got on well, laughing easily together, and with no artifice whatever, or so it seemed to Caroline. She watched as Lydia put her arm through Simon's and took him off to see her husband's library; she had kept his large collection of rare books, and had discovered, through the judicious questioning she was so good at, that Simon shared this love. Lydia had always enjoyed the company of younger men - her husband had been three years her junior - so Caroline was not surprised to see that her new friend and her sister-in-law had taken to one another so readily. There was no need to accompany them - she had seen the books many times before: Lydia never tired of showing them to her family and friends - so she remained in the parlour, sitting in Lydia's favourite cushioned wing-chair in front of the fire, warm and comfortable, but, strangely, a little disturbed.

After they had been gone from the parlour for the best part of half an hour Caroline rose abruptly, laid down the book she was ostensibly reading and marched the length of the room to the door, across the spacious entrance hall and into the library, where she found Lydia and Simon seated close together on the sofa, their heads bent over a large book, laughing.

"It's time we were getting back," Caroline said, sharply.

Simon and Lydia reacted instantly, no trace of guilt on their upturned faces; the smile they gave Caroline was warm. Taken aback, Caroline managed, in return, to bring a faint smile to her lips; her eyes, though, were still fierce. Lydia, catching the look, put the book down and rose from the sofa. Simon was already on his feet.

As they stood at the front door ready to depart - Lydia's groom, John, had brought their horses round from the stable yard - Lydia put her arms around Caroline and whispered in her ear, "He's perfect. Make sure you keep a tight hold of him." She turned away to bid farewell to Simon and did not see the look of amazement on Caroline's face.

"A charming lady, your sister-in-law," Simon said, as they rode away from Bengeo.

"Yes," said Caroline, not looking at him.

"She thinks the world of you. Never stopped talking about you for one minute in the library."

"Oh?" Was he mocking her? She turned her head and looked him straight in the eyes; there was nothing there to suggest he was not speaking the truth. A smile played about his lips.

"I hardly got a chance to look at all those beautiful books," he said.

Caroline felt a blush creeping up her neck. She hung her head, smiling, and when she felt it had gone, she lifted her face. Simon was smiling at her, and the smile was now in his eyes.

Don't be silly, Caroline said to herself. He's too young, and besides, he probably has a young lady somewhere up in Yorkshire. It's for her that he wants to purchase an estate.

"We must ride faster," was all she said. "That sky looks leaden. I fancy we may have more snow."

They rode on in silence. By the time they reached Bull Plain it was prematurely dark, and the snow was coming down in earnest.

18

Mary, gazing up at the lowering sky on the second morning of her 'freedom', hoped it was not a bad omen. She had still not seen Jem.

She had thought he might come looking for her at Yardley Bury last night: all evening in Bessie's room she had been on tenterhooks, awaiting his knock on the back door. What was the matter with him? He knew she was here, on her own, that her mistress was away - in a village everyone knew everything - and he would also know that Miss Caroline would be back the day after tomorrow. Perhaps he didn't want to see her any more and this was his way of telling her.

"What's up with you, girl?" Bessie had asked. "You're as jumpy as a kitten. Do you not feel safe, without your mistress here?"

"No, it's not that," Mary had replied quickly, realising too late that she should have said "Yes" and that would have been the end of it.

"I thought not," said Bessie. She pressed her lips together, then said, knowingly, "It's that lad, isn't it? You're expecting him here, aren't you?"

"No!" Mary said defiantly, and too loudly.

"Good, because I'm not letting him in if he does come. Your mistress has left you in my charge and I intend to do my duty by her! So you can forget about skylarking with young lads on the sly."

"I wasn't!" Mary had exclaimed, outraged.

"I'm very glad to hear it." Bessie had put a hand on Mary's shoulder, and with her voice now softer, had said, "If young Jem does come to see you, you bring him in here, where I can keep an eye on the pair of you."

A lot of fun that would be: sitting in Bessie's room, with Bessie's eagle eyes on them. But Jem had not come.

Her reverie was interrupted by Bessie's voice, now harsh and fretful. "Go on, girl, it's time you was on your way. You won't get Mistress Gardiner's new gown sewn if you stand staring out of the window all morning!"

Mary swung round. "You know?"

"You didn't expect folks not to notice, did you? Course we know. Rector's wife has had that silk stuff for years... and when one of the women saw it laid out on the kitchen table, and you, with your scissors and pins and... Well... you're making her a dress, a smart one by the sound of it, the sort ladies wear, at them fancy gatherings in London, though where Mistress Gardiner's going to wear it round here, Heaven knows. Greys and browns is what she usually wears, though I did see her once in green."

Mary was looking open-mouthed at the housekeeper.

"This is a village. I told you, folks gossip. And now we haven't got a witch to talk about. Don't look so worried; a bit of fancy sewing won't do no harm." She put her head on one side, looked hard at Mary. "Mistress Newell does know what you're doing, doesn't she?"

"Well… not exactly," Mary said, slowly. "She knows I'm sewing for Mistress Gardiner, but she thinks I'm mending sheets… and collars and…"

"Oh, I see." Bessie chuckled. "Ah well, what the eye don't see… Go on, girl, get to the rectory, I've work to do." She straightened her large white apron. "I'm baking one of Sir Henry's favourites." She looked up at the clock on the wall. "He's usually down by this time of the morning."

Mary still looked uncertain; could she trust Bessie?

"Don't worry, child, I'll not say anything. Mistress Gardiner could do with a bit of enjoyment after all that's been going on these past few weeks. It'll do young Anne good, too, to see that silk, blue taffeta from what I've heard, turning into a pretty dress. Do you think if you have the time, you could make something for her? She's a sad little thing, she could do with cheering up."

"I don't know," Mary began. At this rate Bessie would have her sewing for half the village.

"No, you've enough to do with Mistress Gardiner's dress. I expect she'll be wanting lots of frills and bows on it."

Mary just smiled. Bessie knew quite enough already. What Mrs. Gardiner had on her dress was nobody's business but hers. Mary suddenly felt quite protective of the rector's wife; she would not have the whole village gossiping about her new gown!

"I'm off now. Enjoy your baking, Bessie."

"Mistress Sawyer, if you please!"

"Sorry… Mistress Sawyer." It wouldn't do to get on the wrong side of Bessie.

"You've no need to look so sorrowful, Mary; there's no great harm done." Bessie smiled at her. What did she know, poor girl? Treated more like a daughter than a maid.

"You will save some of your baking for me, won't you?" Mary said, smiling back.

"Cheeky girl! Not if it's custard tart; Sir Henry never leaves a morsel of that!"

The rectory kitchen was empty and quiet. Mary warmed her hands at the fire, then turned to the big deal table to set about her work. The sooner I finish the sewing, she said to herself, the sooner I shall be free to go in search of Jem. Miss Caroline will be back tomorrow: I *have* to see him today!

The taffeta, covered over with a clean cloth, had been left on the end of the kitchen table overnight, so that Mary could get to work as soon as she arrived.

She lifted the cloth, folded it up, put it on the dresser, and turned back to the table, pleased that she had managed to get so much done yesterday. All the pieces of the gown were there, the skirt panels, the bodice and the sleeves, cut to perfection - Mary was proud of her cutting skills - and labelled, so there would be no mistakes when she began sewing them together. There was *something* missing, though. She looked hard at the table. Oh no! Not the little doll, in its tiny blue frock, pinned up and ready to be stitched. She had spent such a lot of time getting it just right and in proportion. She bent over and looked on the floor: it must have fallen down when she pulled off the white cloth. She crawled all the way under the table on her hands and knees. There was no sign of it anywhere. Perhaps one of the cats had taken it: despite Arthur's efforts there were still cats about. Serve them right if the pins pricked them! She knew Mrs. Gardiner wouldn't have taken it; she didn't like pins.

"That's very strange," she said out loud, straightening up and looking all round the room. "I'm sure I left it here, on top of the left-over bits of fabric."

She stood, thoroughly perplexed, with her hands on her hips.

"Is this what you're looking for?" a voice said, close behind her.

Mary jumped, and swung round. It was Susan Aylott, a smirk on her face, holding out the fashion doll at arm's length.

"Yes," Mary managed to say: her heart was racing. She reached out for the doll.

"Oh no." Susan Aylott stepped back. "This is evidence," she said pompously.

"Evidence?" Mary asked. "Of what?" *That I have been sewing a fancy gown instead of mending sheets? That a rector's wife is about to flaunt herself in a Paris-style gown?*

"That *you* are a witch, of course!" Susan Aylott's eyes were piercing and triumphant.

Mary forced a faint laugh from somewhere within her trembling body.

"Nonsense," she said, weakly. "It's… it's just… a doll."

"A doll?"

"Yes. A fashion doll." Mary's mouth was so dry she could barely get the words out.

"With pins in it?" The mocking voice was menacing.

"Yes." Mary ran her tongue round her dry lips. "You pin before you stitch."

"I know what you do! I can sew!"

Mary's confidence began to return. "Then you'll know that you…"

"This is a doll, wearing a gown like the one you're making for Mistress Gardiner!" Drawing close to Mary, but holding the doll away from her, she spat the words in her blanched face. "Oh, we know you're making a dress. It's not a secret; Mistress Gardiner's had this silk cloth for years!"

"Then you understand." Could she keep the village woman talking and somehow get hold of the doll?

"Understand? What?"

"Why I am dressing this doll." She reached out her hand towards it.

"No. Miss." She hissed the word, and drew her arm holding the doll behind her. "I do not understand. To sew a gown, I know about, but to stick pins in a doll! That means only one thing: *you* are a *witch*… and you are bewitching *our rector's wife!*" She moved back, satisfied, smiling menacingly at Mary.

"No! I'm not…" Mary began.

"Don't try to deny it! We all know, don't we?" She turned around, called through the open doorway into the passage. "You can come in now."

Into the room, one behind the other, came Alice Gilbert and her daughter Margaret, Elizabeth Field and two other women whom Mary did not recognise. Bringing up the rear was a trembling, flushed Mrs. Gardiner.

"I… I don't think she… she meant it…" she said, speaking to Susan Aylott, unable to look Mary in the face.

"Course she meant it!" Susan's voice was hard and loud. "They don't do things by mistake, not witches; they know what they's doing." She swung round, brought her face close to Mary's. "Sticking pins in our rector's wife!"

Terrified as Mary was - Oh, Jem, where are you? - she managed to blurt out, "I wasn't sticking pins in Mistress Gardiner! I wouldn't ever do that!"

Mary began, very slowly, to move away from her aggressor, hoping to reach the door, but Susan Aylott's eagle eyes were upon her.

"Oh no, you're not leaving here. Madam," she added, her voice heavy with sarcasm. "Not till we've tested you."

"I'm not sure that... that we should do that." Mrs. Gardiner was obviously distressed.

"We'se not letting her go," Margaret Gilbert said.

Yes, thought Mary, jealous Margaret Gilbert; she would want me out of the way. Well, I don't move that easily, certainly not for a grubby-looking country girl with snot on her face!

"You don't frighten me, Margaret." Her eyes took in all the other women, all of them grinning inanely. "Not any of you do." She paused briefly. "Mistress Newell returns tomorrow. She'll soon put a stop to this!" The words were brave and Mary spoke loudly, but she was still afraid.

"That's where you're wrong. Miss."

Mary did not like the predatory look in Alice Gilbert's eyes.

"She will. I know she will."

"She might... if she comes back."

"Of course she'll come back, she's only gone to Hertford to see the..."

"Oh, we know why she's gone," Margaret said, and the village women laughed. They felt safe, with Jane Wenham out of their way.

"It is right, what they say, Mary." Mrs. Gardiner stepped forward and took Mary's hand. "I doubt that Mistress Newell will get back tomorrow."

"Why not?" Mary could hardly speak for fear. Had these evil women harmed her mistress in some way? Were the men of the village going to ambush her and Master Simon on the way home? She had seen the way they treated the old witch woman; they were quite capable of inflicting harm upon her mistress if they wanted to.

"Look outside," said Margaret gleefully.

The women watched as Mary turned her eyes to the kitchen window: snow, coming down heavily, had settled on the path and the grass beyond, and was already beginning to weigh down the spreading branches of the old cedar tree.

Caroline rubbed away the condensation on the window. It made little difference; she still could not see the houses on the other side of Bull Plain.

"It will be gone by the morning," she said. "I know it's coming down fast, but it's not settling."

"It is not settling yet," said Richard, standing with his back to the sitting-room fire, "but when the temperature begins to drop, as darkness falls in the next hour, you can be quite certain that, with no warmth in the ground to combat it, the snow *will* settle, and by the morning there could be as much as four inches on the ground outside the house, more in the narrow side streets which have not had the benefit of today's earlier sunshine, and therefore…"

"That's nothing, four inches." Caroline said, "I can ride in four inches of snow: it's no trouble for the horse with a bit of butter under its hooves. I am sure Simon can do it." She turned to him for confirmation. He nodded at her.

"There. See?" Leaving the window, where a draught was beginning to chill her, Caroline crossed the room to the fire.

"I was about to say, Caroline, that although we may have only four inches here, possibly less, but more in the side streets…"

"You've already said that!" Two days of Richard was more than enough for her.

Ignoring her interruption, but moving away from the fire so that his sister-in-law, rubbing her cold arms, could get warm, Richard went on, "… and in the countryside, without the heat which the many chimneys of the town provide, it will be considerably deeper, and although you may start your journey from here in relative comfort and safety, it will be quite a different matter, in fact it will be dangerous, if you venture into the lanes of north Hertfordshire where you could encounter the most treacherous conditions." He stopped, expecting comment from Caroline. When none came he began to speak again. "So, my dear sister, I think you would be ill-advised to set off tomorrow."

"Thank you," Caroline said. "Let's see what the morning brings…"

"Yes, but…"

Caroline raised her hand. "I haven't finished," she said firmly. Emilia, sitting by the fire with Edward on her lap, allowed herself a secret smile: her sister could give as good as she got in conversation with her husband.

"I do beg your pardon." Richard sounded surprised: what more was there to say?

"If the weather is as you expect, and the snow here *is* four inches deep... then we will take your advice and stay a day longer."

"At the very least," Richard said. "This snow may remain with us for several weeks."

"Or it may have gone by tomorrow! Either way, I cannot stay for long. I have left my maid..."

"Is Emilia's maid not good enough for you?" Richard made no attempt to keep the sarcasm out of his voice.

"I am responsible for Mary... and before you say I'm not, Richard... I have *made* myself responsible for her, and it is not right for me to leave her on her own for long."

"What do you think is going to happen? Is she going to run away with some poor country lad, and leave you without a well-trained lady's maid?"

"Oh husband, that is most unkind!" Emilia slipped Edward off her lap. "Go and find Anne and Charlie," she said to him. He toddled off obediently, sucking his thumb, and for once his father did not admonish him.

Most of the time Caroline felt at ease with her brother-in-law, despite his pedantry which amused and annoyed her by turns, but she always felt at a loss when anything relating to the difference in their backgrounds arose. It was not her fault that she and Emilia came from a wealthier, more aristocratic family than the one into which Richard had been born, and from which he had raised himself through hard work and the use of his brain.

Caroline had no fears that Mary would run off with Jem, but she did fear that she might let herself succumb to his charms… and then who knew what might happen: there could be a… Please not. There must be more ahead for a clever girl like Mary than bringing up a bastard child in a benighted village like Walkern.

"Mary is a sensible girl," Caroline said, giving Richard a beaming smile. "She is helping the rector's wife with some mending during the day, and she will spend the evenings with Bessie in her room at Yardley Bury. She has given me her word on this, and I trust her."

She extended her smile to Simon, who, unlike Richard, saw, in Caroline's eyes, that she was deeply troubled: the sooner they could get back to Yardley Bury the better.

19

Mary turned from the rectory kitchen window to find six pairs of eyes full of triumph fastened on hers; the women, standing close together, had formed a semi-circle from which Mary could not escape. She began to shake with fear. It was these women who were witches, the women enclosing her! One of them was even stroking a black kitten, perhaps training it to become a familiar. Oh, please God, don't let them hurt me, she whispered to herself, her mouth too dry to utter any sound. If she attempted to move past them, they were sure to grab hold of her. Then what? Tear off her clothes, push her to the ground, stick pins into her? And if she stayed still, would they crowd even closer? If she smiled at them, would that anger them? Would they think she was mocking them? If she was silent would they sense her fear? Six women, staring, not taking their eyes off her for even one second, as if... as if they had her in their collective power. Mary shivered - try as she might she couldn't help it; Miss Caroline's deep breaths were of no use, she couldn't even take one! - and when her teeth began to chatter, a satisfied smirk spread over the faces of, first Susan Aylott and then Margaret Gilbert. Very slowly, the woman and the girl began to move forward, breaking the semi-circle.

Through the gap made by their moving, Mary could now see Mrs. Gardiner, standing by the fire, her hands clasped tightly together, the ends of her thumbnails in her mouth, her eyes as frightened as Mary was sure hers must look. Poor Mistress Gardiner, she was powerless to do anything, Mary thought. Or was she? The women would take no notice of anything Mary said to them: might they listen to the rector's wife? They would listen to the rector if he was here. Over the heads of the women, all of them now inching steadily nearer, Mary called out: "Mistress Gardiner!" She felt herself to be shouting, but little more than a hoarse whisper came out of her parched throat. "Please fetch the rector."

"What you say, girl? Speak up." It was one of the women Mary did not know, an older woman, cupping a hand to her ear.

"I said, please fetch the rector," Mary croaked.

"Oh… Well now, that's not goin' to be easy. Is it, Mistress Gardiner?" the woman said, turning round to the rector's wife.

Mrs. Gardiner was finding it hard to answer. "No," she said at last.

The woman turned back to Mary. "'Cos, you see, *young lady*… Rector's not here. He gone to old Mrs. Chapman, gone to say prayers with her… and with this snow… well…" She shook her head, her matted grey locks hardly stirring with the movement, and tutted with what teeth she had clamped together. "… could be a long time afore he gets back." The other women murmured in agreement and Margaret Gilbert was openly grinning. Oh, she was enjoying this!

"So you see, miss, in your fan-cy la-dy's gown," Alice Gilbert spoke the words with disdain. "It's just us."

"We shan't hurt you none." Elizabeth Field, the only woman in the group whose appearance was clean and neat, smiled encouragingly at Mary.

"Don't you go soft on us, Elizabeth Field!" Susan Aylott's eyes flashed angrily. "Depends upon how she behaves. If she don't do what we say, then... we might have to." She narrowed her eyes and brought her face close to Mary's. "*You* don't want to go to the gaol, do you?" Mary shook her head. "Best let us decide, eh?" Mary shook her head again. "No? That's not a good answer. 'Cos we'se goin' test you, whatever happens. You let us test you proper... we might just be nice to you. All right? You understand?" Mary nodded. "Good."

Susan Aylott turned to the other women. "She won't give us no trouble. Will you?" She spun round to Mary.

"No," Mary answered. "But..."

"What? You want to tidy your hair first, do you? Put some colour on your cheeks, or perhaps some perfume... from France, maybe!"

The other women tittered nervously. They knew what Susan was like; she could ruin it, if she got carried away. Mrs. Gardiner wouldn't want another witch in Walkern, but if Susan went too far, slapped the girl or spat in her face, Mrs. Gardiner would be sure to say *something*.

"No! I don't. I..." Mary looked desperately round the sea of faces, searching for a pair of friendly eyes. Finding none, she brought her gaze back to the woman whose foul breath was now so close to her face she felt she might be sick. She took a quick look behind her: if only she could open a window, and breathe fresh air! The wind had got up and huge flakes of snow were now swirling around the rectory garden.

Unable to step *back* - she was already right up against the window seat - she moved sideways; anything to get away from the vile smell engulfing her, but her tormentor had foreseen her action and had moved sideways too. Mary was trapped. What would Miss Caroline do in this situation? She would use what she said was the best weapon of all, words! Mary pulled back her shoulders, and braving the odour, looked Susan Aylott full in the face.

"I am *not* a witch!" she said.

Susan laughed raucously. "We'll be the judge of...."

A whoosh of cold wind, rushing wildly through the passageway outside, and the thud of a door banging back and forth, drowned her words. There was the sound of high-pitched laughter and flurries of snow began to drift in through the kitchen's open door. Thick smoke swirled down the chimney and the black kitten, on the rug in front of the fire, leapt up, yowling, and fled from the room. The women, all but Susan Aylott, drew back from Mary, fear on their faces. Although Susan stood her ground, her face was white and her hands shook.

"There!" Her voice was hoarse. "What more proof do you need?" She pointed her finger at Mary. "You did that! Witch!" and she spat in her face.

Mary wiped the spittle from her face with the back of her hand.

"I did not! What a ridiculous thing to say!" Beneath her brave words she was afraid. However outrageous Susan's imprecation was, Mary was at her mercy, *and* the mercy of the other women who all too easily followed her lead. Her only hope lay with Mrs. Gardiner. She was about to appeal to the rector's wife to bring the village women to their senses, when a wooden pail, half-filled with snow, rolled into the kitchen; behind it, trying to catch hold of it, came Polly, giggling and muttering to herself, "Polly pail run 'way; Polly pail naughty". Her tattered skirt was soaking wet and her bare feet were blue with cold.

"Polly!"

Alice Gilbert pushed her way through the other women to reach the girl, but Mrs. Gardiner had got there first.

"Oh Polly, you'll catch your death!" She put her arm round the girl and drew her to the fireside. "Come, child, sit here and get warm. One of you…" She looked up at the village women, who, apart from Alice Gilbert, stood transfixed, as if they themselves were frozen, staring at Polly. "… give her your shawl."

"Here you are, my dear," Alice said, taking off her grey plaid shawl and wrapping it tenderly around the girl's quivering shoulders. She stroked Polly's wet hair. "Could we have a towel, Mistress Gardiner, please? Poor love, you are soaked. And your feet!"

"I'll do them." Elizabeth Field removed her brown knitted shawl and bound it around Polly's frozen feet.

"Put them by the fire," another woman said.

"No, she'll get chilblains that way. What Mistress Field is doing is right." It was the other woman Mary did not know. They had all turned their attention away from her and were focused on Polly. Even Margaret Gilbert and Susan Aylott seemed to have forgotten her. This was the moment for her to slip away: the witch hunt was over.

Keeping her eyes on the tableau by the fire she moved slowly away from the window, and keeping to the edge of the room, sidled along, her back to the wall, towards the door. As if sensing Mary's movements, Susan suddenly swung round.

"Oh no, you don't!"

With lightning speed the woman crossed the floor, reaching the doorway before Mary got to it. She grabbed Mary by the arm, twisting it viciously. The other women, while still attending to Polly, turned their heads at Susan's words.

"Let go of me! You're hurting!" Mary shrieked in pain, and with her free arm tried, without success, to push Susan Aylott away.

"Well, that's a shame… but I'm not letting you go." She laughed, and caught hold of Mary's free arm. "Very clever! A nice witch's trick, that was. Oh yes, making poor little Polly come here so we'd stop taking notice of you! Well, it didn't work, did it? And don't you start kicking me, madam, or I'll kick you back!"

"Susan, that's enough!" Elizabeth Field was angry. "You've no right to hurt her like that. That's no test."

"All right, you hold her then, you and Margaret, while I get the pins." Eagerly Margaret took hold of Mary's arm, as Susan relinquished it. The girl held it firm in her strong grasp.

"No! NO! Please… No. Don't."

"Not so brave now, are you? Margaret, you keep good hold of her."

"Oh, I will." A huge grin spread over her face. Just a little twist.

"Ow!"

"Sorry." Margaret didn't want Susan cross with her, or her mother.

"Margaret!" Alice shouted across the room, "You got plenty of time to use your strong arms when we start testing her. You just hold her now. No twisting, you hear me?"

"Yes, Ma. Sorry, Ma." Turning her back on her mother the girl stuck out her tongue at Mary, and gave her a surreptitious kick. Mary flinched - the toe of Margaret's boot felt as if it was capped with metal - but said nothing; she stood as still as she could, tears rolling down her cheeks. What did it matter now, if they thought she was afraid? She *was* afraid! Horribly so. She was having the greatest difficulty not to soil her underskirt and her legs. And now Elizabeth Field had taken hold of her other arm. At least with her there, Margaret would not kick her again.

"Bring her to me." Susan Aylott stood, with a long pin in her hand, in the centre of the room. Mary's captors dragged her across the floor, Mary trying desperately to keep her buttocks together.

"Why you taking so long, miss? The sooner we test you, the sooner you can go home." It was one of the women Mary did not know.

Would they really let her go? Mary knew she was no witch: aside from the pain of the pin going into her flesh… a bit hurtful yes, like taking out a splinter… there really was nothing to fear. She *would* bleed, of course she would, and then they'd see she was innocent… and release her. She took a deep breath.

"Go on then," she said, "stick pins in me! It won't do you any good, you'll just get blood on your fingers!"

"Well now…" Susan Aylott grinned and lifted up Mary's left arm. "If do we find you bleed… we shall just have to do some more tests. Pricking on its own don't prove nothing!"

and she jabbed the pin deep into Mary's arm. Mary screamed. It hurt! So much. Susan, her narrowed eyes menacing, twisted the pin in the wound, then, still turning it, she slowly withdrew it. Wailing in agony and close to fainting, Mary somehow found the strength to free her right arm from Elizabeth's hands. Instinctively she pressed her fingers against the hole in her left arm from which blood was now oozing. She could do nothing, though, about the warm liquid beginning to run down her legs.

"What in God's name are you doing?" Jem stood in the doorway, his eyes blazing, his voice shaking with rage. He strode into the room, wrenched Mary, now in a state of collapse, from Margaret's grasp, picked her up in his arms and carried her to the far end of the room.

"You stay away from her, Susan Aylott!" he said. "And the rest of you, don't you come near!"

Tenderly Jem sat Mary down on a high-backed chair and crouching down beside her he began to rub her cold hands. At his touch Mary stirred. Her eyelids fluttered open.

"Jem," she whispered hoarsely. "Oh, Jem," and she sank back into unconsciousness.

"Mary!" Jem called, and gently slapped her face. "Come back to me, lass, come on. It's all right now, nobody's going to hurt you."

"Oh Jem." Mary opened her eyes fully. "Oh Jem ! Jem!" She reached up, wanting to put her arms around his neck… "Oh," she moaned, "it hurts. My arm." She put her fingers on the still bleeding wound.

Jem turned round to the room, his eyes searching among the women for the rector's wife. There she was, by the fire.

"Mistress Gardiner! What can you have been thinking of letting…" His gaze took in a girl at her side, asleep under a quilt… "Polly! So this is where you are. Thank goodness!"

Wanting to go to Polly but anxious not to leave Mary on her own, Jem stood up and lifted the chair, with Mary in it, near enough to Polly for him to keep contact with both of them.

"Polly," he said softly, leaning over her. "Are you awake?" Polly stirred. "I been looking all over for you." He looked up at Mrs. Gardiner. "I found one of her boots sticking out of the snow on your path, and the other one outside your back door," he said accusingly.

"Yes," said Mrs. Gardiner. "She always takes them off before she comes in. She's a good girl that way."

"She shouldn't be out at all," Jem said. "Not in this weather. She knows that." But short of tethering her to a length of rope, it was difficult to keep Polly at home when she had a mind to go wandering. "Why did she come here, d'you know?"

"The witch brought her, of course!" Margaret said, pleased with herself.

"The witch is in gaol." Jem said dismissively.

"Not *that* witch! Her!" She pointed at Mary.

"Mary? Oh Margaret, don't be silly," Jem chided. "Mary's not a *witch*."

"How'd *you* know?" Susan Aylott's tone was aggressive.

"Well… she can't be."

"We was testing her, when you come barging in!"

"That's right," said Margaret, emboldened by Susan's words. "We only done one, we got lots more to do."

"Margaret! How can you be so vicious and… and stupid!"

To the farmer's wife he spoke kindly: he did not want to risk being put out of his cottage on her husband's land.

"Mistress Gilbert, you don't believe this, do you?"

"I don't know, Jem, I'm sure. That wind what brought your Polly in… it was awful strange… and them pins in the doll… was like she was sticking pins in Mistress Gardiner."

"I was not!" Mary, the colour now coming back into her cheeks, struggled up from her chair.

"You stay put, Mary," Jem said, putting his hand gently on her shoulder. With a lift of his eyebrows he tried to warn her to keep quiet; anything she said could only make her position worse.

"Well, whatever she's done, Mistress Gilbert," Jem said, "I'm taking her away from here."

"No!" Susan Aylott was trembling with fury. "She stays here, till we've finished testing 'er. We knows she's a witch, don't we?" She looked for support from the other women. Except for Alice Gilbert and Mrs. Gardiner, they all nodded, Elizabeth Field less vigorously than the others.

"You going soft now, are you, Alice?"

"No, I'm not! I just think that's enough for today. The girl's not well, you can see that… and we're not going be able do a proper test if she's not fit. 'Sides, it wouldn't be fitting to test her for marks with Jem here, and I doubt he'll leave her with us."

Jem looked gratefully at her. "You're right, Mistress Gilbert, I won't."

"So where you takin' her then, *gypsy boy*?" Susan Aylott was never one to spare anyone's feelings.

"There's no call for that, Susan. He's a good lad." Alice might have her doubts about Mary, but she wasn't going to upset Jem: he might leave the farm.

Susan shrugged her shoulders. "You best take her back to Sir Henry's then," she said to Jem. "And you go with him." She nodded knowingly at Margaret.

Margaret grinned. Her cousin Dora, who worked in the kitchen at Yardley Bury, had spied for Susan before, when she had wanted to know what that Mr. Arthur Chauncy was up to.

"You're not going up there, Margaret, you're coming home with me!" Her mother was adamant.

"But Ma, Dora can keep an eye…"

"You can see Dora another day," her mother snapped.

"You can be so silly sometimes, Margaret." Susan Aylott looked at her with disgust.

"I don't…" Margaret began. Then slowly it dawned on her that she had foiled Susan's plan, so obvious to the other women.

"Oh…" she said. "Oh yes, you…"

"Too late, it's done now." Susan turned away from her. She was angry, but this was not the time to lose her temper.

For a moment no one spoke, then Mrs. Gardiner, her voice surprisingly loud, broke the silence.

"I think…" she began forcefully, then, as if realising she had shouted, she dropped her voice to its normal volume. "I think Jem should take Mary to the constable's house. She will be quite safe there tonight, and the constable can bring her back here in the morning, and then… perhaps in his presence… you can resume your questioning, Susan." It was a long speech for the rector's wife, and when it came to an end she began to slump down into her chair. Then, with a jerk, she sat up again. "Besides, there's too many hollows in the ground between here and Yardley Bury."

Margaret grinned at this, imagining Mary struggling along in deep snow, maybe even getting buried in it, but her expression changed to concern as Mrs. Gardiner, looking appealingly at Jem, said, "You'd be putting yourself at risk. And Mary, too. As well as the horse."

"Very true," said Jem, smiling openly at the rector's wife. No more dancing if he broke his leg.

Horse, thought Margaret, her face sour. Jem'll have that… that girl up in front of him. He'll be holding her!

"Best you put her in the Cage," she said. "No one…" She glared at Jem. "… no one goin' get at her there."

"She's not going in the Cage! Not in this weather," Jem said.

Leaving Polly in the care of Mrs. Gardiner, until such time as he could return for her, Jem set off with Mary, just as Margaret had envisaged, mounted in front of him. In normal circumstances it would have taken just a few minutes to walk down the road to the constable's house, but Mary was still very shaken after her experience at the rectory and Jem wasn't sure that she could manage even that short distance on foot.

It was comforting to feel Jem's arms around her as they made their way through the snow; she wished she could stay with him at the Gilbert farm, but that was out of the question. Mrs. Gilbert would not permit it, and Margaret… well, goodness knows what she would do. Probably invite in her crony Susan Aylott for a start. No, Mary must stay, at least until tomorrow, with the constable. Jem would ride over to

Yardley Bury and let Mistress Sawyer... yes, and Sir Henry... know what was happening. Jem didn't tell Mary, but he doubted if Bessie would trouble her master with the news: he had learnt, from young Amos, that Sir Henry had not required either of his stable boys that morning, as overnight he had been taken ill with a fever and was keeping to his bed.

The constable's wife was a kind soul. She took Mary in, fed her, made sure she was warm, and promised her a bed for the night. There was no question of her going in the Cage, the constable assured Jem. Certainly not in this weather: the poor child would freeze! The Cage was for criminals... not a pretty young lady's maid. As for being a witch! Trust Susan Aylott to stir up something like that. Better if *she* was in the Cage!

The girl could stay, secure in his house, but only for one night. The constable made that quite clear. Come the morning Mary would have to leave: it would be up to Jem to find a place where she would be safe.

20

The shaft of light streaming directly on to Caroline's eyes through the gap in the bed curtains was so dazzling it almost blinded her. She groped for the edge of the curtain, and drawing it back, was startled to find the whole room flooded with a silvery whiteness, so bright it threw everything in the room into unnaturally sharp relief. Motes of dust danced in the light, but all else was eerily still. There was not a sound anywhere, not in the house, not outside in the street.

And what time was it?

Caroline reached for her robe which lay across the bottom of her bed, draped it hurriedly round her shoulders, pushed her feet into the slippers on the bedside rug, and went to the window. The heavy curtains here were already drawn back, so someone, probably Rosie, had already been into her room, but for some reason had not awakened her.

Outside on Bull Plain all was sparkling white in the sunshine, as if a fairy hand had sprinkled everywhere with tiny diamonds. The snow lay deep, and the few people who were about were making slow progress, as each foot sank into the snow and was drawn out again. An old man, making a furrow as he shuffled along, was doing better, and as Caroline watched, two women, carrying baskets, abandoned their own painful-looking efforts and followed in the old man's wake.

Caroline laughed out loud and turned from the window. Shivering, she pushed her arms into the sleeves of her robe, ran lightly over to the door, and opening it, went out on to the landing. Still no sound, no sign of life. She tiptoed across to Emilia and Richard's room. About to press down on the latch, she drew back; it would not be right to enter their chamber uninvited... but surely they would not still be abed at this late hour. She knocked gently. No response. She knocked again and Emilia's sleepy voice said, "Come in."

"Are you not well?" Caroline asked, entering the room.

"I am tired," said Emilia. "Oh Cara, I don't know what is wrong with me. I am always tired these days," and she burst into tears.

"Oh my darling, you must not fret so." Caroline crossed the room to the bed, and took Emilia into her arms. "Of course you are tired, you are carrying a child!"

"I was never like this with the others."

"You carried them in the spring; it is harder in the winter."

"It has nothing to do with the weather!" Emilia answered crossly. "I do not want this child and God is punishing me for my wickedness!"

"Oh Millie! God is not punishing you. You have done nothing wrong."

"I have! Oh Cara, I have been wicked... so very wicked." And her tears flowed even more.

"So what have you done...? Said unkind things about Lydia? Smacked the children? Mocked Richard's speech? That is no sin, believe me."

"Oh Cara... I could not bear to have yet another baby die within days of its birth; better for it not to be born at all!"

Emilia was shaken by heart-rending sobs, and for a few moments she could not speak.

"Shush, my dearest." Caroline began to rock her sister back and forth, as if she were nursing a baby. "That's enough."

"No!" Emilia broke free of Caroline's arms and lifted her tear-stained face. "You have to know! I... I tried... to rid myself of it!"

"Oh, my sweet... No?"

Emilia nodded and buried her head in her sister's arms. Caroline stroked her hair and held her close; how desperate Millie must have felt to want to kill her unborn child. A dead child: Caroline's thoughts flew to Hannah. But no, this was not the moment to dwell on her own sorrow.

"You are making my gown very wet," she said, lifting her sister's head.

"And now you will leave me, I know you will."

"I will do no such thing! Don't you dare think such a thing! Besides, how can I go anywhere in this weather? Have you looked outside this morning?"

Emilia shook her head.

"It would be impossible for me to travel to Yardley Bury today, probably not tomorrow either. Besides, I am not leaving you in this state. When the weather improves I shall send Simon to fetch Mary... I cannot do with Rosie's attentions a moment longer! Where is she, anyway? She should be here, attending to you."

"She is minding Edwin for me, so I can rest."

"And the other two, who has them?" Caroline was making no attempt to hide her annoyance: Emilia's servants were a poor lot.

"They are with Mr. Warrender."

"Simon? Where?"

"He has taken them out on their sledge."

Caroline's irritation was gone. "Oh Millie... oh, that is so kind."

"He is a kind man."

"Yes, I know."

"You would do well to..."

"No, Millie, please don't. I am not ready. I may never be... so just put any ideas like that right out of your head." Feeling she may have sounded harsh, she laughed and said lightly, "There, that's two things I've forbidden you to think about! Just make sure you obey me!" She disentangled herself from her sister's arms and propped her up on her pillows. Turning her back on Emilia she crossed swiftly to the window and looked out. "I do believe it is starting to thaw," she said, her voice unsteady. "Yes, look, the icicles at the window are dripping."

"So they are," Emilia said. If Caroline did not wish to talk about the possibility of marrying again, no one on earth, not even her beloved sister, could make her do so. Emilia would not reopen the subject, but she could tell, from Caroline's reaction, that marriage to Simon had crossed her mind, if only fleetingly.

Nor would Caroline speak of it again. She had a more pressing matter to deal with. If she was going to stay here and care for Emilia, which she fully intended to do - there was no reason for her to return to Yardley Bury other than to thank Sir Henry for his hospitality and she could do that equally well by letter - then she must have both her own maid and some more of her clothes - she had been wearing the same gown for days! - brought to Hertford.

No fresh snow fell that day and in the afternoon Simon rode up to Bengeo carrying a letter from Caroline to Lydia, requesting the loan of her groom, John, who knew the area well - his mother lived in Gilston - to ride with Simon to Colonel Plumer's, to let the old man know that he was safe, before riding on with Tom to Yardley Bury. The following morning, with the snow now melting rapidly, Simon and John made good progress across the fields to New Place. John then returned to Bengeo, stopping off on his way to let Mistress Newell know that all was well at Gilston.

"And tomorrow... he *will* go on to Yardley Bury, won't he?" Caroline asked.

"I fear, madam, that is not likely to happen."

"But he must!"

"I think Mr. Warrender will have to stay at least one day more at New Place."

Caroline sighed. "You are right, John. Of course he cannot leave the old gentleman again so soon."

"I feel sure he will go as soon as he possibly can. He seemed to me... I hope you do not mind me saying so... he seemed a very determined young man."

Caroline smiled. "Yes, I think he is. Go on, John, on your way, and do thank Lady Poynter for lending you to us."

"Anything I can do for Her Ladyship gives me great pleasure, Mistress Newell."

"Good," said Caroline, and feeling the conversation was best brought to an end, she closed the door. It was only after John had gone that she realised that the groom had come to Richard's front door; goodness, she had almost invited him in! She did hope he wasn't taking too many liberties in her sister-in-law's house.

Two days passed before Simon was allowed to leave Uncle Plumer. Not only was the colonel concerned for his godson's well-being, quite unnecessarily Simon thought - he had never felt better in his life - but he wanted to hear every detail of Simon and Caroline's visit to Hertford gaol to see Jane Wenham, and to hear news of dear little Emilia and her young family. It was noon of the third day after leaving Hertford before Simon could set out with Tom to fulfil his mission. Sensing his anxiety on Caroline's behalf, the colonel promised to write to her immediately Simon had left Gilston and get his own trusted groom to deliver it directly to her.

True to his word, Colonel Plumer despatched a letter to Caroline just one hour after he had waved goodbye to Simon at the front door of New Place. Once they were out of sight round the bend in the long carriageway he had gone straight into his study and put pen to paper.

Caroline was relieved to hear that Simon was on his way to Sir Henry. By tomorrow afternoon, if there was no further snowfall - the sky was now grey and the clouds promised rain rather than snow - Mary would be here and she would have fresh clothes to wear. Caroline's spirits lifted, to the extent of listening right through to one of Richard's long tales of the misdemeanours of the none-too-honest merchants he met in the course of his work, without mentioning any names of course; that would be both indiscreet and unprofessional, as he was sure Caroline would appreciate.

The streets of Hertford were by now filled with a mixture of dirty, melted snow and mud, and as Caroline walked to the apothecary's for a soothing salve for little Alice, who had come out in a nasty-looking, prickly rash, she inwardly cursed those carters who added to the mess underfoot by letting their horses foul the street whenever they pleased. It was bad enough having the hem of her cloak caked with mud, but to have dung clinging to it as well was more than she could bear. If only respectable women could dress like men, in breeches of some kind, and high boots! Long trailing skirts were fine in ballrooms, but not in the streets of a country town! She collected the salve and returned to Bull Plain.

With Mary here, Caroline thought as she picked her way along the streets, trying to avoid the worst of the slush, she could happily settle down in Hertford for the rest of the winter, with, of course, a few visits to Bengeo. Much as she loved Millie, to be with her in her present gloomy frame of mind for days on end would try her patience, so a few hours spent with Lydia now and then would be good for both Caroline and Emilia.

Then, in the spring, when Millie was well enough to travel - when those first few dangerous months of pregnancy were over - Caroline would send for her own carriage and take Emilia and the children to Amley for a month or so. It was good to have formed a plan, she said to herself, as she reached the door of the Olivers' house. Pausing there on the doorstep, with the sun coming out and bringing a much-needed sparkle to the vestiges of clean snow left clinging to the windowsills and rooftops, she had another pleasing thought: if Simon felt so inclined - after all, he did want to find a property in the neighbourhood - he could join them.

21

Simon and Tom arrived at Yardley Bury to find Sir Henry ill in bed, Bessie distraught to the point of incoherence, Arthur in a state of agitation and febrile excitement… and no Mary. Was Yardley Bury always like this he wondered, recalling his former visit.

With difficulty and much prompting Simon finally managed to elicit from Bessie the few facts that were available: Mary had gone to the rectory to sew for Mrs. Gardiner, Susan Aylott had accused her of witchcraft, she had spent a night at the constable's house… and had not been seen since.

"Except, perhaps, by young Jem," Bessie said reluctantly.

He was now in the snug, and a slightly calmer Bessie had just brought him a dish of hot chocolate.

"Jem, the gypsy boy?" Simon looked up at the housekeeper, her old face drawn from lack of sleep.

"Don't tell Mistress Newell, please," she said. "It's bad enough that… that the girl was left in my care, and now she's missing. Oh, Mr. Warrender, sir, I think… I think she has gone off with the lad! It was him what rescued her, you see, from Susan Aylott and the other women. I can only pray that…"

The housekeeper began to mumble to herself, but whether or not it was a prayer Simon could not tell.

"All right, Bess... Mistress Sawyer... please do not blame yourself. I am sure we shall find Mistress Newell's maid very soon. In this weather she cannot have gone far."

Simon had done his best to sound confident, but he had absolutely no idea how or where to begin searching for Mary. Perhaps if he could speak to the constable... or possibly to Arthur? He was well in with the villagers. The phrase 'crossing your palm with silver' came to him. Well, if bribery was required, although Simon disapproved of it in principle, he would have to resort to it: the girl must be found and returned, unharmed he hoped fervently, to her mistress. His first port of call would be the farm where the gypsy lad worked. No farmer would countenance his worker going off without permission, which Simon doubted Jem would have requested. From what he had been able to gather from the various accounts he had been given since arriving at Yardley Bury, Mary, with Jem, had disappeared in the early hours of the morning, after spending a night in the care of the constable.

Warmed by the chocolate and a slice of Bessie's damson pie, Simon and Tom remounted their horses, also refreshed with food and a rub-down, and rode across frozen fields - the cold was intense out here in the countryside - to Walkern and on to the Gilbert farm, a mile and a half north of the village.

Expecting to find an angry farmer berating his farm hand, Simon was surprised to be told, "Of course Jem is here, he's got a good job and a cottage, he's not going to risk losing that for a silly little lady's maid. Not right, what they did to the girl, though, at the rectory. Best the lass is out of the way." But where she was, Joe Gilbert could not say. "None of my business. So long as Jem's here and gets on with his work...

that's all I care about. If you want to speak to the lad you'll find him over there," and he waved his hand in the direction of the stables. "Don't keep him long. I don't pay him to talk."

The farmer need not have worried; Jem had nothing to say. Nothing of any use to Simon, that is. Oh yes, he knew where Mary was, but nothing would persuade him - no, certainly not money - to tell the gentleman where he had hidden her.

Yes, he had met the gentleman before, he was sure he was trustworthy, but he had promised Mary he would tell no one except her mistress, and there was nothing he could do about that until Sunday when he had a day off. He could then ride to Hertford, if that's where the lady was, and tell her, but until that time his lips were sealed, and even if the gentleman chose to try beating the information out of him with his riding crop he would not break his promise to Mary.

"Leave us a minute, Tom," Simon said when Jem had finished speaking and had turned back to the old chestnut horse he was grooming.

"Right, sir," said Tom, and withdrew to the far side of the stable yard, taking both their horses with him.

"Now then, Jem," Simon began, as soon as Tom was out of earshot.

"It's no good, sir, you'll not move me."

"Is there nothing I can say to…?"

"No, sir. I promised Mary and I will not break my promise."

"Well, that's good… and I admire you for it."

"Thank you, sir. If you'll excuse me, sir, I need to move on to the next stall. There you are, my lady, well-brushed and clean." He spoke softly to the mare and rubbed her nose gently. He picked up his tools, shut the half-door of the stall, and opened the door of the adjacent one. The horse, a grey, whinnied with pleasure as Jem began to groom him with firm, tender, confident strokes.

"Yes, you like that, don't you. Good boy."

Caroline was right, there was something very special about this young gypsy; he was wasted here in this out-of-the-way village. But those thoughts must wait.

"You're very fond of Mary, aren't you?" It was a risky question. The boy might close up even more… or it could be the way to get him to change his mind.

Jem paused in his task, the grooming comb resting gently on the horse's flank.

"Yes, sir. I am."

"So you want the best for her."

"Yes, sir," Jem said. Slowly he began to draw the comb through the long hair of the horse's mane. "I'm still not going to tell you where she is."

Simon sighed. "Very well. I won't force you. Don't look at me like that, lad! I could if I wanted to, and you know that. Let us try to keep this as amicable…" He resisted the temptation to say *friendly*. If the boy did not know the word *amicable* it would only antagonise him if Simon offered him a more common alternative. "… as we can. You are right to keep your word, but the girl has to come out of hiding sometime."

"I know that, sir, but if you'd seen the things that been done to her in the rectory kitchen…" and Jem proceeded to describe, in graphic detail, exactly what Mary had experienced that day. Simon felt his stomach knot in revulsion.

"Nasty," he said. "Very nasty." He paused, and turning away from Jem he spat out on to the stable yard the bile that had risen into his throat. "Nevertheless, we have to find a way to get Mary back safely to her mistress."

Jem did not respond, other than to groom the horse under his hands more vigorously. Simon sighed; he would try another approach. "All right then, if you won't tell me where she is, I suggest you write a letter..." Oh Lord, could the boy write? "... to Mistress Newell, and I will take it to her."

"No, sir." Jem shook his head. "Can't do that." He looked challengingly at Simon.

"We shall have to think of something else then." For a moment neither of them spoke. "Perhaps we could meet, away from here..." In his own time, the lad might be more inclined to talk.

Jem nodded. "There's a spinney halfway between here and Sir Henry's house," he said. "I'll meet you there, tomorrow morning, sir. Half-past five."

It would still be dark, Simon thought.

"Why not come up to the house?"

"No, sir. Sir Henry's kitchen maid is Margaret Gilbert's cousin."

"Ah. I see. Well, I suppose I could be taking an early morning walk. That, surely, won't alert suspicion, will it?"

"No, sir. Gentlemen do sometimes take early morning walks."

"But not usually in the winter, I imagine."

A tiny smile flickered across Jem's normally serious face.

"And then what?" Simon asked.

"Then..." A few more long strokes of the comb on the horse's mane. Simon could see that the boy was having a battle with himself. "Then… I'll let you know in the morning. Sir."

It was as much as Simon would get from Jem today. It was very frustrating, but Simon, having dealt with country people of one nationality or another all his adult life, knew better than to push the lad, if he was to be taken into his confidence.

"I will see you tomorrow then," he said.

In the meantime, he would embark upon his own investigations.

With Tom at his side he rode into Walkern, under a darkening afternoon sky that threatened sleet or more snow. At the sound of the horses' hooves, the few people making their way along the still partly frozen main street, shoulders hunched against the cold, stopped to stare at them - unknown men on unknown horses - and here and there, in those cottages where a meagre tallow candle had been lit, but no curtains had yet been drawn, an indistinguishable face, with the light behind it, peered out at them.

"They know something's up, sir," Tom said.

"Yes, perhaps they do. But not why *we* are here."

"I think they do, sir. I spoke to one of the lads at that farm."

"Oh?"

"Yes, sir, when you was talking to the gypsy. He said, 'You come 'bout that girl, the one's what's disappeared.' Then he said, 'You don't want get mixed up in that; she's a witch, that one.' And when I asked him how he knew, he said the master's daughter had told him, and she knew because she'd been there when…"

"Yes, yes. That's enough, Tom."

"No sir. You need to hear this."

"Oh, go on then."

"Well, from what this lad said, sir… the girl, Margaret, didn't like the maid, not one bit. *And* she is sweet on the gypsy."

"Oh… Thank you, Tom. She might be worth talking to."

"You want me to do it, sir?"

"No, I do not. Now you just keep out of this. And don't start running after any of the village girls either. If you do I shall send you straight back to New Place!"

"Yes, sir. I won't, sir." Tom wasn't going to spoil what could be a real adventure, the first of many he hoped, just for a quick tumble in a hay loft. Besides, that lady's maid, the missing one, she'd taken his fancy, and he was a much better catch than that gypsy lad. Been nowhere he had, not like Tom, who'd been to sea, seen a bit of the world. And he would see more.

"First stop, the constable's house," said Simon, dismounting.

A curtain moved in the cottage across the road.

"They're watching, sir," Tom said. He got off his horse and took Simon's reins.

"Let them. If, as you say, they know why we are here, then a visit to the constable is a logical thing for us to be doing. Now you wait outside… and no gossiping!"

"No, sir." Tom, beginning to understand young Mr. Warrender, allowed himself a wide grin.

"I'm sorry, sir," said the constable a few minutes later, "but there's nothing I can add to what you already know. The girl stayed here the night, and in the morning when my wife went to wake her… she'd gone. And there's only one person could have taken her. And before you ask, sir, I know 'twas young Jem, 'cause he told me. He wasn't hiding nothing... 'cept the girl."

"Well, thank you, Constable. I'll try speaking to him again."

"You'll get nothing out of him, sir. He's a stubborn one. Gypsies, you can't make them do what they don't want to do. No one can. If he's a mind to tell you he will; if not, you'd best look for some other way to find the girl."

"Couldn't you arrest him, Constable?" Simon asked.

"Well, I could," the constable answered slowly, stroking his beard, "but I don't think Farmer Gilbert would like that, taking his man away from his work... and it wouldn't bring the girl back. The boy still wouldn't talk. If he's a mind not to..."

"Yes, I understand." Though Simon had no wish to have the constable go through it all again he did not want to antagonise him. "You have been very helpful, Constable, and I much appreciate it. I am wondering... is there a fund... for helping the poor children of the parish perhaps, to which I could contribute?"

"That would be very kind, sir. Thank you very much."

"Half a crown, would that be appropriate?"

"Oh yes, sir; thank you very much, sir. Glad to have been some help to you, sir."

"Next stop, the rectory." Simon swung himself into the saddle. He wasn't quite sure why he was going to call on the rector and his wife, but as Mrs. Gardiner had been present, so Jem had said, during Mary's testing, she might have something to add to his small store of information. He also had the tiniest niggling feeling of doubt about Jem: had the lad really hidden Mary away for her own safety, or was he spinning a tale to cover some misdemeanour of his own? Why was he making such a mystery of it? Was he, Simon, being prejudiced because Jem was a gypsy, and everyone *knew* that gypsies were untrustworthy? Simon wanted to believe him, and he did, but just in case… It could be, of course, that Jem felt the same way about him.

Still under scrutiny, the two men rode up the main street to the rectory at the far end. A cluster of villagers who had gathered outside one of the bigger cottages began to follow them.

"Looks like we're providing them with some excitement, sir," said Tom, sounding excited himself.

"I expect we are. Not a lot happens in villages like this."

"Oh, I don't know, sir. A witch and a lady from London, then maybe another witch and a kidnapping…"

"Tom, that's enough! You behave yourself, or this is the last ride you'll have with me." Simon hoped he sounded fierce and admonitory, but inside he felt that same ripple of excitement that Tom was obviously experiencing. They were embarked upon a serious quest, but even so he had to admit to a frisson of… yes, excitement was the word. He might feel guilty, but he could not deny it. As a boy Simon had been timid outwardly, but in his solitary moments, and there were many of these, he was a gallant knight, always on a white charger, slaying dragons and riding to the rescue of fair ladies. The present reality did not quite measure up to his imaginary adventures, but it had its merits: he was, if all went well, about to restore *to* a fair lady her personal maid. He smiled to himself at the thought. He would, of course, never tell Caroline any of this; she was such a practical person, she would only laugh at him. And thinking on a practical level himself... it was four days since he had left Hertford, and Caroline would be getting worried. And even if Mary came out of hiding tomorrow, it looked like being at least another day, if everything had to be arranged secretly, before she was back, safely, in Caroline's care.

The visit to the rectory added nothing of importance to Simon's knowledge.

Mrs. Gardiner, though sounding contrite about her part in the testing of Mary - they were in her kitchen after all - seemed more concerned about the unfinished gown that lay in pieces at the end of the table than the welfare of Mistress Newell's maid. Simon felt unable to sympathise with her, but she had given him an idea for a small lie which, as far as he could see, would do no harm: he would write straight away to Caroline, explaining that the reason for the delay in Mary's return to Hertford was simply that she wanted to complete the sewing of Mrs. Gardiner's taffeta dress before she left Walkern.

Satisfied with this outcome he rode back to Yardley Bury, to spend a quiet evening with Sir Henry, who now felt well enough to leave his bed and come down to the snug.

"A game of piquet, my boy?" the old man had asked, and Simon was happy to comply: he had had more than enough of talking for one day.

Arthur, thank goodness, was not at home. Once Jane Wenham had been taken to Hertford Gaol, Francis Bragge had no reason to stay with his grandfather, but before he returned to Biggleswade he was paying a visit to his mother, Arthur's half-sister, in Hitchin. Now that the furore in Walkern had died down, Arthur had taken very little persuading to accompany Francis, and Sir Henry was glad to see the back of him for a while. Knowing, from Caroline, that Arthur took pleasure in taunting, and testing, anyone thought to be a witch, what might he have done to Mary had he been here? Simon shuddered at the thought.

"Bring the table near the fire, my boy." Sir Henry smiled at Simon and reached for his pipe. "Oh, I am going to enjoy this!" he said.

22

A tramp over frosty fields at five-thirty on a February morning was not Simon's idea of pleasurable exercise: the cold was penetrating right through to his bones.

Bessie was right. "You need to put on some more fat, Mr. Warrender," she had said to him the day before. Wishing he were on horseback, he began to walk more quickly, the ground crackling under his boots; at least his feet were warm.

He felt the land beginning to rise slightly and looking ahead he saw that he had almost reached the spinney, a small wood of what appeared to be, in semi-darkness, silver birch, holly and some conifer he could not identify. Although the birch trees were bare of leaves, the evergreens provided enough cover for this to be a good meeting place for people who did not wish to be seen together.

Spotting a natural opening in the trees, he strode towards it, eagerly seeking whatever shelter the small wood might provide. He was not surprised to see Jem already there, but he had not expected to find him holding the reins of two horses, a young black stallion with a piece of blanket thrown across its back, and the old chestnut horse, now complete with saddle, that he had seen at the Gilbert farm.

He acknowledged Jem with a nod of the head. Jem nodded back.

"I'm taking you to her. Best you mount straight away, sir," the boy said, handing Simon the horse's bridle. He sounded nervous, but there was also determination in his voice.

Having made up his mind to disclose Mary's whereabouts to Simon, Jem was anxious to get moving: he hoped to be back in Walkern before Joe Gilbert missed him. Simon did not argue or ask for an explanation; it was enough, for now, that Jem had decided to trust him.

"Where to?" he asked, as he adjusted the stirrups and settled himself into the saddle.

"Don't matter *where*," Jem said gruffly, swinging himself on to his mount with the ease of someone to whom riding was second nature.

Simon, torn between annoyance at what he regarded as Jem's rude answer and admiration of his horsemanship, was about to speak when Jem said, in a softer voice, "It's not somewhere you know, sir. So just follow me… please."

They rode in silence, mostly across fields and always travelling north, the sky gradually lightening to their right. From time to time they came out on to a well-beaten track, with high hedges, mostly hawthorn, showing the first touches of green, on either side. A flight of birds, dark against the sky, flew up with noisy wings from a lone tree, wheeled around and came back to their perch once the men had passed. As daylight approached more birds began to take wing and here and there their morning cries were heard. They had been riding for nearly half an hour, Simon judged, the past few minutes on a narrow lane, when Jem suddenly pulled up, jumped off his horse, and said, in little more than a whisper, "We're here."

Here, at first sight, appeared to be nothing more than a gap in the hedgerow and a rickety moss-covered gate, which Jem now pushed open. Back on his horse, Jem led the way along a track which, to begin with, lay at right angles to the lane. After no more than a quarter of mile, with poor-looking grazing on either side, the track suddenly turned left by a clump of tall, overgrown shrubs, to reveal a farmhouse, which appeared to be as broken down as the rest of this property. Surely Mary was not here! The farmyard itself was excessively muddy, but the hens, most of them brown, pecking among some straw which had been laid down to make a safe pathway from the farmyard gate to the door of the house, looked healthy and were clucking contentedly. Jem dismounted and opened the gate.

"What is this place?" Simon could not keep the agitation and annoyance out of his voice. "Surely this is not where you brought Mary?" He paused. "You owe me an explanation, Jem." The boy looked at him boldly, his black eyes suddenly aggressive. "Now!" It all felt so wrong, and yet... Why would the boy have brought him to this desolate place if the girl was not here? Was he, Simon, about to be kidnapped too? He dismissed the thought as soon as it came... but nevertheless, something here *was* amiss and it was as well to be on his guard.

"She *is* here!" Jem said. He seemed reluctant to go on.

"Yes?"

"And I brought her here because... because I know I can trust these people, Mistress Towler and her sons."

Simon waited: he felt that Jem had more to say.

"I've worked for them. I still do sometimes... now and then." The boy looked anxiously at his questioner.

"It's all right, Jem, I am not going to give you away to Farmer Gilbert."

"Thank you. Sir."

"So, go on, tell me the rest."

"There is no more, not really. They are tenants of Fording Hall. They are devout people."

"Devout?" Simon asked, wondering where this conversation was going.

Jem met his gaze unflinchingly. "Yes, sir. They keep the faith."

"I see." What that faith was Simon had the good sense not to ask. Suffice that the people at this poor-looking farm were kind-hearted Christians of some kind or another, people whom Jem obviously trusted.

"Will they be up at this hour?" It was still not fully light.

"It's a farm, sir."

"Yes, so it is. Come on then, Jem, let's go and fetch Mary."

The two men rode into the farmyard. The hens scattered, flapping their wings in protest at the invasion of their pecking place, and two of them, one brown, one speckled, squawking loudly, flew up on to the moss-covered roof of a low shed attached to an open barn housing a hay cart and assorted rakes, which was to one side of the front door. Jem dismounted and moved to take Simon's reins.

"No," he said, "I'll stay here, you go ahead. I'll let you tell her why we are here."

Jem grinned at him and turned to the door. Simon averted his eyes. If Mary hadn't seen Jem since he brought her here three days ago, it was bound to be an emotional moment for her... for both of them.

"Jem!"

"Ma Towler."

Of course Mary wouldn't come to the door, she was in hiding. Simon turned round, and saw, standing in the low stone doorway, a small, rosy-cheeked woman. She wore a coarse apron over her dress, and looked to be in her mid-forties.

"Oh Jem," she cried, and stepping out from the doorway, she flung her arms around the young gypsy's neck. "Come in, come in!" Then seeing Simon, still mounted, she bobbed down in a curtsey. "Oh, I'm sorry, sir. I didn't see you, sir. Beg pardon, sir."

"That's all right. You carry on, Jem. I'll follow you," and he began to dismount.

"Thank you, sir," the woman said, bobbing down again. She turned round and called into the house. "Nathaniel! You come out here now and see to these horses."

A boy's voice that was in the process of breaking answered her. "Comin', Ma."

A gangly lad in mud-spattered, out-grown breeches appeared in the doorway.

Seeing Simon, he lifted a hand and touched the lock of dark, stringy hair which fell over his swarthy face. His resemblance to Jem was striking... but only at first glance: this boy's face and hair were dark because they were dirty.

His mother looked at him in disgust. "I told you to wash before you came in the house, boy!" she said angrily. "I beg your pardon, sir." She turned to Simon. "He been doing the pigs, sir, and he do like to get down with them."

"I quite understand, Mistress Towler," Simon said, handing the reins of his horse to Nathaniel. "But if you wouldn't mind…" It was time, he felt, to assert his authority. "… we should like to speak to Mary now. Our time is limited: Jem has to get back to work." He had no wish to become involved with the whole family, however kind or devout they might be, and he wanted Caroline's maid safely back at Yardley Bury before the whole of the countryside was up and about to see her.

"But she's not here, sir." The woman looked perplexed. "Not any more."

"*Not here*?" Jem's voice shook with anger and distress. "I left her with you! You said you'd keep her safe!" He took the woman by the shoulders and began to shake her. "What you done with her?"

"For God's sake, Jem. Stop that!" Simon grabbed hold of Jem's hands and pulled him off the woman. "Just calm yourself down."

"Calm!" yelled Jem. He banged his fists so hard against the wall of the house that his knuckles bled.

"You're behaving like an idiot, Jem. Just look at your hands, look what you've done to them! Losing your temper's not going to bring Mary back… wherever she is. Now get that blood off your hands and have the decency to listen to what Mistress Towler has to tell us without flying off the handle again."

Jem shook his head violently. "Sorry, sir, but…"

"No. Stop. If you want my help… then you behave." Simon turned to the woman. "Mistress Towler, I do apologise."

"It's all right, sir." She turned to Jem. "I wouldn't have done it, only the master said…"

"Master? *Your* master? What's he got to do with it?" Jem's face was black with rage.

"*No*, Jem!" Simon put his hand on Jem's now upraised arm. "This is not the way." He felt as anxious and troubled as Jem was but he must not show it: he needed to be positive and objective... or at least give the appearance of being so. "Now, Mistress Towler, please tell us where Mary is, before Jem does something he, and I, will regret."

The gentleman might look a weakling, with his slim build and pale colouring, but Jem had seen him on a horse; he was probably quite good with his fists, too.

"She's at the Hall, sir, the big house up the road." Mrs. Towler seemed neither upset nor guilty at the absence of Mary. Simon decided he must take comfort from that. "The young master said... he said it was all right."

Simon, sensing Jem was about to interrupt, raised his hand to deter him.

"Go on." He nodded at the woman.

"The master came, sir, with his... his cousin, I think he said, sir. A lady, sir."

"Yes?"

"The lady had no maid, sir, and when they heard we had a lady's maid staying here..."

"I said not to tell anyone!" Jem glowered at the woman.

"It was Mary what said! She told our Lizzie, you know, what cleans for us. She has a sister works up at the Hall, Fording Hall, that is, sir. It was her must have said about Mary..."

"It was *you* let her go!" Jem was having difficulty keeping his anger under control. "I trusted you, Ma!"

"I couldn't keep her! I didn't have no choice, Jem. The young master said… he said he was a friend… of Mary's mistress. He knew her… in London, he said."

"And you believed him?"

"He said Mary's mistress had asked him to fetch her." She turned to Simon. "Mary did know him, sir."

"I trusted *you*," Jem roared again. "And you…" He balled his fists at her.

"Jem, don't…!" The woman shrank back against the door, fear and anguish on her face.

"For God's sake!" Simon rose, grabbed Jem's upraised arm and pulled him away from the farmer's wife.

Simon had seen out of the corner of his eye the boy Nathaniel move towards his mother, then draw back once Jem had been restrained. He began to feel out of his depth. As a gentleman he should be able to order these peasants to do his bidding, but he was afraid to make the wrong move. Jem was a gypsy and they had their own rules of behaviour, and the woman was a farmer's wife - or widow, was it; there had been no sign or mention of a Farmer Towler - and he was unsure of her exact social standing; it had all been so much easier in the West Indies.

"Cullion!" Jem said, and he shook off Simon's hand. "Come on, sir, let's go!"

He grabbed the reins of his horse from Nathaniel, and was away.

"Oh, be careful, Jem!" Mrs. Towler called. "Oh, sir, do take care! I wish now I'd not said…"

Simon followed suit, with barely a moment to lift his hat to Mrs. Towler. He had no idea where they were or where they were going. He didn't want to lose sight of Jem, who was already out of the farmyard and up the lane, urging the stallion on so fast that Simon, on the slower chestnut, was finding it hard to keep pace with him.

"Jem! Wait!"

"Cullion! I'll kill him!"

This careering around the countryside in the wake of a cursing gypsy boy had all come about because of the impetuosity of a London lady insisting upon doing good, or so she thought, by visiting an old witch-woman in prison! This was not what Simon had come back to England for. The sooner Mary was back with her mistress the better. There was something not right, though, about Mrs. Towler's story, but Simon couldn't quite put his finger on it: was it something the man she called the young master had said? Yes, that was *it*! 'Mary's mistress had told him to fetch her'. "Jem!" he shouted, and pressed his heels into his horse's flanks.

"Jem!"

The boy, though well ahead, had heard his shout. He wheeled his horse round, and at a trot, came back to Simon.

"What? Sir."

"How could the man at the Hall have a message from Mistress Newell? She thinks Mary is safe and sound at Yardley Bury, not hiding away in a farmhouse."

"That one! He'll say anything to get what he wants."

"You know him?"

"Yes, sir. I've worked for him; wish I hadn't." He hesitated. "He's not like... like you or me, sir. I don't like to think of Mary... in that house."

"Then let's get there!"

Riding fast, side by side, it took only a few minutes for them to reach the elaborately fashioned iron gates of Fording Hall. The gates were open and they rode, more slowly now, up the wide drive. Simon was amazed at the grandeur of the building facing him. There were turrets and pinnacles, a stone portico surrounding intricately carved wooden doors, and a variety of windows, everything from narrow slits to oriels and casements, as if the frontage was a catalogue from which a prospective home-owner could choose the kind of windows he wanted. As they drew nearer Simon was struck with the narrowness of the edifice; this stone and brick confection was, he soon discovered, a mere façade. Turning right past a long raised shrubbery which, until now, had hidden the rest of the house from view, he was astounded to see a large Tudor house attached to one end of the stone structure.

If the man was anything like the house... Poor Jem. To have left Mary in what he thought was safe keeping... and then... He was a good lad. Gypsy he might be, but Simon felt strangely drawn to him.

"Jem," he said. "When you're ready to leave Farmer Gilbert, will you come and work for me, with my horses?" Although it had been in the back of his mind for some time now, he suddenly knew exactly what he wanted to do with his life, and how to go about it. "I want to breed horses, and I think you are the right person to help me." There, it was out, the decision made, put into words. He felt his heart beating furiously. He could see it all: stables, paddocks with young horses, Jem schooling them, orchards, a stream with fish... He was getting carried away, which he did not allow himself to do, not any more. His dreams had gone wrong so many

times: America - he had hadn't even got there - the West
Indies, Yorkshire. But this time… He didn't know why, but it
felt different.

"I'd like that, sir," Jem said, "to work for you."

"Good. It won't be for some time yet though, I've got to
find a place." His heartbeat was almost back to normal.
"We'll talk of it later."

"Yes, sir."

The men walked their horses past the shrubbery on to a
wide, gravelled area in front of the Tudor house. The side of
the house faced east and a myriad of tiny mullion windows
blinked in the light of the rising sun. They dismounted and
tied the reins to a rail by the studded oak front door.

"You wait here, Jem."

"But, sir…"

"I don't want you killing him before we have Mary safe
and sound!"

"No, sir."

The boy laughed, not as a servant, but as an equal. Simon
wondered if he been too free with him; he was after all an
illiterate peasant, not his equal in any way.

But this was not a time for etiquette. And he *had* just
asked the boy to work for him, in a position of some
responsibility. They must pull together now, as a team, two
men with a purpose. Perhaps he should have brought Tom as
well.

"I mean it. I've seen your hot temper, and I think just the
sight of… What's his name, this man?"

"Mr. Clifford, sir. "

"Mr. Clifford… Christian name?"

"Roger, sir. Mr. Roger."

"Well, the sight of Mr. Roger Clifford might have you raising your fists again. Let's at least try it my way first."

Simon lifted the heavy iron knocker and banged it down twice. There was no response. He banged again, louder this time.

From somewhere in the depths of the house, barking was heard, then a raised voice, and the clattering of footsteps on wooden boards. A bolt was drawn back, a key turned, and the door was opened.

"Yes? What do you want?"

The young servant, a slip of a lad who had barely begun to shave, looked as if he had just risen from his bed, as well he might: it was barely six o'clock.

"Good morning." Simon was at his cheeriest. "My name is Simon Warrender. I'm a friend of Mr. Clifford's, from London, and out for a ride this morning I thought it would be pleasant to call on him."

It sounded so fatuous to Simon's ears he almost wished he had let Jem go to the door, fists raised, but if Roger Clifford liked artifice, perhaps this was the right way to approach him; he was bound to be curious, and if what Jem had told him was true, most of the time he was in London he was in his cups and wouldn't know one friend from another. If the ruse got him inside the door, that was sufficient. He might then let Jem loose on him.

Roger, it appeared, was not up yet, but if the gentleman wanted to wait, Simon was told somewhat churlishly, the master would be told he was here.

Nearly half an hour passed before the servant returned, half an hour during which Simon, with the cold of the entrance hall's elaborately decorated marble floor - so out-of-keeping with this part of the house - seeping into his bones, see-sawed between annoyance and boredom. Twice he made a move to leave, but thinking of Jem, waiting outside - probably warmer between the horses than he was here - and Mary, goodness knows where, he took to pacing up and down the hall as noisily as he could. Eventually the servant lad returned, looking no tidier than before, and with an abrupt "Come this way" ushered Simon up the oak staircase, along a landing with soft rugs on the floor and into a large, low-ceilinged room, where a young man, without a wig and wearing a yellow silk robe decorated with bows over a frilly-cuffed nightshirt, lay indolently on a gold painted bed, sucking an orange. He is living in the wrong time, Simon thought. He must think King Charles is still on the throne.

"Yes?" Then, seeing that Simon was a gentleman, he raised himself up slightly.

"I don't think I know you, but you say we have met... I meet so many people you see... in town, you know; I'm there much of the time. Do sit..." He waved vaguely, with curling fingers, to a gold-painted chair near the bed.

"Thank you." Simon would have preferred to stand, but it was no good antagonising this foppish young man unnecessarily.

"I have come..." Simon began. The young man's attention was now taken up entirely with his orange, from which juice was spurting on to his robe. Piqued, he threw it from him and reached for a candied cherry in a dish on the table by the bed. Sensuously he licked the sugar coating.

"Go on, I am listening," Roger Clifford drawled. "Although why, I really don't know."

Simon had had enough. He stood up and moved towards the bed.

"I am here for Mary. I have come to take her home."

Roger Clifford lifted his eyebrows and pulled his thin lips into a sneer.

Simon knew his words had sounded feeble, but he had no idea how to speak to this young man, several years his junior. Oh, hang it, he would just be himself!

He took a deep breath. "Now... I don't know exactly what has been going on, but I do know that Mistress Caroline Newell's maid, Mary, is in this house. You lied to Mistress Towler when you said that Mistress Newell had spoken to you; she did no such thing. She is presently in Hertford, caring for her sister, and she sent me to fetch her maid from the farm."

Which was near enough to the truth, except that Caroline was expecting him to fetch Mary from Yardley Bury.

"Well, well... That is most interesting. So you want the girl back, do you? Is she yours, your little bit of...? "He tilted his face up to Simon's. "No, perhaps not. I fancy you like them a bit rougher. There's some quite good farm girls round here. And boys." He took another cherry, and keeping his eyes on Simon, he licked off the sugar as before. "Oh, once I start on these I can't stop!"

Simon's stomach was in knots and his shoulders were tense but he said nothing.

"Oh dear, you are a starchy fellow. Pity, I thought we might have had some fun together. God knows, one needs a bit of recreation in this dull place." He sighed languorously. "Oh well, you'd better take her then, the girl. She's not a lot of fun. She reads! Would you believe it... and really, she's quite useless as a lady's maid. Pricks her fingers, sewing. Made such a mess of dear Virginie's white gown. So take her."

Relieved, Simon relaxed his taut muscles.

"Thank you," he said.

It had been unbelievably easy. He had been firm and polite… and now he would take Mary back to Caroline. Simon allowed himself the tiniest wisp of a smile, as Roger Clifford turned away to reach for another cherry. He turned round, the sticky fruit held between thumb and finger. Slowly he put the fruit into his mouth, waved a hand at Simon and pointed his sugary index finger at him.

"No, I think not."

"But… You've just said…"

"I know. Tiresome, isn't it? I do change my mind, so often. But there you are, that is how I am. So… what is your name, Warren was it?"

"Warrender! Not that it matters. Just say what you've got to say, Mr. Clifford, and let's get on with it, whatever it is."

The man was a silly, degenerate fop, but he held the whip hand. Simon knew he must stay calm and not lose his temper, which he would so like to do with this excuse for a man now simpering at him.

"Well, Mr. Warrender… of course you can have the girl…" He pointed the now still finger at Simon, "but… I require a letter, from Mistress Newell, signed by her, to say that you are a fit and proper person to take her maid away from my care.

"You see, I don't know you. You could be anybody… and I am sure that dear Caroline… Oh yes, I do know the lady… would not want me to hand over her precious Mary without some authorisation. So just go away now, and come back when you *have* the authorisation, and then… we will talk. If you don't mind, I'd like to get dressed now, so if you would… Unless, of course, you wish to stay… and watch?" He began to undo the fastening of his robe.

Simon, too angry to say a word, strode out of the room, down the stairs and out of the front door, which he banged shut as loudly as he could. Jem, hearing the door, looked up from his place of shelter between the horses. A quick glance at Simon's face was enough to tell him that all was not well.

"Let me get away from here; then I'll tell you."

Simon took his horse's reins from Jem, climbed into the saddle and rode off, not seeming to care if Jem followed him or not. Once well on to the road he stopped.

Jem drew up beside him.

"I don't think I have ever been so angry in my whole life," he said.

Jem listened, his own anger growing, as the conversation in Roger Clifford's bedroom was related to him. He was all for turning round, breaking into the Hall, thrashing the fellow with whatever weapon lay to hand, and not leaving until he had rescued Mary.

"I know just how you feel, Jem, but we must do this legally."

Then, admitting to each other that as well as being angry and frustrated they were also both hungry and thirsty, and that without some sustenance they would not be able to think straight about the dilemma they were in, they rode, as fast as the terrain would allow, to the Towler farm. There, in the kitchen, at the long deal table, they ate warm bread and strong cheese and drank ale… and began to feel they could now deal sensibly with the situation.

Much as they both despised Roger Clifford, they would have to do as he asked.

He did *not* know Simon, and he would not have taken notice of anything Jem might have said, had Simon allowed him anywhere near. They were at his mercy… and they sincerely hoped he had some.

Refreshed with food and drink they set about putting into action their plan to rescue Mary, which they had devised over their meal with the help of Mrs. Towler and Nathaniel. It was not a spectacular or dramatic plan; it simply involved a great deal of riding back and forth between where they were now and Yardley Bury and Walkern. On no account, Jem made very clear, was he going to leave Mary for another night in that house with Roger Clifford.

"He won't be expecting us to act that fast, Jem, so if we do, we shall have the advantage over him." Simon, feeling he had failed in his mission, hoped to cheer himself, and Jem, by saying this.

"Then let's not waste any more time, sir!"

Simon asked for paper and pen. He wrote to Sir Henry Chauncy and to Farmer Gilbert. From Sir Henry, Simon requested a letter, written in his capacity as a magistrate, requiring Roger Clifford to hand over Mary Butcher into the keeping of Mr. Simon Warrender, godson of Colonel Plumer of New Place, Gilston. The letter to Jem's master begged his pardon for keeping Jem from his work, asked for his understanding, and promised that Jem would return to the farm by nightfall. It also asked that, if Polly became upset at Jem's absence, Mrs. Gilbert would take care of her. The graveness of the matter would be explained later, by no less a person than Sir Henry Chauncy, if necessary. The wording of Simon's letters was very formal, he knew, but this was a serious business, the abduction of a young girl, and it was important that they should reflect this.

It was now not quite eight o'clock; the journey to Yardley Bury was about three miles, which Jem and Nathaniel could cover at a canter in twenty minutes, in an hour at the most, if for some reason they had to walk their horses part of the way.

The snow had almost gone and apart from some ice-lidded puddles here and there, the paths and fields were soft underfoot, and therefore reasonably safe.

Giving themselves a good hour and a half in Walkern and Yardley Bury to rest the horses and have some food, and allow time for Sir Henry to write his letter to Roger Clifford, with another hour added for the return journey, they expected to be back at the Towler farm by midday at the latest.

In the meantime, Simon and Nathaniel's brothers, Michael and Adam, both of them as lanky as their younger sibling, would take turns, as work allowed, keeping an eye on the Hall.

Was there really a female cousin there? Or had her relationship to Roger Clifford been invented, to make Mary's abduction appear respectable? Lizzie, the Towlers' servant, couldn't say; she'd never been into the Hall. Her sister, who worked in the kitchen, said there had been a young lady, but the girl didn't know who she was, or whether she was there now. She thought the old master and his wife were away, because there was very little proper cooking being done in the kitchen, just some strange foreign dishes that the young master would call for, even at night sometimes, when the servants had gone to bed. It was all a bit odd.

Having met Roger Clifford, Simon was not surprised.

Much to Simon's relief everything went according to plan. Now all they had to do was rescue Mary from the clutches of that evil man at the Hall. In the intervening period since Jem and Nathaniel had ridden off with the sealed letters, Roger Clifford had grown into a monster in Simon's eyes, and he was eager to confront him… and if necessary fight him!

"Come on, Jem," he said, mounting his horse, "let's deal with the… what did you call him?"

"Cullion," Jem grinned, taking the reins of the fresh horse, a cob, that Michael was holding out for him. It was not the kind of horse Jem liked to ride, but the stallion needed a rest before he bore Mary proudly back to Yardley Bury. Roger Clifford, now dressed, in pale blue brocade, lace cravat and high-heeled shoes, his head covered with a long black curling wig, sat stretched out in front of a roaring fire in his dining hall. He was just finishing a meal. Several small birds, torn carelessly apart and half-eaten, lay upon a plate and there were bones on the floor around his chair. Bits of food clung to his cravat and the hand that he raised to take the letter from Simon was shiny with grease.

"Well, give it to me," he said.

"First I will read it to you, and then I will give it to you."

"D'you think I cannot read?" He leant forward and re-filled his wine glass from a decanter on a small pedestal table by his chair.

"I am sure you can, but if you decide to throw the letter on to the fire…"

"Oh, what a brilliant idea!"

"… I want to be sure you have been made aware of its contents first."

"You have thought of everything, haven't you. What a pity you are so dull. Go on then, read it if you must." Holding his glass of wine in one hand, the other, heavy with rings, draped carelessly over the arm of his chair, and with a bored expression on his rouged face, Roger Clifford leaned back and shut his eyes.

Simon, feeling increasingly uncomfortable in Clifford's presence, broke the seal and opened Sir Henry's letter. He cleared his throat and began to read.

"To Mr.Roger Clifford. Dear Sir. I, Sir Henry Chauncy, Justice of the Peace…"

The young man sat up. "What did you say? Chauncy? I asked you to bring a letter from…"

Simon was in no mood for a conversation.

He cut in sharply, "This is an order from the magistrate. You will do what it says. Now please listen while I read it."

"Oh, don't bother." Clifford lay back in the chair and began to laugh. "Take the girl," he said, waving his hand dismissively at Simon.

"What?"

"Take her. I don't want her. Silly little bitch; totally useless as a lady's maid. As for bedding her, oh no! Far too flat-chested for my liking; nothing there to look at all. And as for squeezing or sucking, well…I'd rather have an orange any day."

"You brute!" Simon wanted so much to hit the man, to hurt him, to humiliate him… but knew he must not.

Scrunching up the letter in his right hand he clenched the fist of his left hand until his fingernails bit into the palm.

"Quite a joke, don't you think? You deserve it, you know. Making me think I was getting a letter from the delectable Caroline… She would suit you; I fancy you need a strong woman. I suppose you *have* had one, or are you one of these puritan fellows, holding it all in until you…"

"Enough!" Simon's voice was hoarse, harsh and loud. "Just have Mary brought here… please."

It was hard to add that final word. This creature was so despicable, so low, so nauseating.

"Oh, don't look at me like that. It's over; we've both had our bit of fun. Don't tell me you didn't enjoy being the knight on the white horse … or whatever colour your animal is. Red, I think my servant said, and the other two fellows, yokels by the look of them, who came and went, on farm horses. You don't think you weren't seen, do you?" He laughed softly, pleased with himself. "It has been most amusing, passed the time delightfully. I am almost sorry it has stopped." He drank deeply from his glass, and reached forward to the decanter.

"Oh, how very rude of me," he said. "Do help yourself. Sorry there's not another glass, but I wasn't expecting you back quite so soon. I'm sure you won't mind drinking from the decanter."

Simon stood, seething with fury, not daring to move or speak until he had his temper under control. Let the odious fellow say what he wanted - he felt there was more - and then he could go. If he interrupted Clifford's flow, Simon was afraid he might turn nasty… nastier… and impose some fresh conditions upon him.

"Vandal!" Clifford shrieked. "Here! Now!" He banged his silver-topped cane on the pedestal table so hard that the decanter flew off and shattered in pieces. The young servant who had let Simon into the house came running into the room. He bowed to his master, and it seemed that he was about to kneel in front of him, when Clifford spoke.

"Not now. We have company."

The boy straightened up quickly. "Sorry, sir," he said.

"Fetch the girl."

"Here, sir?"

"Yes, here. And any baggage she has, too."

The boy took a step back. He began to bow.

"Not now, Vandal. Go!"

"Yes, sir."

The boy - Vandal, was that his name ? - turned and ran from the room.

"I do love the letter V. My second name is Victoire, you know."

Simon said nothing. Clifford smiled at him. "Aren't you even the tiniest bit curious?"

"No."

"Ah. Determined to remain aloof. I like it. I must play that part sometime. Just stand still a moment; let me see how I shall need to dress." He looked Simon up and down. "Not quite sure I can get your scornful expression. Let me try." He pursed his lips and drew in his cheeks in what he hoped was a representation of the disgust on Simon's face.

Simon was in no doubt: the man in front of him, now sitting upright and turning his head from side to side whilst maintaining the expression he had adopted, was insane, and needed careful handling. If Clifford had been a straightforward villain, Simon would have known better how to deal with him. The man's delight in his perverted pleasures not only sickened Simon, he was unsure how to respond to it. Any demand made of him, he felt, might put Mary in danger. At a word from his master the boy could quickly whisk her away to some other part of this forbidding house... and then what? It was best to say nothing.

After a few more minutes of silence during which Clifford pulled a series of faces, adopting first a haughty expression, followed by a hangdog look and then a clownish grin, two sets of footsteps were heard on the marble floor of the entrance hall.

"Ah, here she comes!" The man sounded unbelievably genial, as if he were about to welcome a dear friend into the room.

Simon gasped as Mary entered the room behind the servant boy. Her silk dress was dirty and torn around the hem; her hair, usually so bright and shiny, was lank and dull, her face was smeared and her eyes had no life in them.

Until she saw Simon. Her face lit up and she ran to him.

"Oh sir! Sir!" She buried her face in his chest, sobbing.

"Ah. Isn't that charming! Man and his mistress united again."

"Do you have no decency?" Gently he disengaged himself from Mary's embrace.

"Not a lot," said Clifford. "Life is so much more fun without it."

"Come, Mary, let's get you out of here."

"Oh yes, sir. Please, sir." The girl was trembling and on the verge of tears.

Without another word to Roger Clifford - he didn't dare speak for fear of what he might say - Simon, holding Mary's arm gently, propelled her out of the room. The boy, with her baggage, just a cloak and a small cloth bag, followed them. Clifford began to laugh, almost hysterically. Simon took the cloak, a strange garment made of some kind of hide and lined with rabbit fur, and draped it around Mary's shoulders. From the dining hall Clifford could be heard banging his cane on the floor and shouting, "Virginie! Virginie, come here, you little trollop!"

"I'm coming, master," the servant boy called back, in a high-pitched voice.

Seeing the startled, but suddenly comprehending, look on Simon's face, in a deeper voice the boy now said, "Coming, sir," and dropping Mary's bag on the floor, he scuttled into the dining hall and shut the door hurriedly behind him.

Simon lifted up the cloth bag.

"Just one thing, before we go outside," he said, handing her the bag. He should be able to ask this easily, but he was having difficulty finding the right words. "He didn't... Mr. Clifford... he didn't...?"

"Sir?"

"He... he didn't...?" Surely the girl knew what he was trying to say.

"Oh, no sir. No."

"And the... the boy?"

Mary laughed. "Him? No. Half the time *he* was a she."

"Oh. Yes." It was as Simon thought.

"It was only words, sir, really... the both of them." She lowered her head. "There was a bit of... a bit of looking, sir, but... not much, and it wasn't..."

Reassured that no harm had been done and not wishing to hear any more details, Simon said, briskly, "Good. Good. Now listen, Mary… Jem is waiting outside…"

"Oh, sir! Oh!" Her expression was rapturous. She made a quick move towards the door. Simon put out a hand to restrain her.

"Before you get too excited… You are not to say a single word to him about anything that has gone on in this house. No mention of Virginie, or Vandal, or any of that. That man in there…" He nodded towards the dining hall, from which raucous laughter was emitting, "… is depraved, and I think he may be mad, too. He is best left alone, but that will not be enough for Jem." Simon's voice was harsh, in keeping with the words he spoke. "Jem will want to kill him, and detestable as the man may be, Mary, that would be murder… and Jem would hang."

When Simon felt certain that Mary had taken in the gravity of what he had said, he went on, in a kindly tone now, "We don't want that to happen, do we?"

"No, sir," Mary said. There were tears in her eyes. "I'll do what you say."

"Good girl. Now pull up your hood. You don't want Jem to see your hair in that state. And wipe your eyes, too." With the heel of her hand Mary removed the dampness from her face and in doing so brought back a touch of much needed colour.

"Well done."

Simon opened the front door and they stepped outside together. Mary ran to Jem's waiting arms, and Simon, very quietly, closed the door.

The ride to the Towler farm was both short, and. for Mary, very sweet. Seated on the cob, in front of Jem, and with his arms held tight around her, she was warmed and comforted. The nightmare of the past three days was over. Tears of joy and relief trickled down her cheers. With her hands clutching the cloth bag, given to her by Mrs. Towler, when she thought, so innocently, that Mary was off to the Hall as a temporary lady's maid, she had no choice but to let them dry on her face.

Mrs. Towler had also given her the fur-lined cloak, made for her by her sons who had killed the rabbits and cured the pigskin. That, like the bag, must now be returned. Mr. Warrender was right to insist that Jem should know nothing of her treatment at the Hall; Miss Caroline must not be told either. If she found out that Roger Clifford had kept her a virtual prisoner... well, she wouldn't want to kill him, but she could make sure he was never received in London society again, proper London society that is, not the lowlifes and mollies he often went about with. She had been a bit worried when Clifford came to the farmhouse, but the young lady with him seemed so pleasant, and so in need of a lady's maid, and Ma Towler had no qualms about letting her go to the Hall: she appeared to hold the young master in high regard. Mary could only think that out in Hertfordshire he behaved himself, at any rate when his parents were at home.

It was all over now, and she would *not* think about it any more. She snuggled herself closer to Jem; he responded first by bringing his face down to her neck, then lifting a hand from the reins he pulled back the edge of the hood that shielded her face, and pressed his cheek against hers.

"You're not crying, are you?"

"No, it's the wind; it makes my eyes run."

"There's nothing to cry about, now."

"I know."

"I'm here, and you're safe."

"Yes. Dear Jem," she whispered.

"What was that?"

"Nothing."

"I'd swear you said dear Jem."

"Why would I say that?"

Jem grinned, and tucked Mary's hood back around her face. That was what he'd been waiting to hear… a cheeky answer. If that man had broken her spirit he would have Jem to answer to. He was pretty sure he hadn't hurt her physically - he was such a spineless milksop of a creature - but even a few days in that weird house could hurt this lovely girl, his lovely girl, in other ways. He knew so well from caring for Polly what harm just being shut away in a dark room could do to someone.

Simon, riding a few paces behind Jem, smiled to himself at this small show of affection. Given a bit of education and a proper home for his sister, this lad had the makings of a really good man. He might be a gypsy but he was worth ten of that so-called gentleman they had just left. Had he done the right thing there?

Should he have brought Jem into the house and, between them, horse-whipped Clifford till he begged for mercy? It would have felt good, oh yes, there was no denying it, but it wouldn't have served any purpose other than allowing Simon and Jem to rid themselves of their anger. And the man would then probably sue them, and no court, not even one presided over by Sir Henry Chauncy, would let them off scot-free: you

369

did not attack an English gentleman in his home, no matter what he might have done!

Ma Towler was greatly relieved to see Mary riding into the farmyard on the cob.

She ran out of the house to greet her, enfolding her in her arms like a lost lamb.

She greeted Jem almost as affectionately and for Simon there was a deep curtsey. Once in the house and divested of her cloak, which the farmer's wife was pleased to have back, Ma Towler, having gasped at the state of the girl's dress and hair, took Mary away... "for bit of a tidy-up," she said. She washed Mary's hair with warm water scented with sweet herbs, and sponged and mended the hem of her gown.

When they had eaten - the Towler sons came in to join them - and been told as much as Simon wanted them to hear, and Ma Towler had taken Mary upstairs "to get her ready for the journey", they set off for Yardley Bury, again with Mary on Jem's mount, this time the black stallion... but not quite in the way that Jem had envisaged: Mary was wearing rough breeches and her hair was tucked under a farm boy's cap.

"With a lad riding astride behind you no one will give you a second glance," Ma Towler had said when she brought Mary downstairs, "but a pretty lass upfront... Just think about it, Jem. And you, Mr. Warrender, sir, it would be well if you was to keep your distance from these two... just a bit."

It was a trouble-free ride: to avoid meeting anyone from Walkern Jem had taken them by a slightly longer roundabout route, Simon keeping Jem within sight but far enough away to appear to have no connection with a couple of swarthy gypsy lads - Ma Towler had taken the extra precaution of smearing a mixture of onion juice and goose grease over Mary's face and hands.

Well before dark - there was daylight till nearly six o'clock - Mary, in fresh clothes and with her face scrubbed, had recounted her adventures, as much as she felt she should tell, to a wide-eyed, open-mouthed Bessie.

Reassured by both Simon and Sir Henry that Bessie was not to blame in any way, she had now promised - "...on my life, Sir Henry!" - that she would not let the girl out of her sight for one moment. No longer wanting to have Dora in her kitchen, but afraid to dismiss her for fear of angering Susan Aylott, Bessie had already despatched her to the village of Wemsted End, three miles south of Yardley Bury, to 'give a bit of help to my old sister, for a few days'.

Sir Henry, greatly relieved that Caroline's maid had come to no harm, and that Arthur was not at home, heard Simon's version of events, again a doctored one, in the comfort of the snug.

The only small fly in the ointment now was Tom. Simon had had enough of being angry for one day and he was far from pleased to hear that his lad had been making a nuisance of himself in Walkern, flirting with any girl who came in sight, and, more seriously, trying to pass counterfeit coins in the village inn.

Simon should have taken Tom with him to the Towler farm, but it had all happened so quickly - he had no idea when he met Jem in the spinney that he was about to spend almost the whole of the day away. Perhaps it was just as well. If this was Tom's behaviour, left to himself, then he was not the man for Simon, which was to be regretted, because he was a bright lad and Simon liked him. He would let him sweat tonight: he had given Tom a severe dressing-down and forbidden him to leave the house. Simon had never been one to dismiss a servant out-of-hand, neither here nor abroad; he would give the boy a second chance.

Sir Henry insisted that Simon take Mary and all Caroline's boxes in his own carriage to Hertford, with Samuel driving and William in attendance. The servants were to stay the night - there was plenty of room in the stable block at Lombard House - and return the following day, bearing, please, a letter from Caroline assuring him that all was well, and that she would be returning to Yardley Bury as soon as possible, so that they could enjoy together the visits they had planned.

Simon, of course, was welcome to stay at Lombard House as before.

Both Simon and Sir Henry slept well that night.

The next morning a tightly-held-on-to Mary, wearing one of Caroline's hooded cloaks, was brought out to the carriage by Bessie. Simon climbed in beside her - for her protection, please sir, Bessie had said - and they set off for Hertford. The air was crisp and the sun was shining. It augured well. Simon waved to Sir Henry until the carriage rounded the bend in the drive and he was lost from sight. Simon withdrew his waving hand and let out a deep breath. It was nearly over, this adventure that had been thrust upon him. Once he had returned Mary to her mistress he would set about looking for an estate on which to keep and breed horses. His epiphany moment on the way to the Clifford house was still sharp and clear in his mind. All he had to do now was find the right place for his dream to become reality. He settled back in the carriage and shut his eyes. He had no intention of sleeping but fatigue overcame him.

When he awoke - Minutes later? Hours later? He had no idea - he pushed aside the window curtain, lifted the waxed skin blind and called out to Samuel.

Both Simon and Mary - poor girl, she too must have been exhausted - had been asleep for a very long time: they were only an hour's journey from Hertford.

Mary stirred and opened her eyes. She had been fast asleep, weary after a night with Bessie prodding her every five minutes to make sure she was still there, in the bed. Quickly she shut her eyes. Mr. Warrender was a very nice man, a real gentleman... dignified, that's what Miss Caroline had called him... but she did not want to talk to him, and she knew that if she appeared to be awake he would speak to her. All she really wanted to do was think about Jem.

Oh Jem, when would she see him again? She had been bustled away by Bessie the moment they had arrived at Yardley Bury and they had had no time to make any plans. If only she had asked him when and where they would meet when she was behind him on the cob, but it hadn't felt right then, with her dressed like a stable lad. She should have asked him when he had his arms around her on the way back from that dreadful house... No, she must not think about either of those things: the thought of that house sent shivers of disgust down her spine and the thought of Jem's arms brought on that other, delicious feeling... and it would be quite wrong for her to feel like *that,* alone in a carriage with a gentleman! She opened her eyes to find that Simon's eyes were closed. She settled back into her seat. So many thoughts, both good and bad, began whirling around in her

373

brain that she decided a conversation with Mr. Warrender, however difficult, would be preferable. She coughed, Simon opened his eyes, gave her a brief smile and went back to sleep... or to *his* thoughts.

How much further? Mary's thoughts turned away from what *had* happened to what she suddenly realised was happening to her at this very minute: she needed to piss, and although she knew that Sir Henry's carriage carried a piss-pot, she could not possibly use it!

"Are we nearly there, sir?" she asked.

Simon stirred. "What did you say?"

"Is it far, sir, to Miss Emilia's?"

Simon looked out of the window; in the place of the countryside there were now streets, and they were beginning to descend a steep hill.

"I think this is Bengeo," he said, "so it won't be long now." Simon smiled at her.

Poor girl, she had had quite an ordeal. "I expect you'll be glad to get back there."

"Oh yes, sir. Very much so, sir. It can't come too soon for me... sir."

As the carriage rolled down the hill into Hertford, Simon reminded Mary of her promise not to say a word to Caroline about the events of the past few days.

"But what if she asks me, sir... you know, straight out?"

"You'll have to lie."

"Oh, I can't do that, sir! Not to Miss Caroline!"

"You want her to be upset, do you? Worried about you, when her sister needs all her care and attention?"

"Well, no sir, but if I lie God will..."

"I know. But sometimes, Mary, it is kinder than telling the truth… and I feel sure that God would see it that way. Later perhaps, you *will* be able to tell her, but not *now*."

Simon leaned forward and patted the girl's hand. He looked out of the carriage window again; in just a few minutes they would be in Bull Plain.

"We're almost there. Put a smile on your face, Mary."

"Yes, sir." She forced her features into a grin.

"Not too much. Just… try to look natural."

"Yes, sir." Mary looked across at her fellow passenger. "You too, sir," she said gently.

"Yes." Simon nodded. "It's not easy, Mary, but we must do this."

The carriage came to a halt. William sprang down from the box and opened the door. Simon climbed down, then reached in his hand and helped Mary out.

"Oh, thank you, sir." These courtesies would cease, once she took up her duties as a lady's maid; she wished she could enjoy this one more, but she was terrified that she might disgrace herself in front of Mr. Warrender. She stepped down, keeping her legs together as much as she could.

"Ready?"

"Oh yes, sir."

"Good. Then let's go in."

23

Caroline, knowing nothing of Mary's frightening and humiliating experiences in the past week, was enraged that her maid had refused to return to Hertford until she had completed the gown she was sewing for the rector of Walkern's wife. A taffeta gown indeed! She was meant to be doing plain work, mending sheets and collars, not setting herself up as a Paris dressmaker! All Mary would say was that she was sorry, truly sorry, but she couldn't disappoint Mrs. Gardiner. There was definitely something amiss: Mary accepted Caroline's upbraiding so meekly, *and* she was disinclined to chatter, which was not like her at all. Jem? Yes, she had seen him, once. Anyone else? No mistress, just... just the people in the village. Oh. Where? At the rectory, mistress. Caroline wasn't getting anywhere; best to leave it. If Mary had something to tell her she would, in her own time. And Simon, what about him? He had changed too, somehow; with her he was more jolly, which didn't suit him, yet she had seen him deep in what appeared to be a serious conversation with Richard, the two of them, heads together, walking along Bull Plain towards Sir Henry's house, Simon doing nearly all the talking, Richard nodding from time to time. *That* was odd! She was certain something was being kept from her, but what? Sir Henry had been ill, but he was now well: what else was there to know? Anyway, she had other, more important things to think about: should she stay in Hertford with Emilia, or take her and the children to Amley until after the baby was born? And then there was the trial of Jane Wenham… next month.

Although the woman had been far from welcoming when Caroline had visited her in the gaol, she felt she ought to attend the trial. To what purpose? To see justice was done? Much would depend upon the judge, and his views on witchcraft. Nearly a week had gone by since Mary's return to Hertford. The weather was warm and spring-like, so welcome after the snow. Caroline knew it could change at any minute and they could be plunged back into winter; it was, after all, still February. Simon had gone to Gilston, but promised to return for the trial. If the old woman was set free, he wanted to be on hand to escort her safely to Uncle Plumer's estate: he had promised Sir Henry that he would undertake that task.

With Caroline taking the children off her sister's hands each afternoon Emilia was able to rest, and being less weary she was now in better spirits. The only thing troubling Caroline was Mary's behaviour: no gossiping, no sudden peal of laughter as she recounted some small incident of provincial life that she found amusing. The girl was withdrawn and sombre-faced, and once or twice when Caroline had caught her unawares, she could swear Mary had been crying. There was a lot of gazing out of windows, too.

One bright sunny morning towards the end of that week Caroline had walked into the parlour to find Mary standing by the window, holding a candlestick.

"Mary?"

The girl jumped at the sound of her name and swung round to face her mistress.

"Miss Caroline! Oh, you did startle me."

"What are you doing with that ?"

Mary looked down at her hands and seemed surprised to find herself holding a brass candlestick.

"I don't know, Mistress, I…" Slowly she put it down on a nearby table.

"I don't think it goes there, Mary."

"Oh."

Caroline stepped further into the room, picked up the candlestick, and placed it on the walnut bureau, where its twin was standing. Then she turned back to Mary and took the girl's hand tenderly in her own.

"I think it's time you told me exactly what has been going on. I know something is wrong."

"No, mistress, I *can't*. I want to, but I *mustn't*. I promised Mr. Warrender. He said you'd be upset, and with Miss Emilia's baby coming, and her not being well, I wasn't to worry you."

"That was very thoughtful of Mr. Warrender, but Miss Emilia is quite well now, and you are obviously not, so come on… tell me."

"Oh, Miss Caroline!" Sobbing, Mary clung to her mistress.

"Go on, have a good cry." Caroline could feel the relief in the girl's body as she let out the tears she had kept back for so long.

Eventually the sobbing subsided and Mary, now looking embarrassed, lifted her head from Caroline's shoulder.

"Oh, Mistress… Oh, look what I have done to your gown! Oh, I must see to it straight away, otherwise it will leave a stain. Oh, Miss Caroline! I am so, so sorry…" and the tears began to flow again.

"Oh, for goodness sake, girl, stop this blubbering!" A few firm words were needed to restore Mary to normal.

"Sorry, Mistress."

"And that's enough sorries, too. What I want now is an explanation."

The sun, which had brought into the parlour slanting rays in which dust motes swirled, suddenly went behind a cloud, and the room became dark and cold.

"But not here, I think," Caroline said. "We'll go up to my room."

"Yes, mistress." Mary was at her meekest.

"First, though, you go and make us a couple of nice tisanes, ginger I think… and bring them upstairs."

Mary was relieved to have a mundane task to perform before she faced the ordeal of retelling her horrible experiences to her mistress. As she prepared the tisanes she decided on the extent of her confession: that was how it felt, even though she had done nothing wrong, other than lying about the nature of her sewing for Mrs. Gardiner. She would tell Miss Caroline, in full, what had taken place at the rectory, but not a word would she breathe about that disgusting Mr. Clifford and his weird man-servant.

They sat, mistress and maid, warmed by a log fire, on either side of the bedroom fireplace, their tisanes in their hands.

"Go ahead; tell me," Caroline said quietly. She had already sensed that what she was about to hear would not be pleasant, but as the tale unfolded, and Mary recounted her gruesome experience in detail, Caroline gasped with horror and covered her mouth with her hand; her eyes were wet with tears. The tale came to an end with Jem's gallant rescue, the night at the constable's house and the flight to the Towler farm.

"Oh, how could they! Sticking pins in you! Oh!" There was both anger and pain in Caroline's words. "Oh Mary… you poor, dear child!"

Caroline put her tisane dish on the small table to one side of her chair, and reached out her arms to Mary. Still holding hers, Mary slid off her chair and moved towards Caroline's waiting arms.

"Oh, do put your dish down first! I don't want another wet gown!"

Mary swiftly moved back and placed her dish carefully on its saucer on the floor beside her chair. What might have been a moment of tender, intimate embrace had passed. It was, though, a time for rage: how dare they, those women in Walkern, treat Mary like that! What a blessing it was that Jem had arrived in time to save her from even more horrors - what on earth would have happened to her if he hadn't turned up at the rectory in search of Polly? - but, and Caroline didn't like herself for thinking this, it was also unfortunate that it had been Jem, and not someone like the rector or the constable: Mary, already infatuated with the boy, was now positively in love with him! The way her eyes shone when she spoke of him - even when she just said his name they lit up.

Was this the time for Mary to be told who her real father was? She really was too well-bred to marry an illiterate gypsy lad, however chivalrous he might be.

Mary was now going into great detail about the Towler family, their farm, their animals, how kind they had been, especially Ma Towler, lending her a lovely warm cloak when... Abruptly she stopped talking and turned her face away.

Why had Mary stopped, so suddenly? "Is there more?" Caroline asked.

"No, mistress," Mary came in quickly, "there's nothing else."

Caroline sensed that there was, but this was not the moment to probe. "Tell me some more about Jem," she said. She needed to know what his intentions were towards Mary. "You're obviously very fond of him. Is he equally fond of you?"

"I don't know, mistress."

"He hasn't given you any indication of...?"

Mary sighed. "No, mistress, not... not really."

"And you haven't heard from him since you got back here?"

"No, mistress, but that's because he can't write, and he can't take time off to come and see me. I'm sure he would if he could."

Mary might be convincing herself, but not Caroline. It was easy to see what had happened on both sides: for Mary, Jem was exciting, so unlike the servant boys she met in London, and for Jem... Mary was not the sort of girl he would normally come across in Walkern, and the circumstances in which they found themselves had heightened their feelings. The fact that Jem had not contacted Mary cheered Caroline. Another week without hearing from him and the romance would begin to fade, and she would not yet need to tell Mary the true details of her birth.

"Perhaps so," Caroline said, giving Mary what she hoped was a reassuring smile. "Whatever happens in the future, I shall always be grateful to Jem for taking you out of the clutches of those terrible women, especially that Susan Aylott. I'd like to run a needle into *her* arm! And keep it in there until she cried for mercy!"

"Miss Caroline! That's not like you!"

"Injustice and cruelty are things I cannot abide, Mary, and if they make me say wicked things… well then, Mistress Aylott can just be thankful that I am in Hertford and not at Yardley Bury or my words might well be translated into action!"

Children's laughter in the hallway of the house and then their voices, loud and clear… "Auntie Cara, where are you, we've got something to show you!" brought the conversation to an abrupt end.

"I'm glad you told me, Mary," Caroline said, hurriedly getting up from her chair and going to the door. She walked along the landing and started down the stairs, as the children, seeing her, began charging up. She put a finger to her lips. "You mustn't wake your mother," she whispered. "Stay there; I'm coming down."

The children halted, looking upwards, their little faces glowing from their walk with Rosie in the fresh air. They waited while Caroline made her descent, with Mary, carrying the empty tisane dishes, following close behind. As she reached the foot of the stairs Caroline was immediately engulfed in two pairs of arms and legs as Anne and Charlie threw themselves at her. "You noisy darlings," she said, hugging them tight. Over her shoulder she looked at Mary, poised on the step above. "Oh, Mary, I wish my life was as uncomplicated as theirs."

"Yes, mistress, so do I."

24

It was now March and one spring day followed another. It won't last, people said, as they met in the street. While the good weather was here, though, it was an opportunity to leave front doors open for a few hours and let the warm, sweet air into houses that had been shut up all winter.

Richard Oliver's front door in Bull Plain was wide open and Mary, with one of Anne's smocks in her hands, was standing in the doorway. She was supposed to be sewing in the children's nursery. It was bad enough being asked to do *children's* mending without having to be cooped up in that stuffy room under the eaves on a day like this! If she got the sewing done it didn't matter where she did it. She had crept past the parlour where Caroline was sitting reading and hadn't been standing at the open doorway more than two minutes, feeling both guilty and resentful, when a black horse with a long feathery tail galloped past the house, going in the direction of Sir Henry's town residence, Lombard House.

Astride was a young man - only a young man would ride through a town at that pace - head down, urging the horse forward, regardless of the people in the street who hurried out of his path. Up and over the little bridge they went, and disappeared behind the back of Lombard House. Mary dropped her sewing and flew after them, holding on to her cap with one hand and with the other lifting up her skirt of her blue dress to give herself more speed.

Caroline, coming out of the parlour, saw the sewing flung down on the passage floor.

"Mary?" she called out. She picked up the sewing and went to the front door.

Strange, Caroline said to herself. She had heard the galloping horse - she had even caught a glimpse of a waving tail through the parlour window as she shut it after releasing a trapped moth - but she had no reason to connect it with Mary.

Caroline had heard another sound following the thudding of the hooves: a startled cry, and then one word, which she now realised had been a name.

"Oh dear, if it *is* Jem..." She sighed. "...we're going to need to have that talk."

Men, and women holding the hands of young children, were standing in threes and fours enjoying the sunshine. It was obvious they were talking about the horseman who had just thundered past and the young girl, that lady's maid, who had run like the wind after him: an old man was pointing with his knobbly stick at the bridge and a woman, careless of the live chickens in her basket, was swirling her skirt in imitation of Mary. A few minutes passed and when nothing more happened the onlookers went on their way.

Once they had gone Caroline, with the sewing still in her hand, stepped out on to the street, about to go in search of Mary, when she suddenly came in sight, walking very slowly, head down, over the bridge. Caroline didn't know whether to be pleased for herself, or sad for Mary that the horseman who had so raised her spirits was not Jem. She went back into the house and stood in the parlour doorway.

Mary came in and shut the door behind her; she was in no mood for sunshine.

"Mary, come in here."

"Yes, mistress." Mary's words, and her eyes when she lifted her head to look at Caroline, were devoid of expression, and when she entered the parlour she moved as if sleepwalking.

"Sit down."

Obediently Mary sat on the nearest chair.

"This has to stop. Your mind has not been on your work ever since you came back from Yardley Bury. I can understand that you are missing Jem; he's been very good to you, but really, Mary… it's time you stopped pining for him. He's not for you."

"Why not?" Mary's eyes were now alive and her words were challenging.

"Because… he's a gypsy boy who can neither read nor write, and you… you have been brought up almost like a lady. You are refined… and intelligent and…"

"I'm still a country girl, Miss Caroline. *And* I can teach him to read and write!"

"Maybe, but could he learn?"

"Course he could learn! I did, didn't I? You taught me."

"Yes, but you are…" The girl should not be left in ignorance any longer. Besides, Caroline had not nurtured her since she was twelve just to have her spend her life in a remote village where they still believed in witches and meted out punishment to anyone they suspected of being one.

"I'm a cowman's daughter, Miss Caroline. How is that better than what Jem is? I know he's a gypsy, but that don't matter to me." She was letting her speech slip on purpose.

She'd never before heard Miss Caroline put someone down just because of their lowly birth.

"That is the problem, Mary." She had to be told of her parentage, otherwise she might throw herself at Jem whether he wanted her or not, in a fit of pique.

Caroline took a deep breath. "You see…" she began hesitantly, "you are not really a cowman's daughter."

"I am! My father was Mr. Robert's cowman, Thomas Butcher. You know that, mistress."

Mary was looking puzzled, but not worried. Caroline's heart was beating fast, her hands were clammy and her mouth dry. This should be such an easy thing to do, but suddenly Caroline wasn't sure she had the right. Was she about to turn the girl's world upside-down? No, of course not. For the past four years Mary had lived among gentlefolk, and how well she had fitted in, even, on one occasion, being taken for Caroline herself by a too avid suitor! This flirtation with Jem was no more than that, something to pass the time in a dreary village; it was just unfortunate that she had got caught up in that dreadful witchcraft nonsense.

Which is all my fault, thought Caroline: if I hadn't rushed off here to Hertford, 'doing good', none of this would have happened. It is up to me to put things right.

"No, Mary, Thomas Butcher was not your father." Mary's eyes opened wide, and she began to shake her head. "Oh, I know he brought you up as his own, and he did it well, too, but… your true father was a gentleman, a friend of Mr.Robert's brother, Harold. He…" There was no way she could tell the girl what had really taken place; neither was there any need for her to know the sordid details of Susan's rape, for that was what it had been, on the floor of the barn. "He... made love to your mother and..."

"I don't believe you!" Mary's face was blanched, her hands and voice hoarse and trembling. "You're making it up 'cos you don't want me to see Jem. Well, I will! I don't care what you say! He's a good man and I love him!" Mary picked up her skirt and flounced out of the parlour. Caroline heard her charging across the hall, followed by the very loud banging of the front door. Looking out of the window she saw Mary running full pelt down the street towards the river.

"Oh no! Please God, no. Oh, what have I done!" Without thought for her own appearance Caroline raced down the street after Mary, calling out her name as she ran, causing pedestrians to halt and every eye to turn towards her. She caught up with Mary on the far side of the bridge, where the girl had paused, panting, tears streaming down her cheeks.

"Mary, Mary, oh my dear child, I didn't mean to hurt you!" Her attempt to cradle the girl in her arms was rebuffed savagely. Mary pounded her fists on Caroline's chest and began to kick at her.

"You are right to hit me, but please stop. This won't make it better. Oh, Mary, I have done a terrible thing; please forgive me. I never thought for a moment that you wouldn't want to be the child..."

"Of a gentleman? Mr. Warrender's a gentleman, Mr. Robert's friend wasn't! Why should I want to be *his* child? He's no better than that horrible Clifford man!" Oh no! I've broken my promise to Mr. Warrender!

"Mr. Clifford? What's he got to do with it?"

"Well..." It would serve Miss Caroline right if she said. "*He's* supposed to be a gentleman, but he's... not *nice. You* said he wasn't nice. I don't want no gentleman, and not that sort of gentleman - Sir Gilbey's a gentleman! - to be my father. I've got a father! Oh, Miss Caroline, tell me it's not true."

Mary lifted her tear-filled eyes to her mistress's face, and grabbed her hands in hers. They stood there, hands and eyes locked together, totally oblivious of the crowd that was gathering around them.

In a small voice, barely above a whisper, Caroline answered. "I'm sorry, but it is."

Mary let go of Caroline's hands, and pushing past the men and women who were relishing the spectacle being presented to them, she fled, sobbing, up the street and into the Olivers' house. For a moment Caroline stood where she was, numb with distress. Gazing after Mary's retreating figure, she became aware of the faces of the people around her, all of them, it seemed, waiting for the next bit of the drama. First the horseman, now this.

"What are you looking at?" she said crossly. "Can't I stand by the bridge without being stared at? Go away, please, all of you."

Mumbling their apologies, the men lifting hands to their hats, the women curtseying, the onlookers dispersed. One or two of them, walking away, glanced over their shoulders at Caroline, but seeing the fierceness of her returning look, turned round quickly and hurried away. When they had all gone Caroline walked slowly back along Bull Plain and into her sister's house, her steps ordered and her carriage dignified; her mind, though, was in turmoil. Having held back for so long in revealing to Mary the truth of her parentage, she had now blundered in at quite the wrong moment. Everything was ruined: Mary would leave her and go after Jem. At sixteen she would rush into an unsuitable marriage. Caroline had a vision of her dainty lady's maid in a sacking apron, her hair dirty and straggly, with a horde of tiny, grubby-faced children clinging to her ragged skirt. Caroline shook her head to dismiss the picture, only to have it replaced by an even worse one: Mary, unwanted by Jem, wandering the lanes around Walkern, collecting herbs and… No! None of this must happen!

"Mary, where are you?" Caroline had reached the front door of the Olivers' house. "Mary?" The hallway was empty. She called up the stairs. No response.

From somewhere nearby she heard a small hiccupping sound, as if a sob were being kept in check. She went into the parlour. "Mary?"

"Yes, mistress." The answer, barely audible, came from a huddled form in the far corner, its back to the room.

Caroline crossed the room, lifted Mary up and for a moment held her close.

Then, still holding her, but now at arm's length, Caroline spoke, softly, but with a firmness she felt necessary if this situation was to be rectified.

"I know I have upset you, and for that I am sorry, but the fact remains: you are the daughter of a… I won't call him a gentleman, for that he was *not,* but he was… he was a clever young man from a good family…" Even as she uttered the words Caroline knew how feeble they must sound. Mary's sharp retort came as no surprise.

"I don't care how clever he was, or what sort of family he had, he shouldn't have done that, not to my mother!"

"No, of course he shouldn't, but going over the past isn't going to help us, Mary. It is what you are going to do now that matters." There, that was more positive.

Caroline smiled at the sad, angry girl facing her.

"It don't alter nothing, Miss Caroline, you looking at me like that. I can't stay with you now, not after this."

"Why ever not?"

"'Cos… I don't know who I am no more! If my father was from the gentry, then I'm not really a servant, am I? I know my mother was a farm girl, but…"

Mary looked with troubled eyes at her mistress. Caroline's heart ached for her.

She, Caroline, had brought this about; it was her duty to resolve it, and if she lost her maid, well, so be it.

"If you truly love Jem and he loves you, then you must marry, and with my blessing. I will find somewhere for you to live, and…"

"Oh, Miss Caroline, I don't want to leave you!"

"You can't have it both ways, Mary."

Caroline sat down; oh, how weary all this was making her feel. "I will write to the rector," she said, "and ask him to speak to Jem and tell him… no, ask him… to come here, to Hertford. I will say that you… no, I… would like to see him… to thank him… for rescuing you and looking after you. Yes, that should do it. And then when he comes here, we can find out what his intentions are."

Caroline smiled at her maid, hoping to transfer to the girl some of her apparent confidence in a happy conclusion to the matter. It would all hang on Jem. Did he love Mary? Would he leave his present life to go goodness knows where with her? And what about his simple-minded sister, Polly? That was a complication Caroline had not considered. Oh, let's get Jem sorted out first; somewhere suitable could be found for Polly.

Mary, confused and anxious, took her time in answering. If only Miss Caroline had not told her that dreadful truth about her father, but that's how her mistress was, forever plunging into things without thinking what would happen next, like she'd done with the witch-woman, promising her a safe place to live. She must *not* know about Roger Clifford: she would want to ride up there, astride probably, and shoot him! *And* she would do it! Not that he didn't deserve it.

"Well? You're very quiet." Caroline leant forward, bending her neck, trying to look up into her maid's face, but Mary's head was down, her eyes fixed on her hands clasped tightly together against the front of her dress.

"I'm thinking, mistress," she said, without looking up. "It's good to think before you speak."

"Yes. You are right." Caroline sighed, stood up and walked over to the window.

The activity in the street had returned to normal; just a few people going about their everyday business. The incidents some of them had witnessed would provide a fragment of gossip to be retold in the marketplace or over a pint of ale that evening, and maybe even the following day, but no more than that. For Mary and Caroline there were likely to be repercussions, and recriminations, and if not cleared up now these could go on for a long time. Caroline turned from the window.

"Mary, we *must* put this behind us, and we must do it now. I will write my letter to Mr. Gardiner and this afternoon I shall ride up to Bengeo; Lady Poynter's groom will deliver the letter." Caroline's tone was business-like, but now, bringing sympathy and understanding to her voice, she said, "And Mary dear, while I'm gone, try to find something that will occupy your mind, as well as your fingers. Will you do that?"

"Yes, mistress, I'll try."

"Good girl." Caroline patted Mary's hand and turned away, ready to leave the room.

"What about Mr. Warrender, mistress? Will you write to him?"

Caroline turned round.

"Mr. Warrender? This has nothing to do with him." He had brought Mary to Hertford, yes, but what happened to her now was no concern of his.

"It does, Miss Caroline. Jem is going to work for him."

"*What*? Of course he's not! Wherever did you get that idea from?"

"He said."

"Who said?"

"Mr. Warrender. He said… when he gets his new place, he wants Jem to look after the horses for him and help him to breed new ones. And he'll find a place for his sister!" she added defiantly.

"Oh! Did he? Well…" Was there no end to the things being kept from her? How dare her maid and the man she thought was her friend conspire against her! "In that case, Mary, if what you say is true…"

"It is, mistress!"

"… then I *had* better write to Mr. Warrender! I am not pleased about this, Mary, all this fixing things up behind my back!"

"It was Jem, Miss Caroline, not me."

"Oh Mary, d'you think I can't see where this is leading? Jem goes to work for Mr. Warrender... and you go, too. I'm glad you have the decency to blush."

"You wouldn't have to find somewhere for me and Jem to live if Jem went to..."

"Enough! We don't know if Jem even wants you. Let me get my letter written. No, not to Mr. Warrender. First things first. And the first thing I need to know, is: what are Jem's intentions, because if they are not honourable, then that's the end of it, and however much you sob or cajole you will not see him again. Don't start crying Mary, please. Save your tears in case you need them later. Now go and do something useful. You are still my maid, you know."

"I know! Most of the time I like being your maid, but..."

"Don't be cheeky, I won't have it!" This comes of treating Mary more like a daughter than a servant. Would I allow a daughter - Oh, Hannah! - to speak to me like that? I'll never know.

Mary, with tears streaming down her cheeks, ran from the parlour and up the stairs. Distantly a door banged shut. Caroline leant back in the chair, a sick feeling in her stomach, a feeling of self-reproach coupled with anxiety, and annoyance with Simon, too. Needing to calm herself before she went upstairs to write her letter, she took several deep breaths and shut her eyes. It didn't help; an image she didn't want to see floated behind her closed eyelids - Mary travelling back to Hertford in Sir Henry's carriage... with Simon. That really was most unseemly. What else had they been up to, what other secrets did they have, this man she had thought so highly of and this girl she had nurtured? Oh, this was unbearable: if there *was* anything else, she didn't want to imagine it, she wanted to *know*!

Caroline leapt out of the chair and went to the door.

"Mary, come down here this instant!" she yelled.

Emilia, roused from a nap, called out, "Cara, are you all right?"

"Yes, go back to sleep. Mary, come here."

Caroline stood, trembling, at the foot of the staircase.

"Coming, mistress." Her cap askew, her feet bare, Mary ran down the stairs.

"Come in here." Caroline could barely get the words out. "And shut the door."

Mary closed the door.

"Now, you tell me exactly what this is all about. I don't want any more lies, any more hiding things from me. I want the truth, Mary."

"I don't like truth! You told me *truth* and…" The girl was trembling even more than her mistress. "I've told you the truth!"

"Some of it, perhaps. Not all." Caroline was torn between compassion and anger. Anger won: how could Simon… ? "Come on, tell me."

"I don't know what to tell you." Mary began to feel afraid. She had no idea how to respond; whatever she said or did was sure to be wrong.

"Tell me about you and Mr. Warrender."

"Me… and Mr. Warrender?" Mary's heart beat very fast. I can't tell her; I mustn't; I promised.

"Yes, you and Mr. Warrender. What did you talk about?"

"We didn't, mistress. Most of the time we slept."

"Oh!" Caroline's heart skipped a beat. "You slept. Oh, very nice! You slept! My maid and my friend... well, I thought he was my friend..."

"Oh, Miss Caroline, how could you ever think such a thing?"

"Well, you seem to have got very close, whatever it was you were doing!"

"Oh, dear Miss Caroline."

Very tenderly, as a loving daughter would, Mary reached out her arms to her mistress.

"No." Caroline shook her head. "That's very sweet, but I have to know."

Mary dropped her arms. She walked past Caroline to the fireplace. "This needs making up," she said. "I'll get some wood."

"It is not your job to see to the fire! Turn round and tell me!"

Without taking her eyes off Mary Caroline moved to the armchair by the window and carefully seated herself. Very slowly, Mary turned round to face her.

Caroline took a deep breath: at last, the truth.

"I made a promise to Mr. Warrender, and you are making me break it."

"Yes, I am."

"A promise should not be broken. You taught me that."

"Yes."

"So how can you ask me to break a promise made to a gentleman... a *real* gentleman!... who... who cares for you?"

It was taking a risk, saying that. Mary had wanted to say *loves you* but love was too strong a word. Beside, how did she know that he did? Miss Caroline had spoken of loving Jem as a serious thing. This too was serious; Mary needed to be cautious. How Miss Caroline reacted could affect all their lives.

"He… cares for me?" It was no more than a whisper. Colour began to rise from her throat to her lips, to her cheeks, to her brow. "Nonsense," she said.

"I have given my word," Mary went on, as if the last few words between them had not been spoken, "… and if you feel you need to know why… It is in no way harmful to you, Miss Caroline, I swear… then you will have to ask Mr. Warrender to release me from my promise, or tell you himself."

The two women were now unashamedly crying.

"Come here." Caroline held out her arms and eagerly Mary went to her.

"You are a good girl. I should never have doubted you." Caroline caressed her maid, as if she was indeed a daughter, then gently she pushed her away and rose from the chair. "I must write… to Mr. Gardiner."

"Yes, Miss Caroline."

Neither of them mentioned a second letter.

"And you have some sewing to do."

"Yes."

"Make sure you do a good job on Anne's little smock; it's her favourite."

"I will."

Mary gave a small curtsey and left the room.

A smile she could not control spread across Caroline's still pink face.

"What nonsense!" she said aloud. She stood up, and walked briskly out of the parlour, up the stairs and into her room, humming. Mary, in the small sewing room across the landing heard this unusual sound. Oh, Miss Caroline, please write a good letter, she said to herself. The chances that it would be, Mary felt, were now greatly improved.

Her letter completed to her satisfaction - it had taken several drafts to get the wording right - Caroline rode straight off to Bengeo. If she delayed she might have second thoughts about what she had done... written to a village rector about a gypsy lad!

Lydia was delighted to see her sister-in-law and happy to comply with her wishes. Caroline was determined not to mention Simon, for fear she might blush, and prayed that Lydia would not mention him either. They took tea together and Caroline admired Lydia's newest settee, made of the finest walnut with beautiful scroll arms and needlework upholstery; they looked out of her large sash window with its new silk curtains, at the daffodils just coming into bloom, and at the place where a fountain and fish pond were to be built.

"If he goes today and stays in Walkern tonight, you will get a reply by tomorrow," Lydia said.

She was all for her sister-in-law staying overnight in Bengeo, to await Mr. Gardiner's letter, but Caroline did not want to leave Mary alone that long, so if John could bring the letter direct to Bull Plain that would be most helpful.

"Goodness, you are in a rush," Lydia said, as Caroline mounted her horse, ready to depart. "We've hardly had time for a proper chat, and there's so much I want to talk to you about. The charming Mr. Warrender, for instance. Such a nice young man. You have made no mention of him; has he gone back to Gilston?"

"Yes, he has," Caroline said, bending down to check on her stirrup.

"Will you be seeing him again?" No answer. "Is he coming back to Hertford?"

"I don't know." Caroline's head was still down, as she now checked the girth.

"You have no need to do that, Caroline. The boy will have checked everything."

"Of course."

Caroline raised her head, the pink colour in her cheeks and neck easily attributable to having bent her head down.

"I must go," she said. "Goodbye. And thank you so much. Dear Lydia."

"You're keeping something from me, I know you are."

"Oh Lydia, I wouldn't do that."

"Oh, you *would*. I shall get it out of you, though! You could always write me a letter, if it makes you blush to tell me to my face!"

"Lydia!"

"Go now, but kiss me first."

Caroline bent down from the saddle and kissed Lydia's cheek.

"He won't come unless you invite him," Lydia whispered in her ear.

"Lydia!!"

"You really shouldn't have bent down to see to that girth, my dear: your face is quite red."

"Oh Lydia."

Caroline gave a tug at her reins, turned the horse's head and rode off.

Lydia, giggling like a little girl, went into her house and shut the door.

25

Caroline's reply from Mr. Gardiner, delivered by John the next morning, was brief.

He thanked her for her letter and promised to 'see what he could do'. The rector, the groom told her, was too taken up with gathering together all the witnesses for the forthcoming trial of Jane Wenham to concern himself with Mistress Newell's problems, whatever they were. Caroline was not pleased with the way John passed on this information, with a hint of disdain and annoyance that he should have been sent upon such a trivial errand, implying that it was only because Lady Lydia had asked him to do this for her dear sister-in-law that he had gone at all.

He reminds me of someone, Caroline said to herself, watching him ride away, and as she went into the house, to read again the rector's note, hoping to find in it something more promising that she had missed at the first hurried reading - she had broken the seal and opened up the sheet of paper there and then at the front door - it came to her: John was Malvolio to Lydia's Olivia! He certainly had ideas well above his station. Caroline was all for John making the most of his life - a former footman, albeit a Royal one, now owned a fashionable London grocery shop - just so long as Lydia wasn't hurt in the process.

John's words, though, and the rector's note, came as a rebuke: with her concern for Mary she had put to the back of her mind the trial of Jane Wenham that would be taking place in a few days' time. She should make another visit to the gaol; the old woman might like a prayer book, even if she could not read. As Caroline knew from her servants at Amley, just the holding of a holy book could bring comfort. She would go today; Richard was sure to have a spare prayer book, or even a bible, that she could take.

Now that the time of the trial was fast approaching Caroline began to feel apprehensive for the old woman. So much would depend upon the judge, and of course the jurors. There were judges now, following the lead of the late Lord Chief Justice, Sir John Holt, who completely repudiated the idea of witchcraft.

The jurors though, if drawn from the local people, farmers and suchlike - even clergy, she thought with disgust - were sure to be prejudiced against the prisoner.

She would just have to pray for a sensible, modern-thinking judge.

What Caroline had to do *now*, this minute, was break the news to Mary that there was, as yet, no word from Jem.

Mary took the news calmly, with just a small lift of her eyebrows. Tears and tantrums Caroline could deal with, but the girl's withdrawing into herself again, as she had done when she came back from Yardley Bury with Simon, was worrying.

The sooner this business with Jem was settled the better. If he wanted her and they married, Mary's country ways, those of her mother, could come to the fore. If Jem rejected her, then Caroline would need to groom her to become, though not for a few years yet, the wife of some middle-class man, a clerk perhaps or a merchant in a small way, for whom Mary could keep the accounts, someone who would have a few servants in his household. Mary's pedigree would probably be acceptable to such a person, but, sadly, not to a member of the gentry, unless - Caroline smiled as her imagination ran riot - some young blood were to fall madly in love with her and whisk her away one midnight!

For now Mary was still Caroline's maid, and a normal routine of sewing and laundering, though dull, would be best for the girl. Having imparted the news to Mary, Caroline sent her upstairs to sort out all her collars and cuffs, petticoats and gowns to see if any of them required mending or refurbishing.

Any major trial at the Hertford Lent Assizes in the Sessions House brought visitors to the town, and the trial on March 4th of a notorious witch who had been held in the gaol here for several weeks was causing a lot of excitement. London folk would be attending, it was said, on account of the presiding judge being Sir John Powell, a friend of the writer Jonathan Swift. But Hertfordshire folk knew better than to be taken in by a Londoner: the woman Jane Wenham was guilty, of course she was, and any judge would see that. Sixteen witnesses were being called, and not just country people. There were three clergymen testifying and Sir Henry Chauncy's son. It was a foregone conclusion that the woman would hang … and that would be another spectacle to draw people to the town. The inns were well-stocked with ales and wines, the shops had put their most attractive goods in their windows, there were hawkers on every street corner and extra stable space had been found for the expected influx of horses and carriages.

Richard Oliver deplored the sensational aspect of all this - a woman's life was at stake; a trial was not a circus performance! - but neither he nor his household was immune to the atmosphere of excitement, with so many people hurrying up and down Bull Plain. Caroline was as dismayed as Richard, but not surprised after the scenes she had witnessed in Walkern. She could only hope and pray that Jane Wenham would be set free to begin a new life, safe in a cottage on Uncle Plumer's estate. She had said as much to Richard.

If the old woman *was* set free she must be got out of Hertford as quickly as possible, before Susan Aylott and her coterie could harm her, as Caroline was sure they would want to do, whatever the law had decided.

And where was Simon? Only a day to go before the trial began and there was no sign of him, nor had there been any word from him. Caroline was troubled: he hadn't seemed the sort of man who would break a promise. Enough of musing... it was time to choose her gown for the trial day: nothing too smart or too colourful - she didn't want to stand out in the crowd of people in the courtroom - but she must still be well-dressed. The trial was to start at nine in the morning and go on, if necessary, until the late afternoon. Caroline would need a comfortable dress, suitable for daytime, not too warm, because it was sure to become stifling with a great press of bodies in a confined space.

Mary was called and together they decided on a suitable gown: the russet brown silk with brocade panels in the skirt, one of Caroline's favourites.

Distinguished-looking but discreet, was how she summed it up to Mary.

"What should I wear, mistress?"

"*You're* not going!"

"But mistress, you can't go on your own!"

"I want to do this as... as unobtrusively as I can. So you don't say a word to Miss Emilia, and certainly not to Mr. Oliver. Do you understand?"

"Yes, mistress, but you should have your *maid* with you."

"No, Mary! You cannot attend the trial! Susan Aylott and some of those other dreadful women from Walkern will be there. It will be bad enough if they notice me, but if they see *you*... just think what will happen if Mistress Wenham is set free. They will want you as a scapegoat! You do know that word, don't you?"

"Yes, mistress."

"I cannot risk it, Mary. No, don't start begging me! Anyway, why would you want to be there? He's not coming, you know. Nor is Mr. Warrender, by the look of it. So just run an iron over that lace for me, and give the gown a good shake."

"Yes, mistress."

Mary watched her mistress retreating down the stairs; with a sigh she turned to her task. It had all gone so wrong, and she was helpless to do anything. Hard as it was, she would just have to forget Jem; he didn't care for her, and that was that. Out of sight, out of mind. And it looked as if Mr. Warrender was no better.

From first light next morning the town was buzzing and fizzing with life and noise and activity: the rumble of carts, the neighing and stamping of horses, the cries of street vendors and the smell of cooking, the tramp of feet and the sound of voices raised above the hubbub... and around it all an atmosphere of excitement and anticipation tinged with fear - who knew what dangers the trying of a witch might unleash?

Mr. Gardiner had had a difficult time assembling the witnesses. Not the other clergymen, of course, they could be relied upon to get themselves to Hertford, and Mr. Chauncy was only too eager to play his part. He was there, by the farm wagon in the main street of Walkern, before daylight, as was Susan Aylott. The rector hoped they would behave themselves, Arthur especially. He might be a gentleman, but he had the brains of a simpleton, a vicious one. It was the other witnesses who worried the rector: would they all turn up, or would some of them, afraid of what Jane Wenham might do to them if they spoke up against her in a court of law, fail to appear? It was one thing to say what they felt, and knew to be true, in the rectory kitchen, but at Hertford, before a London judge...

He wished that his wife was not a witness; her health was very poor these days, with constant megrims, for which there seemed no cure. Feverfew eased her pain, but did not prevent their occurrence, and the thought of standing up in the courtroom had several times in the past few days reduced her to tears. Alice Gilbert, who was, on the whole, a sensible woman, had promised to look after her. Fortunately her daughter, who had become Susan Aylott's acolyte, was not coming; someone had to stay with Polly, now that Jem had gone.

Jem Dakers. The rector sighed. No one knew where he was… and the rumours flying around Walkern and Yardley, and up as far as Cromer, were causing Mr. Gardiner and Sir Henry great concern. If they were true, then Walkern would be known not just for witchcraft, but for another, even more serious, crime.

26

Bull Plain itself was almost empty, but the road that led from it to the courthouse, just two minutes' walk away on a normal day, was thronged with people jostling and shoving, trying to get as near to the scene of the trial as they could. It was only by elbowing her way through in a way that appalled Mary, watching from the doorway of the Olivers' house, her hand to her mouth to stop herself calling out, that Caroline managed to reach the courthouse in time for the start of the trial at nine o'clock.

Exhausted, her hat askew, her temper frayed, she took her place amongst the other visitors in the gallery and looked about her. Below, in the body of the courtroom, the jurors were filing in, all twelve men - property owners, as they had to be by law - strangers to her. Not so the witnesses: Arthur, Francis Bragge, Mr. Gardiner, and his wife… in a blue dress, the Rev. Strutt and another clergyman she had not seen before; then nearby a crowd of Walkern villagers. She spotted Susan Aylott and Elizabeth Field and Farmer Chapman… and that poor girl, Anne Thorn. Oh dear, was she going to testify against the old woman? One of the village men looked up at the gallery and Caroline drew back quickly, fearful of being recognised. She turned her attention to the people seated around her; many of them were of her own rank, but fortunately none of them was known to her. They were there, she felt sure, to gawp and gossip, with no regard for the prisoner who was now being brought into the room by the gaoler and a constable.

The volume of noise, which was already considerable, rose to a roar at Jane Wenham's appearance, then instantly died away, either for fear of the prisoner - the look of hatred on her face was enough to quell all but the most scornful of onlookers - or respect for the law, in the person of Sir John Powell, whose august presence was now heralded by the clerk, calling upon everyone to rise to their feet.

By leaning forward Caroline had a good view of the judge, on a dais to her right, his relaxed manner and twinkling eyes suggesting that, although this was a serious trial, he was not about to be browbeaten by a trumped-up young curate who fancied himself as a witch-hunter, nor badgered by a group of prejudiced villagers.

First though, there were prayers conducted by the clergyman Caroline did not recognise, a tall, elegant man, who looked to be in his forties. The prayers were followed by a sermon from the same gentleman. This, to Caroline's mind, tedious part of the proceedings over, the trial itself could begin.

Francis Bragge, among others, had been hoping for a straightforward indictment for witchcraft, and was both disappointed and angry to learn that Jane Wenham, although pleading guilty, was to be indicted only for 'conversing familiarly with the Devil, in the shape of a cat'. There was no mention of Anne Thorn, nor of any of the other people in Walkern whom the old woman was said to have bewitched.

The fury on Francis's face brought a smile to Caroline's. She wiped it off quickly and resisted the temptation to look at the judge, feeling sure she would see a corresponding smile there.

The first witness to be sworn in was Anne Thorn. Asked by the judge to relate exactly what had happened to her, she immediately fell to the ground in a fit, causing uproar in the whole court, from the visitors in the gallery down to the jurors and the other witnesses waiting to be called. The only person remaining totally calm, as far as Caroline could see, was the judge. When the noise had subsided - the clerk of the court had to call three times for silence - Sir John Powell said, to the court at large: "Never in all my experience at the trial of a witch, have I seen the person said to be afflicted fall into a fit in court."

The jurors and the other witnesses were so disturbed by Anne's fit that they would not hear of the trial continuing until the judge had given permission for Jane Wenham to be brought from the dock to stand in front of Anne, to bring the fit to an end Sir John was told, but on seeing the old woman Anne flew at her and had to be pulled away and removed from the courtroom. When the clerk had once more restored order the next witness, Mrs. Gardiner, was called.

So that's the dress that Mary was sewing, Caroline said to herself. Lovely silk, but the gown looks poorly finished, and it doesn't fit properly; it's not up to Mary's standard. It was obvious what had happened: when Mary had been taken to safety by Jem, some of the village women must have finished the sewing. With an effort Caroline pulled her thoughts away from Mrs. Gardiner's dress to listen to what she was saying.

With surprising confidence - perhaps the new gown was responsible - the rector's wife recounted in detail the sad, but to her audience thrilling, story of Anne's bewitchment: the crooked pins, the leaping over gates, her meetings with Jane Wenham, the cat that had a witch's face, the screaming, the exploding bottle of urine - that part of the tale brought cries of amazement and awe from the gallery and much screwing-up of disgusted faces, but not so disgusted that their owners didn't want to hear the next bit! - the bone-setting, the fits and the near-drowning in the River Beane. Mrs. Gardiner's evidence was very long and very detailed; no judge or jury could have asked for a better witness. She had started off this trial in a spectacular fashion! When she stepped down from the box to retake her place beside her husband she was roundly cheered by the Walkern villagers, and from the gallery came the sound of the discreet clapping of hands.

Oh yes, thought Caroline, this is theatre at its best! There was more drama to come. The applause for Mrs. Gardiner had barely died down when a piercing scream rent the air. Anne Thorn, now returned to the courtroom, was having another fit. A request for permission to 'pray over' Anne was refused by the judge.

"No, no," he said. "She will come to herself by and by. Let us get on with this trial."

The second witness was the rector. He related in detail the quarrel between Jane Wenham and Farmer Chapman, and concluded his evidence with an account of the old woman's confession in the presence of the Vicar of Yardley, the Rev. Strutt. When called as the next witness, Mr. Strutt, now recovered from his severe cold, but still with a croaky voice, gave a dramatic account of the several attempts which had been made to get Jane Wenham to say the Lord's Prayer, mimicking her replies to great effect and general amusement.

He then described how he had said prayers for poor Anne Thorn at the rectory, to bring her out of her fit.

Caroline sat forward: this was something she had not heard before.

"Oh," said Sir John, "what prayers were those?"

"Prayers, my Lord," Mr. Strutt replied, "from the Office for the Visitation of the Sick... and some other parts of the Book of Common Prayer."

"I see. Mm. A form of exorcism, you might say?"

"Yes, my Lord."

"I have heard of forms of exorcism in the Roman liturgy, but I did not know we had them in *our* Church." He paused. "Very interesting. Mm. It is good to know we have such virtue in our prayers, too."

Anne's fit showed no sign of coming to an end; reluctantly Sir John gave permission for a prayer to be said.

"If you would be so kind, Mr. Chishull?" the judge enquired, inclining his head towards the clergyman who had spoken the opening prayers.

"Most certainly, Sir John." Possibly Sir John had not heard him, but he had offered to perform this service when Anne had had her earlier fit. In a deep and sonorous voice, well suited to both the pulpit and the courtroom, the minister - the Vicar of Walthamstow and a great scholar, Caroline heard the lady next to her whisper to her friend - intoned a prayer, beginning with the impressive words, 'Oh Lord, who is a most strong tower to them that put their trust in him, to whom all things in heaven, in earth and under the earth, do bow and obey...' After the chorus of Amens which followed the prayer, seeing no change in Anne, he raised his hands, palms outward, in the gesture of oration.

"Our Father, which art in Heaven," he said, and the - audience, congregation, it was hard to know what to call this collection of people, Caroline thought - murmured the words after him in unison. As they did so, miraculously the colour returned to Anne's cheeks and she, too, repeated part of the prayer after the minister.

Relief and admiration showed on the faces of the whole assembly, not least on the face of the judge, whose expression said to Caroline, 'At last we may be able to get on with the trial'; a witness with fits and a succession of prayers had not been on his agenda.

"Thank you, Mr. Chishull. That was well done." The vicar gave the judge a deep nod and the judge returned it.

"Call the next witness," Sir John said.

"Call Mr. Arthur Chauncy," the clerk bellowed, quite unnecessarily, as Arthur was seated only a few feet away.

Oh dear, thought Caroline, this is going to be embarrassing. And it was.

Caroline cringed as Arthur gave his sworn testimony, recounting proudly, incident by incident, his involvement in the exposure of Jane Wenham's witchcraft: the crooked pins, the cats, the fits, a story about strange feathers in a pillow and, finally, Anne's leaping over a five-bar gate 'as nimbly as a greyhound', at which Sir John raised his bushy eyebrows.

"Please remember, sir, that you are on oath," he said.

"I do *know* that! My father is a magistrate, my Lord."

"Quite so. It is a pity he is not here today. Please continue, Mr. Chauncy."

But Arthur was not ready to continue.

"He sends greetings to you, Sir John."

"Thank you." Sir John nodded his head at Arthur.

"He is not well, or I am sure he would be present. As you may know, he…"

Raising a hand to emphasise his words, the judge said, "Enough, young man. Enough. Let us return to your testimony, please. You were saying that the maidservant had vaulted over a five-bar gate." He looked quizzically at Arthur. "Did she? Truthfully?"

"Yes, indeed, my Lord. I affirm upon my oath that she went over it as swiftly as I have seen a dog, a greyhound, leap over such a gate."

"Very well. I will accept your word. Is there more?"

"Oh yes, my Lord."

The judge sat back in his chair.

"We are waiting, Mr. Chauncy."

Arthur seemed to have been put off his stride; he needed prompting.

"I believe you tested the prisoner in some way. Is that right?"

"Yes, my Lord, I did."

"Then tell us about it."

And he did, down to every last grim detail. He had the courtroom in his hands as he described how he had seen Anne Thorn in several of her fits, including one, 'the worst of them all!', when she was 'given over for dead!' but recovered when the prisoner approached her. He told them about the howling cats and how he had killed one of them with a threshing-staff, and then, to the horror and thrill of everyone listening, he described, graphically, how he had *several times* run a pin into Jane Wenham's arm and when he drew the pin out there had been *no blood*! Arthur had more to tell, but Sir John was already calling for the next witness.

"Thank you, Mr. Chauncy. That was most interesting. Let us move on, please."

Francis Bragge now took the stand.

"Good morning, my Lord," he said, and gave the judge one of his most sweeping bows, flicking up the tails of his obviously brand-new silk coat to great effect.

"I hope today finds you well."

"Thank you. Yes. Your testimony please."

"Ah, well…" said Francis, beaming at Sir John, "There is so much, it is…"

"Then the sooner you begin, the better, Mr… er…" He glanced down at his papers. "… Bragge."

"I shall endeavour, my Lord, to give you and the court…" At which he extended his left arm in a large, sweeping gesture that encompassed the whole courtroom.

"… a full and accurate account of all that has taken place in Walkern since the prisoner commenced her present persecution of the worthy, God-fearing folk of this village. I have, of course, a great deal to disclose, but I shall try to be as succinct as possible without omitting any information which I consider vital to Your Lordship's conduct of this case." Another, lesser, bow to Sir John.

"Mr. Bragge…"

"I shall begin with the first occasion on which I was present when the rector's maid, Anne Thorn, as a result of being bewitched by this evil woman…" Francis turned his eyes upon the old woman in the dock, "…was forced to run around the countryside searching for sticks."

"*Mr. Bragge!*"

"My Lord?"

"We have heard all this, Mr. Bragge, from other witnesses. Have you no new matter for us? Mm?"

"Indeed my Lord, I have."

"Then let us hear it."

"With pleasure, my Lord." Another, smaller, bow. Francis straightened his shoulders: this was his moment and he was ready.

"But before you begin…"

"My Lord?"

"Let me just remind you that I am the judge, not you. When I have heard all the evidence *I* shall decide, with the help of the jurors, whether or not the prisoner is evil and whether or not she may have bewitched anyone."

"My Lord, I…"

"Just your evidence, please, Mr. Bragge. Nothing else."

"Very good, my Lord. You wish for new evidence: I have it." He paused. Yes, there was the respectful silence he deserved; he would continue.

"On Tuesday, the 19th of February, desirous to see the cake of feathers which had been taken out of the pillow of the maid, Anne Thorn, I went to the rectory. I took two…"

"Mr. Bragge." The judge's voice was gentle.

"… of the cakes and…"

"Mr. Bragge!"

"… compared them. They were… "

"*Mr. Bragge* !" The judge's voice was harsh and loud.

"My Lord?"

"At last." Sir John sighed and leant over his desk. "Mr. Bragge. Putting aside your ill manners in continuing to speak, *again*, when I have addressed you, we have already heard about feathers in a pillow from Mr. Chauncy."

"Ah yes, my Lord, but Mr. Chauncy only *saw* the feathers. I examined them!"

"No, my Lord, that's not true," said Arthur, jumping up from his seat, to the delight of all the visitors and the annoyance of Mr. Gardiner, sitting next to him:

Mr. Bragge was their most important witness; he must be allowed to give his full testimony. Mr. Gardiner gave Arthur's coat tails a tug and he sat down, mumbling angrily.

"If there is more of this misconduct…" Sir John glared at Arthur, "… or any more prevarication…", with his eyes were now on Francis, "… I shall clear the court!"

He could stop the trial, Caroline thought. What then?

Sir John, apparently restored to the good humour for which he was known, gave a great beaming smile to everyone - Caroline could swear he even chuckled - and turned to Francis.

"Now, Mr. Bragge, please continue, but not too much detail, please. I should like to have finished here before dark."

"Thank you, my Lord," said Francis, in his humblest voice. "I am most grateful to you."

"Just the testimony, please." The judge's smile had gone.

"Yes, of course. Er… where was I? Ah, yes. The cakes of feathers. Yes." He paused, for effect rather than to collect his thoughts; he knew precisely where he had got to when that idiot Arthur had had the gall to interrupt him! "Both the cakes were of a circular shape, something larger than a half crown in size, with the smaller feathers placed at equal distances from each other, making so many radii of the circle in which the quill ends of the feathers met. I endeavoured to pull off two or three of the feathers, and in doing so, my Lord..." He nodded at the judge, whose eyes were shut. Concentrating on my words, Francis thought; that's good. "... I observed that they were fastened together by a sort of viscous material, which would stretch...", and here he demonstrated with his fingers, "... into a fine thread, some seven or eight inches, before it broke, a material which, my Lord, I believe to have been taken... from the flesh of dead men!" The villagers nodded sagely and the visitors in the gallery gasped appreciatively. The judge opened his eyes briefly, raised his eyebrows to their full height, gave a quick glance around the courtroom and shut his eyes again. Satisfied with the reaction to his words, Francis resumed his speech. "With my finger I removed the viscous matter, and found, under it, in the centre..." a longish pause, a glance at the jurors, another glance up to the gallery, "... some short hairs, black and grey, matted together, hairs which I believe, my Lord...", his voice rose, full of emotion, "... to be cats' hair!"

The gasps from the gallery coupled with the nods of affirmation from the villagers of Walkern brought a satisfied smile to the curate's face. He did not look again at Sir John; he had approbation enough. "Then," Francis continued, "I examined the other cake and found it to be exactly the same. There were ten or twelve cakes in all, my Lord, but I did not trouble to examine all of them."

"How very sensible," the judge said quickly. His impatience had been growing during Francis's speech. "I would very much like to see one of these 'enchanted' feathers. Such startling… mm… evidence!" Sir John beamed at the court. "No doubt you have one with you, Mr. Bragge?"

"Er… no, my Lord."

"No? You did not keep even one?"

"No, my Lord. It was not possible. I should very much like to have done, but the opinion of the assembled company was that the maid, Anne, would be eased of her fits if they were all burnt."

"So you have none to show me?"

"Regrettably no, my Lord."

"That is a pity, Mr. Bragge. Call the next witness."

"But, Sir John, I have…"

"Yes?"

"I have more to say!"

"Do you? Well, unless you have any fresh evidence - no more pins please, no more feathers - then, I am sorry, Mr. Bragge, but I have no more time to listen. Next witness, please."

Barely containing his rage, Francis, without so much as a hint of a bow, turned his back on the judge and stomped back to his seat. Caroline was unable to resist a giggle.

"What an unpleasant man," the lady sitting next to her whispered.

"Yes, isn't he," Caroline whispered back. Oh no, she had promised herself that, no matter what, she would not express an opinion of any kind.

"Fancy being so rude to that nice young curate."

Caroline held her hands tightly together in her lap and said nothing.

The next witness, now being sworn in, was Thomas Adams, whose testimony covered the same ground as that given by previous witnesses. After him came Matthew, with his account of Jane Wenham's request for a handful of straw and the consequent actions which he said he was forced to take. The only thing she had not heard before was that the old woman had been wearing a riding-hood when Matthew met her. I wonder where that came from? Caroline thought.

John Chapman's testimony backed up Matthew's story, but from a different viewpoint, with the added, aggrieved information, solely for the benefit of the judge - everyone else in the court knew this - that he had lost over two hundred pounds worth of livestock because of 'that woman!'.

Susan Aylott, in a surprisingly subdued fashion, Caroline thought, told of the terrible things that had happened to the wife of one Richard Harvey, and to his child, because of the woman in the dock. Elizabeth Field, following her, also had a doleful tale to tell, of a child in her care who had had distorted limbs and convulsions, and then 'pined away until he died'… and all because of the spells that Jane Wenham had cast upon him. Both accounts brought 'Ohs' of sympathy from the visitors and nods of agreement from the Walkern people.

There was now little chance that Jane Wenham would be acquitted. The corroborating testimonies of the final witnesses, four village men whose faces and names were not known to Caroline, all added to the weight of evidence already piled up against the prisoner. They all made much of the old woman's association with cats; two of the men, Uriah Wright and Thomas Harvey, had questioned her about her visits from the Devil, who appeared to her, she told them, 'in the shape of a cat'.

Sir John turned to Jane Wenham. She had no one here to speak for her.

She could speak for herself she had told the clerk: now her moment had come.

Everyone waited, breath held: would she curse them all? The sense of danger in the courtroom was at its most palpable in the gallery, where women fanned themselves and even strong men sweated. Or perhaps that was occasioned by the heat rising from below. Caroline was thankful for her lightweight gown, its dark colour hiding the fact that she, too, was perspiring. It was, though, becoming difficult to breathe in the increasingly foetid atmosphere.

Jane Wenham, to the general disappointment of the court, had little to say.

"I am told that you can fly," said the judge, prompting her. "Is that so?"

The woman shrugged her shoulders; she seemed not to care what anyone said; she was resigned to her fate.

"They say so," she mumbled.

"I can't hear you, Mistress Wenham."

Jane lifted her head. "Yes, I can!" she shouted.

Sir John looked hard at the jurors, who had begun to talk excitedly among themselves. The woman has said she can fly: this proves she is a witch!

"So you may… if you will," the judge said. "There is no *law* against flying. Gentlemen of the jury, did you hear me?"

"Yes, Sir John," they chorused, subdued.

"Good." he turned to the woman. "Have you anything else to say, Mistress Wenham?"

"No sir, except…"

"Except?"

"I am a clear woman, sir."

"A clear woman. Mm. And by that you mean... that, despite all the evidence, you are not a witch?"

"Yes, sir. No, sir."

"Thank you, Mistress Wenham; you may stand down."

A constable came forward and took a bemused Jane Wenham - how much of all this had she understood, Caroline wondered - out of the witness box. If only I knew any of the jurors, she thought fleetingly, I might be able to suborn one of them!

Sir John, after shuffling the papers, and then writing for some minutes, lifted his head and addressed the court. He first summed up the evidence in a short speech, then, having taken a long drink from a carafe in front of him, he spoke directly to the jury.

"You have heard all the evidence, gentlemen. It is now left to you to decide whether or not it is sufficient to take away the prisoner's life, upon the indictment."

The court again held its collective breath, while the jurymen gathered around their foreman. Caroline's heart was beating wildly. Just one little word could end this poor old woman's life; two words would spare it. Please say 'Not guilty' she whispered.

The foreman of the jury rose to his feet.

"My Lord, if you please, we should like some time to consider our verdict." So, thought Caroline, they have not *all* decided that the prisoner should die. Thank God, there is a small ray of hope for her.

"Very well." The judge nodded; he seemed relieved. "This is a good time to stop. I am sure we could all do with some fresh air, and... Mm..." He peered at his travelling clock. "I see it is past one, so some of you may also wish to take this opportunity to eat. I know that I shall!" His words, spoken with a smile, eased the tense atmosphere of the courtroom. "We will adjourn these proceedings until three in the afternoon," he said, and rose from his seat.

"Mistress Newell!"

Caroline had come down the stairs from the gallery, and now, in the street outside the courthouse, she had stopped to take in a breath of relatively fresh air; even a faint whiff of horse dung was preferable to the stuffiness of the courtroom.

Oh no, she thought, I know that voice. She turned round.

"Mr. Gardiner! Mistress Gardiner! How lovely to see you both!" She smiled her broadest smile and wondered how she could get away... and still be polite. "I do hope you will excuse me if I do not stay to talk but my sister, with whom I am staying, is not well, and I need to be at her side." It would do, and it was, partly, true.

The rector's wife expressed her dismay at Caroline's news, and would have happily let her go on her way; she appeared to be embarrassed - by her gown perhaps? She kept smoothing down one side of the skirt where a panel was not hanging properly - but Mr. Gardiner had more to say.

"Mistress Newell, I trust you will accept my apologies for such a brief reply to your letter. There were matters I had to attend to, prior..."

"Of course, Mr. Gardiner, I understand perfectly."

"I am now in position to answer your query concerning the young gypsy."

Caroline wanted very much to hear news of Jem, but not here in this crowded thoroughfare.

"If we might just step into Bull Plain," she said, pushing her way through a knot of people and hoping that Mr. Gardiner would follow her.

Once out of the mêlée, she stopped. The Gardiners were close behind her.

Courtesy told her she should invite them to Emilia's house, common sense told her otherwise: if there was bad news of Jem - for all she knew he could have become betrothed to Margaret Gilbert by now - it was better that Caroline should hear it first, and break it to Mary later.

"It is not good news I bring you, Mistress Newell," the rector said. "Young Jem… so good with my mare… has left the village." He shook his head sadly.

"Oh!"

"And young Polly, too. No one knows where they are." Well, that was that then.

Mary would just have to stop pining for him and get on with her life.

"I expect Farmer Gilbert is glad to be rid of them, with all that's been going," Mrs. Gardiner said.

"Oh, why?"

"Regretfully, Mistress Newell, it is not just that the boy has gone…. there has been a murder in the district…"

"Oh, how terrible!" Oh no… No.

"And it is generally supposed… that the crime was committed… by Jem."

Mr. Gardiner had found that hard to say. Tenderly Mrs. Gardiner laid a hand on her husband's arm.

"A murderer, Jem? No, I can't believe that. He seemed such a nice lad. Very polite… and open, too."

Unless there was proof she would not say a word of this to Mary. "Who is he supposed to have killed?"

"This is what makes it so terrible, Mistress Newell. His victim was a gentleman."

"A victim is a victim, Mr. Gardiner, whatever his rank!"

"You misunderstand me, Mistress Newell. The murder of a gentleman is taken more seriously than that of a peasant, and if Jem, a gypsy into the bargain, is brought to trial he is unlikely to be freed, whatever the circumstances."

"Who was he, the gentleman?"

"A Mr. Clifford."

"Clifford?"

"Yes, Mr. Clifford of Fording Hall; it is near Sandon."

"Yes. I know the family, slightly. Goodness, how terrible. Have you any idea why?" It can't be true, but I might as well get all the information I can.

"No. Not really." Mr. Gardiner looked abashed; he does know more about this, thought Caroline. This was not the time, though, to pursue the subject; the crowd from the courthouse was beginning to spill over into Bull Plain. Caroline caught a glimpse of Arthur, and beside him, Susan Aylott.

"Mistress Gardiner, I trust you have somewhere to rest, and to partake of some refreshment…" Oh dear, how stiff that sounded. "… before the court is in session … before we hear the verdict?"

"We have, thank you, Mistress Newell. Mr. Chishull has invited us to join him at the… ?" She looked to her husband for help.

"The Bell, my dear." He turned to Caroline. "It is a hostelry near by, I believe."

"Just across the square; barely two minutes walk away."

Caroline smiled at the rector's wife. "I am so sorry not to invite you into my sister's house, but her condition…"

"Of course, Mistress Newell. We are well provided for, by Mr. Chishull."

"Yes, he will look after you, I am sure. Well… I think I had better be getting inside."

Caroline smiled broadly, willing the Gardiners to move: she did not want them to see which house she entered. She knew Mrs. Gardiner liked to gossip, and the thought of an impromptu visit from the witch-hunting women of Walkern made Caroline's already knotted stomach tighten even more.

Thankfully they turned away. Only now did it register that the Gardiners had not spoken of the trial: for them there was only one conclusion, and on the strength of it they would enjoy their meal at The Bell. Caroline watched them disappear into the crowd. When she was sure she was out of their sight, she walked as quickly as she could, without appearing to rush, to the door of the Oliver house. She opened the door and let herself in. She stood inside the door and let out a deep breath. Oh God: Jem. She would have to tell Mary. She shook her head violently: no, it couldn't possibly be true. Why would he kill an old man like Mr. Clifford? A mild-mannered gentleman, Caroline recalled, from the few times she had met him. It was hard to believe he had fathered that dreadful son. Could it be *Roger* Clifford who had died? 'That nasty Mr. Clifford' Mary had called him. No, he would be in London.

Mary, who had been watching for her mistress from an upstairs window, came running down the stairs towards her, eager questions in her eyes.

"Is she dead, Miss Caroline?"

"Who?"

"The witch."

"Don't be silly, girl! She's being tried, not hanged! Bring me a tisane. I'll have it in my room." Caroline strode past Mary and began to make her way up the stairs.

"Is everything all right, mistress?"

"No, Mary, everything is very *wrong!"*

"Shall I bring you something to eat as well?"

Caroline turned sharply and glared at her maid. "If I had wanted something to eat I would have said! Just do as I've asked, please." Caroline fled up the rest of the stairs, flung open the door of her room and threw herself on to the bed. The day was already fraught enough, without this! Was this what Mary and Simon had been keeping from her? That Roger Clifford - or his father - was dead? No, no!

She was not thinking straight. If Jem *had* murdered one of them surely Simon would not protect him? And why would he kill either of them anyway? Was that why he had not come to see Mary? Dear God, none of this made any sense. She refused to believe that Simon would…

Caroline got up off the bed and dragged herself, trembling in every part of her body, to the landing. She began to walk down the stairs, but her legs shook so much they gave way under her and she collapsed on the staircase, saving herself from tumbling to the bottom only by holding on tight to the banister.

"Mary," she called faintly. "Come. Please come."

There was no answer. She could call again, loudly, but that would disturb Emilia, who was again not well. She would just sit where she was, and wait. Mary would be

427

coming up the stairs soon, with the tisane. And when she did come…

Oh, dear God! How could she tell Mary that her beloved Jem had… had killed a man? She could *not*! Not now. The trial would be starting again in just over an hour's time and she must be there. She must try to put aside all thoughts of Jem, and the dreadful deed he may have done.

There were so many responsibilities weighing down on her: Emilia, Jane Wenham, and now this. She remembered a line from Shakespeare's play *Hamlet*, about sorrows coming in battalions. How true that was. If only she had someone to lean on. If only Robert were… No, she must stop this. She pulled herself to her feet and walked slowly down the rest of the stairs and into the parlour. Mary brought her the tisane and, soon after, some bread and smoked fish. Caroline was suddenly hungry and she ate greedily.

No windows in the courtroom had been opened during the adjournment and it still had the musty, musky smell of the morning session. It was also cold. Outside the sky had clouded over. Perhaps, thought Caroline, taking her seat in the gallery, God doesn't want to see what horror man, in the form of the jury, is about to perpetrate on his fellow man, in this case… woman. Crazy thoughts! Anything to stop herself thinking about Mary: she had been completely unable to look her maid in the face when she brought her food and asked about the trial.

All was now ready for the verdict. Judge and jury were in their places; the sixteen witnesses had their eyes fixed on the foreman; Jane Wenham, in the dock, stood with her head bowed; the onlookers in the gallery craned their necks forward for a better view: this was the moment of high drama and they did not want to miss it.

"Are you agreed upon your verdict?" Sir John asked the jury foreman. His voice was without emotion.

"We are, my Lord. We find the prisoner guilty upon the evidence."

The judge turned his eyes to the old woman, then back to the foreman. "Do you find her guilty upon the indictment for conversing with the Devil in the shape of a cat?"

"Yes, my Lord. We find her guilty of that."

The courtroom erupted. Hats were flung into the air, there were shouts of "Hurrah!", hands were shaken vigorously and backs were slapped; women kissed one another.

Susan Aylott, making the most of this emotional moment, threw her arms around Arthur's neck; Mrs. Gardiner rocked back and forth, tears streaming down her cheeks; Matthew and Farmer Chapman, linking arms, danced a jig; Mr. Gardiner shook hands with Mr. Strutt. Francis, his fingers steepled together in prayer, looked up to the gallery and smirked: oh yes, he knew Mistress Newell was there. Alone among the hubbub Jane Wenham stood, unmoving, silent, looking straight ahead of her. The noise spread into the road and the crowd outside raised *their* voices.

What a triumph! What a cause for celebration! Thank God for a right-minded jury.

In the courtroom, once silence had been restored, Sir John Powell, looking as grim as any man could look, took the black cap from his clerk. He placed it carefully upon his head and spoke the solemn words which would bring the prisoner's life to an end.

"Jane Wenham, the sentence of this court upon you is that you be taken from this place to a lawful prison and thence to a place of execution, and you be there hanged by the neck until you be dead. And may the Lord have mercy upon your soul. Amen."

From every section of the court triumphant Amens rang out. Here and there were fearful voices: until she *was* dead, the witch still had the power to harm them. Caroline's trembling, whispered Amen was lost in the uproar that followed.

The Walkern villagers raised their voices in jubilation, the visitors in the gallery clapped their hands and smiled at one another; some of them shouted hurrah; and in the body of the court everybody milled around, shaking hands, chattering wildly and loudly. The witch would die!

Francis Bragge preened himself and, with deep bows, accepted the congratulation that came from all sides. This was his personal triumph; of course it was. Without him, this glorious day would not have dawned!

The judge removed the black cap and handed it back to his clerk. The usher called for silence; the court had not been dismissed - how dare these people make all this noise! It was several minutes before everyone had calmed down, and sat down.

Sir John Powell took his time. He surveyed the court, studying every section of it carefully, his eyes sometimes resting on an individual face, then taking in a bunch of people at one glance. No one escaped him. When he sensed that he had everyone's full attention, he spoke.

"I am going to say something now that most of you will not like. You will kindly remain silent while I speak. If you *do* interrupt, you will be charged with contempt of court." He paused… and waited, as feet shuffled and a few throats were cleared. Then, the moment judged precisely, Sir John spoke again. "The prisoner is reprieved… until I give further orders. Constable, take her to a place of safety."

The judge stood up. The usher called, "All rise."

Stunned by Sir John's words and moving as if in a stupor, everyone got silently to their feet.

The constable, assisted by the gaoler, took hold of Jane Wenham by her arms and escorted her from the courtroom.

Sir John gathered up his papers, stepped down from the dais, nodded to the clerk, and began to make his way out of the chamber.

"You have not heard the last of this, my Lord!" Francis's voice was loud and clear.

There was a collective gasp and a sudden stir as dozens of hands were raised to cover open mouths.

His Lordship paused in his short walk to the door.

"I am a man of God, and the power of my pen is greater than your law!"

Slowly Sir John turned round.

"Who is this person who disturbs my court?"

"The Reverend Francis Bragge, my Lord!"

"Ohh…! Mis-ter Bragge. Mm." He nodded his head sagely several times, then turned to the clerk. "Dismiss the court," he said quietly, and left the chamber.

The clerk, obeying the judge's order, struggled to make himself heard above the great surge of noise that erupted the moment the judge passed through the doorway to the ante-room.

Caroline, her hands clasped together in front of her face, shook with sobs.

"You might well cry. I said he was a dreadful man!"

"No!" It didn't matter what she said now. "He is a wonderful man!"

Her first instinct was to rush down the stairs and intercept Sir John, to thank him for his judgment, and to tell him that, should Jane Wenham's life be spared, there was a home for her on the estate of Colonel Plumer. She was prevented from carrying out her plan by the great crush of people on the staircase, all hoping for a glimpse of the prisoner as she was escorted back to the gaol, the only place where she would be safe from the inflamed mob in the street below.

Among the angry faces, Caroline had seen, fleetingly, that of an excited, but not angry, young man, whom she felt sure she knew. He disappeared from view and his place in the crowd was taken by Susan Aylott and Margaret Gilbert.

The bulk of the crowd had moved on to the gaol and were now filling the High Street. It had taken three constables, as well as the gaoler, to convey the prisoner to safety. Once inside the gates she was out of the physical reach of the mob but they continued to taunt her with curses and insults. A group of young lads began to throw stones and bricks, and glass bottles, and anything else they could find, at the gates of the gaol. Only a very brave constable would be prepared to come out and accost them. No such officer appeared, and after a while, with no more fun to be had, the lads moved off. Gradually the rest of the crowd dispersed.

The Walkern villagers who had been witnesses had not followed the prisoner to the gaol; they had crowded round Francis Bragge and Mr. Gardiner. Not only were they angry, they had no idea what to do next. They could not leave things up in the air like this, not knowing if the witch might be eventually be hanged, or - Heaven forbid! - be sent back to Walkern. *That* they would not have!

It was while they were clustered around Francis, listening to his great plan to write a pamphlet, a series of pamphlets possibly, on the treachery and wickedness of witchcraft, with particular reference to this trial and its disastrous verdict, that Susan Aylott spied Caroline making her way towards Bull Plain. She signalled to Margaret, and to another woman close by, to follow her. The three women broke away from the main group, and keeping a tight hold on one another, they threaded their way through the crowd until they were within calling distance of Caroline. Starting to run, they hurled angry words at her.

Caroline knew that she was in danger, and so would Mary be if they found her.

She must get back to Emilia's as fast as she could. The top end of Bull Plain was filled with people, but the narrower part lower down, where the Olivers lived, was almost empty. If Caroline stayed in the crowd she might elude her pursuers, but if she made a dash for home she was bound to be seen. She took a chance… and ran!

Margaret and her friends, and several other village women, were now chasing Caroline, screeching and shouting at the tops of their voices: "Witch-lover! Witch-lover!"

"There's no Jem to rescue *you*!" Margaret Gilbert was very close now, and gaining on Caroline with every second. "Or your silly little maid; not this time!"

Terrified, but with her fear producing an extra spurt of speed, Caroline reached Emilia's front door. She flung it open, all but threw herself into the house and shut the door fast behind her. She stood, shaking all over, her eyes shut tight, against the door. She began to feel dizzy and hot, and her breath came in great gulps.

Outside the women pounded on the door, still screaming and chanting: "Witch-lover! Witch-lover!"

Suddenly another voice, a male voice, joined them, speaking her name.

Caroline felt so confused and frightened that it was several moments before she realised that this new voice was coming from inside the house.

"It's all right. You are safe. Open your eyes. Look at me…"

It wasn't Richard, it was…

"Simon!"

Caroline opened her eyes wide. He was standing close, in front of her. Her head swam, her legs gave way, and…

When Caroline came round a few minutes later she found herself lying on the sofa in the parlour, with Simon bending over her. In answer to the query in her eyes, he said softly, "You fainted."

"I don't faint."

"You did. Good thing I was there to halt your fall."

"I fell?"

"Yes, but only on to me."

"Oh." Caroline looked down. "Well, thank you," she said. This was so lovely.

And so embarrassing. Her mind was in such a whirl: Simon, the women outside - they had gone; had Simon sent them away? - the trial, the noise, the crowds…

That boy? Who was he? "Tom," she said, looking up.

"Yes," Simon nodded. "He saw you. I was just coming to fetch you back here, when the door opened... and you fell in."

"Please don't keep reminding me," she said, smiling. Simon was here ... but where was Jem? Oh God! Jem.

"What is it? What has taken the smile from your face?"

"Jem," she whispered. Mary, carrying a bowl of warm water and a towel, had come into the room.

"Not now," Simon whispered back. "Good girl, Mary." He stood up. "Now you just wash your mistress's hands and face." Looking at Caroline, he said, "And I will let your sister know that all is well." Interpreting Caroline's look of concern he went on, "Don't worry, she is resting - the noise from those women disturbed her; it was intense - and Mr. Oliver is with her."

"Oh, thank you. Dear, kind Simon." She reached out a hand to him. Unwanted tears began to fill her eyes.

"Now... have that wash, and then a rest," Simon said, briskly. "And later you can have some food."

"Yes, Dr. Warrender, whatever you say."

Simon gave her a quick, embarrassed smile and left the room.

"Well," said Caroline, when he had gone, "That was a surprise."

"Yes, mistress." Gently Mary wiped Caroline's sweat-soaked face. "Miss Caroline, is there...?"

"No, Mary. I have no news of Jem."

The rumour must be true: Simon would surely have spoken to Mary earlier, if he had brought good news. Best to get Mary's thoughts away from Jem.

"Oh Mary, that was so frightening, those women chasing after me, screaming."

"Yes, mistress, I heard what they said." Her voice was flat. Poor girl; Simon's return had made the loss of Jem more keenly felt.

"Have they gone now?"

"Yes, mistress. Mr. Gardiner and a constable told them to stop, and they did. But only just in time; one of them, I think it was that Susan, she'd picked up a stone and was going to throw it at the window."

Mary finished drying Caroline's hands, and lifted up the bowl to take it away.

"Oh, my poor Millie; I must go to her, and then I must go and see Mistress Wenham."

"Miss Caroline! No!"

"Don't worry. I shall not go alone. I shall ask Mr. Warrender to accompany me,"

"No need, dear sister. No need at all." Richard was standing in the parlour doorway. "Emilia is perfectly all right and the other matter is being attended to. Mr. Warrender and I will visit the gaol and take the good news to Mistress Wenham first thing tomorrow morning. We thought it unwise to go today. By tomorrow the locals will have moved on to some other excitement and the Walkern people will have returned to their village."

"Oh! You have been busy."

"Are you not pleased, Caroline? Surely you do not *want* to visit the gaol again. I understand from Mr. Warrender your previous visit there was not at all a happy occasion, certainly not one to be repeated. I believe that the gaoler was most…"

"Of course I don't want to go again! I was just surprised to learn that you had already made arrangements to…" She sighed. "Thank you, Richard. I am most grateful." And, strangely, she was. She could now concentrate on Mary. She would have to be told: Jem was a criminal and he would not be coming for her.

But first she must talk to Simon.

It was nightfall before Caroline managed to get Simon on his own. They had all had a meal together, adults and children, and it was then, sitting round the table in the dining-room that Simon had told them his great news: he had found, and bought, an estate, High Green, on the Essex-Hertfordshire border.

"High Green? But that's…"

"Yes, Caroline, it is. We shall be neighbours."

"Oh Simon! How wonderful! Oh, that is …" They were all looking at her. Was she sounding too thrilled? No, of course she wasn't. "It will be lovely to have you as a neighbour," she said. So that is what he had been doing.

He had such plans for his new abode; it was good to see how eager he was get started on them. The property had been neglected for several years; an enthusiastic young owner was just what it needed. The orchards, the fish-ponds, the ice house, the stables, the horses; he spoke of them all, but there was no mention of Jem. As soon as Richard had left the parlour - the adults had all adjourned there after their meal - Caroline spoke.

"Jem," she said. "Tell me."

Casually, too casually, Simon got up from the settee, where he had been sitting next to Caroline, and began to poke the fire.

"Simon, stop poking that fire and look at me." She knew she sounded harsh. "Please," she added. "I need to know."

Simon laid the poker down on the hearth and turned round.

"I was hoping you wouldn't ask," he said, grinning. "Not yet, anyway."

"There is nothing to *smile* about! Do you not realise what this is doing to Mary?"

"I know she wants to see him, but she will have to wait."

"Simon, how can you be so insensitive! *Do you know where he is* ?"

"Well… not at this moment, no, but…"

"You don't *know*, do you?"

"Know what?"

"Jem is accused of murder!"

"What?" The colour drained from Simon's face. "No. That is nonsense, he is… Who told you this?"

"Mr. Gardiner, the rector."

"And his victim? Who is it?" He spat out the words.

"A man called Clifford; you won't know him, he…"

"Clifford?"

"Yes, he…"

"I know who he is," Simon said abruptly. "Oh God." He shook his head. "It can't have been Jem. He's… I think one of us has got hold of the wrong story."

"You doubt Mr. Gardiner's word?"

"No. I can well believe the man is dead, but not that Jem killed him."

Simon hoped he sounded positive; he didn't feel it. Oh, the hot-headed little fool! God knows he had reason, but… When had he done this? That's what didn't make sense.

There was one person who would know if Mr. Gardiner had spoken the truth: Ma Towler.

"Caroline, I have to get to the bottom of this. At this moment I can't tell you why; you'll just have to trust me. I need to speak to someone, as soon as possible."

"Who?"

"It's… it's not someone you know. I shall set off first thing. With luck I could be back here by nightfall. Now, if you will excuse me I shall go and speak to Tom. And to your brother-in-law."

Caroline reached up and grabbed Simon's hand. "You can't just go!"

"I have to, Caroline. Believe me, if I could think of another way to settle this, I would do it." He began to draw his hand away, but Caroline was keeping a tight hold on it.

"You're doing this for Mary, aren't you? This is part of the secret, isn't it?"

"What secret?"

"The secret you're keeping from me!"

"I am not keeping anything from you." This was not the moment for Caroline to learn what a vile man Roger Clifford was: she had been through more than enough already today. It was worth telling her a *lie* if by this time tomorrow he could tell her, truthfully, that Jem was an innocent man.

If he was not… No. Action, not wild thoughts, was what was needed now.

"Let me go," he said, withdrawing his hand from hers. He could not look her in the face. He bowed stiffly and left the room. He knew he was behaving badly to her; it took all his willpower to stop himself from going back into the parlour, pulling her to her feet, taking her in his arms and… "Richard, are you there?" he called hoarsely. "I need a word with you."

27

Forbidden to leave the house, Caroline spent much of the next day pacing up and down the parlour.

"Do you really want to be attacked again, Caroline?" Richard had asked, when she protested. "If you won't think of yourself, think of Mary, and what they would do if they got hold of her." Although some of the Walkern villagers had gone home, there were still several, Richard said, "roaming around the town and looking for trouble". One of these was believed to be Susan Aylott, and it wouldn't take much for her to get a new crowd fired up with anger against Caroline and Mary, particularly Mary. One witch had got away from her; she would be determined not to lose a second one.

All the curtains at the front of the house were kept closed and the women and children in the house were under strict instructions not to open them, not even to peep through! No one, with the exception of Richard, was to answer the door.

The proposed visit to the gaol would have to wait until Simon's return.

Mary, accepting the restriction as the means of keeping her safe, went about her duties, if not calmly, at least without undue anxiety. Caroline, her heart and mind in turmoil, could settle to nothing, neither reading, nor playing with the children, nor talking to her sister. She could not eat; every morsel that she tried to swallow choked her. So much depended on Simon. If only she knew where he had gone, who he was seeing.

It was late afternoon and raining hard when he returned, mud-stained and weary. Caroline had known it was him at the door, but she steeled herself not to leave the parlour until she heard his voice; if the news he brought was bad she was sure she would break down and sob, and Simon had seen quite enough of her weakness already.

"Well?" she heard Richard asking.

"He's innocent."

"Oh Simon, Simon," Caroline cried, running to him. Not caring who saw her, she flung her arms around his neck. Not even Richard's glare of embarrassed disapproval, seen over Simon's shoulder, could dampen her spirits. She clung to him a moment longer, then, to Richard's relief, drew back. "Just look at you," she said. "What a state you are in! Go and get yourself washed." She turned away, her heart dancing. By the parlour door she stopped. "When you're clean, come and tell me about it," she said stiffly.

"Yes, of course I will." Simon's answer was equally stiff. How could someone display such widely differing sides of their character in such a short space of time? Which was the real Caroline? The one who was rebuffing him now, or the one who had held him close, so very close, just a few seconds before. If only he had had a sister he might understand women better.

When Simon had sought out Richard the evening before to say that he would not be going with him to see Jane Wenham, Richard had demanded an explanation, and Simon had felt it necessary to tell him. So now it was right that Richard should be present, in the parlour, seated on one side of the fireplace, with Simon on the other side and Caroline on the settee, while Simon recounted the day's happenings.

He had ridden with Tom to the farm just south of Sandon where Jem had taken Mary for safety. The farmer's wife, whom he called Ma Towler, had been appalled to hear that Jem was suspected of murder. Oh yes, Mr. Roger Clifford was dead... but he had not been shot or stabbed. There had been a fight. Her boys had been there and they had given the man a thrashing: they had some private score to settle with him.

Simon hesitated. "A girl... a girl they liked... had been treated badly by him."

That would do.

After the beating, which would have done no more than bruise him and perhaps make it hard for Clifford to walk for a few days, the boys had thrown him into his own lake, which was not deep, and his manservant after him, thinking that the man would drag his master out of the water. They had ridden off, and as far as they were concerned that was that. They were as surprised as anyone to learn from their Lizzie, whose sister sometimes worked in the kitchen at Fording Hall, that the manservant had run away and the master had drowned. Terrible shock it was, Ma Towler had said. But why anyone thought Jem had killed him... well, she could only think that the day Jem had ridden off from the farm someone had seen him, and because he had suddenly given up working for a farmer near Walkern, the wrong two and two had been put together. Shame, poor Jem, but that's what rumour does, Ma Towler had said.

There was, of course, more to Simon's story, which he had managed to tell Richard while he removed the mud from his clothes. But that was quite enough for Caroline to hear.

"It's good to know that Jem is not a criminal," she said bluntly, when Simon had finished his tale, "But where is he?"

"At this moment?" Simon asked. "He could be anywhere within…"

"That's no help to my maid!" Caroline sighed. "Poor child. She is still pining for him."

"He's a good lad." Simon smiled across at her. "I feel sure she will be seeing him soon."

"You know, don't you? You know where he is!"

"Please, Caroline. Don't press me on this."

Caroline felt uncomfortable, and suddenly unsure of Simon. What kind of game was he playing? That was all a lie, that tale about Roger Clifford drowning in a lake. Jem *had* killed the man… and Simon was covering up the crime! No, that was nonsense; he wouldn't do that. But what then?

"In the meantime, Caroline," said Richard, getting to his feet and taking up a masterly pose in front of the fireplace, "Simon and I feel that it would be a good idea if…"

Both of them now… plotting behind her back! Well, whatever it was, she wouldn't do it.

"… if you and Emilia, and the children of course, were to go to the countryside, until all this witch hysteria had died down. Hertford at the moment is not a safe place for you or your sister, who by her connection with you, is implicated, nor is it safe for young Mary. Until Mistress Wenham is either dead or removed from the neighbourhood, your maid's life is in danger from those who feel themselves cheated by Sir John's reprieve, and…"

"Yes, yes, we know this, Richard. Just get to the point."

"The point is, dear sister, that the day after tomorrow you and Mary, and my immediate family, will travel to Gilston, and…"

"Gilston?"

"… and from there either to High Green or Amley."

Richard was smiling broadly and Simon, also smiling, but less assuredly, was nodding, in agreement presumably.

"Well," said Caroline tersely. "That's it then, isn't it? You clever men have spoken… and we women must obey!"

She wanted to feel angry, she should feel angry: men, as always, deciding what was best. The strange, even comforting, thing was that she agreed with them: it *was* the most sensible thing to do. She felt, though, grave concern for old Jane Wenham. Yes, she was safe in the gaol, but how long would she be there? Not for the rest of her life, surely: for an old woman accustomed to roaming freely in the countryside, that would be as much a death sentence as hanging. So much would depend upon what Sir John's further orders might be. Until they came there was nothing Caroline could do for the prisoner that Richard could not do just as well. As for Sir Henry… she would invite him to visit her at Amley. She would not, under any circumstances, return to Walkern.

Wisely, the men waited for her answer. Richard turned around and poked the fire; Simon looked down at his clasped hands.

Caroline allowed herself a gentle smile before she spoke. "I think it is an excellent idea," she said, and the men smiled. "But I do have one query: how are we all going to get there?

You don't have a carriage, Richard, and Emilia and the children cannot…"

"It is all arranged," said Simon. "You are travelling as far as Gilston in Lady Poynter's carriage…"

"Lydia's? But how…?"

"If you'd allow Simon to finish speaking, Caroline…"

"I'm sorry. Go on."

"I called on her on the way back today."

Caroline raised her eyebrows, but said nothing.

"From Gilston, where Tom has gone today to apprise Uncle Plumer of the arrangements, we shall have the use of the colonel's carriage."

"Well… There's not much left for me to say, is there?"

"No." Simon and Richard said in chorus.

"I had better tell Mary to start packing."

"I think you will find that she already has," said Richard.

"What! You told her before you told… Oh Simon, how could you?"

"I wouldn't do that, Caroline." His voice was gentle. "She overheard us talking, Richard and I, and I asked her not to tell you."

"More secrets!"

"No, not a secret. I would only ever keep something from you if I thought it would hurt you." He had crossed the room and taken her hand. It was as if her brother-in-law was not there.

Richard coughed loudly. "That's all settled then. Tomorrow I will visit the gaol, on your behalf Caroline, as you appear to consider another visit necessary…"

"I just felt it was the least I could do."

Richard had not finished. "...and if Mr. Warrender is so minded, he can accompany me. Meanwhile, you and Mary will, I beg of you, not leave the house," Caroline nodded in acquiescence, "... and the day after I shall bid you all farewell."

Try as she might, Caroline could not get to sleep that night. Yes, it was good, very good, to think that in two days' time she would be at Amley - oh, how well she slept there! - or maybe Gilston; even that was cheering - the thought of seeing dear old Uncle Plumer again, such a lovely man - but there was still something not right. Finally she gave up any attempt to sleep, took her robe from the foot of her bed, pushed her feet into her slippers and crept downstairs to the parlour. The embers of the fire were still glowing and the room was suffused with a warm light. Yes, better to be here in an armchair than tossing about in her bed.

Perhaps now she could think logically, and she hoped, find out why she was still so troubled. Everything had been arranged, and she had agreed with the plans that Simon and Richard had made. So what was it that was *not* right? There was still some mystery attached to the whereabouts of Jem, something Simon was keeping from her, for Mary's sake, no doubt... in case Jem did *not* want her. But that was not it; there was something else.

She reached forward, lifted the poker from the hearth and stirred the now dying embers back to life. The sudden brief flare of flame lit up the cosy room, the worn sofa, the backs of the books on the shelves by the door, the heavy brocaded curtains that kept out the draughts, and on the mantelpiece, the old chiming clock that had been her father's, and Richard's rack of pipes, well out of the way of the children.

The flame died down; the room was dark again, but in Caroline's brain all was suddenly light. Pipes in a rack... Sir Henry's pipes on the mantelpiece at Yardley Bury. How could she leave... how could she have *thought* she could leave... and not see him again? She *must,* she *had to*... and if that meant going to Yardley Bury - to Walkern even - well, she would have to do it. It was not a comforting prospect, and how she was to get there she had no idea... Yes! She did have! A sort of idea, anyway.

Now, at last, she could sleep.

28

Swearing Simon to secrecy was not easy, but once he had accepted that this was the only way Caroline could carry out her plan, he agreed to say nothing to anyone. As far as everyone else was concerned - and that included Emilia and Mary - she had gone to Bengeo to spend a couple of nights with Lydia before leaving for Essex. Richard was displeased at the delay - and said so - but he knew that once Caroline had made up her mind there was no arguing with her.

The chief difficulty would be keeping everyone confined to the house for the extra days. Mary, annoyed that she was not going with her mistress, would have to help Rosie to keep the children occupied, and Simon was to be entrusted with 'guarding the front door' while Richard was at work. On no account must he ride to Bengeo with Caroline! Richard was adamant. If his sister-in-law wanted to set out on some foolish adventure - he felt sure there was more to it than just seeing Lydia - then upon her own head be it! The delay did mean, however, that Richard would have his dear family with him for a couple more days. Goodness knew when he would see them again, once they had departed for rural Essex.

Taking nothing with her in the way of spare clothing, Caroline rode swiftly to Bengeo. Lydia, though delighted to see her, was dismayed to learn that Caroline would be leaving her at daybreak.

"Oh, Caroline, no! No! It is a ridiculous idea. There and back in one day? My dear, you will be exhausted."

"I won't. And if I am... well, it can't be helped. I have to do this, Lydia. I have to see Sir Henry."

"I understand *that*, but why such a rush?"

"I daren't stay longer, Lydia. I don't want anyone in Walkern to discover that I am at Yardley Bury. It could be..." Caroline hesitated to say *dangerous;* Lydia might make it impossible for her to leave Bengeo, "... unpleasant, awkward."

Lydia got up from the library sofa and went to the long window overlooking her front garden, neatly set out with newly planted box. She paused there for a moment, not seeing the view, imagining her sister-in-law in the hands of the angry women of Walkern; she knew how they had behaved towards Caroline in Bull Plain. She turned away from the window. "Supposing I say you can't take my groom?"

"I shall go without him."

"You will *not!*"

"Then let him come with me."

The two women stared at one another for a long moment, neither willing to give way. Finally, with a sigh, Lydia relaxed her tense shoulders and moved away from the window.

"Oh, very well," she said. "Take him. It's the only way I'll have any peace of mind. Really, Caroline, sometimes you are impossible! I expect you'll now tell me that you want to wear breeches under your skirt again and ride astride!"

"I do."

"You will not!"

"And how will you stop me?"

"Do you have the breeches?"

"Well… no."

"Then there is your answer! Oh Caroline, don't be so wilful…"

"I shall ask John to lend me a pair of his."

"Oh no!" Lydia shook her head violently. "Most definitely not." She sighed. She sat down on the sofa beside Caroline and took her sister-in-law's hand in hers.

"Why don't you ride side-saddle there, and then on the way back, if you *must* ride astride… make use again of that old pair of Robert's, the ones you put in that chest in your bedroom at Sir Henry's."

Caroline's eyes lit up and she gave Lydia a flashing smile. "Oh yes, of course!"

She had told Lydia about the hiding-place, and about the embroidered cloak she had seen there. "I do hope Sir Henry hasn't found them."

"Well, if he has you'll just have borrow a pair from one of the stable boys."

"Lydia!"

"My dear, if you will behave in this ridiculous way, you must expect to take the consequences." She paused, enjoying Caroline's discomforture. "Oh, I feel sure Robert's breeches will be where you left them. Come on, let us go into the drawing-room and have a refreshing tisane. *I* certainly need one, even if you don't."

Lydia drew Caroline to her feet and side by side they walked out of the library.

"You know, my dear, it really is time you were married again."

Caroline halted. "Don't start that again, please." Without looking at Lydia she began to walk on.

"You will... by the end of this year, I should think."

This time Caroline did turn round. "You do talk nonsense!" She could feel her colour rising and her heart beginning to race.

"Is that why you are blushing?" Lydia took her sister-in-law's arm.

"I am not blushing! I am just a bit hot, that is all. Your library fire was rather fierce. I hope the one in the drawing-room is less so."

Caroline pulled her arm smartly away from Lydia's and marched ahead down the hallway. Lydia, following her slowly, smiled to herself.

Sunshine and a light spring breeze made the journey to Yardley Bury the next day a pleasant one. Cutting east across country to approach the house via the village of Yardley rather than go anywhere near Walkern, Lydia's groom and Caroline reached Yardley Bury by mid-morning. They rode into the stable yard and dismounted. No one was about. Caroline left John to attend to the horses and slipped into the house by the back door, closing it quietly behind her. She had not been seen! Thank goodness for that. She leant against the closed door and took a deep breath. And then another. If only her heart would slow down. The danger was over; she had arrived safely and undetected. But that had not been the real issue for Caroline; it was what Sir Henry would think - and say - to find her suddenly appearing in his home without any warning. Well, she was here now, and if he *was* cross with her she would just have to accept it. She knew that, in Sir Henry's eyes, her behaviour might be considered rude, but… oh, what did that matter! She had come to see him, to be with him, to apologise for rushing away before. A smile, a hug, a kiss on his cheek… that should do it! She crept past the kitchen door - she could hear voices, Bessie and the cook probably - and tiptoed down the passage to the snug. She took another deep breath and turned the door handle. Slowly she pushed the door open. The oak settle, its back to the door, blocked her view of both the fireplace and Sir Henry's red brocade chair.

Gingerly she peeped round the settle. The fire was alight but the room was empty.

"Oh," she said aloud. Now what should she do?

"Can I help you?"

There was no mistaking Sir Henry's deep tones, nor the amusement in his voice. Caroline turned to him, relief flooding through her.

"Oh, Sir Henry, I…"

"I saw you, through an upstairs window."

Oh, she *had* been seen. "You do not… mind?" It was hard to get the words out.

"Do I *mind*? I am delighted to see you. I did so hope you would come back… and here you are. Come, give me a kiss." He turned his cheek towards her. She kissed him hesitantly, then drew back.

"Oh, Sir Henry, I was so afraid you would be angry with me for..."

"Angry? My dear girl…" He reached out his arms to her; she moved into them and kissed him, warmly now, first on one cheek and then the other.

"That is much better!"

"You forgive me then, for letting myself into your snug in this… inappropriate way?" She could not believe she had said that word, but the occasion seemed to require it. It *was* inappropriate to enter Sir Henry's inner sanctum when he did not even know she was in his house.

"It was not the most polite thing to do, and if you want me to admonish you, I will."

"No, I…"

"My dear girl, let us put decorum to one side. You are here, and that is all that matters. I'll get Jacob to fetch you some food, and then we can talk."

"Oh no! Please, Sir Henry… I don't want anyone else to know I am here."

"Oh?" He raised his eyebrows. "You rode with your groom - well, Lady Poynter's groom, I imagine he is - into my stable yard, so my stable boys will have seen you. And old Samuel, probably."

"Yes, but John - the groom - will speak to them."

"Ah, so he is a party to your *adventure*, is he?" The old man grinned at her.

"He… he knows I wish to be as invisible as possible. That is all."

"Invisible?" Sir Henry laughed. "You could never be invisible, Caroline, with your beauty and your…"

"Sir Henry! You are embarrassing me."

"Good." He was *so* pleased to see her; she brought such warmth and joy into his life. Realising he was staring at her with goodness knows what silly expression on his face, he coughed and turned away. "At least take off your cloak and sit down. Won't you?"

"Yes, I will." Caroline removed her cloak and placed it on the oak settle. She walked over to the fireplace, took off her long gloves and warmed her hands at the flames, then perched on the edge of the armchair opposite Sir Henry's red one. There was no point in getting comfortable; she was here simply to make her peace with Sir Henry, collect the breeches from the bedroom chest and get back to Hertford as quickly as she could.

"Good. Now you will have some food."

"But… Sir Henry," Caroline implored, "if Jacob…"

"I trust Jacob… and Bessie… with my life, and so should you. They will not tell anyone that you are here unless I ask them to…"

"Oh, Sir Henry, you would not…?"

"Oh, Caroline… what has become of your sense of humour?"

Caroline smiled weakly. "No, of course you would not, but I am so nervous at being here and…"

"Enough." Sir Henry waved his hand, dismissing her protestation. "You *will* eat. By the fireside. And you will explain to me why you have come here in this hurried fashion. I see no boxes. Are they coming later by the carter's wagon?" Caroline shook her head. "No, I thought not. You are not here to stay." He sighed deeply.

"No, Sir Henry, I am not. I am so sorry… I do not wish to hurt you, and if I could stay longer I would, but…"

"You no doubt have a very good reason."

"Yes. I do."

Jacob brought her food - hot parsnip and onion soup, with fresh bread seasoned with thyme and sage - and as she ate she told Sir Henry of her fear, for Mary and for herself, at the hands of the women of Walkern should they discover she was here at Yardley Bury, her anxiety at the disappearance of Jem and her concern for Jane Wenham.

"I feel I am to blame, somehow, for what has befallen that old woman."

"How can any blame attach to you?"

"If I had not annoyed Francis so much he might have been less aggressive and vindictive towards her."

"No, no, no! You simply gave Francis an opportunity to pontificate, which he enjoys. I am sorry to say it, Caroline, but your presence will have made no difference to the outcome. Francis... and regrettably, Arthur... was determined that the woman should be tried for witchcraft."

"But did not my opposition make them more steadfast... in their attacks upon her?"

"It might have done... slightly, but in the end they were gainsaid."

"Yes. Thank God for Sir John Powell."

"A clever man."

"Yes. Very clever."

"A modern man, too." Sir Henry nodded his head several times. "A fortunate man, able to look to the future, and not be... shackled... by the past, as some of us have found ourselves to be."

It was a painful speech - a confession almost - and Caroline felt it would be wrong, and perhaps rude too, to comment. Silence hung between them. Finally, she broke it with a question.

"What will happen to Jane Wenham now?"

"I don't know. She… she may have to stay in gaol, in Hertford or somewhere else, for the rest of her life…"

"I do hope not," Caroline whispered.

"… which, of course, may not be long - she is over seventy years of age now. Or," he brightened up, "she could be pardoned!"

"And then she could go to Gilston, to Colonel Plumer's estate!"

"It is most unlikely that she will be pardoned." Sir Henry's face knotted with anxiety and there were tears in his eyes. "I feel I have been remiss. There are… there are things I could have done and things I should not have sanctioned concerning Mistress Wenham." He took a deep breath and his next words came out in a rush. "I am hoping that I can make amends. As you may know, many powerful people in the county were subscribers to the publication of my book *The Antiquities of Hertfordshire* some twelve years ago." Caroline nodded. "I think I might approach some of them on this matter… and if Sir John Powell is minded to ask Her Majesty for a pardon, they could add their names to his. I don't know that it would do any good, but… it is worth trying."

"Oh, it is. Yes, please do that." Caroline reached forward and touched Sir Henry tenderly on his arm.

"It is the least I can do. My son… Oh Caroline, I do hope he will make something of his life! I am not sure now that sending him to Hitchin, to his sister Jane, was the best thing to have done. He will come under the influence of that dreadful man she married. I must get him away from there."

"He could… come to London, to stay with me." Caroline tried not to sound hesitant.

"That is very kind, but no, Caroline, I will not let you do that. It is not right. I had hoped, as you know… but he is not the man for you."

"No, he is not," Caroline said sharply. "I wish, for your sake, he was," she added in a softer voice.

"Some day, my dear, you will meet someone who is worthy of you. For all I know you may have met him already."

"Yes, thank you." Her possible remarriage was not a subject Caroline wished to discuss with anyone. "That is most encouraging," she said briskly, and at Sir Henry's blank expression she went on, "getting your influential friends to assist Sir John, should he ask, in securing a Royal Pardon."

"Ah. Yes."

"You will send me word, won't you, when there is news… concerning Mistress Wenham? I have no time to visit her now, but I will at some time, if you - or Sir John perhaps? - should think it helpful."

"Caroline, do stop fretting." Though said tenderly, it was an order.

"Yes, I must." She sighed, then suddenly remembering - thank goodness she had - the practical reason for returning to Yardley Bury, she sprang to her feet.

"While I am here, I should like to go up to my bedroom… the room I used, I mean. I think I left something there."

"Of course. And do think of it as *your* room, for when you come here again."

"I will. Thank you." She smiled and turned to the door.

"Oh, and Caroline…"

"Yes?"

"While you are there, go to the chest and take out the cloak, the one we spoke about."

"The cloak?" Caroline hoped that the smile she now turned on Sir Henry was beaming enough to hide her sudden anxiety - what if he had been up there after she had left here for Hertford, seen the breeches… and thought they belonged to… to whom? To Simon? Oh no! "Yes, of course I will."

Without another word she ran out of the snug - Sir Henry knew her time at Yardley Bury was limited, so that would be acceptable, she hoped - raced along the passageway and up the stairs, her feet keeping pace with her pounding heart.

Please let them be there, and untouched, she said to herself, as she entered the room. There was no fire lit and the smell of musty cold was overwhelming. Had she really slept in such a room? With the tattered curtains closed, the room was dark, too. There was just enough light shining in from the landing to guide Caroline's steps to the chest at the foot of the bed. Quickly she raised the lid - nothing, as far as she could see, had been disturbed; the cloak lay as she remembered placing it, with the wide velvet ribbon ties lying symmetrically on either side of the front opening. Carefully she lifted it up, put it on the bed, returned to the chest and lifted out Robert's old breeches. She shut the lid of the chest, picked up the cloak and walked out on to the landing. Her whole body was shaking with cold; the sooner she was back in the warm snug the better. She began to descend the stairs. Halfway down she came to a sudden stop. What *was* she to do with the breeches? She couldn't just walk into Sir Henry's presence holding them, with the cloak, over her arm! She turned and ran back up the stairs. In the bedroom, her fingers now numb with cold, she lifted her skirts and struggled into the breeches. The cloth felt tight against her skin: she must have put on weight since she last wore them! Uncomfortable as it was, there was no other way that she could think of, to get the offending garment out of the house.

With her skirts back in place and the cloak again over her arm, Caroline resumed her descent of the stairs. Just three steps down, and still out of the sight of anyone in the entrance hall below, she heard a raised voice, coming, by the sound of it, from the passageway that led to the snug. She couldn't make out the words, but the tone suggested anxiety. She paused, straining her ears to hear. It was John, Lydia's groom! What was he doing, shouting outside Sir Henry's private room? And now there was Sir Henry joining in, also in the passageway!

Another two steps down and the words became clear.

"No, Sir Henry, we must go *now*!"

"She has barely had time to rest."

"We must get away at once! She can rest later."

"I will not having you speaking of a lady in that… that familiar way!"

Caroline gasped. Oh no, she was not having that. Whatever it was they were saying, they must say to her face!

She hurried down the rest of the stairs, calling out as she ran, "Sir Henry… is there something wrong? Why are you and John talking about me?"

"Come inside, my dear," Sir Henry said when she reached the door of the snug. Taking her arm, he drew her quickly into the room. "And you, John… you'd better come in too," he added reluctantly. Even in what appeared to be an emergency, Sir Henry did not take kindly to admitting a stranger, and a servant to boot, into his most private room. "Shut the door," he said to the groom, "and stay by it. Don't let anyone in."

"Whatever is the matter?" Caroline allowed herself to be led to the fireside, but resisted Sir Henry's effort to get her seated. "I don't want to sit down, Sir Henry."

She shook off his arm and looked crossly at the groom. "I will leave when I am ready, John… and not before!"

"Yes, madam, but…" John paused. He knew he should not be taking the initiative, but felt he had no choice; it was his duty first and foremost to protect Lady Poynter's sister-in-law, and if that meant he had to speak forcefully to her… well, so be it. "There has been a change in the situation, madam, and I feel it is best you leave here at once."

"What situation?"

"It's the kitchen maid, Dora. She saw you riding into the stable yard, madam."

"The kitchen maid!" Sir Henry exclaimed. "You're fussing about nothing, John."

He lowered himself into his red chair.

"No, Sir Henry, according to your housekeeper, this could be serious." The groom turned to Caroline. "If necessary, madam, I will explain everything once we are on our way to Hertford."

"You will explain *now*!" Sir Henry's words, loud and severe, were accompanied by a heavy thumping on the arm of his chair. "I will not allow Mistress Newell to leave the safety of my house to go haring across the countryside, without a full and sensible explanation!"

"Yes, Sir Henry. I apologise for…"

"Oh, just give us the facts."

"It seems…" John nodded first to Sir Henry and then to Caroline, "… sir… madam… that Dora has some grudge against Mistress Newell, connected with your maid, madam, and a girl called Margaret Gilbert, who is her cousin - and she has run off, to Walkern, Mistress Sawyer believes, to seek one Susan Aylott, who was in Hertford and has now returned to…"

"No! Oh no, not that woman! John, we must make haste." Distressed and fearful, Caroline turned to Sir Henry. "She must not find me here, Sir Henry!"

"My dear girl, what harm can she do you? You are safe here; you have my protection."

"Yes, but once I leave here I am at risk from those women, should they come after me! John is right; we must get away immediately, before they have a chance to catch up with me."

"It was your maid they were after, not you! And she is safe… in Hertford."

"She is, but I am not! Mary escaped their clutches… and they are angry. They feel cheated. Jane Wenham is not to hang, and I am sure they blame me for that, as much as anyone. What is to stop them testing *me* for witchcraft if they get hold of me? I must go! Now! Before they can assemble a group of people to attack me!"

"Caroline, you are talking nonsense! No one is going to *attack* you, nor test you for witchcraft."

"They tested Mary!"

"Yes. A maid. And she probably gave them cause, making sheep's eyes at that gypsy boy."

Angry as Caroline was at Sir Henry's words, she felt it best to let them pass.

She took a deep breath and let it out slowly. Turning to Lydia's groom, she said, "I need a few minutes alone with Sir Henry, John, and then I will be with you."

"Yes, madam." John bowed. "I will have the horses ready." He opened the door. "Please don't be long, madam, I beg of you."

"Impudent fellow!" Sir Henry rose from his chair, too late for John to respond to his words; the groom had gone, closing the door swiftly behind him. "How dare he give you orders like that! Your sister-in-law has been far too free with that man by the sound of it. The arrogance of him!"

"Don't let him upset you, Sir Henry. We have only a few minutes together; please let us make them harmonious ones." Caroline stretched out her arm, with the cloak draped across it. "See, I have brought the beautiful cloak, as you asked me to."

Sir Henry looked blankly at it.

"Aunt Elizabeth's. You wanted it brought down... from the chest."

"Yes. Of course. Forgive me, my dear, this nasty business just now... it put it out of my mind. Yes. The cloak." He leant forward and tenderly stroked the soft fabric. "I want you to have it."

"Me?"

"What better person could I give it to?"

"Oh, Sir Henry. Thank you." Caroline's voice was soft. "I shall treasure it, always." She lifted the cloak to her face, caressing it with her hand. "Are you sure?" she asked. "I know how important it is to you."

"If I wasn't sure I wouldn't have offered it to you, Caroline."

"No, of course not." Had she belittled his gift by doubting him? He looked hurt.

"Dear Sir Henry, thank you." Caroline flung her free arm around the old man and hugged him.

"When all this witchcraft business is over," he said, patting her arm, "I shall expect another visit from you… and this time make it a long one."

The last thing Caroline wanted was a return visit to Yardley Bury, but the old gentleman was looking at her so wistfully she had to find some words of comfort for him.

"I have a much better idea!" she said. "You must come to Amley, and stay with me. The orchards are glorious in the spring and summer. Oh, Sir Henry, do say you will come!"

"I should like that very much. And perhaps you will wear Elizabeth's cloak."

Caroline looked down at it. Oh dear, this was all becoming too emotional. If they carried on in this vein she would soon be in tears.

"I will," she answered, "but now I must go." She gave him a quick kiss on the cheek and hurried out of the snug.

The back door was open, letting in cold air. The horses were drawn up, ready, and John, looking impatient, was holding both sets of reins. Drawing her cloak around her, Caroline moved swiftly forward. A sudden blast of warm air filled the passageway as the kitchen door flew open and a distraught Bessie all but threw herself at Caroline's feet.

"Oh, Miss Caroline, forgive me! I am so sorry. It is all my fault!"

"Bessie, do get up! Nothing is your fault."

"But it is, Miss Caroline, it is! If I hadn't turned away to see to those tarts in the oven that girl would never have left the kitchen. I knew what she was like, I should have…"

"That's enough, Bessie." The authority in Sir Henry's voice brought Bessie's tirade to a halt. "Get up from your knees and let Mistress Newell leave!"

"Oh, Sir Henry, if only I hadn't …"

"I said *enough*! Go back into the kitchen and shut the door."

"Yes, Sir Henry." Bessie's reply was whispered and tearful.

Caroline reached out her hand to the old servant. "Don't distress yourself, Bessie, please."

"Caroline…" Sir Henry did not like having his authority flouted. Please don't defy me, his look said.

"Oh, thank you, Miss Caroline… Mistress Newell." Bessie let go of Caroline's hand, then almost immediately reached for it again. "Don't wear that cloak, Miss Caroline, please." She nodded towards Caroline's rich velvet cloak. "Wear an old one of mine, I beg of you."

"Mistress Newell does not want to wear…" Sir Henry began.

"She is right, Sir Henry." Caroline knew he wouldn't like it, but she had to interrupt. "Thank you, Bessie. With your cloak over mine no one will know it is me…" - she turned to Sir Henry - "… and that way I shall be safe!" She turned back to Bessie. "Could you find an old coat for John, too?"

"I'll get him one of Samuel's."

Two riders in worn clothing, hats pulled down against the cold wind, caused no more than mild curiosity between

Yardley Bury and Woodhall, and both riding astride - Bessie had looked appalled as Caroline mounted and bunched her skirts up under her two capacious cloaks, but said nothing, and Sir Henry, unable to watch his dear girl departing yet again, had fortunately returned to his snug - it would be assumed they were two men, farmers perhaps on their way to a sale of livestock, a sight that could be seen anywhere in the county.

John had been relieved when they got away from Yardley Bury; he had no wish to be caught up in any kind of fracas.

"I must apologise for my behaviour earlier, madam," he said, once they were out of sight of the house, "but if a gang of angry villagers were to have waylaid us on the doorstep…"

"Oh, John," Caroline spoke gently, belying her own anxiety; the groom looked so troubled. "You were right to hurry me away - I could have been in danger if I had stayed - but as things are, well… Dora has only just left the house, and it will take her a good fifteen minutes to get to Walkern, and then she's got to round up the village women, and some of the men, no doubt. They will be on foot, you know, not on horseback. We shall be well away from Yardley Bury before they get back there." Caroline hoped she sounded more confident than she felt.

"Yes, madam, you are right, but I promised Lady Poynter that I would take care of you, and I feel that I have failed in my…"

"No, you have not!" and seeing that John was itching to put his horse to a gallop, she said, "We may gallop later, John, but we do not want to call attention to ourselves at the moment." She was as frightened as the groom that they might be overtaken by what had grown in her mind into a rapacious horde of armed villagers, seeking revenge for what they saw as their ignominious defeat, but she was not about to admit it, nor show it. "We shall walk to begin with. We can break into a trot once we are on the road. Is that understood?"

"Yes, madam."

For most of the journey Caroline and the groom, not speaking but glancing behind them every few minutes, their ears constantly alert for the sound of angry voices or thudding hooves, kept their horses to a trot, but when the terrain allowed it and there was no one about, they galloped. Veering off the road into the parkland of Woodhall, in the shelter of a holly spinney close to the road, Caroline dismounted, removed Bessie's old cloak, rolled it into a bundle and hid it under a holly bush - "Some vagrant will be glad of it," she said to John - and remounted, this time side-saddle. Decorously, with John now divested of Samuel's old coat and once more the smart liveried groom of Lady Poynter, she rode into Bengeo, looking for all the world, she hoped, as if she were a lady out for a gentle ride with her groom.

In Lydia's stable yard Caroline had the greatest difficulty dismounting from her horse; she was trembling all over and so dizzy that it was only by holding on to John that she managed not to collapse completely.

"Oh John," she whispered, "I don't ever want to go through…" - it was hard to speak - "… anything like that… again."

"No, madam, nor do I."

"We say nothing to Lady Lydia."

"No, madam."

"I've just been riding fast and hard… in a cold wind. Nothing more."

"No, madam. Nothing more."

29

Two days later, Caroline and Mary, Emilia, the three children and Rosie set off for Gilston in Lady Poynter's comfortable, silk-lined carriage. Caroline, returning to Hertford from Bengeo early that morning, ready for departure, had been surprised and disappointed - and, yes, a little annoyed, too - to learn that Simon would not be travelling with them: he had some very urgent business at High Green to attend to, Richard said, and would meet them at Gilston, and from there he would most certainly escort Caroline, and everyone else, to Amley. In his place, Richard had found "an extremely reliable local ostler to ride alongside you."

It was all rather odd, but there was no time for argument or recrimination; the children were getting restless, and standing in Bull Plain for even just the few minutes that it took for everyone to get into the carriage was making Mary nervous. Lydia had wanted Caroline to stay with her longer, but arrangements had been made, Caroline told her, and she would keep to them. Lydia was sure her sister-in-law was about to succumb to some horrible illness: she shook so much, and looked so pale, yet refused to have a doctor attend her.

"I shall be perfectly all right once I get to Amley," she said, and no amount of gentle words, or strong ones, from Lydia would make her change her mind.

"You are so stubborn!" Lydia said finally. "I hope Simon knows what he is in for."

"Simon? He will be *in for*, as you put it, whatever is required of him as a neighbour, that is all!"

"Hmm," Lydia sniffed.

"And if I do decide, at some time in the future, to marry again - I know that's what you're talking about! - it will be because *I* want to, and not because *you* think I should!"

She had not slept well that night at Lydia's, despite the comfortable bed, her own fatigue after the strain of the day and the almost sleepless night in Hertford before she set off for Yardley Bury. So many emotions had been stirred up by her visit. She had not set out to rescue an old woman from a charge of witchcraft; it had just happened, like so many things in life. Actions had consequences that one could not always foresee. She allowed herself a small smile: if she had not run away from an undesirable suitor she would not have found herself running away from a crowd of vengeful villagers. She had escaped them both... and now she could go home, to the safety of Amley. Sadly, there was no Robert awaiting her. She had learned to live there without him, she told herself, and now she would live there again... without him. And this time she had Emilia with her, and the children... and yes, Simon. Dear, kind, lovely Simon. Not *at* Amley, but close by, so that if she needed... Oh, she must sleep! She would tell herself one of her comforting bedtime stories: an orchard, ripe apples on the trees, girls in muslin dresses, a young man on a horse... No, that was no good; sometimes the man looked like Robert, at other times like Simon. She got up, drew on her robe - this was becoming a habit, one she did not like - paced the room, looked out at the dark, moonless night, then, feeling herself getting cold, climbed back into bed and pulled the covers tightly around her. Finally, from sheer exhaustion, as the light of the new day began to filter through the curtains at the long window, she slept.

Now, settled in the carriage, the older children chattered or slept, Caroline and Emilia spoke together quietly, and Rosie, holding Edwin, played games with his fingers and toes. Only Mary, sitting opposite Caroline, was silent, downcast, as she had been the last time they travelled to Gilston. Oh, how she had cheered up that day at the sight of Jem appearing alongside them!

Nearing Gilston - there had been no sign of Simon - Caroline looked out of the window, and had a sense of what she believed the French called *déjà vu*: there was Jem, riding alongside the carriage, grinning from ear to ear. Jem? What was *he* doing there? And Simon… where was he? There were things going on here she did not understand. Well, Simon could wait; at least now Mary would be content.

"Mary," Caroline called softly.

"Yes, mistress?" Mary lifted her head. Her cheeks were wet with tears.

"I think you should look out of the window. No, the other side."

The tears continued to stream down Mary's cheeks, but now they were tears of pure joy. The carriage had slowed almost to a standstill; Mary flung open the door and leapt out. Jem leant down from his horse and scooped her up into his arms.

The window on Caroline's side darkened. Simon's smiling face filled the aperture.

"Simon! Where have you...? What is going on?"

"I'm sorry to have kept things from you, Caroline," he said softly. "I should have told you that Jem is now working for me."

"Oh!"

"But I had to be sure first... of his intentions towards Mary. It would have been cruel to have said anything earlier."

"Yes, of course," Caroline said, "it would." She was bemused. How had all this been come about? No doubt there had been lots of chasing around the countryside with Tom at his side. In time she would find out, but now... she had a far more important question to ask.

"And *are* you sure?"

It was a simple, straightforward question... about a gypsy lad, nothing else... so why was her heart beating so wildly?

"Yes," he said, looking deep into her eyes. "I am."

"That's good," Caroline said, smiling. "That's... so very good. I am glad you made sure." She took a deep breath and let it out slowly, her eyes fixed on Simon's. "Well..." she said at last, and dropped her gaze. "Let's not keep Uncle Plumer waiting."

THE END

Author's Note

Jane Wenham was a real woman who lived in the north Hertfordshire village of Walkern. She suffered all the indignities described in the book and was tried for witchcraft at the Spring Assizes in Hertford in March 1712. The judge, Sir John Powell, a friend of Jonathan Swift, reprieved her after the jury had brought in a sentence of death. In July of that year she received a Royal Pardon, and went first to live on the estate of Colonel Plumer, where she "was provided (with) an apartment over his stables… and sent victuals from his table…". After the colonel's death in 1719, Jane Wenham moved to a cottage on the Cowper estate at Hertingfordbury. She died in January 1730, aged around eighty-eight, and was buried in Hertingfordbury churchyard.

Francis Bragge wrote several pamphlets, as was the custom of the time, about the trial, notably *A Full and Impartial Account of the Discovery of Sorcery and Witchcraft practis'd by Jane Wenham of Walkerne in Hertfordshire,* etc., upon which I drew heavily for the details of the trial in Chapter 26. This pamphlet was refuted by one entitled *The Impossibility of Witchcraft, Plainly proving, From Scripture and Reason, That there never was a WITCH...* which gave the curate good reason to write another one! And so it went on. There were at least nine pamphlets resulting from this trial, some for, others against, Jane.

Discussion of the subject of witchcraft continued in pamphlets and books until 1735 when the Witchcraft Act of James I was repealed and the practice of witchcraft was no longer a crime.

Sir Henry Chauncy, who had "allowed superstitious belief to triumph over his customary good sense... (and) achieved an unpleasant notoriety due to his involvement in the case" (W.B.Gerish's biography of Sir Henry Chauncy, 1907), lived on until April 1719.

His son Arthur finally married, in 1724. He died in Diss, Norfolk, in 1752. He was described in a document at that time as *vafer* (crafty) and *nefastas* (wicked) which leads one to wonder about his life after the trial. Francis Bragge also married, and had two sons. The Rev. Godfrey Gardiner and his wife remained at Walkern until his death in 1722 Susan Aylott, Matthew Gilston, John Chapman and Elizabeth Field were certainly alive in 1712, but I have found no further record of them, other than the dates of their deaths.

* * * * *

Robert Newell had made notes on the treatment of horses on the battlefield, and it is Caroline's intention to write these notes up in the form of a book for the use of farriers and veterinarians. For anything else in the future lives of Caroline and Simon, Mary and Jem, Emilia's family, the Towlers and the Gilberts, Tom, Bessie, William the stable boy, Lady Lydia and her groom John... you will have to rely upon your knowledge of the characters... and your imagination.

For further information about Jane Wenham and the trial on March 4th1712, go online. Type in *Jane Wenham the witch of Walkern.* This will lead you to a number of sites connected with the events and the real people in the book, but please be aware that not everything posted on the internet is accurate.

Mary Rensten. March 2013

Mary Rensten is a Vice-President of the Society of Women Writers & Journalists (SWWJ). She has lived in Hertfordshire since 1960. Formerly a teacher and a journalist, she now writes fiction, including drama. This is her second novel